Decision Most Deadly

Mark Turnbull

First published in Great Britain in 2009
by Mark Turnbull

Reprinted in 2010

Copyright © 2009 Mark Turnbull

Names, characters and related indicia are copyright and trademark
Copyright © 2009 Mark Turnbull

Mark Turnbull has asserted his moral rights
to be identified as the author

A CIP Catalogue of this book is available from
the British Library

ISBN 978-0-9556353-0-4

Cover designed and typeset in Garamond 11pt
by Chandler Book Design
www.chandlerbookdesign.co.uk

Printed in Great Britain by the
MPG Books Group, Bodmin and King's Lynn

For my daughter, Amara.
with love

Introduction

I n writing this book, I hoped to focus on one of the least publicised parts of the seventeenth century. The English Civil War is frequently written about, describing battles and personalities, but the most critical year, 1641, and the actual reasons behind the war are often skimmed over. It is easy to make quick assumptions over why the war occurred, or underestimate what caused friends and families to go to fight against each other.

Choosing King or Parliament seems immensely easier to judge today, and I aim to show just how grave this decision was, along with the host of consequences it brought to our seventeenth century ancestors. In fact many people tried to escape making this deadly decision for as long as they could.

Hopefully through reading the book you manage to feel transported back in time to savour what life was like in this fascinating period of history, while enjoying the story. All I recommend is that you try to leave modern attitudes and ways of life behind when you read. A King being appointed by God, health being affected by the position of the planets, and the male being the dominant sex were all normal. It is easy to disregard points such as these, or view them with derision, as they are alien to our current society and times.

My fascination with this period extends from childhood and in writing this, I hope to provide an enthralling plot and storyline that entertains the reader, as well as keeping the extraordinary events and activities of our ancestors alive. The history of Great Britain - and indeed any country - is what makes us who we are. It unifies and identifies us and should be celebrated over and over again with pride.

For a full breakdown of historical characters and fictional ones, please view the website. The official site also contains more information about the story, characters and the period. If possible, all feedback about the book would be most appreciated.

www.decisionmostdeadly.com

Acknowledgements

I owe a lot to my editor, Jenny Hewitt, whose expert services have been invaluable.

Thank you also to the City of London Library for giving permission to reproduce the scene of London for the jacket, and Ray Foster for professionally transforming my designs for the cover into reality.

Lastly, I want to express my appreciation to all my friends and family for their support, with special gratitude to my friends Keith Crawford for giving honest advice and feedback regarding the storyline and writing, as well as John Hopper for designing and creating the official website.

At the back of the book, you will find a character list and brief historical background to the period, if needed.

1 June 1639, Near Kelso

As he rode along the track at the head of his troop of horsemen, Lieutenant Charles Berkeley still retained some of the enthusiasm he had been infected with when English force, he was thriving on the challenge of managing the troop of sixty, itching for a fight.

The dark clouds swirled above him, like they were getting ready to close in with one thunderous charge. The wind had been veritably pushing them onwards, but thankfully it had subsided now as they searched for quarters for the night.

Through the gloomy light, he saw a large house overlooking a village and was readily anticipating getting his boots off and putting his feet up. Within a few minutes his superior, Major Anderson, announced his intention of heading towards the manor house with the Lieutenant Colonel. After brusquely telling Charles to quarter the troop, he tugged the reins, turning his steed towards the luxurious target. Charles was now in overall charge of the men behind, and this thrill negated the lax behaviour of the senior command. He gripped his plain sword, pulling it into place and examined his leather buff coat, which covered his doublet for protection. The dark brown leather boots were unfolded to full length, covering right up to the lower thighs. He straightened his back and pointed towards the hamlet ahead, directing the steed up to a canter. The rest of the army lay scattered around the neighbouring areas and despite welcome thoughts of rest, a menacing sensation encompassed him. The black mount he had come to love even seemed hesitant, so he gave 'Ripon' a tender stroke; the name conjuring up images of the picturesque place from where he had bought him.

"Go forward and prepare the inn for our approach," he shouted to the man behind, instructing him to take three others.

Turning round to his troopers, he observed their morose expressions, most of them seeming to have neither any heart in the war, or personal quarrel with the Scots. England and Scotland were one nation now he had heard many argue. The fervent Scottish motivation was much more attractive; protecting their own religion from the King's desire to impose one uniform prayer book and church government. They rode up the street, passing the warm glow from the small windows, horses snorting as they eventually halted. As night closed in, an eerie fog had followed them, like a giant curtain descending in a theatre. The scene was over and he swung his leg to dismount, standing outside the local tavern. For the first time in hours, he saw the troopers look lively and they practically leapt from their saddles, eager to fill their bellies with beer. The sight of the building brought back memories of his father's inn at Colchester where he had toiled since childhood; either he tidied up, served customers or did errands until he was able to take on heavier duties when he was twelve.

Then he heard noises and voices, speeding through the narrow straits of the street like floodwater. He demanded the men stay put and carefully walked forward.

"Not long now, men," was the bellowed reassurance from the distance, in a broad Scottish accent.

Charles's senses were triggered by the dialect and he quietly, but sternly, ordered two groups to take up position on foot at either side of the entrance to the street ahead. He sent a few more to an alleyway nearby, insisting the rest remount with him. The urgency and unusually coherent orders seemed to hypnotise most of the men; he manhandled those who stood idle into obedience. There would only be a few minutes, judging by the sound of the approaching horses and the building clatter of weapons and armour.

His heart pumped furiously - this was the chance for glory and honour and he thought of his Uncle Tom and those war stories he had been told in younger years. He sat on Ripon, squinting through the bleak night, waiting for the right moment to launch his cavalry.

Some sweat beads frustrated his concentration as they trickled their way down his forehead, not daring to breathe for fear of missing the crucial moment. His reactions had been impulsive but reflected common sense. Some echoing noises pierced the silence, giving the impression that an invisible spirit army was in the vicinity.

Just as he began to give way to frustration, a horse and rider emerged, the sight causing him to freeze while more began to materialise. During the seconds that he was completely still, a whole line had manifested from the haze and he cried as loud as he could, ordering the men who had pistols to fire down the street now that the enemy were in range and still hemmed into the cramped lane. He wondered whether his orders had been heard, as for a crucial second nothing happened.

Finally the rapports came cracking out into the night, adding extra smoke to the thick air. He spurred his horse, initially forgetting in his haste to command the rest of the mounted cavalrymen to follow. The noise of horses whinnying and the sight of the enemies leading mares rearing up gave a picture of utter confusion and shock. In an instant, the quiet, sleepy settlement was enveloped with sounds of warfare. Men shouted, horses hooves pounded the ground while armour and swords clanked with the action.

He clattered down towards them, heart racing, hair flowing loosely and eyes wide with excitement; the absolute speed of the encounter allaying any nerves. All cares and thoughts flew away from his travelling body, his sole intention being to crash into the front lines and scatter the Scots before they had any chance to recover from the attack. His sword shuddered as he held it outstretched in front of him, letting out a yell of exhilaration.

Ripon slowed as they bore down into the ranks of bewildered horsemen, but the opponents did not flee as he had imagined. He slashed out at the foe to his right. The man was irate, flinging his weapon at Charles in a fury and taking him aback with the ferocious defence.

Charles locked blades several times, the fellow grasping at him as they now closed in on each other for a split second, and he felt his arm being wrenched. Charles was helpless as he thudded to the ground. At this juncture of cold perception, the din of the battle and utterances of both men and beasts penetrated his mind, now that he was brought back to reality.

His opponent jumped from his horse and Charles responded by getting up and quickly thrusting his blade, but the man was agile and dived out of his way. Charles felt sure he would still win the duel and gave an almighty roar as he cut at him again with his weapon, but the man met it, the clash stunning Charles's arm. The opponent followed this up without hesitation and slashed back with success. Charles jumped aside, shocked at his wound, finally realising his own limitations as his assurance seeped away. He doggedly went back at the Scot though, who crashed his weapon away, blocking his intentions each time and causing Charles to lose energy and method. As the Scot turned to the attack once more, he sliced at Charles, pushing him backwards.

He tried to anticipate the fellow's actions, but found himself losing ground, unable to keep up with the movements or increasing speed of the encounter. Another man was killed nearby and as the body fell from the horse, the mare positively went mad, as though it were one of the lunatics in the Bedlam Asylum, heading towards Charles and his enemy.

Charles saw the man gearing up for a final blow and jumped backwards while this beast galloped towards them, kicking out.

The horse was even harder to predict than the Scottish trooper, and he felt it was magnetised to him. He yelled, just managing to avoid it as he stumbled out of the way, but the Scot was knocked to the ground as it collided with him instead. Charles ran forward, seizing this chance to defeat his foe and slicing across the hand to stop him retrieving his sword. A cry of pain came from the Scot, which did nothing to stop Charles quickly following it up, his blade now at his rival's chest when cheers broke out nearby. He hastily turned, seeing his men roaring happily at the sight of the vanquished Covenanters, and respect for his rival's outstanding swordsmanship gave way to mercy.

While he stood panting, thankful to have beaten the man, he took a minute to recollect his overwrought emotions, even needing to assess what he had just done. He had the sudden heart stopping thought that the enemy could have been a larger army, or even worse, they may not have been enemy troopers after all.

"As an officer, I demand you take me to your colonel. I am Sir Arthur Cotton," an imperious screech demanded.

Unable to fully take in what had happened, he was drawn to a blue banner on the ground, the classic Scottish Covenanter emblem, and he rested against a wall, swearing with frustration over his exhausted state. In front of him his men had driven them away and the defeated officer scowled with hatred, still demanding to be taken note of.

Charles still only just heard him, jubilant that they had won something at long last, and he laughed out loud, ignoring the insolent dog. This was the proudest moment of his life. His conviction that he could make something of his post had been proved and despite the daunting sense of purpose and direction of the Scottish, he had achieved the impossible.

Jubilation overflowed. "We routed the bastards," he cried to his men.

[I am] "Yielding up one of the fairest flowers of [my] garland."

King Charles's comments after finally agreeing to a Bill which meant Parliament must be summoned at least once every three years, ending the monarch's power over when it should be called.

FEBRUARY 1641

Chapter 1

S ir Charles Berkeley felt himself being shaken softly out of his slumber. The room was a blur as he opened his tired eyes. The glow from the flickering candle that lit the bedchamber awoke his senses and he focused his gaze to see his wife, Lady Anne, standing over him. He smiled at 'sweet Annie' who had been through so much lately; sadness still filled their hearts over a stillborn baby daughter, lingering on as heavily as the fatty smell of the tallow candles.

"I was in a dream, with Father finding Lucy had eloped," he said with surprise, "T'is the first dream in years of my sister's folly."

After a second or two he saw the look of agitation on the attractive features of her pale face. Anne's delicate fingers were fondling a folded sheet of paper, held together with a large, red wax seal and ribbon. Recognising the imprint of the crest, as crisp as a freshly baked loaf, Charles sprung out of bed.

Taking the letter from his wife, he listened with frustration as she told him about the strange gentleman who had just delivered it. The seal was the Earl of Holland's, a well known courtier and friend of the Queen's; the same peer who had given

Charles patronage and the chance to get his knighthood a few years back in the war with Scotland.

The wax emblem was easily distinguishable, branding the letter like a burning sunset.

He impatiently gave one tug of the paper and unlike his own immense resolve, the wax easily broke in half, falling to the wooden floor. Unfolding the letter with haste, he wondered to what end he was needed this time. The message was short but simple, in line with the author's character; it bluntly commanded him to accompany the servant to Whitehall Palace where the peer waited. This all seemed extremely urgent and he wondered why he was summoned at such a late hour. It was hard to make out the words on parts of the letter where the wax had greased the paper, making it as transparent as Charles's honest character. He looked at Anne who, devoted as ever, sensed that the state required her husband, and she headed towards the wardrobe for his clothes.

Barefoot and feeling the cold floor against his feet, he stepped onto the fur rug beside the bed. Then realising this automatic act and sensing its weakness, he returned to the chilled floorboards. The image of him as a young boy working in a small room, freezing, but stubbornly enduring the cold, came to the forefront of his mind. His father's spell in the navy battling the enemy had turned into a fight for backdated wages.

He erratically brushed his long dark curls and widened his brown eyes while looking into the mirror for a few seconds to examine his thin moustache. The freezing night had already seen a covering of snow and Charles didn't know whether the shivering sprung from cold, anticipation of this strange message, or both. Was it Holland's impatience that added to it? He was becoming more irritated at Holland's great expectation of him - he may owe his position to the man, but sometimes it felt like he had been anchored to the peer in exchange, dragged along into every choppy sea. The added danger was that the political currents of England were getting decidedly unpredictable right now.

It did soften his anger as he remembered how he met Anne through a banquet Holland had hosted, Charles's healthy appetite being replaced by a hunger to find out more about the lady opposite him. She had more than looks, being intelligent, genuine and caring. An inkling that this woman was extremely special tipped his determination to begin to court her, despite his awkwardness with social gatherings.

* * *

Henry Rich, first Earl of Holland, sat on the plush velvet covered seat in one of the two thousand or more rooms within this centre of government; one fish within an ocean of patronage. It was easy to be lost in the vast splendour of the cold room, where a sumptuous décor did not need the adornments of furniture to look majestic. It contained famous paintings, triangular carvings mounting the tops of the two doorways, and a grand fireplace that held only ashes and embers. In contrast, Lord George Digby's fermenting ambition burned higher as he waited. Digby, son of the old Earl of Bristol was already outwardly confident, despite only being fresh to the King's cause. The long serving Holland sat rigidly, betraying his sense of seniority and a hint of wariness about the other man, who was rapidly gaining favour with the Queen, and by default, the King. He could see his new rival itching to speak as the man caressed the carvings of cherubs, grapes and vines that made up the fireplace decoration. As he traced every leaf and shoot, it seemed he was drawing inspiration to cultivate his own future and entangle Holland's.

"So the King needs a messenger most urgently?"

Holland looked round, jubilant that he had met the royal need before this smirking fellow. Already he sensed the rogue was thinking of opportunities to intrigue for his own ends.

Holland gripped the golden head of his cane like it was the world he held in his hand and remained silent.

"How will the letter get through though, my lord?" Digby probed, persistent as ever.

"It shall, mark my words, sir," Holland tantalised. He would explain his plan and just who he had volunteered for the task when the monarch returned here later.

"But the scales are set against your man's success."

"I would not be too sure," Holland mused, fencing with his opponent.

"Well I would certainly not do it," Digby asserted quickly.

Holland did not bother to look or reply and quiet ensued again for a minute or so. Then the reminder that the King had asked both of them to come up with a suitably skilled and discreet post boy, inflamed Holland's indignation that the monarch would consult this newcomer too.

"I will always manage to serve my King, which is why I will resolve this matter tonight. Remember that my loyalties have been displayed as clearly as these magnificent Rembrandts for over twenty years now. One day you may know what I mean by this," Holland reminded while keeping a calm, courtly appearance, but ramming his experience home.

Digby strolled over to him now, passing the gleaming, black marble pillars that linked the tiled floor with the panelled effect of the stone ceiling.

"I wish you well then, my lord. I would not expect such a master artist to risk himself on any unknown canvass, so I hope you have a suitable fellow," Digby said, persistently meandering closer to Holland's raw nerve, a veteran at manipulating people's feelings.

Holland began toying with the gold ribbons that flopped

about each shoe - he would flick his foot every now and then, tipping the material side to side - trying to calm himself as he observed Digby square on. "Risks? I have other people to take those."

"Ah, so maybe the King's insistence to meet your brave candidate will benefit you, for at least he will not refuse such a ruinous assignment in His Majesty's presence, or I hope not anyway," Digby said with a snort and a snap glance up towards the octagon shape of the central roof decoration.

Holland smiled with restraint, slow to anger, but perfectly prepared to defend his honour as far as a full blown duel.

"Sir," Holland said discreetly, with an ever so mocking, casual shake of his head, "Must I remind you that your family have only just climbed out of that pit of dishonour you have rotted in for so long now. Why, I believe even you yourself as a child had to beg Parliament for your father's release from prison. Handsome and charming you may be to the Queen, but your name shall be your eternal link to that abyss."

Digby's cheeks flushed like a girl, going near to matching the colour of his scarlet suit, stockings and cloak. The gold braiding that depicted leaves curling down each side of his breeches and along the edges of his doublet, had formerly accentuated the impression that his confidence had rooted him to the palace. Now he was instantly upturned like a tree in a storm, the young sapling that he still was. To top the moment off, the King's acting Secretary of State entered, giving the last word and the victory to the Earl of Holland.

Holland knew the King would be pleased that his task had been accepted, but it was damned frustrating that he demanded to see any man they had in mind, to personally scrutinize him. The earl knew of Sir Charles Berkeley's lack of political expertise, but unusually, this did not affect the man's abilities.

But then again, maybe Digby was right in one respect; it was best the King sees this messenger, for he was bound to accept in such a situation.

The piece of correspondence will tie any man's honour within it, in the same way as the crimson seal and silver ribbon clasped the message.

*　*　*

Anne emerged from the closet with a pile of clothes in her arms, and Charles rushed forward to help. As he tipped the garments carelessly onto the bed, she fussed and rearranged them, anxious they remained at their best. Pride in tidiness, was always close to Godliness, or so she would frequently tease him.

Pulling on his doublet, he explained, "I am needed at Whitehall, it must be important but I do not know the reason."

While he spoke, he noticed a stray length of her rich, brown hair, still forming a remnant of the loose ringlets which so complemented her. He gently eased it back over her shoulder, his eyes admiringly tracing her lips, before slipping to her chest. Time froze as he did so, her soft hand tenderly stroking a healing cut on his, before gently easing it towards her lips and kissing it.

"You will be late," she whispered, almost regretfully.

With a heavy sigh he quickly hung his medal around his neck, glancing out of the small leaded window overlooking the street below to see the coach waiting for him.

"Hurry back, sweetheart."

Charles stamped his foot against the floor to help get his leather boot on. Then taking his cloak, he replied, "I shall be as speedy as I can - not even the Earl of Holland can disobey my wife," before hurrying downstairs with Anne following, amused at his quip. He turned to look at her again; she was a lively woman of five foot and every inch of her body was filled with love.

Seeing the servant's gleaming, buckled shoes reminded him of the King's rules that men could not wear boots in the royal palace, so he pulled his off in frustration, grabbing some tanned ones. Luckily he was wide awake, with early rises instilled from his boyhood days working in the family inn - he was able to propel himself into the new day at once, although Anne sometimes needed time to catch up with his energetic approach.

"Damnation, I much prefer boots too," he cursed while rushing through the hall, gripping at his shoe and hopping at intervals.

Once properly dressed, he went to meet the earl's servant with a formal nod. Charles took his hat from Anne and stopped to embrace her warmly, following with a kiss, which they relished for a few seconds longer. She had never shown any resentment at her husband's duties and although only married for less than a year, they felt the same intense love that had never yet been diminished.

"Be careful," she mouthed silently.

Charles smiled warmly, appreciative of her concern, but adamant she should not worry. He knew how to handle himself with Holland, for he had met the man several times and taken stock of him. Although an air of urgency ushered him, he was sure that after all the fuss, tonight would be no different to their other meetings.

Taking his wife's leave, he stepped outside onto the cobbled street, his leather soles echoing in the quiet night. A footman came forward dressed in the earl's resplendent blue and gold livery, a bright splash of colour across the dull, dark shadows, to open the door for him with a submissive nod. The coach was also branded with the family crest on the side of the door, making it clear the noble owned both the carriage and the man, with no distinction between the inanimate object and the human being.

Entering the coach, a small introductory portion of Holland's world, he sat down on the plush seat. Leaning forward, he observed Anne as the coach moved off. He held his hand up, looking back at her petite figure, murmuring for her to close the door and get back into the warmth and safety of the house. Being jostled from the rough ride, he sat back as she left, realising he still tightly gripped the letter - betraying a true sense of his inner feelings. Clattering through the streets of London, Charles's concentration eventually broke as he lapped up the experience of a private coach with its glass windows, normally only for the elite. It was strange not to hear noises and street sounds as vividly. Watching with an eager eye, he passed Old Palace Yard, next to Parliament.

How different the streets appeared compared to yesterday and indeed many days before. Normally bustling with people going about their business, now the mob protested here against the royal ministers and the King's prerogative. Yesterday he had happily signed a petition. It asked the King to give up illegal taxation and imprisonment and he remembered how the father of his childhood friend James had been seized for non payment of a dubious levy. By removing the breadwinner, it had brought the family to poverty, not that the King would be bothered by that, he thought bitterly.

The coach passed through King Street and under one of the large gatehouses that were decorated with a chalk and flint chequer design to arrive outside the portico of the palace gates. Charles let out a sigh, hoping that this remote and uncaring sovereign would eventually come to his senses. A bell struck, chiming the hour and it banished these thoughts of the power struggle from his mind.

The noise brought back memories of the funeral peals that had sadly echoed news of his stillborn daughter.

He never forgave himself for not being able to christen their unnamed little girl, hoping sincerely she had found her tiny way to heaven despite the lack of Christian ceremony. It affected him, but he did not show it and even now was substituting his sorrow for anger about politics, which stopped any sadness seeping through his masculine front. He must be strong, for he was the head of the household and any weakness was as visible as blood to the predatory courtiers within Whitehall Palace.

The coach jerked to a stop and the chassis designed to ease bumps made him feel slightly nauseous, accentuating the motion. Cursing as he was shaken off balance, he heard the noise of the gates opening and the guards talking to Holland's men. He paused, listening to the welcoming diversion of the common, innocent banter.

Passing through, the carriage travelled the short distance to the entrance of this immense splendour, once home to Cardinal Wolsey and then King Henry the Eighth. The palace was separated by a wall from the servants' quarters, kitchens, pantries and wood yards that were the veritable organs of the place, keeping it alive and fed. Gathering his thoughts, he waited for the footman to open the door, before stepping out. The man nodded as Charles put his red feathered hat on, standing on the gravel courtyard, savouring the cool, quiet London night.

Silence was the main and most attractive attribute, until the strict and ruthless ritual of palace life interrupted it, despite the lateness of the hour. Looking around, he could see the marvellous banqueting hall built for the King by Inigo Jones and scene of the masques the Queen enjoyed so much. He thought of the King's pompous decree that only a few candles be lit during the plays, to stop them discolouring the fabulous painted ceiling by Rubens. But what roof could rival the free and natural one he gazed upon now, with a crescent moon surrounded by twinkling, diamond stars.

Finally entering through the arched, stone doorway, he was

9

told that the grand waiting chamber lay ahead. The guards on either side of the doors moved their large poleaxes to one side as he approached. He had grown up in a small, poor village and now he stood in the King's palace, a knight of the realm. But he still felt somewhat two faced, because he did not agree with royal policies - it salved his concerns to remember he was not here for the King's business though, but for Holland's.

Chapter 2

Once in the grand room, he stood in the middle of the expanse of floor, formal and cold, but so magnificent that he simply had to stare in wonder.

Although empty, he tried to imagine ministers waiting in this long, rectangular room with much impatience for an audience with the Head of State, remembering these details from his mandatory etiquette lessons, following his knighthood. His tutor had told him the more senior the rank, the further into the palace and closer to the King's person a man would be allowed.

Tapestries filled one wall, while he was shocked to see erotic art covering the other. Images of Mars, God of War, holding a semi naked Venus, Goddess of Love, both watching their offspring, or another of a naked lady lying in a forest scene, surrounded by men hunting with dogs and a Cupid flying above them all. The sheer vastness of the area was awe inspiring, in a similar way as it had been to see thousands of men marching or fighting in the recent war.

As he walked, he deliberately stepped from square to square on the chequered marble floor, coming purposefully to rest on a white slab and playfully avoiding the black ones. He admired the artistry of a painting of the King above the fireplace, noticing from the date that it was a recent creation. It displayed the royal on horseback in cuirassier armour, his great, mighty steed, the sheathed sword and lack of visor all portraying the monarch as the guardian of his peaceful nation. On the corner of the painting he noticed a discreet marking of the letters 'C R' and he guessed it was the cipher to show it belonged to 'Charles Rex'. While admiring the work, he thought about the strategic location; right in the room where foreign ambassadors and the like would wait for an audience, taking in this display of the King's power and greatness before they saw him.

Lord Holland's arrival soon interrupted this critique, the doors opening in one fell swoop, and he quickly bowed, his attention yanked back to the purpose of his visit.

He observed Holland, whose long, curled, fair hair and good complexion he had become somewhat used to. The richly dressed peer wore a pearly white doublet and red breeches. He seemed as calm as ever and Charles noticed the sumptuous silver lace - the peer much preferred to enjoy this wealth without interruption, probably why he befriended the Queen.

With the usual neutral face, he greeted Charles, "Thank you for your haste, Sir Charles. This is most vital …"

Holland stopped what sounded like a forewarning, as another man strode in. Observing his wry half smile and slow, calculated walk, Charles instantly felt an aversion, despite this being their first meeting. He was always prone to judge people immediately, despite Anne's protests. Holland introduced Lord George Digby and then led them onwards.

Holland tapped his cane intermittently with the men's footsteps as they walked through the room, the sound eerily echoed back through the grandiose corridors. Charles was reminded of the beat of the drum which coordinated the army.

A man of medium build with light hair came past, pausing only for a second to quietly acknowledge them all, before proceeding to another room.

The fellow returned again with a servant who handed him a piece of paper, speaking so quietly that Charles could not hear, no matter how hard he strained out of curiosity. Holland's eyes then scoured the room, Charles guessed for a seat, and he wondered why the servant was so secretive, his inquisitive military mind as forward thinking as ever. Holland as the most senior rank in the room, now sat on an ornate chair.

"That was Nicholas just gone," Holland observed of the man who had entered the presence chamber. Digby rested against the fireplace as Charles moved closer to them; even this man's posture seemed arrogant, he decided, increasing his enmity.

"So Nicholas waits on His Majesty, is he promoted then, sir?" Charles queried.

"No, sir, Secretary Windebank fled to France after Lord Strafford's imprisonment and Nicholas has unofficially been doing his work these last months," Digby added hastily, narrowing his eyes. The expression gave Charles a sense of being weighed up or assessed, the resulting sigh and casual glance away making him feel as though the result was not favourable.

"He is quiet in his endeavours and speaks few words to anyone," Holland stated, lifting his fair eyebrows in surprise.

"They say he is devoted to His Majesty's service, indulges in no corruption, court gossip or vices and gains the respect of all," Charles added, calculating the two men's jealousy.

"Respect and devotion," Digby scoffed, "They will not make him a great man, for the court intriguers do not value honesty, nor do other ambitious men. Weak qualities."

"I hear he has the King's confidence," Charles said with a smile, intentionally contributing to Digby's irritation. Surely it is admirable he has survived thus far honestly in court, Charles observed privately.

As they were about to reply, conversation was cut short when guards opened the two huge presence chamber doors and the King entered the room. Charles gasped, staring wide eyed, before realising this rudeness and looking to the floor. Holland stood and the three men bowed, Charles fumbling nervously with his hat as he kept his head bare in the royal presence.

Through all the delay and talking, he had not even remotely realised they might catch a glimpse of the King, let alone be actually waiting for him.

Now before him stood the King of Great Britain, Ireland and France, who held the power that Charles had signed a petition against the day before, and of whose actions he had shouted about and cursed over the last few years. Never in his life had he seen the King so closely, for this was not a privilege of his rank or employment and right now his body went cold with intimidation and awe, despite his fearless bravery in battle.

Thinking of nothing more than being so close to the man whom God had appointed to rule this part of earth, Charles felt his legs tremble, somewhat to his embarrassment and he knew he must be conspicuous because of his giant six foot, slim frame.

King Charles the First walked calmly and with a gracious bearing. Although no more than five foot four, his regal dignity and countenance more than made up for this. Charles absorbed each fact and observation about the monarch, drawn to it in spite of his political leanings - he had heard how the King mysteriously seemed to transcend any viewpoint and now he began to see why. The royal wore black with a blue ribbon of the Order of the Garter hanging from his neck and the rich, lace collar and cuffs contrasted against the dark material like the two opposing passions this man could inspire. His moustache and beard were auburn, like his long hair, the curls being interrupted by a glint from a drop pearl earring.

Charles felt the magical presence, imbued with feelings of subservience and even strangely, a patriotic attachment to the small figure in front of him. This was one of the most frightening moments of his life and his head buzzed as to the reason for being here; what did Holland want with him that involved His Majesty?

Silence fell as King Charles the First eyed all of the men individually before taking hold of his Garter medallion.

"My Lords, you have found someone for my task?"

Charles concentrated so hard that he felt himself momentarily frown deeply, realising some of the tangled web behind his summons.

"I have, Your Majesty, Sir Charles Berkeley is an able gentleman," Holland announced.

Charles felt his heart sink, enveloped by a chill of reality.

"Alas, I did not wish to risk such an important task so close to Your Majesty's person without more than one night's thought. I am glad Lord Holland feels so confident though, for surely a man cannot fail if he holds so much certainty," Digby excused himself.

Veiled as a compliment, Charles noticed Holland's eyes burn into his rival, before reminding the King of Charles's military career in the Bishops War, the discussion bringing the topic of the Scottish army to the forefront.

The sovereign interjected, "Parliament issue challenges to our lawful authority but despite fresh negotiating with them, do refuse to vote money until we submit, organising mobs to pressure people to support their extreme views," but at this point his slight stutter impeded him, "Would they see the c-country occupied by Scottish rebels for m-much longer? It has now come to pass we cannot dismiss Parliament, for we n-need them to vote s-subsidies."

Following a second major defeat for the English in the Bishops War, the Scottish army had occupied Northumberland.

The Scots would not move back across the border until they were paid an enormous sum of money, which the King's government could not afford.

News sheets gleefully explained that this necessitated the calling of a Parliament to vote the money to the King. Once Parliament assembled for the first time in eleven years however, they demanded change and more power, with a redress of the wrongs they claimed their monarch had committed. They then imprisoned his leading ministers.

King Charles told them he had heard that the incarcerated Earl of Strafford, until last November his principal minister, was about to be put on trial for his life. The King's stutter grew worse as he became more agitated. "A loyal m-minister on trial, it is not s-sense. I spy it as a less direct thrust at myself through innocent m-men and ..."

The King stopped, closing his eyes for a second. Feeling unnerved by the monarch's stutter, Charles began breathing quicker. King Charles did not continue, but sighed, seeming deep in concentration. Worried by now, Charles feared getting too close to the royal service and policies, with which he disagreed and he marvelled at the hypnotic effect he had seemed to succumb to just now.

"Strafford's plight makes it perilous for you, Your Majesty, as you place your trust in him. For the peace of the kingdom, his life might be forfeited as these men wish," Holland quietly suggested. Charles actually thought the same, but was surprised at Holland's boldness, for he normally told the King what he wanted to hear.

The royal expression turned to a glare and Charles saw the anger in those dark melancholy eyes as he discreetly looked at them for a split second. He also noted how any slight appearance of threat to the sovereign's authority visibly disturbed him.

He did know that King Charles believed, like his father, that a King was chosen by God and answerable to him alone, for this had been reinforced in church services around the country. This belief was entwined with extreme dedication to the Protestant religion, but in the form favoured by the Arminians, in which certain parts of church services resembled Catholic practices with beautification. His mind was torn, half wanting to get away from this dangerous situation he was being drawn into, and the other still magnetised to the monarch.

Holland had shown again that he seemed to be partial to Parliament's thoughts - perhaps too partial for the King? Maybe he is trying to get out of declaring support for anyone, to continue to enjoy his wealthy lifestyle, Charles thought.

The monarch raised his voice and asked Holland, "Should we bow down to all Parliament's token demands and be the shell of a King? I grant concession after concession and they are never happy. Strafford has made savings in my revenue and set up a stable government in Ireland and the North of England and this is how he is treated by them, under my nose."

"Your Majesty's whole authority and powers would continue to be gradually removed, I'll wager, for one submission will multiply to others," Digby interjected immediately.

The King's face changed, as though he had found the support he craved from someone who understood his personal actions and concerns. Charles was amazed that the stammer had vanished with the royal sense of outrage.

"Exactly, Digby and where would that leave my people and my coronation oath to protect them? If Strafford is condemned on such ridiculous charges, how can any of my subjects, great or small, be safe?"

Feeling out of place and alarmed, Charles could see Digby sympathising with his master, while successfully alienating Holland. But Digby, might prove himself much more devious than them all put together. Holland's influence would totter at court if he kept his current sympathies and as a patron, this would jeopardise Charles's own position.

Court politics annoyed him; it was the reason why he disliked venturing near the palace.

In Charles's opinion, Parliament had not yet gone too far. What they proposed was supported by a lot of Londoners and the country as a whole, judging by the protests and petitions; the privileges of Parliament as opposed to the outrages of royal power. The King had taxed, raised troops and imprisoned without any reference to Parliament and that must stop.

Edward Nicholas, the man who had passed them earlier, entered the room and handed the sovereign a letter. Taking it, the King looked at the men and held it in the air while speaking, finally betraying the focus of tonight's meeting. "This is the letter I need delivering to Lord Strafford. Parliament threatens all our ministers, our authority and loyal friends," he added with anxiety, "We will not s-stomach an honest man to be persecuted, let alone our friends, so it is imperative that he knows my thoughts on the matter, as written here."

"They parade daily about Westminster, inciting violence, Your Majesty," Digby warned, or rather provoked.

"So when My Lord Strafford is brought to Westminster for his trial, I suggest we appoint Sir Charles Berkeley to command the guards which will line the route. This is why I brought him, for the more sympathetic men we install in the lines, the better," Holland intervened.

"So be it, Holland. Instruct the relevant people that he should be one of the officers on duty, but his colonel will take overall charge. I also command them not to carry an axe before Strafford while he m-makes his way t-to the session, as they usually do with traitors, and I will not back down on this point."

Charles boiled up inside at the task of being an officer in the proceedings. They spoke of filling the ranks with sympathetic people and he clenched his fists to vent some anger. He hated Strafford, so why the hell was he now being classed as well disposed towards him or even the King for that matter?

The royal made eye contact with the two men, ignoring Charles, which made him feel uneasy, unwanted and even more wary. Charles longed to refuse the job, but the nerves and etiquette, dictated he had to remain quiet until asked to speak.

"Your Majesty could use your own lifeguard and the trained bands to forcibly dislodge these people, for they will only comprehend force before they fill themselves full of their own power," Digby snapped, much to Charles's astonishment.

"Sir Charles, what say you, as a Lieutenant Colonel in the bands?" Digby hastily asked, looking either for support or trying to show him up.

Charles looked up with a start, his heart booming like a cannon as he began to speak. The monarch's glare moved to include him, but not directly and rather as though he was staring through him, while he awaited the advice. Charles flushed, his frame tensing.

"Such actions would ultimately show that as Your Majesty called them out, you so use them to uphold and force your will on the people and overrule the Parliament and their ancient privileges. It must occasion further counter actions from these resolute men," he added before Digby could interrupt him in disagreement.

The King raised an eyebrow at Holland, prompting the response, "Your Majesty, Sir Charles fought with us in the Bishops War. He is the man I discovered who had helped me win our only victory."

Charles's eyes widened as Holland began claiming half of his own victory amidst this flood of reassurance to the King.

"Resolute men," the King said with a dismissive shake of his head.

"I believe it to be so too, Your Majesty. Clemency from yourself and your distance from encouraging force will attract sane men to the view that Parliament are the ones that threaten the peace. Their attacks will fade as support wanes," Nicholas advised.

The King changed now that Nicholas had backed this up. No longer was it the view of an unknown upstart.

"I desire none other than the security and peace of my people. Violence should be avoided because the kingdom flourishes from my people's happiness," he said with apparent sincerity.

"It may be well to let them amuse themselves in this trial, but the Parliament is deadly serious, sir," Holland solemnly warned, "Perhaps Parliament should be listened to on this occasion, for they want only the removal of this man and the kingdom can be at rest once more."

Nicholas broke in. "Your Majesty, the trial will be no more than show. If you let it follow through, it will demonstrate you are committed to the Parliament's rights. Lord Strafford cannot be found guilty of treason when he still holds your confidence and I greatly doubt the House of Lords will vote to send down one of their own either."

Digby changed tack and erratically abandoned his suggestion of force, "I agree, sir, let them put Lord Strafford on trial and he is such a great speaker he will tie them in knots. He has done no wrong and we may as well allow him a platform to show this to the country."

The King looked to the paintings adorning the opposite wall before speaking. "Gentleman, I hear your views, but mark this; my authority must be upheld throughout. As for Strafford, he is innocent and I have promised him in this piece of correspondence that I will m-maintain his life and honour. Sir Charles, I trust this to you for delivery, on the recommendation of Lord Holland."

The letter was passed back to Nicholas, who then handed it to Charles. It was bad enough being before the monarch, for whom a public holiday was held on every anniversary of his coronation.

To think he had spent time with Anne and friends on the last occasion, feasting, and all in reference to the man before him now. Yet in a strange twist of irony, people seemed happy to attack the royal government, but were still loyal to the monarchy itself. As he stood staring at the sealed parchment, Charles reached out and took it, with the greatest of reluctance, a buzz of dread passing into him.

The King breathed deeply before continuing. "I was handed my rights from my father and on behalf of God and I see no higher earthly authority than the K-King. To see my people protest and be so distempered b-because of these men afflicts me so, out of concern for their own safety as much as my family's. Holland and Digby, I command you both to attend this trial and follow the proceedings for me."

The sovereign beckoned Nicholas closer. "Acquaint us with the details of the trial after our prayers tomorrow," he ordered.

The King then thanked them all and strode from the room, raising his hat before he went, showing the exquisite manners for which he was well known. Most of both the tension and magnificence exited with him.

"Sir Charles, I pray for your success, for politics is a dangerous game and with that letter, you not only hold the fate of Strafford, but of yourself and Lord Holland," Digby warned, before chasing after the King like a small lapdog seeking a morsel of food.

Looking mortified at the letter he held, Charles panicked. "What does Lord Digby refer to in this letter?"

"Only that it is of vital importance to the King."

"Does he not understand these men just wish him to agree not to tax us without their consent, as the laws dictate, not to imprison without due cause and to allow Parliament to safeguard itself?" Charles asked, summarising the main issues.

"No, Sir Charles, I fear he sees it as a personal attack on himself and his power. Anyway, now that you are to be an officer lining Strafford's route to the trial, it will give you a perfect alibi to deliver that. See how I look after your interest," Holland said.

The peer was about to leave, before turning once more.

"And pray make sure you are successful, for Digby will no doubt be planning your downfall. If you fail, it will impact on me, and that I will not have."

The whole world seemed as though it were turning upside down. His gut instinct lay for Parliament and their rights, although his insides were churned up with foreboding.

"How in God's name am I to simply pass this over? My honour and future now rest with this sheet of paper," he hissed in despair, realising Digby's rivalry was tipping the scales even further against the mission before it had even started.

"He hath taken as much care, hath used as much cunning to set a face and countenance of honesty and justice upon his actions, as he hath been negligent to observe the rules of honesty in the performance"

Mr Pym opening the trial of Lord Strafford
MARCH 1641

Chapter 3

Travel was slow going through the intense jams near the Westminster hall. Like the wheels of government, the hackney ground to a halt due to a number of other coaches causing a hold up, common on busy days as he well knew.

People walked past staring inquisitively inside the coach and this invaded Charles's important sense of privacy. The lady in the corner pulled the leather flap over her window, closing the small box off from the madness outside. Once the carriage finally limped close enough to the destination, he stepped out and made his way to Westminster steps, ready to await the barges carrying Strafford.

"Are you guardin' Black Tom, master?" a young lad asked him as he neared his destination.

"Aye, I have that task," Charles said with a smile, ruffling the boy's hair, only realising at the last minute how he hated people doing this to him as a child.

The lad respectfully watched the soldiers milling around with a fixed interest. The sight moved Charles, reminding him of his own youth, fascinated with his Uncle Tom's naval career.

Plus the young boy was behaving in a more responsible way than the hooting and jeering adults around him.

It was just after quarter to seven in the morning and Charles bellowed at the bodies of men, getting them into an orderly fashion and inspecting the lines, awaiting Strafford's arrival. He felt the role was as unpredictable as the English weather, with drizzle starting up again. Unfortunately he knew this would not dampen any of the hatred that the congregation exuded.

Sir Richard was sauntering around in the distance, like the wind was blowing him aimlessly across the courtyard. He sighed to himself at the pomposity of his colonel, who was now adjusting his posture to allow the gust to blow his grey curls back in a dramatic gesture. Such amateur dramatics were a big part of the man, but so was an army career in Flanders, fighting for the Dutch against the Spanish. But for once Sir Richard's presence was quite a reassuring one, for as senior officer, he would take responsibility for all possibilities, without realising he was only here as an afterthought; assigning Charles to this duty meant that his colonel's presence was needed by default.

"Soldier, take another man and make sure the area we are to march through is clear," Charles ordered, returning thoughts to the matter in hand. Then he ran over the timetable again under his breath.

"We walk with him in the middle of us, along with the men from the Tower of London, two officers with him, to Westminster Hall entrance, escort him inside …"

"Berkeley?" a voice growled from behind him.

He turned to see Sir Richard clasping his plump hands and casting a disapproving look with his heavily lidded eyes. Sir Richard did not have broad shoulders, and from this position, his large waistline made him look like a giant pear on legs. Yet even this did not remove any of the air of authority that the man held, as graceful as his groomed, flicked moustache and small beard.

"Yes, Colonel?"

"What are you doing? You are very distracted and we cannot afford for that when such a fellow is due to come into our midst," came the gruff warning.

"I am running through our orders," he said, emphasising the bond of command they *both* held.

"Are you going to go inside to listen to the damn thing after we have taken him in?"

Charles nodded. "Aye, for Lord Holland has saved me a seat in the public area."

"Good God, you know they are like gold. Rather you than me, sounds extremely boring."

Charles groaned. If it was not for his other secret task, he too could wash his hands of it all once Strafford had been conducted back to the Tower. It did feel good though that his commander was so obviously jealous of his reserved place. At that point a shout was heard from down towards the river. Sir Richard's head lurched up, like an attentive dog, the down turned mouth and glaring eyes changing instantly. With age, the man's faded blond locks were changing to grey and cheeks and nose turning ever more pink, yet the pride and self importance remained as youthful as ever.

"Berkeley, you and your chatter. They are arriving now, come on."

With his longer legs, Charles deliberately paced ahead of the plump colonel, towards the stairs that led down to the River Thames. A man climbed the stone steps and raised his hat in greeting as he emerged from below like an apparition of a long dead mariner.

"We have the prisoner," he said, pointing to the barges beneath him.

Charles stepped forward to see six craft with the centre one hemmed in. In an instant, he could guess about another hundred soldiers were spread amongst the vessels, and he anxiously searched for Strafford. His heart thumped and a chill came over him at the thought of this evil man being so close.

He rarely got scared but was extremely anxious right now. The heart bobbed as erratically as the barges on the murky water.

Sir Richard was overshadowed the officer addressed Charles, and spoke to assert his seniority, "Lieutenant Colonel, have you prepared the route?"

Charles realised Sir Richard did not remember the name of the man in front of them and he stepped in to rescue the situation, unable to stop a little smile cross his face.

"Our route is clear for Sir William Balfour and his men," Charles confirmed for his colonel.

Balfour nodded impatiently. "Well, can we proceed and get him inside? The sooner they have their prey the better," he said.

Sir Richard laid one hand on his hip, the elbow nudging Charles, following this up with an order to inspect the lines of men and wresting control of this conversation.

Charles watched as Balfour, the Lieutenant of the Tower of London, instructed his subordinates to come up in his Scottish accent, before joining his men and lining them up in two rows to complement the soldiers of the Trained Bands.

As a huddle of people approached with Balfour, he noticed the absence of the axe again. It was poignant that the King could only manage to do away with this small point, but could not do a jot to stop the court; not confident to sever the trial, but wishing to do something, which in the end only irritated both sides. But, thinking back to the nocturnal visit to the palace, he knew they did not take the whole matter seriously anyway.

Then he saw Strafford.

Black clothes and a long, dark cloak resembled funeral apparel - even his Order of the Garter hung on a gold chain, instead of the colourful blue ribbon - and all this seemed to accentuate Charles's nervousness of the peer. He could not bring himself to look at the cruel features, but he was determined to surmount this feeling later. Strafford seemed as though he was limping and Charles guessed it was the gout he was riddled with.

As the guard set off, Charles walked at the back, leaving the head of the march to Sir Richard. Crowds surged towards them, yelling and chanting and in itself, this was quite unnerving, as though they spouted hatred at the troops as well as the prisoner.

It was strange to be momentarily within the focus and sights of tens of thousands of hunters, like one huge stag chase. Within the double lines of two hundred of the London Trained Bands, Sir Richard, Charles and their men escorted Strafford right to the steps to Westminster Hall and left him to enter with the guards from the Tower of London.

The Earl of Arundel called out, "Thomas Wentworth, Earl of Strafford, you are called here to answer the charge of high treason."

The thought gave him a shiver of anticipation and curiosity for the trial, despite his antipathy to the mission he had to carry out, and after a few minutes, he went to begin his second task - delivery of the King's letter. Walking through the people who crowded the way to the hall, he paused again as he heard a great cry, "Stop, thief!"

Examining the crowd, he saw amongst many bodies a man make off towards the narrow back streets with the parish constable chasing after him. Taking his own leather purse from his belt, he walked ahead and entered apprehensively, legs stiff with anxiety. He hoped the gold coins had reached the selected guards who had agreed to do his bidding. Luckily for him, he knew two of them who had served under him in the Bishops War and they still held loyalty to his deeds and hard work. Plus with his attachment to the guard, he had an excuse to approach Strafford - one chance which must be timed and chosen to perfection.

Inside, he was confronted by towers of benches arranged for a multitude of spectators and a cool draught swirled through the vast stone room, feeling like Strafford had conjured up some evil spirits to protect himself. He raised his eyebrows at the difference in the hall as it had no traces of the wooden market stalls and law courts that were usually here. Gazing up at the ornate hammer beamed roof, he didn't see Digby approach him.

"My Lord Holland has failed to rendezvous with me and has taken his seat with the peers, but that is no surprise for I had been suspicious of him."

Charles felt frustrated now he had seen Digby, purposely not replying. He realised the position was more untenable - his patron and indeed the man whose influence had got him where he was today was now distant from these actions.

Digby continued doggedly, "You need not worry, for the King will not allow Strafford's death. Indeed, His Majesty has just reprieved a Catholic priest from death for exercising that religion."

To the news of this reprieve, Charles frowned, impelled to respond. "Catholics are hated more than Satan himself - was that a wise act, especially in the present circumstances, sir?"

"You question the King? You are as bad as these damn people. I hope for both your own and Holland's sakes that you deliver that letter, for it would be terrible otherwise."

"I believe that until a few weeks ago, you were part of those *damned people*," Charles snapped, causing Digby to burn up with outrage.

At that point a man stood up with a confident pose. He was slightly taller than most around him, around five foot eight, with black hair interspersed by grey flecks. The immaculate, deep blue suit made him more distinguishable in the crowd, a silver lining in his cloak being revealed when he cast it over his shoulder with disdain.

Charles looked at the stranger, intrigued by his smart appearance, dashing figure and above all, the seeming interest in him and Digby. After observing Charles's reaction to the other fellow, Digby walked away, taking his seat and calling on the other man to speak with him.

"Well, it had to be said," he thought aloud, justifying his verbal put down earlier. As a boy, Charles's father used to chide him for his opinionated character, despite the man being ten times worse.

The room started to fill and the public began a procession into the massive space that had been allotted to them, and which took up nearly half of the hall. Within the area beyond this, which Charles was examining, he could just see a throne for the King at the south end and spotted the Earl of Arundel taking his seat on a woolpack in front of it. At either side of Arundel, wooden seating extended several rows back, tiered up to a great height and holding the three hundred or so members of the House of Commons. The seventy barons, earls and viscounts from the House of Lords sat below the mountains of benches, while the officers of state waited in the centre of it all, alongside nearly half a dozen clerks to record the occasion. A dock was prepared at the northern most part of the arena.

Charles hastily took a seat on a wooden platform and listened to the conversations flooding around him, trying to get some more opinions about the reasons for the trial.

"The damned fellow told the King to use the Irish army to subdue England. How can any of us be safe with him at the sovereign's ear?"

"I hear he forced the King to appoint him to great offices of state. He got them through pressure, rather than merit," Charles said, interjecting his piece into the discussion.

"Merit? He has not an ounce of it. He has robbed money from the state, swindled, engaged the army in Ireland to force taxes out of people and used his energy to uphold the tyranny he set up over the people of the north. Why, he even backed the Church in their persecutions and I am sure he is a Catholic agent."

Charles felt like tearing the man apart with even greater fervour now, never mind helping guard his way to the hall. He listened to another gentleman who described how Strafford had called Ireland a conquered nation and trounced their laws and customs for his own advancement, the details spurring on his anger like war cries. Finding himself spoiling for the trial and rapid execution as much as these men, he was engrossed.

* * *

Digby addressed Sir Arthur Cotton after speaking to Sir Charles Berkeley.

"Is he definitely the man?" Digby asked, raising one eyebrow in examination.

"Aye, I would recognise him anywhere. You do me the greatest of services to bring me back into contact with him, for revenge will be my tonic, a healing balm that can finally close up my wound."

"He has trumped up the story of his battle with you in the late war to such a great extent that it was a popular anecdote. His fickle army career was built upon it, so it was easy to trace you as his vanquished foe, to lay the chance for revenge before you," Digby explained.

"And with my revenge comes the failure of his mission and your ascent over Holland," Cotton replied, with a shrewd observation.

Digby nodded, casually commenting on the benefits of Cotton serving a man who climbs to higher political heights, no matter who he scrambles over.

Cotton bowed, taking his leave, but on turning back, saw that Digby seemed not to have even noticed him go.

He sidestepped through the people, trying to find a good spot, as though he were waiting for a play to begin. Seeing Charles, he rubbed his hands quickly, before walking over to the sergeant of the guards to raise the opening curtain.

"Sergeant, do we still have an understanding?"

"I believe so, sir, although I feel the sum was too low."

The high, bony cheeks of the sergeant grew more pronounced as he glared, the veiled threat for more money was as cheap as a local whore. Cotton firmly held his sword, which was wrought with twists, patterned crosses and carved lines, proud of his ability with the weapon. He saw this as proof of anyone's manhood, though he was particularly skilled enough to deal a blow to enemies without the need for material weapons.

"Fail me, and you will have no need of money," he warned as he opened his hands to show several gold coins.

To add more glamour to the beautiful objects, Cotton rubbed them with his fingers, gaining the sergeant's whole attention. The six golden crowns, worth a total of thirty shillings was obviously highly tempting payment to simply follow the instructions and change the guard slightly earlier. The glance went back down to the glittering prizes, one showing the present King, whose face was so worn that it made him appear twenty years older, another the quartered shield of the arms of England, France, Scotland and Ireland, and the older coin showing the head of King James the First. He put his hand out to take them, but Cotton clasped them as suffocatingly tight as his ruthless nature, only releasing them when the man agreed to his demand.

"Make sure two men cover that doorway later and let nobody through," he growled, pointing to a stone archway next to an old tapestry.

Chapter 4

C harles could see the faint flicks of the King's ornate writing through the paper of the letter to Strafford, elaborate capital letters, flowing, curls and a crossing out. The hastily corrected error gave him an image of the King's uncertainty and he explored no further. He was curious, but remained reluctant to know precisely what was in the message he was passing on, and it was best he stayed in blissful ignorance. The more he thought of the mission, the more he detested the matter because it was actually aiding this arrogant, monstrous prisoner too.

"The bishops from the House of Lords have decided to stay away, because a life is being tried. I see only a devil being tried," one man muttered.

A loud and majestic fanfare from the trumpets outside heralded the King's arrival with poignant notes that silenced everyone and gave a thrill of excitement. He waited for a glimpse of the royal person, more curious than ever due to his recent close encounter with the monarch, but after a delay there was still nothing. A similar flurry of news spread in the form of whispered gossip, gradually building into renewed chatter like an approach of an army, that the King and Queen had arrived via a discreet entrance. Then he spotted a neighbour of his nearby and he called out, standing up to talk.

"Jacob, where is the King?" he asked of his friend.

"Apparently the lords ordered him to remain hidden, otherwise his presence on the throne would influence the case," Jacob told him, this small formality of the trial suddenly becoming interesting because of the effect it had on the major players around the event.

Charles could just make someone out taking a seat in an area behind the throne, closed off by curtains and wooden screens - this had to be the King, he thought. More snippets came in to create a fuller picture; the throne represented the monarchy, a sign of the power it vested in Parliament. The vacant seat showed that King and Parliament were joined for this legality.

A sidelined King Charles, the individual, could attend if he wished as a private interest and without official capacity, but he must remain hidden, to avoid influencing the proceedings.

Despite the sovereign's presence, the public in the hall feasted, ate and drank, showing little courtesy or respect to him, which strangely enraged Charles.

"Manners go down while protests and anger rise. What a damned awful situation," he muttered. Despite his aversion for the royal cause, he believed wholeheartedly in hierarchy and respect.

Glancing up, he nodded to the two guards near the stone archway. They acknowledged him and he felt a little more secure that they were still in collaboration. The wait here was as bad as that deathly, long and unbearable time just before a battle, where worries festered and bred with ease.

His senses told him someone was watching him and he turned to see the unusual man who had been with Digby some time ago. He stared constantly and Charles raised his eyebrows, meeting the gaze until the man looked away. Again for a second time

Charles noticed the man glaring, but this time a neighbour began to converse, taking his attention away from this irritation. He tried to pass the time, reading the printed leaflet that had been pushed into his coach. Strafford was accused of misleading the King but what if Strafford was executed, would the King then come under scrutiny? Who would take the responsibility and the wrath of the people if they didn't stop at Strafford's death?

His thoughts were getting out of hand and he kept searching this human forest, for Digby's acquaintance, anxious to pinpoint his movements.

How on earth can I be here to deliver this when I agree with the basic principles Parliament call for? He thought, drifting back to the matter at hand, while pulling his cloak around him. A staff was thumped on the stone floor, silencing the hall and startling him. He could not help but compare the shock of that thud to his steely nerve during cannon fire. Watching the proceedings, he observed the clerks and various peers entering the hall and felt more interest at the procedures of the court than the issue itself. He mused about the law, remembering his father's statement of fact to his sister, that a father had legal power over his children until the age of twenty one, and also how it was perfectly legal for a girl to be betrothed at the age of seven. The trouble in his family was that headstrong Lucy had flouted this authority.

His guards were still in place.

Within the leaflet, he had read about how a case of impeachment meant that the lords of the realm had to be judges.

The peers were dressed in their sumptuous and historic red, ermine cloaks - seniority defined, he noticed, by the number of gold stripes on one side. Once they had taken their seats,

Strafford was summoned to the hall. Some people howled and it seemed everyone chattered at the call for the prisoner and Charles himself jeered, waving his pamphlet. As the hall quietened, he sat down, tapping his foot repeatedly with nervous anticipation. Even though he had seen him earlier, the effect of the man was still immense and his presence cast a shadow across the whole place, no matter what distance you were from him.

Slowly advancing into the hall, Strafford took up his position with the familiar heavy and interrupted walk. He appeared sickly, stooping as he moved along the cold chamber. He had a grey beard and wore a fur cap. Holland had mentioned that Strafford was not yet fifty and despite these ailments, Charles reluctantly noted that he behaved with dignity amongst it all, his immense strength of character coming through in the body language and attention to every detail. The hall went quiet, as though a lion had been released and it was clear people were scared, and in awe of the man, despite his situation.

Charles eagerly examined the peer from afar.

The Earl of Strafford stood out conspicuously alone, perhaps the only man on his own in the packed, unwelcoming place and the gentlemen in Parliament must have purposely done it to make him feel exposed. Then the screens which hid the royal family from view were torn down and the hall started buzzing as discussion and animated talk about it began to escalate, until full volume eventually returned again. The move showed that the King was not prepared to be closeted from view and he seemed determined to assert his presence and importance. It was obvious he had strong feelings about this trial, and Charles knew the King greatly valued Strafford's services, but did not really get on with the man himself.

He did not want to be mixed up with the royal policy more than he was already, and he was glad he was way too far away for the King to see him. Watching Strafford and then glancing down at the letter again, he proceeded to fold it twice more, making it fit into his palm, still unable to believe that this needed to get to that remote prisoner. He held it as if his life depended on it, and to an extent, it did.

Nerves frayed the more he thought about the delivery and he focussed on the trial to help reassert calmness. He likened it to a duel, both King and Parliament lined up, eyeing each other warily while brandishing their blades in the sunrise of this new dawn. Now Parliament lashed out with the first attack. Fear of this man made it a ferocious onslaught indeed and seemed like it would secure Strafford's downfall in one go, such was the passion it stirred up. Charles thought it ironic that Strafford should be the one to actually inspire both sides' viewpoints.

He listened as the charges were read out in the clerk's deep voice. The noble was accused of endeavouring to subvert the fundamental laws and government and to introduce an arbitrary and tyrannical regime. Parliament had taken a damned good swipe indirectly at the King and it remained to be seen whether the accused could counter this blow. John Pym, the man who had come to the fore in Parliament and had formulated its actions quickly rose to his feet. He was vigorous, looking around the crowds as though he were a virgin gladiator, here to make a name for himself.

"The Earl of Strafford has taken as much care and used as much cunning to set a face and countenance of honesty and justice upon his actions, as he has been negligent to observe the rules of honesty in the performance."

Charles kept checking the two guards he had bribed, while Pym continued his colossal assault, though he noted it consisted wholly of general accusations.

"My Lords, it is the greatest baseness of wickedness that he dare not put his actions into their true colours. Now he will claim he acted constitutionally, but let me warn you of his true deeds in their honest context, stripped bare of the lies and mask he has built up around them."

Charles smiled, enjoying the roasting Strafford was taking and pinning his hopes on Pym's words, hoping for more precise proof.

"From using martial law to punish his opponents in council, to allowing thousands of Irish children to starve to death, the man is evil through and through. He might implore in his replies that his behaviour was judicious, but the habit of brutality in him is more perfect than any act of cruelty he has committed."

Applause broke out amongst the lines of people, few daring to remain silent. Charles sounded his agreement.

"Pray give me leave to call witnesses to speak on the subjects of breaching our Parliamentary privilege, illegal billeting of soldiers upon the populace and misappropriating revenue," Pym continued unabated.

Although he could not see John Pym fully, Charles could sense in his words and actions that failure to condemn Strafford was his prime fear.

"We will reveal Lord Strafford's intentions in all their natural blackness and deformity," Pym claimed, slashing his last sentence through Strafford's public image.

"Sir Piers Crosby," the clerk boomed, calling for the first witness, while Pym finished his introductory offensive.

A man moved forward and instantly, Charles could see Strafford raise his hand to speak. He could not fully hear what was going on though and a murmur sailed through the sea of people, flying around like a stray seagull.

"He says Crosby is prejudiced against him, so is not a fit witness. Apparently Crosby has recently lost a libel case against Strafford," was one man's commentary.

After a few minutes silence, Crosby resumed his seat, repelled by the prisoner with ease. The Lords must have backed Strafford's concerns. Pym was deep in discussion now, readying himself for a second pass. The air became tense and everyone now realised that their quarry may be on trial, but by no means was he powerless.

"John Clotworthy," was the next call.

Charles could hear little details of interest and then Strafford began cross examining witness on matters concerning his own post as Lord Lieutenant of Ireland. The man stuttered and could not answer some points. Pym's friend interrupted the spiralling scene and asked for leave to read the remonstrance of the Irish Parliament, extricating Clotworthy's evidence from certain death.

Strafford raised an objection again and Charles tutted, irritated at his constant complaining.

"That remonstrance has no bearing, it is not in any of the charges made against me," Strafford insisted.

The reply came back that it had reference to what was being discussed and Lord Arundel duly overruled Strafford this time. From his dealings with Holland, Charles knew that although the two men were peers of the realm, Arundel abhorred Strafford.

The prisoner was incensed at the use of the remonstrance from Ireland, which had finally been announced in full, giving the impression the Irish Parliament wanted his death. "Your Lordships may observe that this remonstrance is fallen out *since* my impeachment of High Treason here. It is a conspiracy."

The hall went silent at Strafford's claim of a plot and he seemed to realise the effect of his accusation as soon as he said it - even the most vocal critic froze.

John Glyn, Pym's right hand man jumped up and waved his arm, seizing what he thought to be a chance to marshal people against Strafford's accusation of foul play. "My Lords, these words are not to be suffered. Charging the House of Commons with conspiracy? We desire your lordship's justice in this."

Strafford went slowly down to his knees, as though he were scrambling around looking for something and Charles felt some relief that he had made a fatal mistake at last. "My Lords, forgive me, I never intended to charge the House of Commons with that. I wished only to point out that there are such groups at work outside of Parliament to conspire against me."

Glyn resumed his seat, appearing embarrassed at asking for justice on Strafford's words, before he had accused the prisoner of anything specific. Pym moved the proceedings onwards, leaving this behind.

The Vice Treasurer of Ireland was giving evidence against Strafford now, backing up Parliament's charge that he had misappropriated the revenue of that country until the prisoner got the chance to question him.

"Tell me, sir, how much was the finances of Ireland in deficit before I turned it all around?" Strafford demanded of the Treasurer.

Pym stood up now, anxious to save the situation from deteriorating again. "My lord, I object to such discourses between the accused and our witness."

Again Arundel nodded his agreement to the prosecution, swiping away another of the prisoner's defensive moves and forcing him to call for extra time. But the fact still remained that the Vice Treasurer could not deny the peer had cut down inefficiency and actually added to funds.

"My Lords, so far the questions I have faced have not been in my original charges. Pray give me some time to collect my thoughts before I answer further questions which are likewise new to me," Strafford interrupted, clearly desperate to stop further surprise attacks.

The House of Commons signalled their disagreement and Strafford persisted, this time addressing his request directly and solely to the men of the House of Lords. They stood and retired to consider it and Charles rolled his eyes at the delay. The longer this took, the more worry he had over delivering this letter.

It was nearly half an hour before they returned and notified Strafford that they would not be siding with him on this point either. With a second wind, Strafford relentlessly began the attack again, telling the peers that he took actions in Ireland based on the law of Ireland, which differs greatly from the legal situation here.

"I beseech you to look in my papers and account books and I am sure you will find all in order and I ask you to verify the spoken evidence these men have put forward against me. Remember there is no proof in mere words. Most importantly, the Irish Remonstrance I have been presented with today was drafted and issued from a near empty Irish Parliament, knowing that I am here on trial. Less than one year earlier a full Parliament was happy to approve my policies and even vote me their thanks. There is more to this new remonstrance than meets the eye and with regards to conspiracy, I meant what I said," the prisoner reminded them all, his attack combating his foe's assault and disabling it.

Pym stood up again, this time with less confidence and self assurance than before. "My Lords, I can promise the accused and everyone here that the articles we bring against him will prove everything."

By now, the day was drawing to a close and Charles felt it was no further forward, disappointed that no damning proof had been levelled to run Strafford through. He was firm in the opinion that Parliament would find a way of saving the country, and the King, from this man, for Strafford was evil and cunning. The clash was over for now, both parties alive to fight another day.

He wondered if the public fear of prisoner was because of the image Parliament had highlighted as a warning, combined with the coincidental riots over the trial.

Toying with his wedding ring and straightening his cuffs, he knew that every second delayed his mission. During the debate the Queen had risen and left the hall, but the young Prince of Wales and the King remained to the end.

Seeing Digby in the sea of faces, he shook his head. That was one man he could never even begin to understand. Digby's complexion was perfect, as good as any lady's and complementing his golden locks of hair, but hiding what Charles thought was the true, twisted nature of the man. Despite having clear eyes, his soul was as dark as the Thames.

After more assertions thrown from both sides and no hard facts, the furore died down as the proceedings were brought to a close.

One man was clear, "Strafford has valid arguments when he says there was no proof of any treason."

The person was set upon in a vicious argument and Charles in the meantime saw the prisoner exchange a smile as he looked over to the direction of the King.

"What was the point of this trial?" he muttered, seeing the accused and his humour as blatantly patronising.

Now it was time to move and he jumped to his feet on noticing the prisoner leaving the hall. Charles's moment of truth had arrived.

Chapter 5

Without further ado, and inspired by hatred of Strafford's sarcastic behaviour, he headed for the Gothic arched doorway, eyes fixed on the two guards he had in his service. His legs felt numb, almost as though he were sleepwalking.

In many a sticky situation, he had used mind over matter to push himself on. Now, as he strode towards his destination, he was aware of others who seemed to be on the same course.

At the far end of the hall, two guards were moving his way, looking concerned, and the possibility they were aware of his plan wreaked havoc with his senses.

He walked faster.

Staring at the doorway, his heart raced, the immediate goal being to walk through that portal and into the Unknown that lay beyond. His analytical and practical mind had subconsciously broken the mission down into such various parts. The divide between him and these unknown troops narrowed and it was clear that they were headed in the same direction. Finally, after what seemed like an age, he approached his two men and saluted.

"We are discovered, sir," one said. The short, simple comment was the final straw for his nerves, tipping the scales of his normally well balanced mind, and he felt panic release from the pit of his stomach.

"They are coming our way," the other whispered.

At the lowest ebb, seeming like his plans were unravelling, he was imbued with an intense determination in the face of defeat, and he faced the newcomers. A full sense of stubbornness, which must have been the by product of his anxiety, emanated from him. This had turned personal - no longer was it a task for the King, but a point of honour that he would not drop in the face of any threat. Always he had a sense of justice for the underdog, and right at this moment, he was just such a beagle. He acknowledged the new guards, who calmly nodded back.

"What is your business here?" he demanded.

The pair stiffened up, the aura of forceful authority changing the tables between the hunter and the hunted in an instant.

"We ... were ordered to relieve the guard here, sir."

Charles waved them away and told them to see that the boats were ready for Strafford, to carry the accused back to his iconic prison. They stood still, looking at each other.

"But we were ordered by the sergeant, sir."

"And I am an officer of the escort. Do what I say, damn you."

As they finally left, he was free to enter the archway, and he did so with a feeling of jubilation, relishing the accomplishment.

The confidence that was injected into him gave the drive and ability to carry on, and he walked to the end of the stone corridor, pausing at the corner. Echoes resonated through the narrow passage and he felt a cold draught swirling around, as though the spirits of all the people who had graced this magnificent building over the centuries were eagerly spurring him on.

Then reverberating footsteps signalled Strafford and his guards' entry at the opposite end of the passage, like gearing up for a joust. He listened closely to the noises, judging the distance as he had done in the Bishops War, when making a cavalry attack at precisely the right moment to ensure success. A cough from one of the men raced its way through the place, and he guessed they must be around eighteen foot away. His vision blurred for a moment.

Charles counted in his mind before stepping forward, clutching the letter as though it were his weapon. Indeed, the small piece of correspondence would be as deadly as a blade to him, especially due to the identity of the recipient. At that point, a shiver came over him as he thought about Strafford and how close he would be to the devil. This chilly atmosphere most probably emanated from the fellow's heart.

Then as he rounded the corner, he saw the peer, accompanied by two men. Charles took little in, but marched on, clashing into the Earl of Strafford. The soldiers flapped around, as though they were two panicked chickens, the sort which chased around the back streets and courtyards of the city. Strafford recoiled and as Charles's fraught body fell backwards, he saw the pale face of the accused, eyes wide as he looked to his chest, anticipating an assassin's wound.

Charles fell onto his backside and the guards recovered from the shock to begin shouting at him, ordering him to rise.

No matter how hard he wished to, his body was temporarily stunned into inactivity. Then the most shocking of things happened; Strafford held his hand out in assistance. He paused, not wishing to touch the man after all he had heard about him, but as his recovering senses gushed back, he grasped the large hand, pulling himself up and intending to seize the moment by pushing the letter into Strafford's palm.

"What the hell are you doing?" a soldier yelled.

"Stop, that man has just conspired with Strafford," another cry came, this time from behind.

No sooner had the words been spat out, than they robbed Charles of all vestiges of self belief. The man who uttered them stood in the doorway, pointing dramatically and flanked by the short sergeant. The two guards with the prisoner stopped dead in the face of such an accusation, hovering over Strafford, bordering on terror.

Crucially, Strafford had quickly withdrawn his hand, severing Charles's plan and leaving the letter still within his own tight grip. At the onset of this interruption, a complete anticlimax washed over the all too short hint of success.

"Who on God's earth are you?" Charles demanded with outrage, while he hastily slipped the paper into one of the gloves he was wearing.

"You should know, Sir Charles," was the mysterious reply.

The audacious clothes and the striking appearance of this man hit home; it was the one who had been with Digby.

As Charles stood speechless, an urge to flee came over him, until reason dismissed it from his thoughts. Indeed, such feelings had never succeeded in all of his twenty seven years. The two soldiers and sergeant came towards him and he warned them off, but their journey proved relentless as hints of disturbance seeped out of the thick, stone walls. Charles adjusted his doublet, ignoring the hollering junior officer. The feelings he had experienced since accessing this colourless, bland area were now added to by anger. It was the way the sergeant was bellowing at him that irritated him, after all the tension of the plot.

"Hold your tongue, soldier," he barked much louder in response, as he pointed to his medal from the late war.

"Forgive me, but what is your position here?"

"I am a Lieutenant Colonel of the Red Regiment, London Trained Bands, in the prisoners' escort party. Now your enthusiasm for guarding this swine has not gone unappreciated, but I take exception when it is extended to myself."

Silence lasted for a few seconds, until Strafford broke in with his own demand, not one to be left out. It was this desire to have the last word that alienated most of his colleagues in government.

"Get me back to my damn quarters."

The soldiers stood amidst this confusion until Cotton swaggered towards him, a look of sarcasm on his face.

"So, we are brought face to face. It is lucky I informed the sergeant of the conspiracy I had heard about out there."

"What are these cryptic riddles, you fool? Who are you?" Charles yelled.

Before anyone could speak, Strafford roared, like the caged lion he was. A peer of the realm, one who was the King's most powerful subject until last year, now cooped up inside a small alley. This frustration was self evident.

"You argue like a gaggle of women. I demand you get me back to the Tower and leave this officer to do his duty."

Taken aback by the thought that he needed help from such a rogue as Strafford, someone who had sought to trounce the rule of law, Charles scorned it, determined to show his opposition.

Strafford began arguing with his jailors and Cotton urged the sergeant to search the peer.

"I have nothing to hide, but mark my words, I will remember this vile treatment when I am acquitted," Strafford threatened.

Charles's heart seemed to stop temporarily, now thankful that Strafford had not taken the letter. The sergeant acquiesced with Cotton's demand and as the troops advanced to the black clad figure, Charles grasped the moment, which hung precariously in the balance. He reinforced his official position of authority within the escort party.

"To satisfy your wild imaginations, I will ask Lord Strafford to show his hands and quickly turn out all the possessions that are on his person. This man, Cotton, has no reason to be here, but I will entertain his ridiculous notions temporarily, if only to disprove them."

Charles took his own hat off and held it out, as Strafford hesitated, before making a sarcastically elaborate showing of one hand, and then the next. After this, everyone staring with bated breath, he put a paper and some coins, along with a miniature portrait of his wife into the hat. Charles handed the paper to the sergeant, who scrutinised it with Cotton peering over his shoulder, only to announce it was simply notes made about the trial. Then Charles saw the two guards in his employ appear, promptly ordering them to escort Strafford onwards, while he himself began marching to the end of the corridor.

"And take this member of the public out of Westminster Hall," Charles instructed, Cotton's presence now on borrowed time as one soldier loomed ever closer.

Charles entered the vast Westminster Hall again, the commotion and noise was twice as bad to his troubled mind.

The swirling of bodies made him feel he was in a storm, soon to be drowned. Then amidst the maelstrom, Lord Holland appeared, like a ray of hope streaming into the dire surroundings. Holland's face dropped as he stood with one hand on his hip, the other grasping his walking cane. He seemed to examine Charles and his appearance.

The high eyebrows and delicate mouth accentuated every mood of the noble, who was adorned with a red suit and abundant gold lace. Charles hoped to speak to him, but

Holland walked briskly away as though he could not wait to leave.

During the Bishops War, Charles's victory was a rare success story, and came at a point when Holland's capacity for command was being questioned; it had helped save the man's post as General of the Horse.

The retreating peer tapped his cane impatiently against his leg, spurring on an invisible horse and making it ready to charge at the people who parted for him with all sorts of polite gestures.

"He knows," Charles murmured with further distress, sure Holland could tell the letter had not been delivered.

By this time, Strafford and his orbit of guards appeared and Charles commenced leading them through the now structured bodies, a way carved through with the troops on each side. Accompanied by a new stony silence, continuously unnerving in itself, Charles stepped into the daylight, squinting for a few seconds, while the actual truth became apparent with the illumination; his hands were still impalpably bound to this mission.

He descended the steps towards Sir Richard, a wall of observers cursing and muttering, while the small, folded letter in his hand seemed to burn into his skin, branding him permanently. As he continued through the populace, it felt like the letter stood out, his leather glove transparent around the message and he could not help but grip his fist together. He passed Sir Richard and nodded to him, turning after a while to check the black shadow of a prisoner, head held high. The breeze came up and Strafford wrapped his cloak around him in a flurry, like a crow making ready to fly away. It was at this point that he watched the sergeant talking to Sir Richard, both men marching along together behind, the old colonel's eyes fixed upon Charles.

Chapter 6

Sauntering quietly into the black and white tiled hall, turmoil still repressing any sort of happiness to be back within his home, Louise took his hat and gloves. Charles then passed into the dining room, finding Anne with his old friend James and wife Elizabeth. After the initial surprise at seeing him, he threw his arms in the air, seizing the chance to leave his troubles behind and yelled his name.

James was now a merchant in the city and Charles noticed by the fact he had a sumptuous lace collar, rather than a plain linen one, that he was successful. The green coat and breeches were as outlandish, bright and flamboyant as the man himself, a contradictory colour considering he always bad mouthed the boring countryside and its meadows and shrubbery. The tight doublet that clung to the silver buttons echoed his elaborate claim of always eating double in remembrance of the hardships from when his father was imprisoned for not paying the latest tax the King had conjured up. Elizabeth and Anne cooed over the couple's child, like two blackbirds fussing over their brood and making ready for the young's feeding time.

He kissed his wife's welcoming pink lips and then Anne took hold of the baby, gently gliding over to show Charles with one arm wrapped round the precious bundle like a protective wing. "Isn't she gorgeous, sweetheart?" she exclaimed, beaming happiness over the little girl.

"He is telling her the catechism already," Elizabeth said of her husband, with a smile.

"I'll wager you can't remember the wording?" Anne challenged Charles, with high spirits.

"My duty is to love, honour and succour my father and mother; to submit myself to all my governors, teachers, spiritual pastors and masters; to order myself lowly and reverently to all my betters ..."

"All right, you can stop. To think we used to say that every Sunday. One day, like James, you will have to teach our child to swear it well too."

He watched the baby and her petite face as she slept, features like her father's. He wished it was his own little girl that he gazed upon, as content and delightful as this, but even the lovely sight before him could not stop a flash of that awful image of the lifeless, tiny body. With every view of it, he could feel pain, like the memory had been brutally carved so vividly into his mind. For a split second he pulled back from Anne and the baby, before realising his actions. His eyes darted to his wife, desperate that she should not have experienced the same, or caught the horror like a spreading illness, but Anne was obliviously stroking the baby's fine hair.

"We have left Tom with his wet nurse. No need to employ another though, for Elizabeth says she is going to breastfeed this little lass herself," James told him, knowingly providing a welcome break from the impasse that had come over his friend.

Charles smiled, then took Anne's hand, rubbing it gently. She looked up, as though heartened by him.

"Have you heard the maids around Westminster, Charles, their tongues run on wheels," exclaimed James, "They are all a flutter about this trial."

With a sigh and a playful roll of his eyes, Charles nodded, commenting with more truth that he wished the whole issue would fly off, to really give them something to flap about. The government and James were playmates that had fallen out long ago and James loved nothing more than immersing himself in the waters of politics, the only thing to rival his appreciation of the opposite sex.

"Anyhow, Charles, if you are not engaged tonight, please come and visit us; we can play music and sing. Let's reminisce about the old days."

"Yes, Charles, let's go, we seldom get the opportunity," Anne echoed. Her happy face made his mind up yet again.

James's last comment about musing over their boyhood seemed to detonate a wild rhythm of excitement as he now threw more ingredients into the cooking pot. Matthew Thatcher was a mutual friend who he revealed he had invited too.

"Old Straw Locks always has a *towering* list of stories he can tell," James joked as he stood up to leave, "We must be gone now, Charles, we shall see you both tonight."

Charles groaned at the joke about Matthew's interest in the Tower of London, where he worked. Elizabeth said nothing, except giving one of her sparkling smiles, the only betrayal of what a jewel of a personality lay unpolished and overshadowed by her husband. She was much the opposite of James and he saw the scar on the right cheek, the visible reminder of her battle with smallpox, one of the few times James had come to him in tears. They saw the couple out and as he shut the door, Anne hugged his slim body, brushing some dirt from his woollen breeches. He smiled warmly and cuddled her back - it was good to wind down from today's events.

"Old Straw Locks?" she laughed.

"Aye, but anyone is given the title of 'old' by James though; why he'd probably even call that little darling of his the same in a few months."

With his arm around her, they went back into the room and stood together while he told her about Matthew, who he and James would see every week browsing the same old stalls at the exchange. She undid the wooden buttons on his doublet, before tugging frivolously at the two linen cords which interwove each other to fasten up the top part of his shirt. He fell into the chair, hardly feeling the clash against the wooden frame, barely cushioned by the embroidered Berkeley coat of arms that adorned the thin fabric padding. He had adroitly pulled Anne onto his knee, surprising her, with handiwork of a different sort to the crest she had created. He kissed her playfully; tickling her while she laughed and squealed unconvincingly for him to stop.

Like a divine message, a small white object dropped to the floor as she hit out at him in merriment and she leaned over to get it, Charles keeping one hand on each breast as she did so. With a slap of his hands and a mischievous smile, she asked what sort of love letter she had retrieved. Charles froze, almost forgetting about it.

"It is nothing," he said quickly, going to take it from her. Anne continued her joke, snatching it away from him at the last moment.

"Promise you will not breathe a word to anyone if I tell you."

Anne laughed, clearly thinking it was a continuation of their fun, with a nod of her head.

"The King wrote it, handed it to me personally."

Her face dropped, astonishment lifting her eyebrows as she mouthed the words 'the King'.

He nodded, but she tilted her head in disbelief, asking for the truth because she knew that he disagreed with the monarch's political stance.

"Who is it for?" she asked, as if testing his claim.

"I cannot tell that to anyone I care for. Trust me."

Anne was not to be put off and like a corkscrew, the type he had just bought recently from the blacksmith, she made ready to drill into his secret as she leaned ever closer with intrigue.

"That is where I was called to that night. I had to deliver it to Strafford, but I am not going to do it now, I am done with it."

She looked stunned at the name he had mentioned and Louise entered the room, asking permission to clear the empty glasses away.

"I love you, Anne, but do not ask any more questions," he told her, wishing to end all discussion over the odious task.

"Would you not like a son, Charles?" she whispered, the deep sincerity and longing pouring out of her tone.

"Of course, my darling, but with all this protesting, I would rather wait."

Taking Anne's hand and sensing the fact she had been moved by the presence of the baby, he waited to hear what she had to say.

"My only wish from childhood was for children. Why do you not allow me to bear any, while other women produce regiments of them?" she asked bitterly.

Stroking her head, he embraced her trembling body.

Deep inside, he ached for his little daughter who had been snatched away and Anne had never let out such a torrent of raw feeling before.

"My sweet, I am sorry," he said, lost for words.

Anne said nothing. It felt as though she was crying sporadically recently, or getting irritated at the smallest point, and from childhood he did not know how to handle such emotion; children were all that Anne spoke of right now. Plus, once she had made her mind up, she was not to be changed.

"At least we have a nice evening ahead of us that will cheer us up," he said softly.

"You risk yourself with this letter, yet you will not have a child because of the apparently dangerous times. You contradict yourself all the time," she shouted as she walked away from him.

Feeling he had to do something about the child issue, he called after her, "Try and be reasonable, we will someday, but there is no urgency," and he meant it, for he loved nothing more than the thought of being a father. He told himself again that it must have been God's will, though he would never understand why their first had been snatched away and indeed why the Almighty had been so cruel. The pain was still too much and he had no desire to risk going through it again so soon, God forbid, losing Anne. Nevertheless, he felt a rush of selfishness. Reluctantly, he retired to his study.

Louise tapped and entered after him, handing over a letter. "This came when you were out, sir."

"Louise, I know you do, but will you look after my wife?"

She glanced at him warmly and nodded. "Yes, Sir Charles, of course."

The writing was small and precise, grandly announcing his invitation to an informal banquet, hosted by Lord and Lady Holland, in two days' time. He had already been fitted and measured for a new shirt, with a grand lace collar, and shoes with a flourish of material on the front, in the form of a silver flower. His tailor should finish making the shirt in time, having already told him his son was helping. The banquet would be an ideal location to mix within, and plans to retrieve his reputation with Lord Holland would be best served up there.

He then sprang to his feet and walked through the passage to the kitchen, which had white walls and a large fireplace. It seemed like a pot of aromatic plants were in every place, to keep flies and smells at bay, battling for superiority with the scent of the herbs hanging in a row. Opening most of the cupboards he searched for a candle, but found nothing but foodstuff. Again he noted the cupboards were lined with blue paper to keep flies away, for they were scared of the colour blue; that he did know.

He amused himself at last because Holland's coat of arms was the same colour, and he vowed to keep the same aversion as the flies to any future 'missions'.

Finding a candle on the shelf, he lit it in the roaring fire and placed it in a holder on the table. The flames and the light reflected their orange tint into the pewter cups and dishes, injecting warmth and a sense of homeliness into everything.

He remembered how as a child in his father's inn, he would lie in front of the fire and watch the rain or snow outside. It was safe and snug until their dog jostled him for position, his father settling it by dragging him to his feet to start work on some job or other. Examining the way the fire beautified normally bland objects, he saw some sand grains, used to clean the stone floor, congregating in the cracks, like the idle youths outside. He was glad his father had encouraged him to work. Without that discipline, he would never have managed so well with his military role.

He held the cursed letter up, marked at the edges now from the travels it had faced today, contemplating throwing it into the flames that seemed to call out for something to consume.

He unfolded the letter, to see the seal still intact, the whole thing looking somewhat sorry for itself now, as it remained in limbo with him. No matter how hard he hated the fact, he felt like a guardian trying to reunite it with one of its parents. This item had been given to him by his King, whether he supported him or not, and the bond of honour, duty and courage that this small scrap embodied could not be ignored. With a subdued roar of frustration, he resolved to deliver it tomorrow, casting it into his leather purse, though the whole matter went deeper than this. As his heart raced with determination, a thump on the door pealed out alongside it and he walked into the main room to see Louise showing a man in.

"Sir, this gentleman is from Lord Holland," she explained, curtseying as she left them both.

The man nodded, removing his hat in greeting, though the long face and hook nose gave a certain bleakness to his presence. His bland clothes betrayed the fact that this was not a social call.

"Sir Charles, my lord wishes to know whether you were successful?"

"Ah, a verbal message is more convenient in the situation, eh?"

"Should I report a failure to him in that case, sir? He was not very hopeful anyway, following a sarcastic jibe from Lord Digby."

Charles snapped indignantly, "Nay, I have not delivered it yet, though I shall succeed, and when I do, then I shall inform his lordship immediately. There will be no need to send any hounds out."

"Well I pray you will accomplish it as speedily as possible. Lord Holland expects the King's displeasure, for His Majesty always presumes his wishes will be carried out immediately. My lord also instructs me to tell you that his honour rests on this as much as your own … and he guards his own reputation without mercy, if you understand the meaning, sir?"

"Perfectly. Though I disagree with the King, I will carry this matter through and Lord Holland's reputation will blossom, while I enjoy the fruits of my labours … if you know what I mean, sir?"

The man stared for a short time, his protruding lips tight with concentration, like a small beak, before he gave a sharp nod of his head. After this, he replaced his hat and stepped into the night again, leaving Charles to ponder tomorrow's court session and a different way of delivering the letter in view of today's setback.

He went upstairs to the bedroom, putting his candle down on the small oak table at the bedside. While changing his black doublet and breeches to rich red ones with silver lace, he took time to examine the paintings on the wall, which he had not done in detail for some time. One portrayed him and Anne dressed in various apparel and rich silk clothing, especially used for the sitting. The garments hung across their bodies like an elaborate nightdress, in luscious waves, mingled with sumptuous cloaks, shawls or jewels. He remembered the artist's statement that this enhanced his social standing, prestige and riches, but above all for him, it depicted his beautiful wife.

The other was completely different and less skilfully done. It showed a family scene of two children with their parents, the mother's eyes gazing sadly at a skull that represented a dead child.

The father was standing proudly straight, pointing to a sword, indicating his military career. The little girl watched her parents admiringly, while the son seemed sullen and rather scared, having his father's huge hand resting on his shoulder, as if to steer him in life. Charles was, of course, looking at himself as the child with his family around him, although everything had changed beyond recognition since his father had commissioned this modest work. Despite the amateur attempts at scale, or the limited colours, it was a priceless and unique image of his mother, all he had left to remember her with outside of his thoughts.

He moved on and combed his hair, before taking his medal from the mantle, holding it with reverence, proud of how he had earned it nearly two years ago. It was for his men he wore it he said then and it was still the same now. As he heard Louise leave the dressing room, he strode into the bedchamber, immediately kissing Anne's head as he sat with her. As she continued to dab her cheeks with indifference, it came to him that he and Anne were the only people who could know what the other was feeling and so far they had continued to grieve on their own.

"All this talk of children, Anne; we do have a child, just being cared for by God."

Her chest heaved as her breathing intensified, igniting a furnace of feelings that had been clouded for some time, and she gave a gasp of relief as her soul was resuscitated. For a moment they looked at each other until he embraced her, Anne pressing her head to his chest.

"I thought you would never mention her. I felt like she had gone forever until now."

Charles nodded. "She will always be here between us," he whispered, placing his hand between their bodies.

"I know that most parents go through this several times and Mother warned me about stillbirths and infantile deaths, but I am devastated, Charles."

"If she had breathed for but one minute, I would have christened her, but I feel sure God has still taken her to him."

He eased her closer, explaining how much more unified they seemed, her emerald eyes even twinkling light into the darkness, though his royal task still managed to creep like a spider into this touching scene. He examined her delicate round face and petite lips, before caressing the ringlets of her silky hair. He traced his fingers round her pearl necklace and to her chest. They had not looked so meaningfully at each other for quite some time, and now the emotions that had been overshadowed by grief began to gush forth as he admired every small detail. The way she held her head and the sparkle in her eyes transferred the thumping from his head to his heart.

Chapter 7

She asked if Charles had instructed Louise to make sure the cook maids had left the kitchen sound, or told her that they would be back at around eleven tonight. He nodded as they walked up the narrow street, arm in arm, as though they had just began courting. Charles was on the outside while Anne walked inside, under the protruding upper storeys of the buildings, which provided some shelter for her. Her prized position in the street was proven when some excrement sloshed all over the stones after being thrown from a window above, with Charles casually jumping out of the way at the warning shout. He was starting to become adept at escaping the descent of such waste, especially the rubbish his superiors were coming out with lately.

"Last week I saw two grown men disputing over who should take the covered route," he told her with a chortle.

They went towards the narrow alley, which ran between some run down timber framed houses, checking for approaching hackney carriages first as they crossed the street.

He noticed a man ambling behind, as though lost, but looking in their direction, dismissing him as a drunk.

Charles caressed her hand as they approached a sign hanging from the passageway with a picture on it.

With unusual precision, James had given directions by telling them his new house was next to the sign of the Cock and Bottle in Aldersgate Street. Once they left the street, the noise died away, the run down buildings in front providing a cover to noise and dirt from the main thoroughfare. James even had a garden of a modest size, though the pruned trees and roses would owe their life to Elizabeth.

"He has done extremely well for himself, merchants must be the money makers nowadays," Charles jested.

While he waited, he saw the same odd man pass by the opening and glance over, before striding away out of view. He turned quickly, anxious now to get a good look at him, but only caught a glimpse of the brown hat and dark clothes. The door opened as he was still scouring the distance, eventually giving the maidservant his hat.

"Good evening," Charles said, greeting the hosts, immediately noticing the huge, gilded mirror that hung in the hallway, looking like it had been banished from any intimate rooms. Under the great object, two somewhat battered pewter candlesticks clung piteously to some candles.

Elizabeth smiled in reply to their arrival and he observed her take Anne's arm, coming alive in an animated way. "I must show you my embroidered mirror frame."

Charles tugged his leather gloves off and followed them over to the chair, watching as Elizabeth handed Anne the partly finished cover. He was intrigued to see what her creation looked like, knowing so little about the woman. Embroidered with untwisted silk, it portrayed lots of flowers and a scene from the bible and he thought it well done from what he could see - it was clear the house was Elizabeth's domain. Charles overheard her saying how grateful she was that their four year old had threaded the needles for her, her own eyesight being too poor. It was a shock to hear that her vision was impaired until he remembered she was over thirty now.

James put his arm round him and led him to one side.

"Damn embroidery, she thinks of nothing else. What about the wants of my needle, I often ask her."

Charles shook his head, unable to stop himself laughing at his dejected friend's expression. This characteristic bluntness let anyone know exactly what James was thinking.

James guffawed as he spoke again, "Did you hear about the fellow who had his purse snatched near the Goat and Compass in Bishopsgate Street?"

"Nay," he said as James carried on with the story, his face betraying an amusing ending.

"Well what he failed to mention to the constable was that the thief was a whore and she moved quickly from his codpiece to his purse without a trace."

The two laughed heartily, James bellowing so much the women turned to investigate.

"So, Charles, let that be a lesson and always keep a tight hold of your purse if not your breeches," whispered James.

"Was he frustrated that she played with the wrong bag?" Charles jested.

At that point the maidservant entered with freshly decanted wine from Spain. Charles sat down and the women carried on chattering to each other about their clothes, with Elizabeth proudly showing off her new petticoat. Her dress was fashionably revealing the hem of it, reminding Charles of the ladies at the palace. Anne showed her galoshes in turn, talking for ages about these backless shoes with high platform soles.

"They are wonderful for raising my feet above the dirty streets," she praised.

While tasting his drink, he overheard Elizabeth talking about the rabbit's foot she wore around her neck, to ward off future bouts of smallpox and he thought about getting one for

Anne. Far from hiding her scar, Elizabeth practically seemed to point it out in subdued pride; she had no jewels on, preferring this plain talisman that was as simple as her tastes.

"To privileges of Parliament," Charles toasted.

James grinned and quickly raised his glass. "Aye, I'll drink to that for sure and let's hope they stop this King from pulling them apart like a fat man tugging a chicken's legs off."

Charles clinked his glass with his friend's. "Fat man with a chicken," he repeated with humour, while James shrugged his shoulders.

Then his glance rotated to Anne like a compass and he winked, exchanging a cheeky grin.

While sipping his wine, James asked him, "How does this trial go?"

"It proceeds slowly, but doggedly on. I grow weary of it already," Charles said, rolling his eyes.

"Well that Strafford, they should hang him up from London Bridge. We kicked the Jews out of this country hundreds of years ago for their greed, and now he is as insatiable as most of them put together," James retorted, and with a quip, he added, "A bumble bee in a cow turd thinks himself a King."

Anne seemed puzzled at it, which caused some merriment again. Her cheeks turned red as she grew more embarrassed.

"Stop it," she pleaded playfully.

"It just means he is pompous, Anne," James clarified, teasingly nudging her.

With James and his political boat gusting across the sea of conversation, Charles listened, waiting for the breeze to die down and agreeing with him on this issue.

"Aye, this King has resurrected mediaeval taxes from the grave in a bid to squeeze out more money to support his favourite ministers, buy lavish paintings for his palaces and pay for troops to attack the poor Scottish because they dared to resist his changes to their prayer books," James said, anger growing with each point listed. He had nodded his head tellingly at the point about the 'poor Scots' because Charles had enlisted to oppose them.

"No wonder Parliament have turned on him now - he needs curbing. At least Strafford is under lock and key," Charles mused.

"But judging by what he has done already, he will just order Strafford's release whatever way this trial goes," Anne added.

The two men looked at the women. "I never talk to Elizabeth about politics and business. That was the way my father behaved too," James told them, eyes wide at Anne's trespassing into a male domain.

"I am not most women," she chipped in quickly.

Charles smiled. He felt fired up when Anne became as feisty and determined as this. She was now lecturing James on how her father always allowed her to help with his trading activities and the financial books, in the absence of any son. Charles laughed as James hung his head, meeting his match. Anne's mother had died during childbirth and her father doted on her, showing a decent side that was often clouded by his laziness and affection for evenings involving alcohol and large card games.

"Public opinion is the reason, Anne. Parliament has the support and the right to levy taxes and the King desperately needs money, so he is not strong enough to release him. They grant money if he agrees to secure our rights, so Strafford is at their mercy with a powerless monarch watching helplessly," Charles explained.

James moved on, as though they were arousing Elizabeth's interest in it all, commenting on the full hackneys that were monopolised to go to Westminster for the event.

"I have a mind to own my own coach someday to save us having to keep getting hackneys. Fifty pounds is one quote I have heard," Charles said.

"Fifty pounds? It is a waste of money," James announced as he frowned and puckered his lips up in shock, always careful with money. He had once said that cash was like a child; if nurtured, it would grow into a large profit. Now the reason for the contrast between the showy mirror and the pewter relics became apparent.

"Can you imagine, our own coach?" Anne mused.

"I see I have stirred something here. There will be no going back now she is eager for one," Charles said with a smile, quite happy to accede.

"I would sooner buy a license for five pounds and get my own hackney, than pay fifty for a personal one. At least if I became a hackney driver my license would last for life," James said.

"You as a hackney man? It would kill you being sat up on a coach all day with nobody to speak to."

"Lady Berkeley, remember that if a woman is found guilty of controlling her man, they can be liable to be ducked in the river," James said provocatively, completely ignoring his past defeat.

Charles playfully pointed his finger at Anne, not at all insecure in his position as master of his house, for without each other, there would be no house or household. James was always stirring contentious matters and Anne flicked the cork of the bottle at him with a grin. This prompted Elizabeth to chortle when it bounced off his head. Despite it being hard to relate to James, depending on what mood he was in, the man could always laugh at himself and had an open heart if his friends and family needed help. Like his house, his own genuine and caring nature was shielded behind a different façade.

"You have missed your profession. Get him to enlist you into the musketeers," James advised.

Then the two ladies mimicked holding a musket and made to shoot him a second time.

"How fare Lucy and William?" James asked, changing the subject.

Charles's face turned sour at the mention of his brother in law and as he spoke, he felt his eyes narrow with anger. But when he eventually talked of Lucy, who was still estranged from their father, he lost the negative feelings just as quickly.

"Lucy is fine, although I do not know how her children are, for it is weeks since I received a letter."

Casting his memory back, he sat thinking and closing off from the room. He pictured a scene, sitting with his parents in their inn, when a carriage drove up outside.

* * *

His father was gazing out of the window like it offered a view to a different age, frozen in that time until, with a start, he shot back to life. Charles could not believe that Lucy had eloped and not told him anything and he felt utterly empty and distrusted.

"Here's the bastard and his wife in person, come to rub our noses in it," his father howled as he ran for the door.

His mother sprang forward, while Lucy appeared with the man behind her. What a coward, Charles thought, watching him push his wife in first. For this reason he felt immediate scorn, regardless of what his true qualities may be.

Grabbing Lucy's wrist, his father yanked her away whilst eying the man with contempt. Charles nervously watched them, and then his father bounded forward, taking hold of the stranger's throat in an iron grip.

"Leave him be, Father, lest you be charged with murder," Charles yelled.

His tearful mother tried to take hold of Lucy and

screeched for the struggle to stop. Screaming hysterically, Lucy hit her father's arm, but this was useless. Charles pulled his sister away, as he wanted to part the two men himself. His father's face was practically purple - it was as though he couldn't find the words he had longed to bellow. Although Charles felt revulsion for the man who had taken Lucy from them, he was too busy trying to stop his father doing something he would later regret and stubbornly pushed himself between the two.

"Father, cease this - he be not worth it," he shouted as Hungerford struggled free, having the advantage in his thin frame.

"You will pay with yer life, show my family up, eh?" his father shouted as he threw the wooden doorpost, which they used to bolt the door. It smacked against Hungerford's back, crashing him to the wall. Charles followed this up by booting the man out of the doorway. He naively thought Hungerford would leave and Lucy would stay. When he saw her run back to her husband his heart sank.

"Will, let's be away, I knew it was a bad idea. Thank heaven you rescued me from this damned house," Lucy shrieked.

Will Hungerford was pale as snow and shot back into the inn, trying to get Lucy, while Charles's mother clung to his father's now stationary body.

"Aye that's right, I see you have poisoned my daughter against me. In fact she is no girl of mine," his father said with a sting.

"Father, do not speak about Lucy like that," he demanded.

"Grow up, Charles. Your sister has betrayed us all and shamed the Berkeley name; your name. Let me never see her face again."

His mother looked terrible, hanging limply as though life had seeped out of her body. Her long, auburn hair had come loose, making Charles feel even more upset as he took hold of her. He held her tight while she broke down into deep rooted sobs and outside, Lucy and Will ran back into the carriage.

*   *   *

Chapter 8

"Charles ..."

He looked at James while shaking his head. The room went silent, for Elizabeth was normally quiet, and he knew James was simply worse than he was for handling such situations. Charles quickly asked after Elizabeth's new pendant, guessing it held a miniature of James. Encrusted with small blue jewels, it shone magnificently in the candlelight.

"Jamie chose it for our anniversary this year; it is most precious to me," she said.

"Aye, I shall expect favours in return for it though, mistress," James said in a cockney voice, rubbing her leg as he imitated the customers of the brothel houses.

Taking his friend to one side, Charles whispered, "What you said about the trial before ..."

"Aye, what about it? You have some news?" James asked impatiently, waiting for a large morsel of juicy gossip.

"Well, I cannot help feeling I have endangered Anne by such involvement?" he asked, searching for reassurance.

James bellowed in a dismissive way, "Why, you fool, you only attended the blasted thing."

"No, not that … ah never mind, you are right," Charles agreed, as he saw James's intrigued face.

"What are you not telling me?" he demanded curiously, with Anne clearly wondering what the debate was about.

"Let us forget it," he said, realising the fatal slip. He bit his lip. Like a dog with a bone, he knew James would be infinitely picking away at this secret.

In the nick of time, like a column of reinforcements, the maid showed another man in, who Charles recognised instantly; Old Straw Locks. James shouted loudly, taking him by the hand and practically dragging him into the room, striding across the polished pattern of the wooden floor. Matthew Thatcher was a creature of habit, lacking spontaneity, which was probably the reason he remained unmarried, but with a cutting humour. More important still, he often supplemented his wages working for the Lieutenant of the Tower of London with private tours of the place.

"You remember Charles? After he spoke of you today, I was determined that you should come."

Charles was happy to see the man, instantly recognising a way of access to the Tower. This was the ideal moment he needed to seize. Such a valuable opportunity had seemed to come to him on a silver platter, but like the ripe, sweet strawberries which he enjoyed so much, the chance could easily degenerate if left for too long.

Meanwhile the ladies' conversations moved from how Elizabeth used a mixture of sugar and water to keep her curls in place, to medical remedies and use of wild rocket seeds to control armpit odour. The three men drank a few more glasses of wine, sharing stories, gossip and politics, mixed with a few rude jokes. James sent the maid to a shop for more tobacco for his clay pipe, hoping to catch them before they closed this evening at eight o'clock.

When the maid began laying the table, Elizabeth and

Anne led the way, James forgetting his responsibility as host; he could only ever focus on one thing at a time, but would make a success of whatever that was. The men filtered to the table, Charles first, sitting on the wooden bench with Anne, Matthew on the one opposite and James taking the chair at the end of the table, with Elizabeth already enthroned at the other end. A crisp, white tablecloth covered the whole table, a refreshing change to the constant, dark, oak world. Casting their eyes over the dishes including carp pie, sugar cakes, lamb and almond tarts, James poured his apple and honey drink, brewed to perfection over three months, or so he bragged.

As Charles sipped reluctantly at the sweet smelling brew, he was surprised at how refreshing it was, energy levels surging.

"Do you still arrange visits to the Tower, Matthew? I would love to see the history within its walls."

He observed the man's clean shaven features, which highlighted his broad jaw, the brown eyes lighting up over talk of the iconic fortress. The moat that ringed the building was like a wedding band to Matthew, always eager to talk about the place.

"Aye, only too happy. You can see some carvings from Walter Raleigh, where Guido Fawkes was interrogated, Traitor's Gate, or I could try and let you see the crown jewels, though it would carry an extra fee that I would have to supply to the custodian."

Anne looked at Charles with wide eyes at the prospect of seeing the actual jewels which had adorned the royal line for generations, deeply religious and symbolic. The thoughts of the stunning pieces set an unyielding desire to go, injecting an addictive element of interest to his dangerous ploy. Anne nodded firmly, adding her own desire to his and effectively sealing their visit as a certainty. As he faced Matthew he realised that if his delivery failed a second time, he could find himself in the midst of the architectural, historical beauty of the prison.

Ironically, his proximity to the crown would be literal when they saw the jewels, having already met the royal person and now the symbols of the position.

"If you tell me when I can expect you, I will secure admission," Matthew promised.

"Secure admission? Normally people try and break out, yet here I am desperately attempting to get inside. How about on Friday? "Charles said with a laugh.

Matthew signalled his agreement with a nod of his head and wave of his hand, taking a swig of his drink for the first time. No sooner had he done so than he groaned, screwing his face up and roughening his soft, rather feminine features. It was not long before he complained about the new and strange taste the drink offered him.

"Good God, do not say you disagree with that sublime flavour? You have to try new things, Straw Locks, for believe me, it keeps a certain variety in life. Eh, my darling," James hooted, cuddling Elizabeth with a wink.

"Why do they call you that, Matthew?" Anne queried.

As Matthew shrugged his shoulders, denying knowledge with a humorous look in his eyes, James broke in to tell them about the state of the man's messy, blond, wiry hair as a young boy. The jumbled locks looked like straw and were very apt in view of his surname, and needless to say, James had coined it.

"Now, shall we play? My big belly is unsuited to sitting in this damned hard chair much longer," James suggested as he pointed to the virginal in the corner.

Anne clapped her hands, quite excited in anticipation of the melodies. Elizabeth eagerly handed out some Italian song books and Charles flicked through the tunes, interested in the lyrics.

James proceeded to play the instrument, the notes echoing out into the room and adding joy and life to the gathering, the ladies humming and getting into rhythm.

"I want everyone to sing heartily, for I have waited weeks to appreciate this tune sung in its full glory by many people, as it was written for," James warned with a point of his finger, while he lifted it from the keys in an elaborate gesture.

As the beautiful music glided around the people, it reminded Charles of the processions of dancing milkmaids led by musicians, and the wedding processions that often proceeded through the city. James played the virginals well, and with pride, judging by the way he puffed out his chest with a straight back. It was strange to see him so encapsulated, rarely taking such an interest in culture, but again, he had mastered the art of playing them as quickly as ever. Charles, on the other hand, could not hit a note at point blank range, never mind generate a tune, therefore he had never owned a virginal.

Matthew and Elizabeth began singing along, surprising all of them with their happy vocal unity, arm in arm and enjoying themselves immensely. James waved his hands in the air and mouthed at Charles, ushering them into the energy he was creating, and he joined in. Ever since he sang at church as a little boy, he had been reticent about it all, while his father boomed above those surrounding him in a gruff voice, still singing the peaceful words of worship well. His mother would often sing him and Lucy to sleep at night and this music seemed to foster happy memories, hypnotising everyone into such a cheery state of mind. It was even enough to dissolve his solid worry over Strafford for a time.

The singing continued until Elizabeth coughed and held her hands to her face, James stopping his finger work abruptly, before the ladies burst out laughing at the reproachful expression on his face. James rolled his eyes and this made Charles give way to mirth himself. Nevertheless, they all agreed with James that the various pieces had sounded magnificent; the tune the virginal exuded seemed made up of several different notes at once. Charles inspected the rectangular instrument that was placed with extreme care on top of a cloth on the table, the lid lifted and secured open, displaying a painted European hunting scene, with part of the front cut away to house the keys. The vibrant colours of it added a visual attraction to the sound too.

The clock chimed midnight, with its own little melodious addition, as if anxious not to be left out. He couldn't believe it, for there would be few hackneys due to the time and they had finished off several bottles of fine wines too.

"We had best be gone, Anne," he decided and thanking James and Elizabeth for their hospitality, they made their way out, leaving Matthew to gather his belongings after confirming the forthcoming sightseeing. Then the way James walked past the doorway reminded him of the strange man who had been outside when they arrived, wondering where he had managed to wander to now.

The maid brought their things and outside Charles put on his hat, the red plume of feathers waving its own farewell. He handed some money to James to be distributed to the servants, making sure he gave enough to suit his status, following the custom. After embracing the couple, he held Anne's arm while they walked through the garden. Their hosts gave a final wave and as they shut the door, the small amount of light they were using to navigate disappeared.

Through the narrow alley it was especially dark and Anne's grip became tighter as she held him with both hands. Once into the street the stars and the moon afforded some visibility.

Few seemed to bother to obey the order that all people hang a light from the window after dusk.

"I do not know how you two are such good friends. You are both so different," Anne told him.

"Aye, I suppose. But I could always talk to him as a boy, where I could not talk to Father much. I think we learned from each other, gave each other a balance; his overconfidence spilled onto me and I curbed his wilder moments with common sense."

"But you have me to talk to now when you need to?" she queried with an incisive look.

Pausing, he rolled his eyes. "My darling, I did not mean I still only have him. You are my world now; I was talking about when we were children, though I do still greatly value his friendship."

She looked up at him. "And you have enough confidence. You courted me from the minute we came into contact and you had come along on your own to that dinner party. That must have been daunting?"

"I was only shy as a child. Besides, Cupid's arrows were as deadly as the English archers at Agincourt."

A smile lit her face up, before he shouted as low as he could, "Boy, over here." At that moment a bright faced young lad walked slowly into view holding a long stick.

"We would like to hire you and your link."

The boy put the long wooden pole down, lighting the lantern on the end of it, wiping his nose on his cuff in celebration as the flicker took hold.

"We are away to Queen Street, you know of it, near the Cat and Fiddle tippling house?"

The child nodded without speaking and walked in front of them outstretching the pole and it shone illumination into the murky distance, brightening the way. Anne smiled warmly, nodding at the cute little fellow. Charles had heard of horror stories where the boys were in league with criminals to lead travellers to them, however he had his sword by his side tonight. After the wine he had drunk, he jokingly hoped he would not have to use it.

They walked past Saint James's Park, Charles sniggering with mischievous delight as he took the link off the boy. He shot over to the boundary and pushed the pole toward some trees, causing them to sway as darkened figures leapt out of sight.

"Charles, we do not wish to unearth all that," Anne said impatiently, knowing her comment would have little effect on his merry attitude.

"Ah, t'is only a joke. Sodomy, harlots and extra marital affairs - the park takes on a whole new image at nightfall."

"Sodomy," Anne grimaced in disgust, commenting on the absence of the parish constable and the offence that carried the death penalty, until Charles told her that the official would probably be in there too.

Then a deep voice echoed out a drunken tune, making them both turn sharply to see a stumbling man emerge from the shady realm to tell them, "I hope to see you signin' a petition against yonder King's autocratic ways, for if you don't then you will be a marked man, sir."

He pushed Anne ahead and out of the drunkard's way, watching the fellow closely as they walked on.

"Out of our way, you rogue," Charles ordered as he swiped the bewildered man aside, "He is as bad as your father for getting befuddled with beer."

"Very rich coming from you, after drinking so much wine. You are the one who encouraged him out of his pit with that prank. Besides, father deserves to enjoy his retirement."

As they followed the boy, the only immediate noises were his leather soles resonating on the cobbles, with Anne's small quick steps following. A dog barked in the distance, which as the only sound, was a welcome change to the din of daytime.

Arriving in their street, the boy stopped and Charles took the money from his purse to pay him. The youth's face expressed satisfaction as he glanced at his earnings. Continuing to stroll down the street, Charles grabbed Anne's arm, making them both stop, and kissed her. Then he whispered in her ear, causing her to move away as it tickled her, but his words ceased her amusement.

"Someone is following us. When I make a move, you get to the house, *do not* hang back."

Charles led her to the side of a building, into the shadows, a few feet past a small alley and kissed her again. He looked over her curls, catching a brief glimpse of sinister movement in the dead end passage nearby. By pausing where they had done, it made the place the only natural hideaway for a stalker. With a whispered instruction to push him playfully, Charles laughed and staggered backwards before darting for the shady lane. A figure sprung away, but too late for Charles's swift reactions and he raced onwards, grabbing the person, punching him in the face as the man struggled out of his grip. In the scuffle, he pushed the head to the wall, cheek pressed against the whitewashed plaster and blackened timber frame.

"Stop, Sir Charles, I beg you."

"Who the hell are you and what is your business?"

"It is me, Corporal Conway."

Charles recognised the voice now, flinging the man away and demanding answers as the corporal held his face, moaning and whining as he leant against the building.

A window opened above and a dark head popped out to shout, "Get ye gone, damned fools."

"And God be with you too," Charles cried back sarcastically, before moving back to his colleague from the Trained Bands, "Now why are you here?"

"I am only following orders, sir, Sir Richard instructed me to keep track of your every move."

Charles growled, wanting the reasons why, when Anne came round the corner with a knife, wielding it determinedly as she approached haphazardly.

"Anne, get inside," he ordered, dragging Conway with him as he spoke.

"Now tell me Sir Richard's reasons, God damn you."

"I do not know, sir, I swear. He would not tell me a thing and I would never question him, for he is such a martinet, yet here I am with a black eye in the end for abiding by his command."

"Piss off then, your duty is done," Charles commanded as he thumped the man in the back, thrusting him away.

Entering the house and locking it, embracing Anne silently and tightly as he thought of her bold move. He proceeded straight upstairs to change, asking Anne to let Louise know they were back, so that she could retire to her room in the garret for the night. He was in his nightgown when Anne came in, shaken with the night's events and taking a long time to comfort and reassure as they cuddled into each other, Charles feeling her curves through the night dress. Yet despite the intimacy something made him sober up and stop the enjoyment as anger and indignation gave way to worry about Sir Richard's underhand instructions.

Casting his mind back, it was the words the drunkard had also used that echoed this feeling.

"Marked man," he repeated.

He then thought of the full enormity of what he had done; he had attended the trial and attempted to deliver correspondence to the most hated of men in London, whose blood all the mobs were chasing. No wonder no one else wanted to do the job.

Instantly feeling the most ignorant and stupidest of men in Christendom, his face flushed. How unwittingly he had got so closely involved in something he had hitherto constantly stayed clear of, for fear this quarrel should have interrupted his marriage. Yet now he was involved to such an extent that it was impossible to back out, or at least more dangerous to do so than it was to see it through.

Taking the candlesnuffer, he extinguished the flame, though his worries were impossible to cut out so easily now.

Finding it unusually difficult to sleep, he was eventually dozing off when a loud voice shouted from the street below, "One of the clock and it be dry."

It was the night watchman bellowing. His back pain

returned and gradually got worse as he lay, prompting him to get up. Its origin was from the wound he had received in the Bishops War, when a Scot hit him with the butt of a musket, and he hoped this was not a sign from God of further trouble.

As he flicked through the old book by his bedside, the published play called *The Duchess of Malfi*, he realised that a small book would be the ideal location to convey the letter. The bible would be such a publication above all scrutiny too.

This kept him thinking all night about how his life would continue - it was definitely not the time for children and he prayed, "Dear God, please do not let my actions today trouble my wife."

Chapter 9

A noise of a dog barking outside woke him, enough to pierce his light sleep like a bullet. He rubbed around his lower spine, pondering whether to see that new astronomer to check if he could do anything for his back. It might be because of the wound he received nearly two years ago, from the Bishops War, or simply the alignment of the planets. He stared at the lumpy mattress, knowing he could not dispose of the bed, for it had been passed down Anne's family for generations, and was part of their status.

Not even sleep could give him respite from his damned mission, for he had dreamed about the Tower and Strafford; he was trapped within the fortress and the peer was trying to murder him. With a deep sigh he licked his finger, laid some salt on it and proceeded to rub his teeth, trying to make them as white as he could. It was six o'clock and Louise would probably be up now so he called on her to light the fire. Anne was still sleeping when the flames propelled dancing shadows around the room. He took the ceramic chamber pot and relieved himself.

Glancing outside through the thick, plain curtains, he saw

that the country had begun to waken and tradesmen prepared for the day ahead, while apprentices opened their masters shops for business. The usual dogs and pigs were sniffing around, eating any small morsel of foodstuff that littered the cobbles.

He also noticed the numerous signboards that infested London's streets were still.

"Must be no breeze," he deduced aloud, looking at the board hanging off the building opposite.

Sitting back down in a chair and observing the fire, he watched a puff of smoke rise, clouding the surround and its ivory Delft tiles. He could think of nothing else but demanding answers from Sir Richard for sending Conway to spy on him.

He was definitely a morning person, but especially with so much urgent business, every hour of sleep seemed a waste.

"You look tired, my love?" Anne murmured as she rose.

"I have been up for an age," he said, while walking over to kiss her.

Anne rubbed her eyes, despairing with the early hour as she left to go downstairs. As his mind began to churn with deeper thoughts and questions, he changed, no longer able to put off his visit the colonel. Just why had he posted a guard on him, he wondered again. He was adamant that action was needed, yet knew that it would be folly to attempt to deliver the letter at court again today, and an idea came to him about his forthcoming trip to the Tower. He bounded down the stairs, buoyed up with his new plan, but it was short lived.

He found Anne hunched up on a chair, with red eyes.

Placing his arm around her and stroking her shoulders, he asked, "What is the matter, my sweet?"

"The maid we hired last month has taken one of my best petticoats and pearl necklace. Louise has just told me," she said with a tremble in her soft voice. He felt her take hold of his hand.

"Do not worry yourself, I will spread the word and offer a reward for her. They are only objects;" he whispered comfortingly, "James had his gold watch stolen by a valet, so it is widespread."

"I trusted her though. Oh, she could have handled this dress I wear now. I feel sick, as though the place is foul with disease from her presence."

"If I should so much as see that damned harlot, I shall punish her for you," he swore, unable to appreciate Anne's full feelings over the matter, but irate with the thief.

She looked at him tenderly, appreciative of his care and concern, pouring forth in an outlet of anger.

Louise brought some wine and filled a glass, the stem like an elongated heart, and she touched her mistress's shoulder in comfort.

"Edward my tailor was telling me about the lions in the Tower of London. Have you seen them?"

"No, but I know of them. We will have to go sometime, sweetheart?"

"Aye, it might make you forget about this," he agreed, happy he had found something to help comfort her.

"Did you see the new suit he made me? Apparently his family were on making it for two months. Can you imagine that for a living, all huddled round making clothes, stitching and sewing for a lifetime, and at the end of it you have to give your work of art away," he continued.

She nodded at him, mouth breaking into a gleaming smile at the chatter. She asked him if he was late, but Charles told her he would not go to the poxy trial today after all.

"But, darling, you must go, it is important," she insisted, standing now to assert the matter.

Her hair hung to one side as she looked at him, head tilted slightly, leaving her neck and upper chest exposed. His own strength of feeling seemed to have brought out a mighty force of her own. He nodded in final agreement with her resolve, and as Louise left the room, Anne pointed at her with a grateful look.

"If it were not for her, I think I would lose all faith in servants."

Charles nodded. "How long had she been with you before we married?"

"Five years. She is practically part of the family. I know we give her a clothing subsidy in her wage, but I think she needs a little extra, as she wants to impress an apprentice she chats to at the market," Anne hinted.

Immediately presuming she meant a pay rise, Charles sighed, for money was tight at the moment; Anne's birthday had not long past, plus Saint Valentine's Day, and the cost of the banquet.

"You can be so miserly at times, all she needs is a nice new dress," she said with a frown.

"I thought you meant a pay increase. I was just going to say she is well paid already, and I had to pay out ..." Charles stopped short of telling her five pounds had just gone to Anne's father to settle another debt the man had incurred. The money had been despatched with a terse and honest letter to state that this was the last time.

He reached into his purse and handed over some silver shillings, Anne beaming with gratitude, eager to help Louise impress her lad. She had a big heart and often the monthly housekeeping accounts she passed over would include donations to a poor man, or a blind beggar, and he knew the true cost of this would be higher than she let on in the figures. With a kiss and a cuddle, and a reminder about the time, he left for Sir Richard's before day two of the proceedings started.

Outside, donning his hat, he searched for a hackney. The stench from the dirt was strong today in the sun and he wiped sweat from his forehead, barely noticing the excrement that was caked to the cobbles, such was his single mindedness.

Glancing round, he sidestepped as a man on horseback passed him, an encounter that would never have come so close normally, when his full wits were unclouded by other worries. The hackney he managed to attract was mercifully empty, as his head was pounding.

The extreme noise of the street traders and the shaking of the carriage accentuated the pain and irritation. Passing down one street, the coach stopped and Charles thumped the seat, complaining about the hold ups.

Looking out of the window, he saw that the obstruction was due to the number of people, women as usual, gossiping near the public water supply in the centre of the road, which was always holding him up on important days. The coachman gave them a mouthful of oaths, Charles nodding in frustrated agreement, and they soon moved aside. Carriages passed by, some coachmen being bareheaded and he bowed his head to these ones out of respect for the noble passengers, some pretentious people choosing bald coachmen to make their transport stand out. As he disembarked at his destination, he saw a female peddler and called out. She was carrying a basket of various foods on her head, with cherries and asparagus being two types he could see.

"I will have some cherries, madam," he said, while the woman placed the basket on the cobbles, handing them over with a respectful nod. Paying her, he walked away, being glad to get them so early before it was busy. Apart from the many fingers that would have prodded and examined them later, he also avoided the possibility of filth landing on them from what people threw out of the windows above.

"Any kitchen stuff have ye, maids?" came the next familiar cry as he turned into a street.

This fellow seemed weighed down already with old waste, paper, food and excrement, looking to trade with passing maidservants especially. It was anything but quiet. He pushed by an ink seller, so continuously yelling his price of seven pence, that Charles cried that he would pay him that to go away.

Dodging two dogs, he slowed and avoided some cows being driven to the slaughterhouse and all the while his impatience was growing. Being amongst the shouts of the street vendors and apprentices, the clattering of coaches and horses, the signs squeaking above him, along with all the people talking and going about their business, his pace quickened, the noise seeming twice as loud as normal. Then at last, he paused for breath, finally allowing himself a brief respite at Sir Richard's.

Knocking on the door, he was confronted by their surly maid. Thinking that she would make any man terrified, he told her, "I am here to speak with your master."

"An' who shall I say is callin'?" she asked rather improperly.

"*Sir* Charles Berkeley," he barked.

The maid's face changed at his forcefulness, announcing, "This way, Sir Charles, I will see if Sir Richard is engaged."

Walking inside, he removed his hat and gloves, giving them to her. Clasping his hands, he rubbed them together to get them warmed up, while the maid went into the study. The doors eventually opened and the maid walked through to the kitchen as he heard Sir Richard's deep dull voice shout, "Come in, Berkeley."

Incensed, he utterly detested the way Sir Richard called him 'Berkeley'; after all, was he not a knight of the realm too? Sir Richard liked to assert his position as his superior, and Charles thought it seemed to be the only reason why he clung onto the post.

Walking in, he took a deep breath to allay the offence and anger he knew was bubbling near to the surface of his current mood.

Sir Richard was seated at his desk, and pompously as ever, he announced without glancing up, "I am very busy, sir, so I hope you will not keep me long."

Charles sat down without an invitation, which prompted the colonel's large brown eyes to leave his work, sunken and absolutely piercing, like one of those officious and arrogant parish constables. The serving boy stood next to him sealing the envelopes he had just written, as if they both represented two different eras. As he warmed the wax over the candle, the lad spilt some onto the paper his master was writing on, cheeks flushing. Sir Richard threw his quill down instantaneously, as though ready for any slightest mistake, and hit the boy with a backhander several times. He screamed and Charles tightened his frame, sitting bolt upright.

"You bloody fool of a child," Sir Richard bellowed.

Charles frowned at the boy. He should be able to do such a menial task without any accidents by now. Sir Richard stood up and the boy cowered as he took his sword belt from the chair and whipped it right across the side of the lad's body. Charles looked in astonishment, as he had not expected any lashing after the smack the boy had just taken. The punishment was repeated, with the child begging forgiveness, almost choking on his tears as he tried to speak, but not daring to walk away. Charles winced at the extent of the punishment, and the brutality coming from the man.

"Sir Richard, we have much business," he said, distracting his colonel. The boy ran out of the room, and Sir Richard resumed his position with refreshment and near relish, like he had just taken some medication.

"Damned child, if it were not for me, he would be a beggar. I like to keep my household in order, the same as my regiment," he bragged.

Charles cut his hand down through the air, bringing it to rest, palm upwards, and pointing at his colonel. "What in God's name did you assign Corporal Conway to trail me for?"

Sir Richard sighed, repeating the question under his breath, before pushing his fat finger against the desk several times.

"You have some sort of strange way with the Earl of Strafford, for God's sake, is that not enough?"

"Who on God's earth told you that? " Charles questioned with shock, unable to deny it, and now wondering how much Sir Richard knew.

They glared at each other, eyes attempting to extract information from each other, and remaining quiet for a while longer.

"There is no such thing, it is all fantasy. I did not think you would believe such rot either," Charles snapped, instantly causing his colonel's shoulders to straighten in an effort to distance him now that his hunch was being challenged so ferociously.

"Well it does not matter what I think, for you have no further part on the prisoner's escort. I received orders from the Lord Mayor, originating from the palace, to dismiss you from the party. If I had my way, I would cast you out of the regiment too, not just this temporary role we have. So someone other than myself has cause to suspect you."

Charles felt outraged at this scant regard for the perils he had faced for the King, cast aside like a failure, picturing immediately the way the monarch had seemed to look right through him as though he were expendable; there if he needed him, but invisible if he did not.

Standing up, Sir Richard walked towards the wall, which was mounted with various weapons. Swords were hung decoratively, with his leading staff and poleaxe in the corner.

Pointing to a portrait of himself in full armour, he explained, "I have been a soldier all my life, and now we have new masters in the Parliament, who rival the Lord Mayor himself. Do you approve of them?"

Sir Richard was either testing the water or beginning some elaborate scheme of his own; almost jealous of the interest influential people had in Charles.

"Well, we need to get the wheel of power turned more towards them."

"Although I am a veteran of wars, I still remain active for future ones. It will come to blows," he said, dismissing Charles's reply and waving his hand.

Charles was not prepared to listen to his self righteous imagination of past glories.

"I hope for your sake that you did not try anything yesterday."

Sighing under his breath, Charles refrained from comment and stood, head held high in disregard.

"I must get on; I have important business seeing as I am not distracted by this trial anymore."

"Then I bid you good day. Now that I know you are shunned from those above, let us just say that I expect your full cooperation with me in this regiment," Sir Richard said as he clasped his hands together behind his back.

Charles stood up slowly and spoke calmly, "If I thought that was a threat, I would smash my fist into your fat face."

Walking towards the door, Charles left with a strained bow, determined to retain his manners, despite this unbridled enmity. His colonel gazed on with an open mouth, astounded at the throwaway remark that had destroyed his own parting shot in one go. This was a prime time for that quip of James's; a bumblebee in cow turd thinks himself a King.

Chapter 10

Outside, groups of unemployed apprentices ganged together again to drone on about Strafford. More traders passed by too, carrying sacks of sea coal, water in wooden pails or used clothes. Hailing a hackney, he was about to step in when a man jumped out, somewhat red faced. He got inside and found a woman rearranging her dress, struggling to tie it up against the buxom figure that was rebelling to get out of it, body and garment as repellent to each other as himself and Sir Richard. Rather embarrassed, he fell into the seat as she spoke.

"Where you be off to, sir?" she asked, leaving her clothes to rub his thigh.

"Aldersgate Street, madam, though I dread to think where you have been," he announced sharply, unable to resist the light hearted response. His heart beat faster as he opened the leather flaps that covered the windows, letting light enter this mobile underworld.

"I like a gentleman with a sense of humour," she cackled.

"I'm sorry, but you'll get no business from me."

"Why, d'ye prefer boys?" she screeched.

"How dare you insult me like that, I am not a sinner," Charles growled, gripping her hand tightly and removing it.

She winced and as he let go, he saw her ogle him, as though excited by the use of force. After she whispered her name, he ordered the coachman to stop, unable to stand her loose morals any longer.

The streets were choked with people, which did nothing to allay his turmoil. Despite the King's easy duplicity, Strafford's rebuttal of the letter, and Sir Richard's arrogance, they all only served to increase his urge to deliver the letter, if nothing more than to prove them all wrong about his ability. Not long afterwards, he spotted James walking the other way, and the two men greeted each other.

"Your face is as sour as the Queen's," James joked.

Feeling unable to talk about what worried him, Charles made up an excuse.

"My back is tormenting me; it's that damn bed, passed down through the family."

"Well I married into good stock then - the cloth hangings on my relic allow the four posts to show on our bed, so that proves it is absolutely ancient," James said, nudging him with a smile.

"Let us go in here then, eh?" he said excitedly as he nodded towards a tavern, "I'll wager it's full of drunken braggarts and women."

Charles cut in, "No, let us go to the inn over there. I am famished."

James disagreed, but Charles persisted, "God favours my choice, for inns serve all days except Sundays and that settles it," he said playfully.

Inside, they sat down on a wooden bench; the large fire behind them warming the room as effectively as the alcohol fired their discussions. Some men puffed on pipes in a corner of the chamber, deep in conversation, with the smoke clouds shutting them off from the room in their own private atmosphere.

"Two pints of ale, mistress," James ordered, eyeing her rear as she turned to acquiesce.

"Make mine beer," Charles corrected.

As James took a mouthful, he shared his wisdom with Charles, "Beer, eh, stick with the traditional ale, man."

"I was mighty pleased with beer when I first tried it, although it's the Dutch method," Charles said as he perked up a little, looking forward to quenching his thirst.

"That stuff's made with hops, water and malted grain, is it not?"

"Aye? Do not tell me you are not aware of that, for the damn drink has only been in England for forty years now," Charles said sarcastically.

James raised his eyebrows in silence, admitting his friend had a point.

"I'm thinking of taking Anne to Father's house in the country for a few days – we haven't seen him for a long while and she needs a rest. I am hoping while we are there to work on him face to face about seeing Lucy again."

"Why not write to Lucy and see if you can effect a reconciliation?" James asked as his eyes darted around the room.

"It is hard when she does not read very well and cannot write. I do not fancy the thought of the local clergyman knowing my business when he reads it to her. Anyway I'll be damned if I've not tried that option before," he said with regret.

"What you need is a child - you have not got over the stillborn one ..."

Charles interrupted, "Not you too. Be quiet about children, James, Anne is always talking of them. It would be folly to bring a child into a chaotic city that London is right now."

"But you can both have fun in the meantime though, eh?" James joked.

Charles laughed, but James turned morose in an instant.

"What is wrong now?" he asked.

"Elizabeth," he replied tersely.

Charles shook his head in frustration, feeling sorry for her.

"She is lovely. And I am sure you blow things out of all proportion, for she was so charming when we visited recently."

"Charming? Only the other day she threw a pot at me, screaming that I was going to bed the maid."

"Would you?" Charles queried.

"Elizabeth will not sleep with me, so I may as well."

"Well I think you need to show you love her by being patient, for I know you will be pestering her day and night for it. Either that, or get a divorce."

James spluttered, taken aback by Charles's shock tactics.

"Divorce," he whispered, "By which Parliament would have to sanction it, the washing aired in public to my shame."

Charles knew his friend loved his wife, for the pair had known each other since childhood, betrothed at fourteen and married at sixteen.

"Buy her some flowers and do not ask for sex. That way she will feel you want her for love too," Charles counselled, as James raised his head in deep realisation.

Before he could comment further, a man walked over to them and was greeted by James enthusiastically jumping to his feet, as though all the trouble he had spoken of was trivial.

"Jeremiah Brandon, I do believe?" James asked joyously.

Brandon's grin betraying a missing tooth, the arrogance and angry poise also displaying a certain lacking in his emotions.

"Now here is a Puritan icon before us, but what brings you to our table?" James queried, inflating the reputation of the man even further beyond reality.

Charles nodded at the plain, solemn man. He unwittingly stared at the marks 'SS' that were branded on his cheek, the two letters interlinked with each other. The markings were striking, and the grooves they made were the colour of red wine, certainly intoxicating the man with a sense of martyrdom.

"I see you notice my punishment for not supportin' those wicked servants of the divil," Jeremiah said with bitter temper.

Charles raised his eyebrows. He felt instant suspicion and aversion to the man because of his manners and branding, and until recently, it would have been surprising to hear someone utter such an extreme comment as this. He realised his expression would display his antipathy, so he took another mouthful of his drink to distance himself from the newcomer.

James recapped on the sentence, not that it was needed though. "For his support of Puritanism and publishing a pamphlet against bishops, he had an ear hacked off and those letters on his cheek, a sower of sedition. The Archbishop of Canterbury fined him ten thousand pounds in the Star Chamber Court; I am surprised you did not read about it in the new news sheets."

There would be no way in five lifetimes that Brandon would find such wealth, but the authorities would make sure he was ruined for life with it. The man exuded lack of respect for authority, and Charles rapidly summed up that this lay behind his rebellious nature, rather than any intense devotion to Puritanism. Once he had made his mind up about the thug, his opinion may as well have been set in a mould, rarely to change again.

Then with a glance to Brandon, James said in explanation of Charles, "He keeps out of the news about events, you see."

"That accursed Star Court is the scourge of us all, formerly controlled by Archbishop Laud to uphold the King and 'is lot," Brandon said with a furrow appearing between his eyebrows.

"Aye, it is very harsh, but you remember when a poor man from our village was let off with ship money tax, James," Charles reminded them, unable to help himself from issuing such a contentious statement, and receiving a glare from Brandon.

"Aye, I suppose so. At least we are not a despotism like France, where Louis basks in his magnificent palaces and the poor starve," James mused.

"Ye mean we are not a full despotism yet," Brandon bellowed, his high cheekbones tensing up with fury.

James coughed, looking to Charles, then back to Brandon. Silence ensued.

Charles itched to say something to wind Brandon up, but he restrained himself after seeing James sweat with uncertainty.

Deep down he agreed with Parliament, but he was certainly not going to say this, for it would appear he was only doing it because of Brandon's presence. Such a stubborn streak often swayed his actions.

"Do you passively support the King and 'is Star Chamber?" Brandon asked of James, with further outrage.

"Erm, no I wasn't supporting it. I merely, well I detest it actually … " James spluttered, to Charles's disgust, his opinion falling as easily as the men who were cut down in retreat during the Bishops War. Charles himself ignored Brandon's overbearing attitude, folding his arms and examining the place. Brandon's narrow eyes observed Charles up and down.

"Ye are a King's man, is that so?" he asked, staring for a response.

"Definitely not. I am nobody's man, except perhaps my wife's," he retorted sarcastically.

"Ah, a coward," Brandon jibed with a shake of his head.

"You go too far. How dare you speak to me like that," Charles snapped, reeling his indignation back as much as he could.

"Respect for a coward?"

Charles smashed his fist on the table, making Brandon's beer tip over, spilling out as quickly as James's fear; he was wide eyed and apologising profusely. A cool wave rose from the pit of Charles's stomach, through his upper body and to his head, making him feel icy cold. Brandon remained seated while James stared at them both.

"Ooh, I sense the little Lord Berkeley is upset 'cause I poked fun at his King," Brandon said pushing Charles's chest, "Ye cannot be hard if you tried and I am talking about ye cock an' all."

Charles's vision went blurry with temper as he quickly wrenched Brandon's hand away and slammed it to the table, the position twisting the fellow to one side. The customers stared and the keeper panicked at the scene.

"What in the name of God are you doing?" James spluttered.

The customers began whispering and muttering under their breaths to one another, like a theatre audience dismayed by the performance.

"Answer me then - I have never seen you like this. You upset his type and you will know about it. He already suspects you of being a royalist. You really must show Parliament sympathy and let your true feelings out," James snapped, trying to be as quiet as he could. A woman had stood up in the corner at the instant that Brandon shouted Charles's surname.

"Damn it, I am for nobody, especially not the King's policy - I want him to give over power as much as you. But I do not have to put up with remarks on my character and you should not *expect* me to sympathise with Parliament either."

"Charles, he just jests," James said, excusing Brandon, as he grabbed his sleeve in desperation.

The woman approached the male battle, gliding right through the middle of them all and approaching Charles. The opposite sex could be mystical at times, he well knew, but this female attracted his whole attention. He seemed to recognise the mischievous glint in her dark eyes, mounted with thin eyebrows. Her petite lips were situated just above a small and rounded chin, the defying face without any fashionable fringe.

She repeated his name with a tilt of her head.

"Aye, that is me," Charles confirmed.

James stood gazing in wonder at the large breasts. They were emphasised even further by her thin figure and rather creased, but expensive dress. Brandon began howling at the woman, making Charles direct her to one side, attempting to get past to shut the insolent man up once and for all, his temper encouraged by the presence of a lady in all of this.

"Always the soldier; thriving in war, but eaten up with inactivity in peace. Will you forget your obstinate honour for once," she said, stopping Charles in his tracks with mere words.

"Bess."

The woman grinned, then laughed and walked right up to Brandon, unfurling her fan in an elaborate flick, like she was unsheathing a sword.

"Begone, sir, for I am not too much of a lady to hitch my skirts and kick you, and believe me, you will lose more than your teeth where I intend to aim for."

Charles inadvertently let out a chortle at this feisty comment and Brandon hooted at her, walking away, but yelling about a woman saving Charles. Before he left, Brandon cried out in one last act of defiance, "I spoke out against the papist whore, yer Queen. I be not the coward."

The customers dispersed, others looked at him and spoke low, while the keeper and his maid ran around tidying the place up. Then the keeper came over to him.

"I am a poor man, sir, see all this damage. You need not come back again, for you destroy my inn and attack such a brave man as 'im. Mister Brandon is the mob's idol."

Charles handed him some coins in recompense. As he straightened his doublet, he felt the money hit him and clink onto the stone floor, rolling around. He looked at the innkeeper who had just cast them back.

"Why?"

The keeper glared, full of hatred. "Coins do not buy what you have nearly jeopardised for me. I am a true Parliament man. Money is your answer to everything, but principle is mine and I for one will support Parliament openly."

Charles felt a wave of guilt more than anything. How right the keeper was, and he thought of how casually he had handed money over to smooth things out. Then he grew jealous of the fact that he had no such high principles in the matter of King or Parliament.

He was tired of James's constant sighs of disapproval. His friend could not stop fiddling, scratching his arm and pacing around while Charles finally hugged Bess tight.

"I would never have found his balls anyway, Charles, but yours are a different story," she said quietly.

He laughed, remembering their times together with fondness, his first foray into the realms of the opposite sex came at the same point as his march into the Bishops War and the manhood that brought.

"Will you just relax?" Charles shouted to James, with a swipe of his arm, the other inviting Bess to sit with them.

"He is married, you know," James warned, as this pretty, unconventional creature fluttered around Charles, now subordinating herself as quickly as she could spring to the attack.

"As am I, sir. But Charles and I go way back."

"You must do, for he is Sir Charles now," came the playful, jealous mutter.

A song drifted out from a flute, catching people's attention and prompting claps in intervals and in tune with the chords. The serving girl sang as she cleared the table near them and Bess joined in, "Then take warning boys, from me, mark well what I do say. So take a warning, boys, from me, with other men's wives don't make too free."

The keeper approached again, signalling for them to leave, though Bess ignored him and spoke out. "Well I must love you, and leave you, my dears, for I need to collect some things for a social evening with the Earl and Countess of Holland."

Charles laughed out loud, taking her arm and revealing his own invitation to the same event, both taking great delight in catching up with each other.

As he parted company with Bess, excitedly telling her of his forthcoming chance to view the crown jewels later this afternoon, he stopped suddenly and raised his hands.

"Ah, he has seen the light and the true foolishness of his actions just now," James mocked.

He had remembered his earlier plans around this opportunity to get near to Strafford again. The chance dangled enticingly, with as much allure as Bess's triangular, opal pendant, stones shimmering like the clearest of seas. Tactics and ideas gushed forth with the chance to approach Strafford during this trip to the prison. Then he realised he was still looking at Bess's jewel as it responded to her every breath, lazily propped up by her ample bosom, in a way anything but subtle.

Chapter 11

They gazed on in wonder, Matthew Thatcher's glowing candle illuminating a scene that only a privileged fraction of the six million English people would ever see. Though the light was dim, the priceless objects of beauty created their own twinkle, even from the small, hollow golden orb, mounted by a cross which represented the power that the King held from God. The cross emblazoned itself on the sight, glorifying the sanctity of the jewels.

Matthew whispered details about the crown, almost reverently, moving his arm over to it, and casting shadows of the majestic outlines across the walls. The most striking feature of the crown was the one hundred and seventy carat, oval ruby that separated the four arches of the headpiece from the cross which completed the centre. Matthew's historical facts seeped into their subconscious as they observed every detail; the ruby had originally been the Black Prince's, later the main jewel in the helmet that Henry the Fifth wore when leading the first of many crusades against France, mining through the bedrock of their resistance, until triumphing at the Battle of Agincourt in fourteen hundred and fifteen. The present King's father had incorporated the gem into the current crown, the body of which was a sea of gold, with shaped fleur de lis at the foot of each of the four arches. Pearls highlighted the flowing shape of the fleur-de-lis and between each one were larger crosses, each encrusted with a rainbow of precious stones.

Soon it was time to cut short the breathtaking visit and even while Matthew was turning the giant, black, iron key in the lock, they still had the exquisite visions in their mind, both speechless. Those items had adorned every monarch for over three hundred years, symbolising their power and spiritual appointment, and now in this small, dull, capsule, they truly felt like they were at the beating heart and sacred core of the nation.

Matthew stood describing the endless prisoners that had been ferried through Traitors Gate. His smooth, gentle complexion and large blue eyes were rather too soft in comparison with the rough, stone walls behind him, or the severity of the tale. As he spoke, Charles examined the small, cavernous chamber they were in, bereft of any regal feeling and quite austere. He looked deeper through the plainness, as simple as his own tastes, and into the immense character of the Tower of London. The walls were chipped, patchy and worn from the descent down the slopes of history, sometimes so irregular that the journey seemed to have turned into an avalanche.

Matthew walked through the Gothic archway that led to a spiral staircase and Charles let Anne through first, running his hand over the glossy wall, so aged and brown that it took on the appearance of an old vellum document - it was just like the calfskin deeds for his house. Matthew chased the candlelight into the stairwell, leaving the sensation of spirits lurking behind in the darkness, while Charles's quick footsteps echoed out as he caught up.

"The crown jewels were the most magnificent sight I think I shall ever see," Anne could not help but point out.

Stopping dead in his tracks for a minute, Matthew nodded enthusiastically, as excited as they both were, his own joy being from the chance to reveal the splendid items to newcomers.

"And where does Lord Strafford live now?" Charles queried with bated breath, following discussion of past prisoners.

"He is on the floor above us."

The reply sounded hollow as it veritably spiralled its way up the stairs, to warn Strafford of their arrival. Matthew continued his tour. He leaped onto the first step, reeling off details of the only woman known to be tortured here, her crime being that she was a worshipping Protestant. She was so brave and courageous that the Constable of the Tower refused to continue the punishment, leaving the Lord Chancellor to take over grinding names of fellow Protestants out of her. Anne praised the courage of the woman making a stand against the officials of a man's world. Charles added with bitterness that all governments and their officials enjoyed that part of their role.

"You will have to come back during the daytime and see the ravens," Matthew added, his face now hidden by his blond straw locks.

Next they came to a narrow passageway, the floor continuing the theme of stone slabs, but thick, circular, stone columns interspersed the walls, mounted with carvings that reminded him of their church. A window offered a respite from the claustrophobic sensation of such an impregnable shell, with tall iron candle holders providing signs of more homely habitation.

Like a widowed old woman, the place seemed to have been forgotten by the family it had once been at the centre of. The plainness of the former royal home did give a more earthly feel though, compared to glorious Whitehall Palace, for the interior and its detail was all made of one material in its raw state, bereft of fancy adornments.

"I would give anything to face Strafford and confront him about his sins; why, I even brought my bible should the occasion arise."

"Rather you than me, for the very sight of him could curse you. James would be very jealous of you if you did though, I'll wager," Matthew said, remembering their mutual friend's extreme views of the government that the imprisoned peer had headed.

Anne gave Charles a knowing glance, widening her eyes, and increasing the sparkle of those emerald gems, while she made a comment.

"Come on, darling, no dallying, otherwise we may indeed run into Lord Strafford," she said, the statement instantly hooking him as much as the almost seductive look she gave out as she momentarily looked back again.

Matthew stormed ahead with his royal blue gown in pursuit, like the night sky which was rapidly descending over the evening's events, though they were far from over judging by Anne's obvious plan. At the summit, she called for their guide to slow down in a soft, melodious tone that hinted at her harmonious singing voice. She was leaning near the small slit in the wall that narrowly eyed them all. Cold, refreshing air whistled through it just then, the noise reminding him of how his father used to call for their dog, and Matthew reluctantly returned to hover around the couple. Further down the small passage were some soldiers.

"Tom and Jacob guard the old bugger," Matthew commented as he saw Charles observing the sentries' scarlet uniforms, a reminder of the Tower's heyday, the dress being their bond to the place.

As the guards ambled closer, Charles could see the thistle, rose and shamrock on their chests, within the King's initials of 'C R' and all mounted with a golden crown. The first man, middle aged, with a grey beard that merged with his white ruff collar, gave Matthew a grin of familiarity. Anne quickly begun pointing out of the small cross shaped window, like she was about to use it for its original purpose and fire an arrow, questioning what area she was now overlooking. For Charles, the very sight of her hourglass shape, as sensual and attractive as ever, captured his attention once more. Her humour and underlying strength of character, as flowing as her silky dress, had also attracted him, and seeing her now near another man provoked a touch of jealousy within.

Matthew hastily obliged her with an answer, happy to converse with such a pretty creature. As Anne continued talking, a fresh smile from her confirmed his suspicion that she was distracting Matthew, leaving him free to undertake his own route. Charles approached the guardsmen, one sporting a long, white clay pipe, while the plump one behind puffed his red, veined cheeks out. The leading man guessed they were enjoying their guide's knowledge, still grinning behind the whiskers as he laid one hand on his hip and filled the narrow corridor, his manner as prickly as the thistle on his chest. Nevertheless the mutual support and unified actions of the two sentries highlighted their camaraderie as starkly as their appearance.

"You guard Strafford then, eh?" Charles queried lightly.

"Aye, we do that," the man replied, bushy eyebrows dropping in anticipation of Charles's meaning.

"I have many a complaint with the prisoner and Matthew said there should be no harm in extracting some enjoyment out of the dog's confinement."

"You know young Mister Thatcher well?" the plump one asked as he pointed to Matthew, even the gesture seeming to tire him.

"Good friend of mine, he is with my wife now, we have just seen the crown jewels. I would quite like to read Strafford a biblical passage from Matthew, twenty six, to compare his betrayal of this nation with that of Judas Iscariot, though he will have made a lot more than thirty pieces of silver."

"Ahem, very noble, but I am afraid you will have to cross us with coins first."

Charles half smiled, as if put out that they would even charge for this, but the price would be worth it and he handed over some silver shillings.

"I see no harm in that, Jacob, I'll go with him," Tom stated without any negotiations, passing the coins to his companion in arms, after counting them himself to be sure of the amount. By this time, Jacob had rested his weight on his small stool again, reaching up for them like a beggar.

"This way," Tom beckoned, already setting off without Charles.

As he stepped into a small room, the charred door ahead of him stood out, the wood grain mixing shades of brown with strange black patches. For the first time, the warder's face was neutral and Charles sensed his wariness.

"The colouring gives the feeling that the devil has touched this portal into his servant's den. How do you cope with such a dangerous role?" he probed of the man, using the more frightening reputation of Strafford to good effect.

"I have God's protection," was all the guard could mumble as he seemed to close the door behind them slowly.

"Do you think he will know we are here?" Charles whispered, stifling his own nerves somewhat by chattering.

The man shook his head, a heavy frown appearing as he took the keys in both hands to give extra security to his mind. The guard stood with his back to the whitewashed wall, an archway of cream bricks framing him as his pale face attempted to merge against the backdrop. The tension Charles had helped generate had stopped the man's progress and Charles continued slowly on, raising his bible up to signal his forthcoming intention.

This new preaching and religious overtone did not suit him though and for a split second he remembered the annoying clergyman who followed the regiments during the late war. The bellowing, constant chiding, and above all, the way the man always seemed to get tangled into the running of the unit had been very testing.

The back cover of the bible was pushed tighter by his ever more pressing fingers, due to the letter folded up in the last few pages. He pushed hard against it to keep the letter secure, and although he did not believe some of the more wilder tales of the prisoner's inherent evil, he was admittedly still intimidated. The small window within the thick oak door did have a foreboding air to it, and he fully expected a face to appear there at any moment.

The guard looked on with an anticipation that did not change as the small hole into the cell grew bigger, revealing the sight of white walls, a wooden table, chair, and cupboard and a large portrait of a man. It was a much homelier sight than he had imagined, the table covered with papers and quills, more like a study than a cell. A glimmering candle shivered away within, emulating Charles's nervousness until at last he reached up to knock. Before he could summon the prisoner, two eyes flashed into view, blackness surrounding them as they stared menacingly. He stopped with alarm, blinking the image away, before seeing it return again, though this time with more detail. As if the candles had burned higher, the normal features of a middle aged man laden with worries was illuminated, combined with an air of blunt and honest intelligence, and Charles stood his ground. Black and grey curls framed the small face, the lighter moustache, as sharply modelled as a sword, rose slightly as a smile crossed Strafford's hitherto unyielding expression.

"Do you really find Black Tom Strafford so frightening, sir?"

"Why, no … I have simply come with a message."

The dark eyes narrowed ever so slightly, a recognition overcoming them, connecting to Charles non verbally, before the head raised itself in understanding.

"I wish to remind you of your obligations, sir, of your guilt and urge your penitence."

Charles slowly raised the bible and read a quote about Jesus.

"Verily I say unto you, that one of you shall betray me. And they were exceeding sorrowful, and began every one of them to say unto him, Lord, is it I?"

"And he answered and said, he that dippeth his hand with me in the dish, the same shall betray me," Strafford finished, making Charles stop with some surprise at the man's knowledge of the passage.

Silence ensued before Charles jumped back in to counter attack Strafford. "And while he yet spoke, Judas, one of the twelve, came, and with him a great multitude with swords and staves, from the chief priests and elders of the people. Now he that betrayed him gave them a sign, saying, Whomsoever I shall kiss, that same is he: hold him fast …"

"And forthwith he came to Jesus, and said, Hail, master; and kissed him. Then came they, and laid hands on Jesus and took him," Strafford broke in again, with a strong voice that prevented retaliation, and seeming to relish the debate.

"Then Judas, which had betrayed him, when he saw that he was condemned, repented himself, and brought again the thirty pieces of silver to the chief priests and elders, saying, I have sinned in that I have betrayed the innocent blood," Charles finished, as Strafford voluntarily allowed him.

After a silence, Charles felt obliged to explain his presence again. "I read that because you have betrayed our whole nation, inciting civil war to secure your greed."

"Oh, I know what you mean by it, sir, though it is Parliament who is swindling this nation of its ancient laws and freedom of speech. What's worse is that the people cannot see their deceit; at least Jesus saw through Judas and eventually I hope our nation sees through those few vipers at our heart."

"Enough. At least Judas owned up to his misdeed. This trial is your chance to do that," Charles urged, drawing his passion from the verbal duel with Strafford.

Holding his breath, he heard the guard bang the door, like a gong that sounded the end of the meeting. Charles lifted the bible up to the window, the book almost growing with weight, returning the prisoner's face back to its normal state of sternness as he glared at it. The look was not of disdain, but frustration.

"Read and repent. I draw your attention to Matthew, twenty six."

Far from giving any religious and peaceful message of his own, the soldier cursed in his demand to leave, and Charles was ready to oblige after he had encouraged the letter to slide out of the bible, and through the window.

"I know you," the prisoner tellingly told him discreetly, leaving a pause before continuing at a normal level, "And I know your ways. Your gift of words will bring great solitude to me."

He ignored the comment, only a short hiss and spitting noise from a candle nearby responding to it, as though it endorsed Strafford's recognition of the item he had just passed over. The prisoner paced around, making it easy to imagine how he dealt with official business, for he seemed to examine every aspect of the letter with ease, drifting into an unconscious assumption of his former roles.

A jingling of keys pierced the air as the guard now positively growled, walking out of the room, agitated that the disputing had gone too far. Turning sharply to Strafford for the last time, Charles found the man had digested the information he had been given. The sparkle in his eyes and quickness of the steps had now transformed into a hesitating, gouty movement and he came slowly to the window, a strange friendly expression at the fore, one that seemed so alien to him.

"I think I might have reason to thank you for your sermon. God's words certainly reassure me that my captivity is only temporary, and our Lord looks after all his servants, even you, who preach so unashamedly to me. I am sure he will reward you one day for your devout service."

The poignant words and veiled gratitude caused Charles to reflect for a moment, for in a simple statement, the fellow had even cast away all the lesser images, descriptions and characterisations of him that Charles had believed.

This left him angry; how dare Strafford think that he had done this for the peer himself, or the King for that matter.

"Damn you, I do not need your sentiments."

He strode away, anxious to return to his wife, releasing the torrent of emotions his eventual success had freed up. The tense mission, which could have been discovered at any time, and the stress that brought, had bottled up such strong feelings.

He heaved with energy, relief and pride that he had accomplished everything, overtaking the indignation that Strafford had presumed he was sympathetic to him. It would be truly meaningful now to leave this national prison, for he would be exiting it as a fully liberated man. But then, as if scornfully tearing away all of Charles's achievements, Strafford began laughing.

Charles was puzzled and irritated at such humour from an individual so hated and facing ruin; why was he so audacious, and why did he find the truth of Charles's feelings so humorous?

"I admire your frank honesty, sir. Very admirable and quite similar to my own, which in itself caused so many men to betray me. All but brave men hate the truth, for they fear it."

Chapter 12

J ohn Pym strolled along the small corridor, his allies adjusting their orbit around him to fit within this sphere of influence. Despite its cramped, narrow area, such passages as these played host to some of the most important decisions in politics, acting as arteries, linking the House of Commons with such great organs as Westminster Hall. As they neared the way into the trial arena, Pym saw the cloisters to his right, overlooking a small grassy area. Yesterday he had paced around the square gathering his thoughts, not as one colleague had said, looking for divine support. While they waited for the queue of Members of Parliament to file through the narrow portal, he raised his eyes in frustration to the carved, plasterwork roof that resembled the complex mesh of a spider's web. He heard John Maynard mocking how the people of Westminster now blessed Strafford as he travelled to the court, although this was probably more because the rival city, London, hated him.

"Good God, did you have to threaten one of his witnesses?" Pym demanded with a temper unusual in him, triggered by Maynard's bravado.

"Pennyman needed to be put in his place. Fancy Strafford whinging to all and sundry that he would rather put himself on God's mercy, than call any more witnesses if they were going to be endangered," Maynard stated in derision.

"Aye, I can believe it and I saw that the hall did too. I do not want such tomfoolery today, we have to get a grip of this, otherwise we are all undone," Pym ordered, slicing through their arguments, like the oxen drawn ploughs that carved up the fields of his Tavistock constituency.

The members entered the hall, again lining up in a similar way to a theatre trip as they took up their seats. Pym looked to his far right, at the throne that loftily sat on top of a red dais, significantly without an occupant. He quickly examined the private area behind it, though the shady wooden boxes that housed the royal family merely seemed to create even more mystery and suspicion around them than was normal. As the King and his family sat cramped within that makeshift, wooden gallery, which ran the full length of one end of the hall, he thought about how they had successfully managed to box the King up, in more ways than one. He had been warned off from sitting in full pomp on the throne, for the trial was carried out in the name of the sovereign, so his attendance was as a private person, the official seat solely representing his power. Such an easy acquiescence with this seemed to suggest an innate weakness, and emboldened many of Pym's colleagues. It was not lost on them that the windows of the royal gallery were covered with elaborate grills, like a string of Catholic confessional boxes.

"He infuriates me," Maynard snapped, unable to resist talking about Strafford.

"Will you get this anger out now, lest you vent it again today to our prejudice," John Glyn retorted.

Maynard glared in response, round eyes blinking several times with distaste at his treatment, letting one final comment out before obliging them all, "He casts doubt on all our witnesses, saying they are personal enemies of his and bearing biased grudges.

We should not be questioned by the like of this brute."

The peers had begun to file in now and as they did so, the Earl of Southampton overheard their discussion and commented from under the brim of his large, black hat, "Aye, sir, and so he should question you all, when your witness includes someone who had been dismissed from his service. I somehow feel his evidence would be revenge, rather than truth."

Glyn grabbed Maynard's arm tightly, forcing him to remain seated as Southampton walked away. Maynard's petulant look was reinforced by the way his mouth sagged huffily, in the same way as his jowls.

"You fool," Pym growled, "There is enough worry, toil and work to do with Strafford, let alone controlling such an unruly child as you. This is the most pivotal moment in our lives and this nation's history and you would rather drive us onto the rocks like Jonah. Luckily the Lord is with us and he will not suffer Strafford to escape punishment for his sins."

As the magnificently dressed peers took their places, creating a sea of colour with their red robes and gold stripes, people bowed to them and Pym removed his hat as etiquette demanded in the presence of these nobles. Now the only people to have their heads covered were the peers themselves. Finally Strafford appeared to take up the main part in the act, slowly moving to his small box with the usual calmness, looking his accusers in the face. Pym himself had to turn away to resist losing concentration over his planning and preparation, yet the gaunt face and stooped frame still managed to haunt his mind.

Inside, worry and anxiety swirled around the Parliamentarian's stomach, despite his faith in God's will.

The prosecution began by speaking about Strafford's request to produce his account books to disprove an accusation of impropriety in financial matters. During this exchange, Pym was forced to look at the prisoner, whose habitat was right in front of the prosecution's crammed box; Strafford stood like a preacher in a pulpit, refusing to sit for now and casting his image onto as many as he could.

"My Lords, please block the prisoner from making further impertinent excursions today. He should not be allowed to conjure up these ledgers. I draw your minds back to the evidence of Lord Cork," Glyn interceded.

Strafford quickly made ready to speak in retaliation, hand resting on his chest as he did so.

"I remember my Lord Cork's words, but surely it is not humanly possible to recall words supposedly uttered by me in private conversations near ten years ago? I must admit I sometimes forget what I say, but I can assure you I said nothing like what his lordship asserts. He must have an amazing mind to be able to recite word for word the evidence he has also, by chance, given in writing too. My admiration also is extended to Sir Piers Crosby who similarly drew to his mind words that I had with him at dinner, yet I have never invited him to dine with me. Another man is sure he heard me make threats in Ulster, during a time when I was across the waters in Yorkshire."

There was some heckling from the benches, like dogs barking and howling in support of the beast that was their master. Indeed one of Strafford's portraits had included a great, white hound, which some people were now saying had mystical powers. It stood half as high as Strafford himself, with a head as long as his forearm.

Then the prisoner eased his frame down onto a chair, the smile temporarily stifling the natural ferocity of his sharp, yet petit features. As the whole place paused, hanging on his action, he outstretched his hands and held onto the wooden crate that enclosed him. Only his head and upper chest were visible now, fighting against a sea of accusations, and he examined all around him deeply.

"I thank God I never spoke any unmannerly language all the days of my life, though I confess my tongue has been too free on occasions with my thoughts. My heart perhaps hath lain too near my tongue, but God forbid that every past word should rise up in judgement against me," he pleaded, eyebrows lifted in modesty.

Pym sighed and adjusted his back, which had begun to ache, tired of the charade. It looked like he would have to play his trump card early and cut the prisoner's seduction of the audience, assessing every word and expression to make his final judgement. He looked hard at Strafford, whose mouth tightened, uniting the small sliver of a beard in the centre of his tiny chin closer to his ornate moustache. He wished it would stay so firmly closed. He made to stand, to intercede, but observing his move, the prisoner beat him to it, the spectators turning into moths around the ability and intelligence that veritably beamed from the fellow.

Pym remained on his feet in a stubborn challenge - whether it was Strafford's birthday in a few days or not, he would get no presents from John Pym.

Strafford rammed his point home, tearing into the meat of the prosecution's argument, "As for misappropriating funds, I point out that after my work in cutting waste, there was near one hundred thousand pounds income made from the tobacco monopoly alone and it should be clear from this success that I save money, rather than siphon it away. I wonder at how making a profit is nowadays regarded as treason?"

Pym adjusted his poise, standing with his legs apart, and trying to find some comfort within his close pack of accomplices. Finally the prosecution counter attacked, flashing their own sharp teeth and releasing the pent up frustration.

"Disregarding these comments, we would remind everyone that Lord Strafford has cast down peers of the realm and nobility during his power. His evils are not confined to the common man."

Strafford hurriedly added his conclusion to this point, as fast as the tennis games that took place within the Tudor court at Whitehall Palace, skilfully levering the whole speed of the competition up a level. "So then, does this mean you assert that a peer of this kingdom, as I am, should be beyond the reach of justice or treated differently to the common man?"

Maynard abandoned their position without hesitation, escaping from the prisoner's grasp, before calling for Reinforcements.

"Let us call another witness who heard words made by the prisoner's brother."

Thinking of anything at all, Maynard was desperate to cause Strafford's words to rebound. At that moment, although he feared Strafford, it felt somewhat safer with John Pym's sturdy presence, like a father figure - or indeed a grandfather figure - at fifty six years old.

A witness stood, hands on hips and turning himself left, then right to address the crowds. Someone repeated the Strafford's sarcastic comment that he could not see the strings attached to this man, which linked the puppet with the prosecution boxes. Then at last, the witness began his lines, explaining how Strafford's brother had told him the peer had stated the little finger of the King was heavier than the loins of the law. And then that same sibling of the prisoner began cutting through the benches, weaving towards the front, while demanding to give evidence to correct the tale.

"Nay, sir, I move you are unfit to give evidence," Lord Arundel declared, raising his white staff like a wand, making ready to cast the fellow away.

As Arundel settled himself back onto his woolsack, looking

quite proud of his commanding interlude, and long overdue part in the proceedings, Pym sighed, desperation rising in his soul. He thanked God for Arundel's decision, but thought it ironic that the peer was a Catholic; he hated those just as much as Strafford, if not more. He was well aware that with Strafford's fall, the Catholics would have to be neutralised next, to safeguard the Protestant establishment.

Pym nudged his colleague into action, to address Strafford.

"You are required to answer the following four charges as a whole and not individually. These are the most serious charges, My Lords."

"Let us see him pull each one apart now he has to face them in bulk," Maynard whispered as he resumed his place between Pym and Glyn.

Pym was confident. These were the charges he had personally inserted and now they had come to the crunch, he felt somewhat more secure that he was dealing with his own handiwork. When Strafford protested that he had been given no warning of this, Pym watched Arundel overrule the prisoner once more. Pym breathed deeply, ready to bring Strafford down like a cornered stag with a weapon from his own armoury. The man had threatened the safety of the kingdom, and every man's livelihood and freedom depended on securing a conviction.

Chapter 13

John Glyn began by displaying his indignation. "Never before have I encountered a trial where the prisoner can make demands of the prosecution," he said mockingly, amazed at Strafford's nerve.

Following this taster, designed to outrage everyone, written reports of the meetings of the King's Privy Council were finally produced, dished up in endless courses that the audience never grew sick of.

Strafford was hurriedly noting down comments that were flowing like a torrent, before casting his quill down in exasperation. He raised his hand and shook his head, behaving as though he were once more a student in Cambridge, frustrated by his tutor's lecture. An orchestra of chatter and murmuring started up, changing tempo with Strafford's every move, until it forced the narrator in the prosecution box to look up from his paper, before he had finished even the first charge.

"Am I the lowest felon in this land? By introducing written evidence, you are preventing me from having the opportunity to question the authors of them. Any common man has this right," the accused gruffly stated.

John Glyn threw the matter to the House of Lords like a flaming cannonball, who quickly acquiesced in favour of the prosecution, and ordered the battle to continue.

He remained focussed, as disciplined as a sentry, and Pym praised him with an almost fatherly nod of the head, recognising the same qualities he himself had as a young Member of Parliament.

"Within these papers there is proof that Lord Strafford advised the King to use his Royal Prerogative to impose his will by force if needs be, should Parliament not grant him any money."

Glyn protected the revelations, standing throughout the remainder to bar Strafford from interrupting, until the call went out for a witness to comment on this most vital point. Strafford, they asserted with anger, had tried to cause a civil war.

"Sir Henry Vane."

As they waited for Vane to step up, Pym looked round the hall. He saw a line of men passing some meat to each other, while others drank beer or wine out of the bottle. It shocked his sense of strict Puritanism by its sheer excess, his own desires suppressed with a fast, in recognition of the divine work they had to do today. Old Vane's dull character merged into the vast, grey walls.

"Sir Henry, is it true that during this meeting, the Earl of Strafford told the King that he had an army in Ireland, which he could employ here, to reduce this kingdom?"

Vane hesitated and the question was repeated.

"Yes," he said tersely.

An undercurrent of noise began to circulate through the hall in response to this serious charge. Strafford had sanctioned nothing less than a full civil war.

Pym's eyes narrowed as he stifled a smile of satisfaction and relief, now that the full extent of the prisoner's crimes was being exposed. He thought about the once proud earl's feelings of lying within the Tower of London, and of being ferried out of Traitors Gate to his trial, remembering how the man had been incarcerated as a young politician for his opposition to royal policy. It was satisfying to Pym to know that, unlike his rival, he had stayed on God's path throughout, righteousness being more tempting than self glory.

"Which kingdom is meant, England or Scotland? Remember that at the time of this meeting, the Scots were invading the north, so Lord Strafford could have meant the use of the Irish army against Scotland."

Lord Clare offered this objective warning from the benches of the House of Lords. The crimson decked peer, Strafford's father in law from his second marriage, had drawn blood from Vane's testimony.

"Can you answer, Sir Henry?" Pym asked, taking the challenge on confidently, looking the man square on. Vane stood uneasily. He paused and glanced around as though searching for some more direction.

"I am firm of the opinion that My Lord Strafford had said 'this kingdom' and not 'that kingdom' and I have no doubts," was the best Vane could generate, and even then, with vacillation.

Lord Clare stood up again, unsatisfied, adamant that the words were ambiguous and did not mean England. "At what point during the meeting did these words come up? Tell us the exact wording which was used, for this is necessary before we can judge the context."

Vane's eyes turned to Pym and then his gaze dropped to the floor, almost like a suicide plunge. The Chairman of the Committee then ended the deadlock by declaring there could be no doubt that England was the country that was spoken of. Pym nodded his head, eager to show agreement and anxious to move on.

Next, the Earl of Southampton rose with Lord Clare,

wresting Vane's argument back to the floor for a post mortem.

"Sir Henry could be mistaken in his judgement."

Vane repeated himself and Pym felt irritation cloud his senses, for this evidence was meant to be his personal masterstroke. Once more the trial was held up and being dissected.

"Did anyone else in the meeting think that Lord Strafford had meant England? I ask everyone what could have been meant by the words 'this kingdom' and is Sir Henry sure that at the time, it appeared to mean England, or does he simply infer it?" Lord Clare persisted. The question, flung open to all as it was, caused an instant division in the huge hall, with backers coming forward for both sides of the argument.

Maynard tutted and thumped his seat, thick neck like an oak tree, but with a common sense just as densely wooden. The man was principled, though over enthusiasm often tarnished the otherwise able legal mind. Pym could overlook this, but his patience did not stretch as far as the man's fidgeting, for it was angering him even more as control of events spiralled away, heaven bound. For many, a clear feeling about the whole matter had fizzled out into uncertainty.

Lord Arundel, sitting like a messiah on his raised area spoke over the arguments, attempting to salvage the situation. "Sir Henry Vane has been called here as a witness to the words, not as an interpreter for them."

Pym's rigid body eased ever so slightly as this tempered the atmosphere.

Strafford, though, grasped the moment once more, now that men's minds had been whetted with this particular point. "Look to what is proved, not to what is forced from these gentlemen, for words pass and may be easily mistaken. I do not deny that I advised the King to use his prerogative. It has once been my opinion which I learnt in the House of Commons and it has gone along with me in the whole course of my service to the commonwealth and by the Grace of God I shall carry it to my grave, that the prerogative of the crown and liberty of the subject should be equally looked upon and secured together, but not separately. No lawyer has ever denied that in situations of extreme emergency, there needs to lie a power in the royal prerogative, as a safeguard to the state and its people."

Pym was stunned by the prisoner's words, so much so that an exhilarated Strafford was able to continue unchecked, as if he were on horseback at a hunting expedition.

"Words spoken to friends, in familiar discourse, uttered in one's own chamber, table, or in one's own sick bed. If these shall be brought against a man as treason, this takes away the comfort of all human society. It will be a silent world, a city will become a hermitage and no man shall dare to impart his solitary thoughts or opinions to his friend or neighbour, for fear of them being misused. Sir Henry is but a single witness and I can call three who will testify that he is mistaken."

Shouts in Strafford's favour began spreading in the ranks of spectators behind, still in the minority, but expanding dangerously.

"Alas, poor soul."

In response, Pym stood to try and stop the groundswell of sympathy, manipulated by a menace to society. As he waited, the hall quietened and all lines of sight rested upon him, loading a weight of anticipation upon his shoulders. He had lost his confidence in the trial and could sense Strafford staring at him. He could not bring himself to speak, mind going blank, intimidated for the first time by the immense numbers watching him on all sides with expectation.

Mutterings of unrest began.

Still Pym did not know what to say, so he pulled some notes out and desperately rummaged through them, anxious to maintain the attack, but the worry of it all had taken a toll. He resolved to use elaborate words to remind them of the prisoner's crimes, fumbling through the notes in his fraught state of mind.

"The prisoner's offences are a seedbed of crimes, just as the earth is a seedbed for vegetables. Let no man forget this."

Pym's wording caused momentary quiet, before laughter erupted from the benches of the peers, until enough were engaged in such mirth to inhibit any further arguments for the prosecution. Pym himself resumed his seat, to the embarrassment of his colleagues, and he felt raw from this defeat. Strafford could manage a crowd far better, could use wit much more effectively, and for the first time, the whole of the prosecution were dumfounded. Maynard watched fixatedly, mouth open in wonder at this vulnerability.

One after the other the prisoner's three witnesses backed him up, continuing the trouncing. The third man went further with his time, probably knowing that he was already in the sights of the House of Commons himself, so whatever he said would not make any difference to his own future.

"My Lord Strafford is the greatest friend of Parliament's. He was not the one to advise the King that he was absolved from any rules of government. In actual fact, he always advised the King to stay within the limits of the law, and only use the prerogative to fix the country's ills if Parliament steadfastly refused to vote subsidies of money."

Lord Hamilton even explained that Strafford's constant advice to take note of Parliament's, and to call them frequently, was so monotonous that it grew boring to hear at council.

Glyn intervened on behalf of his recuperating leader, "But, my lords, the royal prerogative has been overused; especially its application over this land for eleven years, when nobody saw fit to consult a Parliament at all. During that time, the views of the people were immaterial and men like Lord Strafford used the royal prerogative as a stick to beat us down with. The sheer notion of allowing the prerogative to exist as a power to be used during extreme emergencies cannot go hand in hand with the people's liberty as he stated."

Pym was thankful at this wording. Glyn had never made reference to the King himself in that accusation, though it was as near as. Attacking the monarch personally would be folly.

Strafford then made a final few skirmishing attacks. "I must pass my thanks to Sir Henry Vane for recalling his part so perfectly, so as to be able to remember the details better than the people who apparently said the words themselves. It seems by speaking in council and offering my advice that I am facing treason. With this in mind, how can any of you be safe in royal service? If your opinion can be used against you like this, order and government will collapse and no man hereafter will serve."

Maynard jumped to his feet. A surprised Pym was sure the inactivity had nearly killed his colleague. "Are we to take Lord Strafford's words, that private conversations should remain so, as evidence that he is guilty and attempting to cover such discussions up?"

Pym folded his arms; events had not gone too well, but they had recovered sufficiently to be on the attack again.

Glyn stood to crank their side back up. "Is this not the greatest treason of all? To claim that being a councillor to the King gives you immunity from prosecution when you mouth advice as treasonous as this? It stains the honour of every councillor of this great land."

Pym was happy to leave the day there, building up indignation within the spectators. In the end, it was Strafford who gingerly pulled himself up, to beg the court to end the proceedings, wincing with apparent pain. The request was eagerly granted, after nearly ten hours without a break; the hunger pains began to rise like demons from Pym's stomach.

As he watched his fellow members of the House of Commons file out, he knew their safety and freedom rested on his burly shoulders. If it were not for his leadership, people kept telling him, they would never have achieved the unthinkable of holding the King to account, after nearly sixteen years of his reign and broken promises. He felt tears come to his eyes and hung behind in the corridor, pondering what would happen in a worst case scenario, should the trial break down.

"Precedents, precedents," he murmured, racking his brains to think of what Parliament had done with past royal servants. Considerations about this took his mind back to his early time in Parliament, when the King was all powerful and new to the throne. He remembered how they had gunned for the royal favourite of the time, the Duke of Buckingham. At that moment John Hampden walked into the chamber.

"Ah there you are. Why the serious face, John?"

Pym looked up quickly. "I was thinking back to Buckingham, escaping Parliament's calls for justice by being murdered by a vengeful officer he had refused for promotion."

Hampden nodded, raising his eyebrows. "The vast wealth that man had, and the array of offices of state he held were disgraceful. Why, he advanced from an ordinary man to an earl within two years."

"I dislike idle chattering when we are in the midst of such important business, but in the name of our Lord, the ghosts of the men who lost their lives in the King's slipshod wars with France and Spain practically call on us to protect the public. So many patriotic souls lost because command was given to the inept Buckingham, and money frittered away on paintings instead of equipment."

Chapter 14

Charles stood waiting for Anne, tapping his foot on the rush mat in the hall to a tune he could not get out of his head. He unbuckled his leather purse that hung on his belt and took out a letter that had arrived a few days ago, still surprised by it even now.

'I am grateful for the bible reading you passed onto me, though your insolent message about my so called sins was not as welcome. However, I have found such comfort in the words conveyed, enlightening me and showing a clear path I can take to deliver me from evil. I pray you pass on news of my agreement to be saved by our Lord, for although he may seem to have struck you down too, you should never lose faith in him.'

Charles had read Strafford's words over and over and he was able to translate the writing, which was masked in a language of its own. It was clear that it referred to the deeper meaning of an escape. The contents of the letter, the King's intentions, the dismissal from the escort party and his own part in it all became transparently clear.

Finally Anne descended the stairs, Louise behind her holding the voluminous skirt, as she stepped precariously onwards.

"Go no more a rushing, maids in May. Go no more a rushing, maids, I pray," Charles sang, remembering the apt song he had been infected with earlier.

"It is still April, my dear," Anne responded with a wry smile.

Her happiness was as attractive an adornment to her appearance as the ceruse paste that included egg white, giving her facial features a delicately pale covering.

She walked slowly towards him, dark ringlets of curls running down her shoulders and spiralling around her chest.

Her ivory, silk dress swished as she came closer, the centre of it decorated with blue ribbons and a jewelled brooch holding the large, lace collar together. It felt like his wedding day all over Again and he held his hand out to take hers, telling her how beautiful she was. She delicately rubbed her eyelid, before looking in the mirror that hung forward from the upper wall, ensuring the blue henna had not smudged. Charles could not help but check whether she had added some veins to her breasts with the same crayon, drawing them on the white make up that also covered her cleavage, waves of passion spreading throughout his body.

Anne pulled her hood carefully up, Louise returning to help, making sure that those exquisite curls that Charles loved so much were not affected. Something about the hairstyle appealed to Charles, and he tugged his brown, leather gloves on, smelling the scent that Anne had soaked these Valentine gifts in before she had given him to them. Anxious to leave as he fastened his calf length cloak about him, he subconsciously edged closer to the door, while Anne took a fur muff to keep her hands warm. With a final lot of instructions for Louise, requesting her to see the cook maid out, secure the doors and expect them back at eleven of the clock, the couple linked arms and stepped onto the cobbles. They got into their hired carriage, Anne lifting the hem of her skirt, trying to keep it from the ground. The short distance didn't warrant pinning it up for protection.

"We will have our own private coach one day," Charles predicted, lost in the world he was creating for them.

"A huge mansion too, with beautiful flowers filling the garden," she said, adding her own wishes with wide eyes. Charles chuckled at the expression, knowing that any smile would crack her makeup.

"But what type?" he asked, touching on her love of flowers.

"White and red rhododendrons, I think," she said, pale, pink cheeks as soft as any petal she spoke of.

"And I will learn geography and take us across the seas to some foreign land, maybe Paris or Venice. My mother's family came from France apparently," he said, whispering a few French words of love in her ear. She playfully slapped his arm, desperately trying to contain her humour again. Instead, he kissed her hands, tenderly tracing his way up her arm, until Anne jumped, eagerly pointing out the sight of Holland House peeping over the trees that kept the dirt, and poorer sort, from its walls. He gazed at the other glorious vehicles in front of them, also making their way through Kensington.

The couple took each other's hands, Charles giving hers a tender rub with his thumb. Flaming torches lit the road up in a warm welcome, the glow giving off a romantic air, with smoke and radiant light swirling around. The fire took him back to his childhood, when the whole town would gather round a bonfire to celebrate Gunpowder Day, the anniversary of the country's deliverance from treason and Catholicism. The carefree joy that had bonded the whole town together had etched this memory on his mind. In particular, it was a few hours away from the drab routine of life, the chance to see his parents arm in arm, as though they were courting again; a rare sight of love during a life full of toil. And young girls were present too, bringing the opportunity to mingle with them, away from the indomitable parental gaze, which was ever present when the youngsters came into contact at church each Sunday.

"Look at you, "Anne said, returning him fully to his senses, and he sat back, resting his head on the seat and looking at her inquisitively.

"You have some of my red lip colour on you," she teased.

He began wiping his face in a rough manner, desperately trying to erase it. Then Anne leaned over, her body touching his, manoeuvring her silk dress as she guided his hand to the mark. In the nick of time the mark was cleaned, and Holland House appeared in front of them in full and sudden glory. The wings of the grand building extended outwards, as though in greeting. Many arches crowned the tops of walls and windows, and the elaborate walkways that encircled the place softened the huge structure, almost giving it a carefree character of its own, and mimicking the owner in this respect.

They stepped out as a footman opened the carriage door, examining the mansion. The servant nodded his head and remembering custom, he tipped the man with a few coins.

Walking slowly forward, he felt his purse, bulging with silver shillings, sixpences and pennies for such gifts. He had especially brought two golden crowns and a golden angel worth twenty shillings in total, to give to Holland to distribute amongst the servants on their departure.

The entrance sported a central tower with two huge bay windows on either side, two storeys high, like eyes. Set back on the main house were two further square towers, the pointing lead roofs of a blue colour topping the soft flowing reddish brown brickwork. The two wings that jutted out from the house created a small, partially enclosed area and Charles and Anne sauntered up the gravel path, wide expanses of formal lawns and boxed hedges all around them.

Charles sensed the sweet aroma of the briar rose hedges as they headed towards the line of balustrades that funnelled guests towards the mansion. The place was brought alive by the fashionable men and women who now milled around the foot of it, making their way into the glittering world beyond. They sparkled with jewellery, dressed in a rainbow of richly coloured materials, like a cluster of semi precious stones surrounding the structural diamond of Holland House. A male peacock caught their eye, and they both could not help stopping and watching the beauty of the tail feathers as it strutted past. Never before had they seen such a creature and the circular patterns on its arrayed plumage seemed to stare back in equal measure.

The interior of the building was no less impressive. Sheets of expensive mirror glass betrayed Holland's wealth, as did the marble floors and the three great chandeliers. It was hard to believe that they were still within the metropolis of London, which was home to three hundred thousand people, made up of all levels of society.

Handing the invitation over gave access to the stairs and on reaching the top, they went into the dinning chamber, still awestruck at the opulence as they marvelled at it all.

Interspersing the dark wooden wall panels were magnificent tapestries portraying biblical scenes, while others elegantly displayed the Holland coat of arms, surrounded by flowers and vines twisting around it, as if declaring that the family fortune would flourish, develop and grow as much as nature itself. As they followed the lines of people, everything reflected in the windows, forming the illusion that the place was even bigger.

Then the vibrant colours of a portrait seized Charles's attention, attracting his artistic interest. He recognised the seafaring Earl of Warwick, portrayed wearing a pair of gold coloured shoes with a sparkling flower on each, and crimson stockings and breeches. In fact it seemed he had a sea of red around him, enriched by his golden doublet. The rugged features of his weather beaten face contrasted with the exquisite attire.

"What a magnificent sight, he looks nothing like his brother Holland. I think one of them is illegitimate," Anne whispered.

The sensitivity of the comment made him grin, wide eyed for a moment, though it was not the same when Anne could not express her humour. Then he put his hand out in front of him, letting Anne rest hers on it, and led her onwards with the flotilla of guests. As they approached the Earl and Countess of Holland, Charles's back was as rigid as the King's pride, and Anne glided as gracefully and effortlessly as the clouds that passed through the early evening sun, which had graced their journey to tonight's event.

"Sir Charles, very good to see you at one of my social gatherings. Lady Anne, your prettiness enhances our gathering," the noble announced, taking Anne's hand and kissing it for a few crucial seconds longer than Charles found acceptable.

Holland's wandering eye seemed to twinkle around her whole body, assessing, exploring and admiring, his fair moustache rising with an appreciative smile. Charles bowed his head and moved closer to his wife. Anne then curtseyed, keeping her upper body straight, but bending both knees to lower herself. Charles took her hand. Lady Holland began speaking to the next couple to move the line on, and to regain her husband's attention, her expression as dour as rumour had described. The only thing he noted about the lady was the rich gold dress, and the pearls that hung around her neck as big as musket balls, ready to defend her matronly bosom to the end. She certainly seemed as straight laced as a corset, probably only coming alive when she worked on her beloved needlepoint, yet despite all this, Charles had one thing in common with her now; he too had taken the measure of Lord Holland. The noble was an exact opposite of his brother; delicate and smooth featured, with a suave tongue and much grace and manners, clearly enjoying both his immense wealth, and the pursuit of ladies. Charles and Anne moved to the corner of the room as others poured in to be received.

Some couples sat down, or stood in the corners and chattered intimately, while two lines of guests formed in the middle of the room. Of course, amidst all this was the odd man or woman flirting like that peacock he had seen earlier.

"Lord Holland seems nice and friendly, a true family man with his wife."

Indignant at this flyaway statement, which Charles knew to be wrong, and which was the final straw to his patience after watching Holland and Anne, he could not help but inhale sharply with a frown.

"A what? Do you know he had an affair with the Duchesse de Chevreuse? He loves the French - literally - and he can do more than talk the language. He was the one who was sent to Paris by the King to arrange his marriage with the Queen."

"How romantic he must be to match make for the King," she said with a continued hint of innocence.

"You are as taken with him as all the ladies. It's a good thing I am with you, otherwise his silver tongue would be all over you. Holland is only interested in keeping a ruthless grip over power and money."

As he thought about Holland in this outraged manner, further justification came to him as he remembered the noble during the Bishops war; the exquisite dress - too showy for any real military man - and his bravado talk were all a front. If there was an easy way out of something, Holland would take that route and he remembered how the peer had made promises when negotiating the King's marriage in France, that the King would relax the laws against the Catholics. All this was done while knowing that the royal policy, and the whole of England, were against such a thing. But he needed the King's match with the young Princess Henrietta Maria to go ahead, for then he would be feted in reward, ever close to both royals as a result.

"Romantic to match make," he repeated, of Anne's earlier claim, summing up his outburst of feeling, "Well the Queen's honeymoon with the English people has certainly ended now, that's for sure."

He saw Anne shaking her head playfully, and with a mischievous look in her eye, she admitted to teasing him, anxious for the display of envious affection. It was the chivalrous protection that she so loved.

He stood relishing the intimacy, mixed with the aroma of her perfume and soon their thoughts unwillingly returned to the Banquet as space became limited; Charles could not place some of the people entering, but he did recognise Holland's brother, Lord Warwick, from the painting outside. His coloured cheeks and somewhat messy hair made him stand out as much as that new warship, the *Sovereign of the Seas*. Indeed like Warwick, the vessel focussed the attentions of many, the first ship with three gun decks and practically a floating castle.

He watched Anne as she fondled one of her own earrings, looking to the direction of the Countess of Arundel. He guessed she was eyeing up the fashions and comparing her own adornments.

"Her husband has twelve thousand per annum to supplement those. My measly fifteen hundred should still buy you some decent pearls though, if that would be good enough for you," he said playfully.

She tilted her head, dark locks hastily adopting a new position as she put one finger to her mouth to ponder the offer, Charles telling from the way she did it that it was an eager acceptance. He had picked up quickly that 'no' or a simple silence always meant an affirmative.

A culinary aroma filled the room as the long oak banqueting table was covered with dishes - even that had the chance to be dressed in its best. Seeing Lord Holland walk to the far end of the table, the other guests followed suit, and Charles nudged Anne. As they stood at their place, Lord Holland's chaplain said grace in his gruff, slow, old voice, making him wonder whether they would ever get any food this night. Finally the guests began to be seated, with a stocky gentleman opposite Charles, another merchant, he was told. This triggered an idea for negotiating a sale of gunpowder for the regiment.

Lord Holland took the seat of honour which faced the entrance doors, resting against the arms of the chair to emphasise this additional privilege of his, compared to everyone else's normal seats. Lady Holland, the hostess, sat with her back to the portal, at the other end of the table. Charles noted with humour how Holland used the distance from his wife to his advantage, as he enjoyed a tête à tête with an alluring female sitting near him.

After everyone was seated, Charles unfolded his white napkin and tucked it in between the buttons of his doublet. He was soon given a succulent piece of venison, but a glance to Anne, highlighted the wizened lump she had been dished up. He turned away before she saw him and stifled his playful amusement - it was as though Lady Holland was definitely adamant that Anne was not to enjoy anything of her husband's - both bodily and culinary. Now composed, he looked back and took hold of her plate, intending to swap it with his, only to feel someone take his arm tightly.

The man next to him frowned and tightened his lips before giving a short, quick shake of his head. Charles looked at the stranger's grip on his arm with disdain and the man let out a low whisper of 'etiquette' as though he were stopping him from committing some heinous crime. A servant now distributed the vegetables around the table as people started tucking into the meal, careful not to let the food slip out of their fingers as they ate. Another servant then came around the table pouring wine in a choreographed performance. As the guests struck up conversations, Charles's neighbour seized his attention again.

"Never do anything to show your disapproval of your hostess's distribution of meat. Tell your wife to leave it on the plate if she cannot face eating it."

He nodded his thanks to the fellow and then rubbed his leg on Anne's as she glared at her meal. Charles discreetly passed the message on, before observing the other men and women, interested in their lives and what they did.

Arundel was obviously talking about art because one by one the table began their own conversations about this topic, mirroring him. A smart looking man with a white moustache caught Charles's eye, as he tucked into some lampreys. Anne turned away from the sight and Charles smiled, knowing how she hated them as much as eels, to which they were so similar.

"There are some masterpieces in Florence. I went there on a grand tour as a young blood," the man commented, stroking his snowy moustache.

Charles was eager for more because he had not been out of England before, and sensing this interest, the man continued.

"Now when I was in Mantua, the duke was negotiating with our own King for works of art. I believe King Charles secured some Raphaels, Titians, Caravaggios and Correggios. A marvellous collection and all sold because the provinces silk industry had declined and the duke was after ready money."

Charles had not heard of the last two artists, but he raised his eyebrows in appreciation at the other names. He had heard a great deal of King Charles's immense art collection; in the circles he moved now, it was admired and spoken of in wonder, but as a young man at the family's inn, some men would rail about its cost to the nation. His father would defend the King to the last, while his mother would agree with the complaints. Sometimes he wondered how his parents got together, when they seemed to have the opposite thoughts about anything, but in manhood he had begun to understand that this was probably what kept the spark in the relationship.

In the meantime, he ate some pigeon and Anne was enjoying her stewed carp, while he eyed up the salmon as his next target. Or maybe he should take some rabbit or ox tongue, he pondered, intending to appease his great appetite.

The silent man devoted his attention to the art lover as the conversation continued. "And what pray did our sovereign hand over for this collection?"

"Near fifteen thousand pounds," he was informed.

Charles gulped as he swallowed a lump of his meat in surprise. The man next to him hissed and screwed his face up like he was undergoing an operation.

"Fifteen thousand, and all when our troops were fighting France and in desperate need of money. No wonder Parliament do not trust our sovereign with finances, considering a meagre forty pounds would pay two hundred soldiers for one week," he growled.

The man who had been talking about the art collection puffed his cheeks out, at a loss with how to respond, but shocked at the severity of the comments against the King. Charles thought the bewilderment the comment had caused was quite funny, and then the man who had uttered the criticism addressed him.

"Andrew Lark at your service, not afraid to say what I think and proud of it."

Charles laughed at the introduction and felt he could get on with the fellow, before introducing himself.

"Do not say you have been to Mantua too?" Lark asked.

"Nay I have not," Charles said sadly, hopeful one day to explore other countries and cultures, if he could further his patronage with Holland. He did not even know where Mantua was because of his poor education.

"Good, because now the art has been swiped, there is nothing to go there for," Lark sniggered.

Charles shook his head, smiling at the man's joviality rather than the joke. He seemed brutally honest and this was so refreshing in a formal, stuffy atmosphere - at least you knew where you stood.

Anne nudged him. "How big is the King's art collection?"

Before Charles could reply, the man with the moustache interjected to add a positive comment to the matter. "My dear lady, it is the greatest in Europe, and not even the Spanish can match it. One day our country will look back and thank King Charles the First for giving us such a treasure that will surely survive for generations. It gives us a prestige over the rest of the world and shows how cultured our great country is. I mean, which other kingdom gets its ships saluted by the dipping of the other vessel's flag, respecting our position as master of the seas?"

"The King has spent enough on it, not to mention the money he pours into his favourite ministers," Charles said to Anne with a frown.

Anne nodded, agreeing with the comment, before resuming her conversation with the couple next to her. As she did so, she rested her hand on Charles's leg for a while, and he laid his gently on top.

As the courses were being eaten, Holland asked Arundel how the business of Strafford went. Charles could just hear it and what he did miss was repeated by some gossiping people nearby, anxiously telling each other what the two peers were talking about.

"Pym has outmanoeuvred the King and Strafford," interrupted Warwick, "Strafford has many enemies, and if the King keeps on supporting him, it will surely tell against him too."

That comment provoked a merchant, who added, "It is a damned disgrace that a loyal minister should be put on trial. Who will be next if they destroy Strafford – will it be Laud?"

"I think your views about the King and his ministers are in the minority, sir. Most men will gladly suffer a few sacrificial lambs for peace and less tyranny, especially if the brutal

Archbishop Laud is the one cooped up in the Tower," said another man.

"The King puts up crucifixes and moves the altar tables; it seems he wants to take us back to Catholicism," another argued.

Lord Arundel looked up in silence. Charles raised his eyebrows and shifted his sight to his food. He knew Arundel was Catholic and discreetly looked again to see how the peer reacted. The natural ferocity in bearing and features was so hardened, that such a comment could not toughen them further anyway.

"Mister Pym seems to have misjudged the nation on this particular issue, for there was a petition submitted in favour of the bishops. The King, of course, will typically think all is well and that the bishops are now indestructible, while Pym simply bides his time."

The man near Anne attracted Charles's attention now. He was an older gentleman, with a round face and Charles especially noticed one of his eyelids were slanted, giving his gaze a doleful air. His mouth was one long line, accentuated by deep furrows at either side of it.

"Mister Armstrong knows where you can buy some globes," Anne informed him.

He waited for the man to give some details. Anne looked at Charles intently, covering her mouth. The fellow seemed docile, but kindly.

"You said you wanted some?" she queried as she took a deep breath to compose herself.

"I do, I am just waiting for the gentleman to tell me about them," he murmured to her.

Judging by Anne's expression, she had obviously palmed the person onto him. He felt a smile of his own breaking through and he tried to restrain it while he looked at the guest again.

"So you want some globes?" Mister Armstrong repeated, in a jittery tone.

Charles observed the way he stuck his neck out a little each time he spoke, as though having trouble getting his voice out. He nodded, but the slow and laborious way the man communicated got on his nerves and he compared the head movements to a duck picking up food, wishing he would manage to collect his conversation.

"Well, you see, I saw a pair. I know a bit about geography myself, Father used to be a master mariner. So, well, I bought some myself around five years ago - no, it was six years. At that time, you see, I was living outside of London."

Charles felt irritated, lacking patience to listen any further. All he could think about was what he could be doing if he were not being distracted.

"Where are these globes?" he interrupted with an outward calm, hoping to put him back on track. Anne diplomatically dabbed her mouth with her napkin.

"Why I saw them at the exchange, but that was six months ago, so I am not sure whether they will ... well, whether they will be there. They might be though. Such a good price ... they were very cheap, in fact, the cheapest I have seen. On second thoughts, they will have been snapped up for sure in view of this."

Unable to help frowning deeply at the waste of conversation, he noticed Anne wipe a tear away as she struggled to hold her napkin steady. Now he himself felt an urge to chortle as he looked at the man, whose pathetic aspect created a feeling of pity. He could see his wife from the corner of his eyes, and with the man looking right at him, he let his laugh out as he gave his thanks for the information.

At precisely the right point, Mr Lark to Charles's other side began a political debate with some men. "What do you think about Parliament's actions? Lord Strafford's head will soon be on London Bridge, I'll wager. Parliament has never been stronger."

Charles stopped dead, the comment reminding him of the letter Strafford had penned to him after the successful mission – it seemed to burn from his purse below.

Taking his napkin, he dipped it into the finger bowl of water in front of him and cleaned his hands and teeth with it.

Other diners did the same, before Gurney proposed a toast to Holland, to which every single guest stood and drank his health, but some with more enthusiasm than others. Another man proposed to toast Arundel and Lord Warwick. Finally the mouthy royalist declared one for the King, which caused a stir, the majority sipping in his honour, still not wishing to insult the monarch personally, despite their strong feelings against his rule.

"Toasts, they provide the opportunity for a refill of wine," he whispered to Anne, holding his glass out.

Then he sensed someone staring at him. He clapped eyes on Holland and bowed his head. The peer gave a haughty, questioning expression and swung his gaze away like a ship tacking in a gale, to give a broadside. Charles sat for a minute or two, rejected and worried at the slighting, before a footman interrupted him.

"Sir, Lord Holland sends you this message."

He hesitated before taking the note, the result of Holland's barrage. Mr Lark examined it, as though trying to unwrap it mentally. Despite the earlier reaction of Lord Holland, Charles was unwilling to imagine anything negative in it. He opened the paper, keeping one eye on Lark and holding it close to him, covering the back with his fingers.

'When I finish at the table, I will adjourn to my closet for a while to speak with my personal acquaintants. Pray join me there a little later and we can discuss your successful conclusion.

I have passed your letter announcing this good news onto our master.'

Charles felt his heart pound and his face flush, the secrecy of the matter giving an air of espionage. He nodded at Anne, hastily folding the paper up, feeling quite proud at his accomplishment and the interest this influential peer had in him.

Chapter 15

Lord Holland spotted the Earl of Arundel enter and began to walk over to him. Arundel's expression was as piercing as ever. The long, pale, gaunt face, coupled with his Catholicism, kept most people at bay. He tugged his cloak off after his saunter outside and the curly black and grey hair, beard and moustache, together with the fur that topped his cloak, likened him to a bear. The aristocrat and his family were anchored in history, tracing their peerage back five hundred years, one of the oldest titles in the kingdom and every inch of Arundel and his bearing emphasised this point. Long forgotten in his mind was the fact that his father, whom he had never met, had died in the Tower of London, imprisoned for plotting against Elizabeth the First and refusing her demand that he give up Catholicism in exchange for seeing his wife and new child. Holland's awkward stance, which made him look unsteady and fragile on his feet, betrayed his own insecurity at the mere sixteen year old title.

"I'll wager you wished Strafford was as dead as the deer that provided our venison?" came the light comment from the older noble, yet without altering his expression one bit.

Holland chuckled softly. "Well at least then I should get his post of Lord Lieutenant of Ireland."

"Such a dismal place, more like an exile in my mind. Are you sure you are in line for it, sir?"

Holland raised his eyebrows, dismissing Arundel's negativity, before taking a sip of his drink. "Well, it is as close as certain. I know the Queen still favours my suit and

Parliament is about to petition the King on my behalf. In the present climate, I suspect he will pass it to me as a concession to these men."

Arundel's body language changed; at last he smiled, albeit faintly. He could be as still, cold and majestic as the marble statues and pieces within his immense collection of art. "Aye, My Lord, I fear Strafford will never perish. He seems to wriggle free from each allegation raised and I do get tired of having to overrule his requests. He wants to call more witnesses, questions the charges, and then tries to turn them against the House of Commons. Such a rude and arrogant man and his very presence provides a block to the King's ear."

"My brother, Warwick, complains about him day and night. To him, Strafford is the devil himself," Holland commented, before moving on, "Now, did you enjoy the food, sir?" he asked with a happy sigh.

"I did, sir, most fine choices. By the way, some little man has been itching to see you, I hear. He was lurking in the corridor when I arrived."

Holland's gaze flicked round for a few seconds to the direction of the passage. By this time, Arundel was making ready to leave and he resented this unknown common fellow for interrupting his canvassing, for he had wished to cement his fellow earl's support. As Arundel left, this well dressed stranger saw Holland observing him and his face lit up. Holland waved him over and casually glanced away while the man introduced himself as Sir Arthur Cotton. Holland's posture adjusted as he made ready to meet the lower ranks, now more assured, casual and haughty.

* * *

He held Anne's smooth, soft hand, as though begging her for something. The very touch of it reminded him for a split second of the same sensual feeling of her whole body, which he would explore with kisses.

"Will you be all right here if I go and see Holland? It is urgent I do so."

Anne nodded, pointing at the couple she had got on well with at the table. He took his wife over to them and after brief introductions, he set out for Holland's study. Charles meandered through the room, careful not to bump into anyone as they sauntered around, or stood in groups. Attempting to navigate the chamber wasn't easy, and as he slowly passed through, the noise of the silk skirts, clipping of footwear on the wooden floor, and voices seemed amplified. He heard Strafford's name mentioned - everybody spoke of the man being as good as dead, and certainly it was as though his ghost was haunting Charles everywhere. Then he stopped as he saw Holland's manservant disappear into a room ahead - it was as though he had vanished like a spirit too. Right now, it felt like everyone here existed in some alternative, glamorous world, gliding around at their heart's desire. He had been told a few times from courtiers that his low birth meant he had no right to be in the locations that he was, and it was fabulous to prove them wrong every day.

He approached the arched, stone doorway, one of the distinct relics of the original Tudor interior, and he hesitated, seeing the rich oak door ajar. Even the way the top of the door curved into a point looked sinister enough to ward him off.

Again, like always in times of crisis, religion came into it and he asked for God's help, this thought somewhat controlling his unsteady emotions. He glimpsed Holland, back to him, sitting in a luxurious golden chair as though he were an archangel. This was the ideal time to catch the peer; divine help had isolated this noble for a few minutes. Charles stepped forward, but froze as he caught sight of another man in there.

It was the person who had tried to betray him in the passage as he attempted to deliver the message to Strafford. Cotton, he remembered the name, the determination for revenge supplementing his already impeccable memory. The man brought on darker feelings and he listened by the door, panicking that the dog was in league with Holland. Then he heard voices and realised that he stood out as much as those new, insolent Adamites, who believed that parading their nakedness was a sign of religious innocence.

Charles stood by the door as if waiting for someone, pretending to admire a bust that sat on a plinth, outwardly studying its workmanship.

"Sir Charles Berkeley?" the words were spoken quietly in mock surprise.

Charles jumped, moving away from an oil painting of a country scene, to see Bess, recognising the blonde curls and curvaceous figure.

"Stand here with me, Bess, pretend we are conversing. I will explain in a few minutes."

* * *

Holland did not look at the man. He felt hostility towards him as soon as he heard the lowland Scottish accent. The defeat and near humiliation that Holland's cavalry had received from the Scottish during the Bishops War of two years ago had not left him. He had an aversion to all things from that country, being as he was a total southerner, baptised in London and educated at Cambridge.

"Who the devil are you, sir?" Holland probed, demanding more.

"Sir Arthur Cotton. I am a Scottish landowner, my lord, here in London to undo the wrongs I committed by fighting against our King in the late wars. I am one of the Scottish commissioners sent down to negotiate a lasting peace. You invited a colleague of mine, Lord Ramsey, who I accompanied tonight."

Holland sniffed, as though the Scotsman's account had done nothing to improve his standing. Indeed, he had failed to retain most of the information, finding it useless to him, but the only thing that grasped his attention was this former enemy's penance of fighting against the King; or in Holland's mind, himself. This attraction grew the more he thought about it. The Scots were such base brutes - no manners and no finesse - and he found the idea of one of their kind who had versed him, coming cap in hand, somewhat boosting to his ego. His command during the war began to be vindicated now as he raised his eyebrows and stared at Cotton.

"So, you intend to right your history of wrongs, sir - " Holland summarised, prompting for his name again.

The dark oak table stood between them like the gulf in their social ranks and the peer leaned forward, resting his clasped hands on it. The evening sun shot out its dying rays through the many window panels and patterned coat of arms, and onto his hands, turning them a variety of shades. Holland's fickle nature could change his colours in a likewise manner, yet the beauty of the golden sun on the dark wood was lost on the two men, repelled by their selfish agendas.

"I hear that you are hoping for the post of Lord Lieutenant of Ireland, once Lord Strafford has been extinguished? I have some contacts that can help you with this, my lord."

Holland laughed sarcastically. "How can such a man as you, help me with a great affair of state?"

"I have channels here. Parliament is desperate to win over Scottish support in their struggle with the King. I understand the Earl of Leicester is also trying to secure the Lord Lieutenant's post. I believe he has bribed Sir Henry Jermyn of the Queen's household to put a good word in for him with Her Majesty.

You will know yourself, sir, how the Queen influences every one of her husband's thoughts."

Holland stayed silent, impressed by the information that had been laid before him in offering, before musing about how the crows were circling Strafford for his positions and offices. He cursed Leicester for unscrupulous methods, mainly because he had beaten him to such a tactic.

"I can find some information about Jermyn to discredit him, which will kill Leicester's bribe outright."

Holland frowned at Cotton, who was trying to direct him, and he rested one of his shoes on the wooden bench. Cotton begged to at least look into the matter and gather facts, and the noble relented, authorising the dirty work with a casual nod of the head and a wave of his hand, instructing Cotton to leave now that the issue was concluded. Both men were using each other and both knew it, but to Holland, he was the power who could make or break Cotton. Like the wind that blows sailing ships; Holland could usher men to rich shores, or cease their journeys and leave them stranded in the midst of the seas.

"I have some confidential evidence coming to me soon which will finish Strafford off," Holland boasted proudly, as though this was the first step to securing the coveted post.

Chapter 16

After hearing Holland's words and realising that Cotton was about to leave, Charles dragged Bess by the arm, out of the corridor and into another room. All she could do was laugh in response, missing the urgency of the action. Luckily enough, the chamber was empty and he pulled the door to, leaving enough gap to see into the hallway they had retreated from.

"Now I always liked it when you showed your domineering side, Charles."

He gave a fleeting, distracted smile. Then his eyes were drawn to Bess's cleavage, unashamedly on show as it always was, and even more so as she moved her arm out of his grasp, making her breasts swell.

"Aye, you have not lost your charms, Bess."

She began chattering uncontrollably, as was her wont, telling him about her husband, a colonel. He missed the name, instead remembering fondly the attention of this pretty woman as he had journeyed home from Northumberland after the Bishops War ended. Bess, the daughter of an officer, had followed the army and kept morale up in her own unique way, especially

Charles's. Her loud, over confident manner did not put him off her, as it normally would do. Something about when they used to be alone together made him realise it was all merely a front, hiding a passionate, caring girl, who craved love. For a moment he pictured their first night together; his nerves had frayed as he sat kissing her, before she unfastened her dress in the candlelight. This first sight of the beauty of a woman, subtly glorified in a golden haze, had made him dizzy with passion.

"Last time we met, you were too busy letting your stubborn nature cause a quarrel, for me to even ask what you are doing nowadays?" she asked, quietly, as she looked up into his eyes.

"I am in the Trained Bands, my wife is here tonight, beautiful as ever. Good God, I need to get back to her."

"You were eavesdropping, Sir Charles," she accused again, teasing him, he knew, in an attempt to retain his company.

He smiled, before telling her his glee at overhearing an enemy of his lay out his plans. "I will foil his mission, as he did mine. Would you help me?"

Charles's gaze moved to the wood panelling on the walls, absently looking at the fleur de lis and cross crosslets, while he pondered his plan. With Bess's prompting, he revealed his idea.

"Can you seduce him?"

"Who?"

"Sir Arthur Cotton – him," he said, pointing to the man outside who trudged back towards the main room. Bess screwed her face up at the vision. "Seeing as it is for you, I will have a chat with him. But tell me why?"

"I don't mean sleep with him," Charles assured her, "I need you to feed some information to him and help me get Holland's favour again. It would be ideal if, during your flirtatious conversation, you let slip that you had been intimate with Sir Henry Jermyn. He will be enthralled by this, and your second gem of indiscretion is that Jermyn was just as excited at a one thousand pound bribe, as he was with carnal thoughts."

Bess laughed audaciously at the thought of sleeping with Jermyn, though she loved nothing more than to act, Charles knew, remembering the way she unsuccessfully pestered the authorities to let her be the first female actress in the theatres of England.

Charles whispered his plan, anxious to keep it short so that he could get back to Anne. She probed and left no stone unturned, until she was fully clear of everything; Bess was always thorough in whatever she did.

"Are you sure you do not mind doing this for me?" Charles confirmed.

"Nay, it will be fun, and if it is brought up, I will deny any knowledge. So what has this fellow done to you?"

They sat on some carved wooden chairs, Bess fiddling with the wicker back of one, and he explained the reason for his revenge, though leaving out Strafford's identity in his earlier mission.

"And now I have a letter from this prisoner in the Tower, accepting the escape offer he has been given. Though he has covered his words well, it is still clear what he means and I suspect Holland is after this proof so that he can secure the man's demise."

Bess tutted with frustration. "Good God, Charles, what do you mean? Who do you speak of and why is he covering his words?"

Charles made her promise that she would not breathe a word of it. "Strafford wrote to me, accepting an escape plan of some sort, and I am sure Holland's comment to Cotton means that he hopes to use this letter to prove Strafford's duplicity. If he can show there is a plot to free Strafford, then Parliament will manage to convert a lot of people into supporting his death; and as a result, Holland will be hailed as a national saviour, thus getting Parliament's full backing."

He undid his purse, Bess laying her hand on his leg as she saw him reach down. "Nay, dear Bess, I am not going for that," he chortled, as he stood up and took Strafford's letter out.

He unfolded the sheet, the signature bringing with it all the memories he had of the man, along with the facts and observations he had made of his own when they were face to face. If he handed this letter on, he would be satisfying one man's ambitions, at the expense of another man's life, overriding a lawful trial with fear and panic and creating more disturbances.

The writing changed from a mere letter, to a premonition, foreseeing so many awful events which would weigh on his conscience.

"Give it on to Holland, Strafford is evil and besides, he would not think so well of you."

Charles knew that, but he could not help but feel he was personally connected to this prisoner now, and the worst thing being that he was not the ogre people had been led to believe. He looked at the flame of the candle, his loyalties wavering just as much.

"It is not just about Strafford. It is honour and honesty, also the trust given to me with that mission - how would that be repaid if I allow Holland to reveal its contents to all and sundry?"

"But what will you tell Holland if you do not pass it on?"

"I don't know."

"Charles, you have to, otherwise you will ruin yourself," she pleaded, taking his hand.

He shook his head and thrust the letter out into the flame, rigidly holding it steady as it turned brown, spreading in a circle until the middle blackened and a light burst from it. Only when Bess gasped and began flapping around did he withdraw it, in the same way as when he had ran an enemy trooper through with his sword. Charred pieces drifted onto the table and he rubbed them away, though leaving dark marks on the furniture, like blood that had seeped from the letter. Bess stepped in and pushed him out of the way to clean the sooty smudges with her handkerchief, while he strode to the fireplace and threw the remains into it. He managed to discard it just before it burnt his fingers, a lucky omen, he hoped, and now it was out, he brushed it around the dead ashes of the grate and mixed them together. For a second he regretted it, though that soon left him, the same as the worry at having such a document on his person; nor had he let his own ambition cloud his honour.

"Well, that is why I was attracted to you in the first place - your honesty. I always know where I stand with you," she said with a tender smile, "Your wife is a very lucky woman, Charles, for it takes a brave man to walk the path of honour."

He took her hand as he walked back over, Bess returning to vivacious discussion about her own part in his new plan, resolving to carry out her role with Cotton. After giving her a parting kiss on the cheek, she glided away, attractive features contrasting totally with the intriguing mission she had just taken. He waited for a few minutes so that they did not leave together, examining the huge tapestry of a classical scene, depicting Noah and his family entering the Ark, animals boarding behind them, and looked over by snow topped mountains. Right now, the scene was apt, for Charles had been caught within the national flood.

Charles left the gilt room he had escaped to, and knocked on the open door, entering and bowing to Holland, ready to face the music.

"May I speak to you, my lord?"

Holland rolled his eyes, complaining that he never got a moment's peace, but inviting Charles in with a last minute knowing look, obviously preparing for the document he presumed Charles had.

"May I ask about the letter I delivered to Strafford, my lord?" he queried.

"It was nothing but a regal promise to make sure the prisoner does not suffer in life, honour or fortune; such a small thing it seems, but what you carried in that letter was the King's own conscience. And for this, he will be eternally grateful, unless of course, Strafford perishes, in which case he will never forgive himself. Ah, honour, such an onerous thing."

"Was it simply that?"

"You were successful delivering it, were you not?" Holland asked, in a way that seemed veiled.

"Yes, I passed it over."

"And he did not give you, or send, any reply?" came the speedy follow up question.

"No? Should he have done so, sir?"

"Of course there should have been a response. I spoke of the King's conscience in that letter, but there was a follow up needed from him."

Charles felt like letting out a short laugh, finally getting the catch he had been fishing for from the start, and also realising how close he and Strafford had just come to the precipice; for if he had handed the letter over, Parliament would have gone for Strafford like a pack of hounds and as the recipient of Strafford's letter, Parliament's shadow would have loomed well over Charles too. He decided to take the opportunity to lay the seeds for his own plan now, using both Holland and Cotton in the same manipulating ways that he had just escaped from.

Holland glared at him, as if he were waiting for another comment. "If I find out that you have had such correspondence, then I will finish you, sir. I detest liars."

Charles felt a chill inside, like the threat had begun to haunt him. "Are you in line for the Lord Lieutenancy of Ireland, sir?"

"Does everyone know my damned business?" Holland expostulated as he stormed into the cover of a bay window, examining the gardens outside.

As he told the peer that he had heard Sir Arthur Cotton discussing it with a young lady outside, the noble's expression changed as he swivelled around. His appearance was of further restrained anger, like the image Charles's father gave to particular fussy customers, and which he used to laugh at so much as a boy.

Charging further into the fray, Charles cast doubt on his rival's ability. "If I may say so, I would urge caution with any service you employ Sir Arthur in, sir. He is indiscreet and deluded in his self belief."

"You can talk, sir; failing initially in your last task and then coming to me tonight empty handed. He has to be more apt than you with my interests, though that is no business of yours. Now when you get the letter from Lord Strafford about his escape, pray pass it on to me immediately."

Holland's tacit confirmation of Cotton's goal was all he needed, slipping out in the aftermath of his castigation.

"If such a response is forthcoming, my lord, for who is to say whether he will. Strafford may feel he can escape Parliament's clutches without any help. I will keep my eye on Sir Arthur for you though - better to be safe than sorry."

Lord Holland sighed loudly and petulantly, as if trying to dismiss the fact that he needed either man to look out for him.

His eyes were like billiard balls from that new indoor game, wide and rounded, ready to pot Charles's very soul. As the peer turned back to the window, he waved his hand, finally ending the discussion, and Charles quickly left, thankful that Holland had too much on his mind to push the issue about Strafford's response.

Charles thought of the painting he had seen of the man's grandfather, the first Earl of Essex. He had wooed the old Queen, Elizabeth the First, with those hereditary manners and good looks, but he had cut that loyalty when he failed to get his own way with her, paying with his head. If Charles was going to be beholden to Holland, he hoped that the noble would not make the same petulant mistake as his forbear.

Finally approaching Anne, she seemed to sense his presence and turned, with a look of disapproval, though even this did not cloud the pretty features. Always she seemed to be planning ahead, able to know where he was and what needed doing.

Charles took her hand, rubbing his finger over the gold wedding band and its small ruby, and kissed it, excusing himself. He remembered the message that was engraved inside it, 'Our hands and hearts with one consent hath tied this bond till death prevent.'

Anne continued the lead role in the same direct way she ruled over the house and introduced him to her newly made acquaintances. Even though she would present the monthly housekeeping accounts to him, she would accept no questioning of them, proud of her financial budgeting. In comparison to her gambling father, she was unique.

"Mister Devonport and his wife are from Oxford and brought back memories from my childhood there."

"Do they know your father?" Charles asked, rather too quickly, wondering whether they knew of his reputation.

Anne gave an ever so slight shake of her head before the Devonports - husband and wife speaking in unison, to create a confusing scene - told him how impressed they were of Anne's knowledge of London.

"Father's merchant activities brought me to London quite a bit as a young girl. Do you know, Charles, London is the third densely populated city in the world?"

Charles was taken aback by his wife's striding talk, left to play catch up. Anne's normally quiet outer shell was completely swept away in social circles. Before he could ask which cities were greater, she had reeled off Paris and Constantinople and was telling him how Mr Devonport supplied the Oxford Trained Bands with gunpowder.

"Ah, we have our own contract coming up for renewal, sir, what rates could you give me?" Charles added, seizing the lucrative lead Anne had introduced.

He began reeling off his prices, during which his wife nodded her agreement, with facial gestures to show just how impressive it all was. The looks increased the wrinkles which surrounded her eyes, giving the appearance that it was her life story written around them. Charles eventually agreed a fee which was a fifth less than the exorbitant price they currently paid. This was only after the gentleman agreed to provide him with a gift of twenty pounds; the benefit of being a Lieutenant Colonel with the role of managing the gunpowder contract. Sir Richard would distribute such contracts between his senior officers, to enable those he saw fit to receive a supplement to their wages, and in theory, an incentive for securing the best rates.

A young man joined the Devonports as Charles and Anne were taking their leave, giving her a shy smile as they left, until the smooth features saw Charles.

"He is such a kind, young man, not like the vulgar womanisers that surround this place. Why, I was speaking to him while you were away and …"

"Were you now?" he interrupted.

Anne coughed. "If you were any longer, I was going to run away with him."

Charles tickled her playfully at this comment as he led his wife through the drawing room, stepping between the tiled floor of black squares, with white circles within each one. Every circle contained a blue 'H' after the owner's title, with a coronet forming the middle line of the letter.

"You are just taunting me," he said with a smile, "Yet I was impressed with your knowledge, and the deal you prepared for me."

Anne hinted at half of the money as commission, prompting

him to reveal his intention to use it to pay for a new dress of her choice. She then recounted a conversation about Holland House being Lady Holland's fathers, and only passing to her husband after the old man's death.

A man abruptly walked in front of them and stopped still, with hands on his hips. It was Cotton and his legs were firmly apart - he obviously had a lot of confidence in himself.

"Can I help you, Sir Arthur?" Charles asked, determined to show that he knew who he was.

"Sir Charles, you did more than attend that trial. Lord Digby mentioned your *service*. I'll wager it would be terrible for you, should this be known," Cotton replied, clearly unperturbed at his identity being known.

The other guests were making their way to the adjoining chamber to await dessert and Charles's heart raced.

"How dare you, sir, I do not know what you insinuate. Now begone," he demanded as he adamantly pushed past, deliberately knocking his arm. Cotton followed him as they left the house and began descending the steps to the grounds.

Just at that point, Bess appeared and Charles looked away as he felt the chill of the colour draining away from his face, anxious Cotton should not suspect. From the corner of his inquisitive eye, he did see Bess hover around his enemy, until the man moved closer, drawn in like a storm driven ship to some rocks. He knew that two prominent, protruding objects would definitely secure Cotton's fate.

* * *

Inside their hired coach, Anne complained at the way women always behaved so loosely at occasions like this, humouring him at her reference to Bess's activity. The enclosed lawns shrunk into the distance as they jerked onwards.

"You have broken your promise," she announced bluntly.

"What?" he questioned, wondering what she was talking about.

"Well, you are hiding something again. He obviously is against you," she perceived, her large eyes observing him from under their lashes.

"I do not even know myself why he hates me so," he admitted, with a shake of his head. He was not bothered about the fact the man had made an enemy of him, but his innate curiosity now nagged him about why this was.

Despite the events tonight - Cotton's plot, his own destruction of Strafford's reply, and the careful plan of his revenge - he was constantly distracted by one thing; how beautiful he thought Anne was and the pride of having her by his side. Anne couldn't help laughing when reminiscing on the conversation about the pair of globes, and to their merriment, her make up finally cracked as her smile grew. Charles saw the damage and he chuckled, the pair shedding tears of laughter.

"Oh, and by the way, I was taking note of young Mister Devonport for my sister's benefit, not my own. If you can, Charles, try and put a good word in for her, as he would make a suitable catch."

He placed his hands on her waist and they came together in a kiss. His breathing was getting quicker and she responded with a groan, letting her head fall back as he kissed her neck. Once the coach stopped outside the house, Charles lifted her down, her cleavage growing as his huge hands compressed her body.

Louise, who had been waiting up, took their outer clothes and then retired to bed, following his permission. On climbing the stairs together, he stroked Anne's curvaceous body, feeling aroused and anxious to see her dress off. His wool trousers restrained him to a degree as he walked up the steps. He thought of Bess and realised just how different that brief young sexual encounter was; with Anne, it was pure love, and the past soon found no place in his thoughts whatsoever. At the top, she turned and he eased her gently to the wall, kissing her lips, before moving down to her chest. He tugged his doublet off, flinging it to the floor.

Anne's breathing became more pronounced as she hugged his body, reciprocating his attention and enjoying the intense excitement. He took her hand and they went inside the bedroom, Anne fumbling and trying to undo the dress. He then finished the job as well as he could, giving it a helping hand to come off and making short work of her petticoat. Next to be removed were her stays, cutting their severe upward push on her breasts. He moaned with pleasure as they came free, and as Anne lay on the bed, he yanked the curtain round the four poster for intimacy, before joining her.

She held his muscles and pressed her body to his in its naked hot state, while he ran his hands through her hair and down to her waist. He kissed her breasts, moving further down and eventually joined her on the bed while keeping firm hold of her eager body. She undid the buttons of his trousers and took them down, caressing his crotch.

By the time the night watchman shouted his weather report, Charles strained, eventually settling back beside her, sweat beads running down his brow. He remained in a high state of arousal, until she helped him unburden himself.

"You make me feel like I have never felt before marriage. I love you," she whispered.

He panted, "My life is complete with you."

She tenderly ran her hand over his chest.

After a few minutes hesitation, Charles murmured, "Did you orgasm?"

"Nay. But why can we not do it all the way again sometime, for I want to please you without using my hands in the end?"

"When we plan a family once more, then we shall. Right now, the city is not in a fit state to be welcome a little miracle," he said, knowing that her answer meant she would not fall pregnant.

"Why not try a sheath? I have heard they are used in France," Anne suggested.

"What happens if it comes off? Anyway, a sheath covers a sword and I do not have one of those down there. Mind you, it is just as deadly."

They smiled and cuddled tight into each other, his arm protectively holding her close.

"These are the Straffordians, enemies of justice and betrayers of their country"

Heading on the posters which announce the names of the 59 who voted against Strafford's death. Somehow the details of these members of the House of Commons found their way to the streets of London for the mob to see.

APRIL 1641

Chapter 17

The crowds had become more regular around Westminster now; Strafford's trial had caused them to step up protests against him. Today, Parliament was in session, so an even greater number of people were outside, which made travel even slower. Charles hoped that the artillery grounds were clear, because people strolled there during bouts of good weather like today. Who would have thought that the grounds were part of a peaceful and serene priory, until King Henry the Eighth destroyed it, would be used for military training?

Passing up the Strand, he admired the one hundred and thirty foot maypole which had just been the centre of the May Day celebrations, the focus for dancing, feasting, drinking, parading and the pretty May Queen. Then some way on, even more groups milled around as though waiting for something. The air felt different here and he became restless, sitting forward in his seat.

While the sluggish journey progressed, he passed a jeering gang watching a woman getting whipped. Charles tried to keep a view of her, but the crowd and the ride only allowed him fleeting glimpses of her naked, slender upper body, the delicate figure being broken by blood. Her hands were bound to the wooden cart, which was being driven through the streets to publicly display the punishment. Remembering this penalty from the past, he knew she would have given birth to an illegitimate baby and he pitied the parish constable who would have to solve the problem of the child and its upbringing. He cringed at her display of pain, before realising that the baby would be lucky, for this was a richer parish than most. The child could get a decent life or trade; the Mother, mindful of this fact, probably moved here deliberately to give birth.

Thankful to arrive at the grounds, he got out of the carriage. Each time he saw a large throng of people now, he would tense up, remembering his mission to Strafford and easily imagining that they had somehow found out about it and were all waiting to get him. In the distance was the regiment, equipped and apparelled in various degrees. The lines of pikemen particularly appeared a miserable sight. He observed the hedgehog effect, formed from the heads of the each sharp pikestaff, as rows of men stood dutifully in formation. They looked like an avenue of newly planted trees, and he looked forward to watching them grow into oaks as their training, which he had fought for, progressed regularly. He felt a lot of responsibility to these men and as he observed every little detail about them, he began to assess the scope of his work.

"For the love of God, some have neither helmets nor armour. And our musketeers, pah, no powder flasks or bandoleers," Charles muttered.

He strode towards them, observing the hundreds of men; noticing immediately that it was under strength. At his guess, there were three hundred pikemen and two hundred musketeers, which was around half the ideal strength of each. The sergeant joined him, holding a halberd that was just over his height, his badge of office.

Breathing deeply, his heart beat faster at the scene before him. He relived the Bishops War each time and the thrill of fighting in an armed force was immense, even if it was simply training. Excitement in his life was as addictive as tobacco and it irritated him when none occurred, as though his brain was rotting away, as all order had done lately.

The sergeant bellowed to the pikemen, "Stand to your arms."

On receipt of the order, the soldiers held their fifteen foot wooden pike poles straight with one hand and placed the other on their hip while the sergeant saluted him. The musketeers were similarly ordered to attention. The other officers of the regiment were here, but Charles was most senior and he nodded at them as he passed.

"Never mind twelve apostles, some of our musketeers have not even got one, or a sword," he complained to Captain Johnson.

At this point he heard Sir Richard approach from his carriage, followed by the scuffling of feet alongside him. He realised that it was Sir Arthur Cotton with his colonel. As they neared him, Charles raised his hat in greeting to his colonel, being careful not to make the inside visible. He wanted his manners to be perfect today of all days. Cotton grinned at him but Charles deliberately kept his feelings locked up so the man would not think he was surprised to see him. Sir Richard raised his felt headpiece in return and observed the regiment.

"What a damn disgrace," he growled, before casually remarking, "Oh, Sir Charles, this is Sir Arthur Cotton."

"We have met," Charles replied curtly, true feelings easily escaping from their prison. Cotton removed his hat, some wind catching his grey hair and blowing it around in a Medusa like manner.

"Have you both indeed, ah well, no need for formalities

here. He is our new captain, recommended by none other than Lord Digby."

A chill passed over Charles. He said nothing and Cotton mockingly put his hand to his mouth to imitate surprise. Then after this, he noticed Cotton glaring at his chest area and he wondered what had caught the fool's attention. He glanced at his clothes and straightened his medal, but found nothing out of the ordinary.

"Sir Richard is most kind in giving me a post in his regiment. I cannot thank him enough. I just hope I can help mould these fellows into half the man he is," Cotton grovelled, causing Sir Richard to positively beam with delight. Charles averted his head in disgust and the colonel let out a bellowing laugh, slapping Cotton on the back. He had never seen the commander as cheerful and outgoing, as though he were a jolly young man who had just slept with his first maiden.

Addressing the sergeant, Sir Richard soon dropped his short lived humour and gruffly demanded, "Get these wretches on the march."

The order was repeated, the instruction reinforced by the other sergeants barking to the pikemen, "Shoulder your pikes," and to the musketeers, "March with your rest in your hands," giving them a few shoves and pushes to aid them on their way.

The pikemen then moved their poles onto their shoulders, the weapons being at forty five degrees. Sergeants manhandled them further. The musketeers copied and held their guns in the same manner, carrying the rests in their other hand. As they moved around the area, Charles cringed at the lack of synchronisation in their step.

But still, he thought, they were better than some of the northern trained bands that he had seen during the Bishops War, for some of those had weapons from the time of Elizabeth the First. One rusty, ancient halberd he remembered, was practically the same colour as the old Queen's red wigs and fiery nature.

"Dammit," Sir Richard observed, glaring at Charles, "They are more like Scottish soldiers."

Charles could not help but smile, looking at Cotton, whom he knew to be from that country too. The colonel stopped in front of his new captain.

"With the exception of you, Scottish soldiers march like dogs," Sir Richard explained, practically apologising.

Again, Charles had never before experienced anything near humility from one so brash and bloody minded. All he knew about Sir Richard was his haughtiness, and that he had fought against the Spanish in the Low Countries - of which the old colonel constantly reminded everyone. He had also heard through gossip that the man's three daughters all looked as masculine as their father.

"You are right, sir, the Scots normally do make poor men," Cotton said, betraying his kinsfolk with ease, if it should benefit his chances. The casualness of the remark cunningly slid out like a snake.

"I told you they needed practice. You expect so much of them in these early days," Charles told the commander bitterly, veritably dismissing the two men's sickening appreciation of each other.

This was his trouble; he was always wont to say what he thought, whether it was a chiding of his commander's view or not, whereas diplomacy needed a more refined approach.

Sir Richard's eyes narrowed and then he evidently heard some children laughing. A deep sense of embarrassment followed; the people of the city had begun to gather, and children impersonated the men and some of the adults pointed and sniggered. Charles felt his pride and honour slip at the poor performance. Instead of the excitement and tingling, he now sweated terribly, losing all patience with Cotton in the regiment.

That whoremonger is out to get me. It is not what you know, but who you know and that means I am done for, he thought, scathing of such underhand methods.

Sir Richard bellowed for them to stop, jolting Charles from his thoughts, and ordered the men to go through the exercises.

The musketeers prepared their matchlocks for firing while the pikemen moved their weapons from their shoulders to be at the charge, holding them vertically and creating a pointed wall that any cavalry regiment would shy away from. Various postures were followed through as if in battle. Charles had bought the drill book for musketeers and pikemen and he knew them all off by heart and had done since he was about sixteen, sneaking a read during his work at the inn. The book became a constant companion and gave him something to occupy his restless mind while his parents slaved away or bickered when their equally obstinate characters clashed over some menial issue like who was to blame for spilling ale on the floor.

He watched Cotton chatting to the colonel. "Crawling round his arse, never my style, but it seems to get you everywhere," he said under his breath.

The red ensign fluttered with the breeze, the noise of the men echoed in the warm air and after half an hour, Charles's spirits began to lift - it all acted as an antidote. The performance may be bad, but he felt a challenge to improve it and he lived for challenges. Cotton and his silver tongued venom was not a problem he could not handle.

"Make ready," came the instruction, as he watched the musketeers blow on the match, encouraging it to smoulder, ready to ignite the gunpowder. The dull glow looked pretty harmless right now on its own.

"Present."

They balanced the ends of their loaded firearms on the rests. Finally, after a nod from Charles, the sergeant yelled, "Give fire," and the guns released a smoke screen as they discharged one by one, the noise scaring some bystanders. One or two weapons fizzled out a hollow crack as they failed to shoot, but none had exploded, which was a blessing. Charles watched the captain, both of them laughing at the reactions of the people.

"Johnson. This is not a comedy play," Sir Richard scolded, about ready to pop himself, "Get at their head, you too, Berkeley. The only amusing thing here is this lot."

As the cloud began to clear, a few tiny pieces of charred paper floated around. They were all that was left of the paper cartridges, which held the measures of powder, rammed down the barrels of the weapons. Observing them, Charles counted in his head, timing the delay between making ready to fire again. Powder was short, so they would not be repeating this exercise today though.

"Three minutes," he tallied out loud.

The men had loaded the pan of the musket with a charge and most were only just pouring the powder down the barrel from one of their apostles.

"Four minutes," he sighed, as he eyed the bulk of them pushing a lead musket ball into the barrel, followed by some wadding, and getting ready to shove the wooden ramrod down to force the ball into place.

"Five minutes," he announced with a shake of his head. By now, the majority were blowing on their match, ready to fire again.

At that, Sir Richard stormed towards the men, Charles quickly following in a smart, straight manner. He moved to the head of the line, while Sir Richard stepped further forward and cast a glare over them. Then Cotton approached to stand next to Charles.

"Get back down the line, you come after me, *Captain* Cotton," he commanded as he ordered him to his place.

"Enough of this tomfoolery, we will march again, and

again, and again until you all get it - the heat of that sun will help your eagerness to improve," and continuing, the colonel stipulated, "Get this regiment's honour back."

Sir Richard gave a wave of his hand and the regiment set off once more, two officers decreasing their pace to join the back of the line to supervise there.

Charles slowed his step, marching at the side of the ranks, shouting to some as they went, "Shoulder that pike," or, "Catch up."

Storming around in the heat was bad enough for him with his uniform, but he pitied the men with the armour and bulky weapons. Then as he fully expected, a man dropped to the ground, pike clattering along with him. He signalled for another soldier to see to the unfortunate and continued the drill.

"Gods wounds, hurry up, man," Charles bellowed as the line began to break.

He lunged at those responsible and pulled them into place, their pikes swaying all over as they changed position. The banging and clinking accompanying their march was as constant as the drumbeat.

"It is the twelve apostles of the musketeers," he overheard one soldier explain to a new recruit, "They rattle like the old bones of the saints too."

Charles smiled at the comment and looked at some of the men's apostles, so used to the noise that he did not spare any thought for it until now. He noted that some of the tubes were wooden and a few others were leather and he hoped the measures of gunpowder inside were dry. They were now starting to get into the rhythm, marching more in tune to the relentless beat and the commands bawled out by the officers. Sir Richard stopped, and then the whole regiment in turn halted. He addressed them with a stern pose and tone.

"Let this be enough today, but mind you this, I expect full

dress next time and you will not dishonour me again."

Looking away from the officer and casting his glare to the men, Charles observed their irritated frowns and stares. Sir Richard's buff coat with gold lace and the gilded tip of his officer's baton glinted in the sun, but his face was red and contrasted with the rich metal. After he dismissed them, some boys and two women brought pails of water for the troops. Charles went over to the commander, not knowing what to expect. He was adamant he was going to use a different approach with the old man.

"Sir Richard," he said. Then as if surprised, the colonel coughed, his face still flushed, like one of the beacons lit to signal the arrival of the Spanish Armada just over fifty years ago.

"Disgrace, dammit, disgrace," he muttered breathlessly.

"I agree, but with your support, they will get better if we drill them more often, sir," Charles reassured suavely, with the manners of a courtier like Holland, yet not the grovelling of Cotton.

"Water, boy," Sir Richard called out as his young servant came near him with reluctance. He took a mouthful and walked back towards his coach, meeting his coachman and other servant there.

Charles shook his head; Sir Richard had still not named the next muster date.

Looking back, he saw that the men had started to disperse and people moved on with their business. He regretted that the colonel had not addressed them with more depth and now it was too late to do so himself.

At that moment a shot rang out and some gravel about three foot from Charles bounced up in a puff of smoke. He got a shock, jumping round to see where it had come from. Cotton held a firearm, laughing at him, even throwing his head back in mirth. The dust from the ground was slowly disappearing as Charles stared, recalling his senses.

He ran over to Cotton and some of the soldiers stopped to observe. Sir Richard began to walk back too. Charles yanked the pistol from his rival, slinging it to the ground.

"You tried to shoot me in the back, you spineless bastard," he said, pushing Cotton on the chest, his face a few inches away from him now.

"Whoa, it was just a bit of fun. I wanted to see a true officer's steely nerves," Cotton said, calmly taking hold of the hand and moving it away.

Charles shook him off, grabbing his opponent's sword belt and pulling him closer still. "I will send you to hell if you ever do anything like that again."

"What on earth is going on here, gentlemen?" Sir Richard asked, eyes blinking innocently, but excitedly, like an owl's.

"This whoremonger tried to kill me," Charles snapped bluntly.

Sir Richard frowned and looked at them both as though he were a judge about to send one of them down.

Cotton's mouth was upturned at one end, as though a piece of string controlled it. "He is exaggerating, sir. I lost my grip of the gun and it went off about six foot from him. It was nowhere near and he ran a mile."

Charles glared at Cotton, pushing him back and back, each time walking forward to meet him again, leaving the adjudicator behind. He was so annoyed that he did not know what to yell at the man, causing further anger as he trembled. That calm and polished act was enough to slither out of the incident, leaving Charles of all people looking like the aggressor.

"Berkeley. What in God's name do you think you are doing? What example do you set to the men who see their officers bickering? You are a hothead and they are dangerous in battle," Sir Richard bellowed.

"Aye, I agree. A lieutenant colonel needs to be sane in mind. I aspire to that post," Cotton said provocatively.

"Piss off, Cotton," Charles answered, unable to emulate the debonair attitude that Cotton had off to a tee.

Sir Richard caught them up.

"Berkeley, cease this. It was a simple mistake. For one thing, I do enjoy the competition you both will bring to the regiment. Rivalry is healthy," Sir Richard announced with a completely blasé attitude.

Charles's expression did not change and he continued to eye his potential assassin, teeth gritted. He commanded himself to simmer down, controlling his own behaviour now as tightly as he had controlled the regiment's earlier.

"You should have seen him jump, sir," Cotton said again.

Sir Richard smiled. "Now go, both of you, but in different directions," he directed. While they were so close, Cotton warned him that he would soon take his patron away too. As the colonel strode away, Charles could resist no longer and he kneed the dog between the legs. Cotton groaned and fell to the ground.

He headed towards the Windsor Castle Inn, the plot involving Bess being his sole thought. Once inside, he ripped off his hat and gloves, hastily taking off his buff coat and doublet, before pulling the sweaty shirt into position.

Feeling a sneeze come on, he took a handkerchief and blew his nose. Half the gunpowder had made a home there by the looks of it, but it was always the same, because he loved the smell of it so much that he would inhale the scent like it was a woman's perfume.

"Can I get you something, sir?" the maid asked, rosy cheeks giving off a welcoming glow, combined with her young, round face and body.

"Aye, a beer. I tell you what, put spices in it too."

He looked around the place, tobacco smoke hanging in

the air like the bleak clouds of a storm. In front of him, the biggest table was taken up with men conducting some sort of business discussion. A large fire roared in the opposite wall and two dogs lay spread out in front of it. Spotting a table by the window, he quickly occupied it and laid his clothes on a spare bench. A pane of the leaded window was open, letting in some fresh air.

The notice on the wall caught his eye, standing out from the rest and he read the latest news from Parliament and then scanned an advert for a new tailor's shop. Glancing around for the serving girl, he saw an apothecary approach him.

"Are you needing some Anderson's Scots Pills, sir?"

"No thank you, sir," Charles said, waving his hand.

When his drink arrived, he gulped it off within a few minutes and then heard a voice from behind, "Hark, the Scots are coming."

Swivelling his body round, he saw the expected face of Edmund Verney who he had served with in the Bishops War. Edmund was the third son of Sir Edmund Verney, a courtier and Knight Marshal to the King and he had not seen 'Mun' for a while now, as he had joined an English regiment in Holland.

Standing shorter than Charles, he was fair like his father and had a long thoughtful mouth, with dark eyes. He had agreed to meet him today to help with the ploy against Cotton.

"Did you manage to find out about Jermyn?" Charles asked.

His friend nodded, telling him he would be in the palace today.

They were drawn to a game of cards going on in the corner, the coins chinking together as one man pushed them into the middle of the table. Edmund raised his eyebrows at the serious value. Charles shook his head at the gamblers and noticed the businessmen stand up, shaking hands and leaving. As they departed, the apothecary approached Edmund, to be met with another refusal even before he could ask.

"Are you hungry?" Edmund asked.

Only for Cotton's blood, Charles thought. "Not really.

How are your father and mother?" he eventually asked, refraining from boring his friend with further thoughts of that rogue.

Edmund ordered some food. "Well, Father is at court but the present distractions cause him trouble. He approves of Strafford's removal, but having served the King so long, finds himself torn. He always complained that Strafford shot anyone down in council with an opinion that went against his own."

"This bloody dispute, I hear nothing else. It changes your whole life. I swear it makes me more stubborn to stay on the fence rather than get dragged in," Charles moaned.

"Should not be long before it calms down, especially as Strafford has little time left on this earth," he observed.

An older serving woman placed the dishes on the table with a scowl, which caused creases on her lips and eyes, allowing some plates to crash onto the surface. Then with a sniff she moved away, wiping her hands on her apron while Charles grinned.

"Must not have had any lately," he joked.

"What, soup?" Edmund questioned sarcastically, making them both laugh out loud.

At that point, Bess came in, wearing her hood, fixated on their table as she darted towards them without hesitation, taking up a place on the bench with Charles.

"Bess, this is Edmund Verney, a good friend of mine," he introduced.

"It is such a pleasure to meet you, Bess. Now take your covering off, and stop hiding such beauty."

She gave a smile and obliged, delicately lowering the hood. With her eyes like a beautiful, faraway sea, she secured Edmund's whole attention away from his food.

Charles tucked into the thick grouse soup, leaving them

to it, Edmund offering some of the other dishes to Bess as he resumed his meal. Charles picked at the turkey, which tasted strongly of the clove stuffing, before trying the goose pie and deciding the fish was the best dish in the end.

"Did Cotton fall for your charms, my dear lady?" Charles queried.

"How could he resist? He is not such a bad looking man. I did manage to feed him the information about Jermyn's bribe though, as you asked," she said, causing Charles to cough at the generous description of his enemy.

Mun handed Bess some sweetmeats.

"And has Cotton been in touch since he asked you to meet him at the palace today?" Charles probed, securing the lady's attention back to the matter at hand.

"Aye, I met him and asked why. He wants to tell Jermyn he has me as a witness to his acceptance of a bribe. Then he will point me out in the crowd so that Jermyn panics at the sight, and agrees to push Lord Holland's case with the Queen, instead of Lord Leicester's."

Charles snorted with laughter, loving the anticipation of seeing his foe humiliated.

"And best of all, Holland has provided Cotton with some funds to pay me, to ensure I go to the palace today and take part in his plans," Bess said, showing off a new ring she had bought with some of the proceeds, eventually whispering the sum of two hundred and fifty pounds.

"Oh, so he has lost some of Holland's valuable money on this illusionary venture too," Charles chortled, as she stood up, indicating that she should be at the palace soon.

"Why, I would not play this charade solely out of the goodness of my heart, Charles," Bess said with a wry look.

He raised his eyebrows, gulping some of the beer the woman had warmed up with a poker from the fire, and then kissed her hand and thanked her again for what she was doing.

Edmund seized it next, holding it reverently before planting a prolonged kiss on the silky, pale skin. A tune started up and Charles saw a man playing a flute in the corner. He tapped his hand to the melody. The effect of music was an amazing thing, he thought, as it enhanced his confidence.

Then not long after Bess left, one of the young serving girls started to dance, and they both smiled as they watched her hitch her skirts up a little. From what he could see, Charles guessed she would have a beautiful pair of legs and commented about them. Just as she got into the rhythm, two merchants interceded, complaining about the interruption to their commercial discussions and the innkeeper emerged to scold the innocent girl and send the musician out.

Charles sighed. He was just enjoying it, but no doubt the keeper was worried his inn would be compared to a measly tavern, where all these things were commonplace. Charles's father had not minded such joviality in his inn, he remembered.

After sharing war stories with Edmund, for both had served in the Bishops War, he ate some more food to curb his returning hunger. Some time after finishing the meal, his friend stood and lifted his hat, drinking Charles's health with it off.

"I am pleased to see you again, Charles, and happy to help you take revenge on that dog. Now tell graceful Bess that I would be honoured to keep in touch with her."

"And I have enjoyed our drink today too, my friend. I shall tell her your intention," he responded with a grin, raising his tankard.

That had been a mighty compliment from Edmund to drink his health, but with his hat off, it was an even greater privilege. He ruefully noted all the food they had wasted and put his doublet and buff coat back on. A few minutes later they left, getting a coach to Whitehall Palace.

Chapter 18

C otton entered the vast, long gallery, watching the crowds milling about the place. The din they made was immense and he stopped for a second, before complaints and prods from behind moved him on, and an impatient man pushed past. He leaned against the wall, looking at the people and assessing the room, thankful to see Bess ahead, swirling amongst everyone with ease and receiving the gallant attention of many. The lady's vivacious manner and assets were extremely arousing.

He was unable to avoid being lured by another beauty; that of the palace, exquisite from top to bottom, crowned with a roof by Holbein that was streaked with gold, as glorious as Bess's curls. He saw a group of men pass by, heading to the stairs at the opposite end of the gallery which led to the bowling green and their forthcoming game. Ever able to spot the most insignificant of things with his keen eye, he also noticed a trio of smaller paintings amongst these magnificent and regal pictures, recognising a portrait of Rembrandt, so presuming the rest were by this artist. Bringing everyday life to the fore, they were totally at odds with this amazing place. Then there were the nine pictures that someone was just speaking of by Caravaggio, portraying Cupid and Psyche in erotic and mythological surroundings, nearly as legendary as the chamber itself. The buxom figures returned his longing gaze to the lady he had arranged to meet, who had fallen into his life and tantalisingly given a glimpse of what love might offer.

Cotton had become practically blinded by her, though she soon brought him round with a nudge. While plumes of feathers from hats, ornate ladies' hairstyles and large dresses and cloaks swept past him like a parade, he strained his neck, now ruthlessly stalking Jermyn like a stag.

He spotted his quarry emerge from a group of people, so ordered Bess to stay put and wait for his signal to move closer.

As nobility swept past with airs of serene grace, he noticed all of the deals, backstabbing, gossiping, alliances and struggles going on in the room, revealing themselves through articulate expressions and body language. If anyone keyed into the atmosphere of the place, they would uncover a whole hub of activity.

He pushed slowly forward, excusing himself to various people as he endeavoured to get to Jermyn. But as he approached, Jermyn unwittingly sauntered out of reach.

"Damn," he hissed, before signalling for Bess to follow. His anonymous letter to the knight had evidently worked, demanding he meet him here and couched with knowledge of his recent acquisition of a four thousand pound bribe.

They trailed through the stone gallery and had to go single file. It was packed with people of all status, for it was a small part of the palace that any respectable members of the public were permitted to access. Eventually, entering the gallery of the public dining chamber narrowed down the admittance levels and they stood in the spectators' area. The marble floors shone in this small gallery, which was raised above the dining room. Opposite them was a long balustrade half Cotton's height, interspersed with huge marble pillars reaching to the decorative roof. In the middle of the posts were some stairs down to the main chamber, blocked by two burly Yeomen of the Guard. The floor there was arranged into black and white marble squares, as though creating a giant chess board, to act out the games both King and Parliament were playing with each other.

The strict protocol observed here was much more formal than any other court of Europe. It was the only European country where the King was served on bended knee, something that many disgruntled people had seized upon lately, claiming that it proved the King's arrogance. He kept an eye on Jermyn, who was watching the proceedings and chatting to fellow spectators, though evidently searching for the anonymous person who had requested he come here on a matter of 'great importance to the Queen'.

"I would not like to eat in front of a crowd of strangers," Bess commented.

"This is not their meal, you know. They retire afterwards for the proper food. I suppose this is a taster. It boosts his image and allows us lesser mortals to catch a glimpse of him for a moment," Cotton replied, admiring her features, while relishing the chance to impress her with his knowledge.

At the precise time, the King and Queen entered hand in hand, with the young Prince of Wales. The genuine love was all apparent in the close body language, despite the marriage being near fifteen years long.

The courses were laid out, with the monarch signalling the dishes he wanted. Next they quietened down for a sermon that was read before the meal began. The King was as devoted to the Church of England as his Queen was to Catholicism and the sovereign listened attentively with a grave face. As all eyes were drawn to the feasting royal couple, which Cotton had known they would be, he wandered towards Jermyn, who seemed completely sensitive to his approach, facing him questioningly.

"Sir Henry, I am Sir Arthur Cotton. Pray forgive the uninvited approach, but I need to speak with you urgently."

Jermyn stood still for a while, as though pondering the request of this foreign knight from a faraway land, before walking to the corner. Cotton followed calmly, knowing the location would serve to add an additional pressure to Jermyn that secrecy be maintained. While onlookers focussed on the fine royal meal, servants respectfully brought wine and dishes to the table in a steady stream. There was an absence of seating, as technically no one but the monarch's consort was allowed to sit in the royal presence. Even the royal dogs, which ran loose around the chamber, seemed to behave pompously.

Cotton was eager to drop a morsel of information and cut to the chase.

"It is vital, sir, regarding Lord Leicester and your service. Finding you here was the only way I could make contact with you," he whispered, a demand for the man to listen, veiled with a somewhat threateningly direct reference to the earl.

"What is it that you wish to inform me of?" Jermyn asked, without any exchange of pleasantries, suspiciously looking down the length of his nose. Such an intriguing approach was unorthodox, but the curiosity was enough to entrap his gambling instincts, like a hidden hand of cards.

Jermyn's small, muscular frame altered course as gazed at the man, with his large eyes, framed both by heavy lids and deep bags. He rubbed his delicate fair moustache, appearing to understand that he was the key to some issue, such was his astute mind in all political matters. Despite the immense quantities of alcohol that he consumed, his senses always remained sharp.

"Well, I have been told by a certain lady whom I believe

you know very well, that you are, shall we say, pushing Leicester's suit for a particular official post?"

Jermyn puffed his stomach out at this whispered comment.

"Know very well?" he hissed with outrage, eyes widening from the audacity of the details, before presumably wondering which whore the stranger had spoken to.

"She speaks of the details of the bribe, which you let slip to her, and will bear witness to this fact."

Jermyn frowned for a second with an angry look, closely followed by a thoughtful stance confirming he was assessing whether he had let anything slip to a loose woman. "You are a lunatic, sir, belonging in Bedlam."

Seeing he was going to be hard to crack, Cotton lifted his hat towards Bess, prompting her to nod her head in reply.

Jermyn strained to observe her and then laughed at Cotton.

"Who the devil is that? I should remember if I had met her before. Your ludicrous claims are nonsense."

Now Bess was on her way over and Cotton was rapidly losing patience with Jermyn's continuous denials. As she neared them, Cotton stood straight and raised his head high again, ready to demolish the man's silence.

"Sir Arthur, nice to meet you again. How is Lord Holland? And pray introduce me to your friend," Bess said as she swirled up to them, cream dress as innocent as her new part.

"B-but - you know this man," Cotton stuttered, attempting to correct her.

"No, I would have remembered his noble face," Bess said flirtatiously, causing a nod of appreciation from Jermyn. She was now the only thing keeping Jermyn here.

As Cotton hesitated and held his hands out to her in disbelief, Jermyn piped up with his own question, "Madam, do you know this man well?"

"Well, I have only met him once at a banquet, when I interrupted his intimate discussion with Lord Holland. He gave me such a chiding, though he did escort me back to the dining chamber, which was so kind. I had gotten lost in that vast mansion …" Bess chattered, as though Cotton was invisible.

"Well let it be the last time you meet him, madam, for he is quite mad. Talks about spurious slanders," Jermyn interrupted.

He then bowed, taking Bess's hand and kissing it. She giggled as he intimately doled out his passion, moving down her fingers for another kiss. He may have come from Bury Saint Edmunds, but Jermyn certainly had no saintly halo.

"I will take your advice, sir," Bess said, as she took her leave of the men. She fluttered her fan of yellow and red patterns painted on the vellum, moving off like a butterfly.

Cotton felt his face burn and Jermyn stepped forward, crushing his foot under the leather sole. Jermyn's whole, small, muscular frame bore down upon his toes, but he took a deep breath and gritted his teeth firmly. He made no attempt to extricate his foot.

"Get out of my sight, Sir Arthur Cotton, for if I see you again, I will make you wish you had never tried to meddle with me. God only knows what you are trying to accomplish, but with Sir Henry Jermyn, you only get one warning."

And with a twist of his foot, Jermyn gave a gracious smile and made to walk towards the balustrade to watch the monarch.

"And pray pass my message onto Lord Holland," was his final polite but ruthless jab.

Cotton went to speak again, but Jermyn's physical appearance and words rang in his head, a man who combined manners and elegance with a common, volcanic temper. He whispered some oaths, unable to comprehend what had happened and wondering whether his earlier conversations with Bess had been a dream. He was livid at the betrayal, more so because she had coaxed and opened such other emotions that rarely saw the light of day.

He looked for her, eager to demand an explanation, to

grab her and look into those captivating eyes. Then thoughts of the money he had paid her up front exploded into his mind, replacing any physical images, sending his mind hurtling back to personal career and gain. How was he going to tell Holland that he had lost part of the peer's money, and through Bess's chatter, compromised Holland's own part, possibly wrecking his chances for the post of Lord Lieutenant completely?

She had told him Jermyn had received a four thousand bribe. That was probably misinformation too, but he had already passed this detail to Holland as well.

Finally he saw Bess, who had linked arms with none other than Sir Charles Berkeley, and now this enemy was giving him a smile. Cotton inhaled quickly, heart stopping for a moment as every vestige of warmth and life seeped out of his body. Within a few minutes, a fire incinerated inside, feeding on resentment and hatred. No doubt Berkeley would be gleefully reporting back to Holland about the debacle.

Chapter 19

I t was now April the tenth, nineteen days since the start of the trial. Westminster hall was crowded to capacity for the last day of Strafford's defence. The prisoner still had enough strength to fend off his assailants though, and Lord Digby was pondering what the final throw would involve.

As he sat with the other members of the House of Commons, Digby felt sure his days with these men would be numbered soon enough. His recent change of political tack had sailed him close to the course his monarch was set upon, as he vied for position amongst the dwindling amount of ministers and royal supporters. He aimed for a peerage before the year was out, and some of the King's ministers would undoubtedly fall from grace after their failure to back Strafford, leaving gaping holes in the array of official posts.

The buzzing and chattering died down, voices turning to whispers as Strafford appeared at the bar. To most Members of the House of Commons, his person represented a whole regime of terror. He slowly kneeled down, still somehow inciting fear, even in this submissive position. The man stayed there for what seemed like an age, before Lord Arundel finally gave a flick of his hand, barely concealing his enjoyment at keeping the earl waiting for permission to rise.

Then the peers of the House of Lords filed in two by two, their red, ermine robes and gold stripes splashing beauty and colour upon the black cloaked clerks, and generally sober dress of the members of the House of Commons. The stream of crimson flowed through the aisles of seats like blood, gushing from their usual chamber beyond.

Digby's careful eye missed nothing and he scrutinised Pym, who quickly nodded to John Glyn. Pym was looking around at the dozen or so colleagues from the House of Commons that had joined him near the bar of the makeshift court, leading the prosecution with him.

"My Lords, I wish to call two new witnesses to articles fifteen and twenty three," Glyn bellowed, commencing hostilities, his Welsh voice still managing to sound melodious, despite the seriousness of the words.

Strafford calmly raised his hand, slicing into the proceedings, as though dividing up a cake. "My Lords, I call on the same privilege. If the House of Commons call new witnesses, I wish to have the same granted to me."

Silence ensued from a majority of the six hundred people within Westminster Hall, more shock at this extremely early foray.

Digby was intently tracking every point, expression and movement, noting them down. Having a vast knowledge of the proceedings would bring him almost uniquely close to the King, who would wish to discuss every detail afterwards, an ideal way to help His Majesty on a personal level. Also he wished for Strafford's freedom; in that event, his part in suggesting the escape plan that Sir Charles Berkeley had delivered would be uppermost in the regal mind too, for Holland had distanced himself more and more. Digby recognised the look of grit determination on Pym's face, as though it was personal between him and the accused. He remembered how Strafford had once been a close ally of Pym's in their early Parliamentarian careers.

By now the peers had retired to consider the matter of new witnesses, and Digby's eyes had followed his father's journey out of the chamber. The old Earl of Bristol had served more than thirteen years in Spain as English Ambassador, and now the cold weather here seemed to bring on his arthritis. He had limped along, Digby guessing that the pains would add venom to his father's short temper. Already today, he had used his favourite phrase *'El Diablo los toma'* several times about Pym's party. If the devil did indeed try to take the man, Digby unwillingly accepted that it would be no mean feat, judging by Pym's skill and cunning.

After waiting for what seemed like an age, he had to wriggle and stand again, the penitence of sitting on the hard benches was like being in church. Then the words 'West Monastery' came to mind from his father's rambling stories, reminding him that Westminster did take its name from religious roots.

"We grant the request for new witnesses and allow both sides to call them, although should the House of Commons wish to withdraw the desire for these witnesses, they can do so now and neither side shall have any."

These decisive words echoed with poignancy, right through the length of the two hundred and ninety foot hall.

Digby smiled at this Straffordian victory, for it brought the two parties head to head, in a battle of wills. Who would back down first, out of fear of the opposite party's witnesses, and what they might unleash?

Pym kept his head high, despite the setback, and his large hairy hands clasped his arms like a vice. With Glyn, Member of Parliament for Westminster, it was additionally precarious to know that his constituency supporters were observing his performance at first hand.

Strafford's eyes wandered to the direction of the Members of the House of Commons and the resultant expression of dexterity told Digby that the man was not finished his attack yet. He was almost goading them into taking the plunge.

The scene could not have been more gripping to a man like Digby, wily and always inquisitive, and it was just as though it had fallen out of one of the political plays he wrote in his spare time. Even this had honed his eloquence and own acting onto a master level, masking any personal shortcoming completely.

"May I query whether my new witnesses will have to be in regard to the same articles as the House of Commons, or could I call them for any article?" Strafford added, mind as sharp as ever, and without any hint of pain from his bladder stone, or gout.

This resulted in a murmur of consultation before the peers once more departed to ponder this fresh question. Pym looked to the ceiling, before shaking his head, while Maynard stood up and left the hall. As the audience waited on the peers, cheese passed down the row of men and Digby wondered whether that would be easier for Pym to stomach, than Strafford's string of blows. He also saw other spectators drinking beer or wine, eating onions and relieving themselves in the public area below, against the wooden stalls.

As normal, Digby began comparing his own strength to that of Strafford's, before vainly declaring himself to be superior.

Strafford was fighting for his political life, and Digby had also been incarcerated in the past; the less serious reason, a duel with another courtier in some gardens, passed him by quickly. Then he remembered how he had freed his father from captivity in the Tower, by making a speech to Parliament at the age of twelve. He still proudly recalled the awe at his charm and presence, which aided the acceptance. Soon, in his own little mind, Strafford's intellectual ability was now well below his own.

After passing more time in contemplation about his family, he looked up and examined the clerks of the court, three sitting at a table, while another three kneeled on the floor, bent over a platform in their submissive posture to the nobility around them, ready to resume their scribing. Then he scrutinised Strafford, who sat enclosed in a wooden dock, doubling as a makeshift prison, guarded by the Lieutenant of the Tower of London. Black, he constantly wears black, Digby thought, aware of the way Strafford was manipulating his own image.

The grey hair, curled and out of control, looked like it had not seen a comb for days - he was like an accustomed actor in a Shakespearian tragedy.

Then the peers came back once more, greeted with a fanfare of whispering and murmuring, to agree that Strafford could indeed call witnesses to any point he wished. Digby leaned forward in anticipation, as Pym called the prosecution together, chattering furiously. After a minute, Digby straightened his doublet, running his finger in a comforting manner around the gold lace embroidered on the edges. A glance at the scruffy Parliament men made him compare the cost of his own clothes to their incomes, and he sat back with a feeling of pride and importance.

"My Lords, we wish to consult each other before deciding whether to call new witnesses or not," Pym said loudly, notifying the court. Digby frowned as the Parliamentary leader seemed to fall back into his seat for a second, face as grey as ash. It was as though he was overcome with illness or pain.

Eventually the small congregation of the prosecution mimicked the House of Lords, slowly filing out and relishing the hold up they were now causing. Since Parliament first met in Westminster Palace, in twelve hundred and ninety five, this year was going to be the most crucial, and this was made clear from the behaviour and actions of these men. During their temporary absence, Digby pictured the vital discussions with his active imagination. Just before entering the hall today, he had overheard Maynard discussing John Pym. A missile of evidence was aimed at the powder magazine of Strafford's defence, to blow it apart, but apparently they were unsure whether it would be best to use it here in the trial, where it could be questioned. One man had argued it would be best to save it until later when it would be taken for gospel.

Once the group of close colleagues returned, like a committee, Pym explained they would be calling their witnesses, and in effect, the prisoner's bluff. Almost as soon as he had finished speaking, Strafford struggled to his Feet. Asking for witnesses would come easily to the accused, for he had already solicited so many things in his life so far, in his indomitable, Yorkshire way; titles and positions from the King, the daughter of the Earl of Cumberland first, followed by that of the Earl of Clare.

"In that case, my lords, I have further evidence on articles two, five, twelve and fifteen and I request these be heard first," the prisoner adeptly announced.

Though he had northern roots, he was very much in tune with government, as though his birth in London had set him up well from an early age.

At the words, Pym stood up with an expression of shock and surprise. The trigger had been pulled and Maynard flung his arms in the air and began shouting, and before long, Pym and his colleagues were chanting in unison.

"Withdraw, withdraw."

Some peers stood and joined in, shouting over to Lord Arundel to adjourn. Other men who had already taken sides began to yell their views. Now those who sought allies or favours began to mimic those they craved support from, and most of those left without any clear view were forced to join in, albeit half heartedly. Chaos had seized the event from its organisers and Digby stood up, exhilarated by the tension and division, compelled to add to the voices in support of Strafford.

A great many of the spectators were on their feet.

Enough was enough; the House of Commons could not allow Strafford to continue to make fools out of them and their case, nor could they let so many unsympathetic witnesses take the stand. As some peers rose to petition Arundel to adjourn, Pym and those closest to him began to leave the hall without any command. They were followed by a large group of people made up of members of both House of Lords and

Commons, though Digby stayed put. He saw 'Black Tom Strafford' smiling up towards the King, no longer seeming like a solitary figure.

After Digby was sure that the King had seen his active applause of the prisoner, he slowly made his way back to the House of Commons.

The jeering and chattering continued as other members walked back to their chamber, or broke away into small groups, buzzing with excitement, outrage and wonder. Maynard was here, telling friends that the difficulty of trying to prove Strafford's guilt was over. Pym handed a paper to John Glyn, and Digby instinctively knew that Strafford's end was about to be proposed in another way.

He sought out his friends and sat with them, casually hanging his hat on the end of the old pew, gossiping about the trial and watching everyone filtering into the place. The oak panelling, which covered the walls and the small gallery that circumvented the chamber above, gave an impression of a wooden warship. Men piled back in, ready to man their stations, while the speaker sat on a high, white chair, which looked like an elaborate plinth.

The statue that adorned the top was the royal coat of arms, the lion and unicorn looking down on everyone, proudly holding up the old quartered shield of England, France and Ireland.

Two clerks flanked the speaker, sitting at a table covered with green cloth, ready to record the momentous events, for nobody quite knew what would happen next.

When practically all of the members had reached the Commons, Glyn stood to address them, calling them back in to the fold, now they were on home ground. An usher locked the doors on Pym's command, lending an historic air and sealing them all in, bonding the men together in one cause.

This had been done nearly twelve years ago, during the last Parliament, when the King had decided to rule alone. They had sealed the doors and refused to disband at the royal order, holding the Speaker down until they had passed certain resolutions, a move which the monarch never forgave.

"Gentlemen, the trial is over," Glyn shouted, before being drowned out in roars and stamping feet, "Mister Pym has some startling information which we did not manage to bring up within the trial."

Digby held his breath, now contemplating dropping his support of Strafford. If Strafford went down, he felt sure the King would come under the influence of Pym and his colleagues, and that meant the Digby family needed to ally with the Parliamentary leaders.

Pym stood up anxious to release his ammunition, and the noise lowered. He held the letter above his head, like a flag signal, and eyed the chamber from top to bottom, reeling the members back in and extending his hold over them once more with simple silence and a serious expression. They waited upon his actions, as though he were their saviour, the minority who did not support him observed with suspicion.

"Honourable members, this document was given to me by Mister Vane, son of Sir Henry, the King's Secretary of State," he yelled, unleashing the earlier frustration.

As if echoing his sombre personality, the members remained deathly quiet.

"What does it contain? Well, it was found amongst Sir Henry's papers by his son and is notes of that fateful meeting of the King and his councillors from sixteen hundred and forty. I will read you some," Pym growled as he held the document closer to his eyes.

Silence ensued, Digby sensing a brief weakness in the leader, in the same invisible way as animals in the wild. Pym, the sturdy elephant of Parliament did not seem to be able to focus on his attack. The pause seemed to last a long time.

"Under the heading, Lord Lieutenant of Ireland, and we all know who that is, it says curiously 'you have an army in Ireland you may employ *here* to reduce *this* kingdom' and with this we see how Lord Strafford views us and our liberties in England. He clearly does *not* refer to subduing Scotland, because the meeting was in England, the only place which could be meant by 'this kingdom' so let us punish this attempt at civil war."

Pym sat down following his blunt warning, to cries from all over the chamber. Men howled with panic and anger.

"Nay," Digby shouted, immediately feeling let down by this vague claim. Pym had told him personally before the trial, that he had sure evidence to prove a national danger from the prisoner. This whimper, rather than a call to arms, instilled an instant desire to switch allegiance, his fickle character making the snap choice all too easy. His father in law, the Earl of Bedford, was already sure that he could patch issues up between the King and his Parliament, so Digby was now absolutely positive that he would not expose himself by siding with such a weak case at this. The King would always be King, after all.

But further than this, he would tell Pym of all his frustration, quoting the personal assurances he had given too. He was not afraid of him, and would score points with the King by taking this leader on.

Pym took centre stage once more, clearly anxious to carry the moment to climax.

"So we see the truth behind this prisoner, who manages to manipulate his trial and the court. He is a traitor and for the sake of the King and our nation, we need to remove his corrupting presence forever from His Majesty's ear. We require use of a Bill of Attainder, gentlemen, and immediately."

The House of Commons exploded into commotion and outcries. The noise was far too deafening for Digby to hear the din taking place in the streets outside Parliament.

Sir Arthur Haselrig took his chance to ride the crest of the wave Pym had created. "Gentlemen, I shall read the Bill to you all as it stands."

Digby knew that an attainder meant simply that no trial was needed. Strafford would die if the House of Commons, Lords and the King agreed to it.

Haselrig paused to allow the din to recede. "Thomas, Earl of Strafford, impeached on charges of high treason, for endeavouring to subvert the ancient and fundamental laws and government of His Majesty's realms of England and Ireland. For introducing an arbitrary and tyrannical government against law in the said kingdoms, and exercising a tyrannous and exorbitant power above and against the laws of the said kingdoms, over the liberties, estates and lives of His Majesty's subjects; and likewise having by his own authority commanded the billeting of soldiers upon His Majesty's subjects in Ireland, against their consents, to compel them to obey his unlawful summons and orders. In so doing he did levy war against the King's Majesty and his liege-people in that kingdom; and also for that he, upon the unhappy dissolution of the last Parliament, did slander the House of Commons to His Majesty and did counsel and advise His Majesty that he was loose and absolved from rules of government; and that he had an army in Ireland which he might employ to reduce this kingdom, for which he deserves to undergo the pains and forfeitures of high treason."

The whole chamber stayed silent as Haselrig looked around the ranks of men.

"The said earl hath been an incendiary of the wars between the two kingdoms of England and Scotland, all which offences hath been sufficiently proved against the said earl upon his impeachment."

Chapter 20

S aint Mark's Day. He thought it was all a bit strange, for the church was near normal, even though the archbishop was incarcerated. Indeed all Archbishop Laud's ideas were still in force in their particular parish; candles and crucifixes adorned the place and altar rails still protectively cordoned off the altar, creating an aura of sanctity about it. This barrier effectively alienated the plainer, Puritan congregation, who believed the whole practice was a remnant of Catholicism, and they began to form as an opposition to the established church. The King and Archbishop Laud were supporters of the Arminian doctrine, sculpturing the Church of England as a middle road between the tyranny of Catholicism and anarchy of Puritanism, aiming to bridge the chasm.

Sitting in their family pew, the Berkeleys were next to other knights of the same status, while the ordinary people sat behind.

In front of him, were old Lord Ashford and his wife and one or two other peers. He lifted his head after his private prayer and looked intently to the aisle of the church at the light grey slab. Beneath it was the remains of their little girl and he felt whole in this place of worship, not only from the way it bound the country together, but also that here, he was reunited with his departed daughter and in touch with God. Taking Anne's hand tightly, they smiled at each other, sensing a family unity.

After a while, his glance shifted for a second to the tombstone of a woman who died twenty years ago, which he had not really noticed before. The seats must have been moved slightly to uncover it and Charles felt impelled to point it out.

"Sixty seven; what an age," he commented idly, while Anne focussed on the minister and did not seem to hear a word he had said.

The clergyman then began to read the usual homily on obedience to the congregation, as per the age old orders from the King's Council. Behind the solitary figure, light streamed through the Flemish coloured glass of the large window. A rainbow of beauty cast itself over the gold candelabra, as though God was connecting to them, directing His love and grace via the clergyman.

"Almighty God hath created and appointed all things in heaven, earth and waters, in a most excellent and perfect order.

In earth He has assigned kings and princes with other governors under them, all in a good and necessary hierarchy."

As Charles glanced round, he saw a man to his right discreetly groping a woman; such ignorance and debauchery in God's house was offensive to him and he glared, prompting only a muffled giggle from the female. Following a further sermon and a song, the preacher then read the recent news from the country, keeping the congregation up to date.

"Her Royal Highness the Princess Mary is betrothed to the Protestant Prince William of Orange, Stadtholder of all the Dutch. His Majesty will receive the said Prince at Whitehall, in great pomp and ceremony for their wedding next month."

Anne gave him a tender smile and had such a twinkle in her eyes that it brought light to his existence. "I hope they are as happy as us."

He nodded his wholehearted agreement, before noticing that the pew to his right was empty again. Thomas would be getting another fine of a shilling for not turning up today, for there was bound to be no valid reason, he thought. With a deep, throaty cough, the clergyman began to read out the banns of marriage, making sure no objections came from the congregation to the forthcoming weddings and Charles smiled as he heard the names of one engaged couple - the carpenter who lived nearby. Young James must have gotten around her father then, he guessed.

The vicar then reminded them of the two men from the parish who had been captured by Algerian pirates, while sailing back to England last month. The dogs would have enslaved the pair, and the curate called for the congregation to add to a fund for their rescue, before slipping in an appeal for donations to restore the church roof.

He saw the kindly face of a young clergyman with rosy cheeks and a warm smile, who had begun a slow journey, from row to row. He held out a wooden box portraying a colourful street scene, with a rich man passing by a poor beggar who was seated on the stones.

A coin slot was cut out of the roof of one house. As it was politely proffered, Charles put some coins in, the resulting noise clunking as emptily as the rich man's pompous stance.

After the service had finished, a couple let Charles and Anne into the queue that had formed in the aisle, the gentleman nodding his head and offering the space. Charles saluted his thanks as the procession exited. He looked right down the walkway, enclosed with Gothic arches, the delay offering the opportunity to admire the golden Tudor roses which adorned the oak roof. The collection box looked heavy now, the proceeds being carried carefully towards the churchwardens, to enter the ecclesiastical funds for the church and the sick, elderly, or poor of the parish. One or two other men let their wives out of the doors first and groups of friends and neighbours congregated in the churchyard, catching up and chatting to each other. They spoke to the woman who had been Anne's maid of honour, her father proudly linking her arm. Charles looked beyond the old graves, some with moss tops like hair, trying to remember where Anne had said her grandfather was buried.

Then they hurried home in a packed hackney carriage, Charles pointing out that Edward, the driver, was following one of his 'short cuts' that took them near the river. Charles liked to look over the Thames when it was quiet and free from all the ferries, Sunday being the only such day when ferrymen did not work. As they passed by, a group of boys were undressing, while others were bathing in the water, splashing and shouting at each other.

The journey was then held up due to a herd of cows being driven through the narrow street, on their way to the slaughterhouse at Tower Hill. When the couple finally arrived back home, Louise was preparing dinner with the other maid's help. Charles spontaneously picked Anne up and kissed her, and she laughed, letting herself lie freely in his arms.

"You have not been this happy for weeks and it is all because another woman is coming," she joked.

"I do not see her often since she eloped to Bury Saint Edmunds with the mongrel."

He followed Anne into the kitchen, smelling the various dishes that were simmering, or being prepared. Louise swung the cauldron out from over the fire, via a moving arm, which hooked onto the pot. She removed some mesh bags that contained boiled vegetables and Charles searched for more appetising food, rather than these plain garnishes. Anne instructed Arabella to take the chicken pie to the bakers nearby, to cook it over there, for the kitchen was at capacity, and also far too hot as it was. Already the rising sultry air going up the chimney was turning the spit mechanism, which roasted the several chickens impaled on it.

He soon left the bustling room as Louise brought out the beef soup, salmon and lobsters, finally followed by roast chickens, mutton, lamb and some cheeses. Charles felt a good appetite at seeing this food; he only hoped his sister would get here in time before it got cold. He trailed each of the dishes, eyeing their progress and destination, starving mind unable to concentrate on much else until Lucy and William eventually arrived.

He scooped his sister into his arms, twirling her round like a child's wooden spinning top, her rich, brown hair cascading out as she went. In comparison, William, her husband, stood in the doorway like a stiff, metal, toy soldier. As his younger sibling held him lovingly, with tears in her eyes, his own welled up. It was a while before the emotional Lucy composed herself enough to talk, and Charles handed her a handkerchief.

After Anne embraced her, Lucy dabbed her eyes again, before Charles jokingly pretended to wring the handkerchief out.

He leaned towards William, remaining fixed to the spot as he offered his hand. The two did not smile and the man quickly shook it, more interested in removing it from his vicinity as quickly as possible. The veneer of politeness was as thin as the leather which hung on the walls of this dining room, embossed with flowered patterns and highlighted with gold leaf.

Moving into the dining room, they all sat around the table as Anne carved the meat and Louise poured the wine.

"William has just finished serving as Parish Constable," Lucy announced, taking her husband's arm, subtly drawing him into the conversation.

"Oh. I'll wager the parish is regretting that?" Charles said, not knowing what to say, but secretly wondering if they had appointed him to prevent him from being idle.

Just then, he felt Anne kick his leg and he jumped, about to query the assault, until a brief glare made him realise his indifferent remark could be meant both ways.

"Erm, Did you catch any card gamers at the inn, William? Father used to turn a blind eye in his, for they would drink so much while they played; can you remember, Lucy?" he added, genuinely remorseful at his earlier faux pas.

"Yes, he would do anything for money," Lucy added, coldly responding to talk of their parent, whom she had not spoken to for so long now.

"William, last time we had a letter from you, it said your sister was ill. How is she now?" Anne interjected, rescuing the whole conversation.

"A good enema and drawing some blood off her did the trick. Now her humours have been balanced, and she is out milking the cow at sunrise each day again."

Whilst helping each other to the huge amounts of food, Charles quizzed Lucy, eager for more news of the children.

"So do my niece and nephew enjoy school?"

"Elizabeth does, but Edward only goes because she does; she is such a protective older sister. Thank you for the money to pay for the education, it will be a Godsend to prepare them for adulthood. I only wish I could have brought them, though hours in a coach would have driven them mad," Lucy replied in the country accent, which he himself had started to lose.

"So we left them with my youngest sister, to drive her insane," William added with a chortle, "For Edward is so questioning and stubborn, that his only utterance seems to be to ask 'why' about everything."

"They have pulled us through the loss of our other two girls, their needs and innocence has kept us going," Lucy commented, taking William's hand. One girl had only recently died in childbirth, while the other had succumbed to smallpox.

"Do you not think it so filthy here?" William asked, changing the subject.

"You just notice that more by not living here."

"The howling and shouting of those protesters must drive ye mad? They are so loud," William replied, as he worked his way through the pile on his plate. Charles started counting the way the man said 'ye' and it reminded him of some of the other villagers from his childhood.

"Well I agree with their principles, but I grow weary of their methods. I hate the way they organise mobs to parade around to force people into agreeing with them. It is but a two faced thing if they demand the correction of an arbitrary way by employing the same methods," Charles said.

"And how be James?" Lucy asked.

Surprised she remembered his friend, Charles answered, "He is well; we were at his house just recently, singing while he played the virginal."

"I had no idea that feelings were running so high. Those rumours I heard of the King trying to use force upon us must be true," exclaimed William with surprise, "Back home, we had no idea that Secretary Windebank had fled abroad after Strafford was impeached. Believe me, the peace of the country is more attractive than the fanaticism of London," William claimed.

Charles shivered. He thought of the King's letter to Strafford.

"Do you know, one of the ladies who I met in the exchange recently told me she had never seen a cow until she drove out of the city for the first time," Anne recounted.

At this point, the conversation was interrupted by scuffles from the street. William tried to talk over it, but with every second, the march of many feet and sounds of loud voices eventually stopped the group completely. Charles rose and rushed to the window. From it he saw people making for Westminster in droves. Muttering had developed into shouting and sheer panic as shops closed up quickly. The noise level soared while people joined the back of the mob, safety being in numbers. A drum was beat and bells rang out and William came to the window to investigate, his mouth open as he watched the unfolding scene.

"W-what in the name of God is going on out there?" he asked.

Anne took Lucy away from the table to keep her occupied, while Charles went out to the front door. William had followed and stood in the doorway, unusually interested in everything.

Charles listened to the shouting to understand more. He felt an intense panic. The crowd was roaring, pulling tables and any other junk across the street.

"Papist bastards," a couple of men cried, prompting more insults and louder yells.

He pushed William back into the house.

"They're shouting that Papists and Catholics have just set the Parliament chamber afire."

William turned without saying anything and went back into the room. Charles called Louise and told her to secure the doors once he had gone outside again, and to let no one in.

Entering the dining room, he told the women that there were more complaints about the trial and asked William to investigate with him.

"I think it best I stay with Lucy, she may be in danger," William suggested.

Anger boiled over as he looked upon this cowardly weasel with scorn, but he withheld further comment out of love for his sister. He gestured to his brother in law to come into the hall, but while a reluctant William followed, he stopped short of leaving the house.

"You cowardly bastard. Come here and help me protect our ladies."

"I am going to protect my wife, by staying with her, not running off into danger. What if ye were killed - ye would leave Anne forever and is that a good husband? I have had my fill of this damned city already," he told him bitterly.

Charles could not reply. His own opinion was to gather facts, so that he was aware of just how to protect Anne. But as he looked at those dark, blue eyes, a deep pool of emotions that Charles had never allowed himself to peer into before, he felt obliged to recognise the actual love this man truly felt for Lucy. The fair eyebrows, as light as they were, faded away, making the iris of his eyes seem even larger.

"You coward, just run away then," Charles snapped, letting his well established feelings cloud the view of the real William.

"But I am the only man who can make her happy, unlike all your family," William pointed, rising just as much.

"My father is absolutely right about you, we can all see through you, except poor Lucy."

"Thy father can rot in hell."

Charles grabbed him and swung him round against the door, dizzy with rage. William moved his head back.

"Go on, hit me right in the mouth. Go on then, if ye are such a hard man."

Charles stepped forward, fist gripped in preparation.

William was so calm and arrogant and this heightened his temper even more. It would not anger him as much if the man would simply react with passion.

"Do it, 'cause when you do, Lucy will never forgive you and she will be rid of both you and thy father for good."

Charles was desperate to pound him, but the door opened, and as he let go, the ladies appeared.

"What is all the noise?"

"This fool is trying to stop me investigating what is going on."

He pushed William away, disguised as a playful act, before leaving the house. Following the crowds, he made his way to Parliament, not knowing what to expect, jostled along until he was in view of Westminster.

The sight was amazing.

Had he been dreaming when he heard the exclamations, he wondered. He saw no fire at all, no damage, nothing but crowds of bemused people wondering what had actually occurred, approaching the usual bustle of business and servants like a probing, slow tide, before ebbing away again, back to normality. Reality dawned; they had all been duped. Nothing at all had happened and the high passion of the city at this time had only needed one rumour to spark mass panic.

He growled to himself, "I despise these times," and he let out a deep cry of frustration.

"Sorry, master," a young boy said, as he bumped into Charles, waking him from his confused state.

As he went to move on, a man was standing very close within his personal space, always a point of irritation, especially if it was a street vendor.

"Get out of my way," Charles barked, practically swiping the man aside.

"Sir Charles," he pleaded.

Charles looked the man up and down in an attempt to understand his approach.

"Lord Digby saw you and would like to speak with you, should you be able to spare some time, sir?"

The humble request, from a master so haughty, caused a short laugh to erupt from Charles. He had not seen, or heard of the man since the trial, and his intrigue at the invitation sufficed for him to nod his agreement, wondering if he could gain some inside information. The servant led him across the busy street, clearing a path for him, while birds squawked overhead, welcoming cargos of new vessels into the nearby dock.

Chapter 21

Charles and Digby strolled through Westminster Hall, past Saint Stephen's Cloisters and into the heart of Parliament. The two men were silent. Following a polite greeting, Charles had been so distracted that he missed the splendid architecture of Edward the Confessor's palace. Digby's explanation that he had left the House of Commons to investigate the din from outside, only to spot Charles in the crowd, fell on deaf ears. The man now poked his inquisitive head through a doorway, before signalling for him to follow.

They stood alone inside the vast chamber, a large, square table practically splitting the room into two. Charles viewed Digby, whose eyes were shimmering like two wondrous amethysts.

Certainly the man's whole being could alter shade in every light, the same as the mineral, and seemed as unbreakable too.

"How are you, sir?" Charles asked, breaking the ice and eager to speed the discussion up.

"I am well, but it pains me to see one's sovereign so distracted."

Immediately, Charles sensed the nature of the coming discussion, determined to be one step ahead.

"What chamber are we in?"

"This, sir, is the Court of Requests. Rather an apt setting," Digby announced, stroking some of his abundance of fair hair.

The man seemed so precise and methodical and perhaps this was why he was so good at intrigue. Then his quick laugh pierced the formal setting, Charles expecting a judge to hold Digby in contempt of court.

"Ah, Sir Charles Berkeley. I entrust you with His Majesty's intimate worries and all you can do is query an old, official room. I will lay before you the chance to play an important role, to be someone and bring honour to your family."

He was lost for words at this frankness, so unexpected from as complicated a man as Digby - who seemed to be lots of different people rolled into one. He had taken an instant dislike to him when he had first clapped eyes on him, but Digby's words massaged his curiosity somewhat, and flattered him, though not enough to fully cloud his judgement.

"You do me a great honour, sir, but I wonder what you are going to propose, and also whether the King himself is hiding somewhere here to spring out and force my hand?" he countered sarcastically, reminding Digby of that night at the palace.

"Very witty, Sir Charles, you have a suspicious mind, but some humour that could forge your career. I wish to draw on your expertise, nothing more," he said calmly and confidently.

The last part, a serene response and compliment, made Charles feel happier to listen, as though the man had opened up a bare vulnerability. He could not bring himself to break away - yet. Digby's many personalities seemed to split other people's in two, dividing and ruling them.

"So why did you wish to talk to me?"

Digby sighed, as though reluctant to say, yet the small lips did not restrain themselves for long. "I took some air just now after the momentous events in the House of Commons. They are casting Strafford's trial to one side, intent on convicting him by a Bill of Attainder – it is a vote, which if it should pass in the House of Commons, and then in the House of Lords, would simply need the King's approval for Lord Strafford's execution. They need no evidence to convict him and it would be done on the grounds of being for the safety of the state."

Charles frowned, meeting Digby's eyes with a look of surprise, though more due to the way the prisoner was to be exterminated.

"Yes, such a wise, able and loyal neck sliced, the bloodied head being the first one to roll around the ground of the new world Pym is trying to create."

Charles coughed, walking towards the plain, plaster wall and tightly gripping the wooden seat, another old pew. He remembered Strafford's grey hair, the bluntly honest way he spoke to him when he passed the letter over, and above all, the man's knowledge of the scriptures. It angered him that he felt some pang of compassion.

"Lady Anne, your wife, is a true English rose. She would be wasted being sent to the bogs of Ireland."

Charles frowned, exasperated by the man's fleeting mind.

"Ireland, she is not going to that hole."

Digby snorted. "Well, if Lord Strafford is cut down, then your Lord Holland is after the Lord Lieutenancy of Ireland, and I'll wager you will share in that glory, for I hear he gives you patronage. To the bogs of Ireland it would be for the Berkeleys, right into the centre of a political massacre waiting to happen."

Charles was stunned at the details, the scenario building and predictions. Digby smiled within that round, smooth face, the nose as sharp as his mind, alive at the fact that he had caused such a stir. He seemed to be playing a game now, switching from one point to another, causing worry, anger and frustration each time.

Walking closer, Digby's expression became serious. He held out his hand to Charles, palm upward as he finally laid his views bare. "The House of Commons will vote for Strafford's demise, and the Lords may just pass the Bill if they think the King will ultimately refuse his assent. If this happens, who can stop Pym and his cronies from destroying all opposition?"

The sun began to glow again, lighting up the leaded window and the coats of arms which were modelled in the top of each long pane. Beneath the great windows, was a bench, covered in a red cloth, the royal coat of arms embroidered, or rather brandished, in the centre. It focussed his thoughts.

"I do think a balance needs to be found between King and Parliament," Charles said, eager to make his view known.

Digby lapped the comment up, encouraging more opinions and discussion.

"A letter has been received by the junior officers of what is left of our English army in the north - your comrades, Sir Charles. It said they had the backing of their troops to … help resolve everything here with Strafford and all. Unfortunately their commanders appear as though they support Parliament."

Charles glared at the man.

Digby's eyes tried to pierce his armour. "Why do you always appear aloof when politics is mentioned? I thrive on it, Sir Charles, and without it we would never have a chance to prove ourselves. Rumours are flying that the King and Queen are behind a plot to use this army against Parliament. The King did not initiate any of it, but he is obviously most interested now, for it may solve events. The royals need to be totally distant from it to crush this gossip. We need someone with the right connections to investigate whether these minor officers actually do write with the backing of their men, or not. Someone just like you."

Digby looked at him in silence.

Charles laughed out loud, realising what he wanted.

"No, sir, not at all," he said, determined to make himself clear.

"Pym is using the rumour of the King and Queen starting this plot as a lever to frighten Parliament into taking command of the army away from the monarch. Would you as a loyal soldier go along with this, to see law and order uprooted and used against the state? Your actions may save Strafford's life and the ancient laws of this land."

"Do not dare bring my honour into this. Both sides are as bad as each other. My lord, I am no fool," he snapped, irritated that Digby was trying to use him.

"Your loyalty may be with Lord Holland, but believe me, I can assure you that Lord Leicester is in line for the Irish role, should it become vacant. I would say you need someone else to promote your corner at court if you wish to advance, although I am prepared to adopt you, I will not do it out of the goodness of my heart."

"I do not need your patronage, sir, and I definitely do not need to be part of such a conspiracy as this. It will be my head Parliament is after next to Strafford's were I involved."

"Sir Charles…" Digby interrupted.

"Do you hear the thousands of men out there baying for Strafford's blood? I am not going to endanger my wife as I did before. In the name of God, judging by what he was trying to do to this country, he deserves …" Charles growled as he stopped talking, unable to continue his tirade.

"You do not need to endanger anyone. If you were about the court more often than you are, you would realise. Let me warn you, Sir Charles, you are rapidly being perceived as supporting both sides at once, despite your ridiculous protestation to be for neither. Soon you will have alienated everyone on each side and you will be in the most impossible and dangerous position, left with nothing but ruin and accusations of cowardice."

Digby squinted at him, evidently expecting success in this, the final throw of the dice.

"I still have sleepless nights over being so compliant about that letter to Strafford. I am not going to help you, sir, I will not risk my family. Now I will return to them immediately."

As he began to head to the doors, tracing his way back along the route he had taken earlier, Digby followed quietly, seeming much more comfortable in these surroundings that Charles was.

In the hallways, it seemed like that the whole northern army had arrived already, crushing into these narrow, Plantagenet remains.

On hearing the din from outside, he glanced at Digby, unable to believe how flamboyantly and supremely self assured this man was, dressed in red, with a rich lace shirt peering through the slits on his coat sleeves and at the collar and cuffs. It seemed it was like the true character of George Digby; trying to escape into the open, but held back by the show the man put on. Shouts and protests penetrated this inner sanctum from the streets, like thundering cannon, attempting to batter anyone who did not believe the dangers of Catholicism.

Then a marvellous scene occurred when the Dutch Ambassador entered with his African serving boy behind him, and Charles stared at the lad, amazed at the darkness of his complexion. The room hushed temporarily, an amazing feat under such circumstances. The boy had a cross burned into the black skin of his forehead, many seeing the sign and adapting to him more now that he had been Christianised, thus making the child less of an anomaly. The clothes were elegant and made from deep crimson velvet, complemented by a crisp white shirt, both of which seemed to highlight his exotic colouring. Charles stretched his head to continue examining him, temporarily suspending his anger. Some women pointed, jealous of the Dutchman for having such an extraordinary servant.

"The blackamoor is a most unusual sight; such a squashed nose," Digby commented.

He noticed just how golden Digby's hair was - the man had a Midas touch it seemed, but fools gold would be the only metal Digby would create. Yet the flawed character was a trait inherited, as Digby's father had once wildly accused the Duke of Buckingham, and by implication, the present King, of murdering old King James the First. Charles bowed without a reply, and then left Digby behind, the blue eyes giving an icy chill. The impression of this look, scornful as it was, seemed to stay with him as he walked away.

* * *

Back home, he found William escorting Lucy out, telling her, "I think it's best we go. I won't have you exposed to this."

Charles stepped forward and pleaded, "It is all nonsense. I beg you stay, Parliament is not alight."

"Nay, sir, I have never liked this foul place and its gossipmongers or rogues," William exclaimed adamantly.

"Stop, I must speak to my sister privately before you leave," he demanded, surprising William's efforts to speed up their departure. Anne began discussing a painting with her brother in law, which was created by Charles and Lucy's grandfather, allowing the siblings to retreat further into the hall.

"Dear sister," he said stroking her arm, "It pains me greatly you and Father still do not speak. He is now over fifty, an elderly man, and he only has us in the world. I am sure it would gladden his heart to receive you. Not even he can hold a grudge for so long."

They eyed one another, as though waiting for the other to speak. Charles felt desperation. He hoped she would forgive.

Lucy sighed, wiping her tears away before replying, "I see your view, but I cannot promise any results. Charles, I love you, but you put so much pressure on me about this. It is upsetting enough without getting another lot of abuse from

Father. Sometimes I wish I could write, for then I would not have to suffer the indignation of the parson reading the rude words I am sure to receive from the old man. Have a care of your wife though, for she seems very anxious and desperate for children."

"I love her and protect her, but a child will only bring heartache at the minute, if it is raised in this atmosphere."

"I know there is more to your view than that, my brother. You still ache for the last one."

He sighed. "You know me too well. Anyhow, what of your husband?" Charles said, looking to the window to stifle his emotion.

"He is called Will," Lucy reminded him curtly.

Charles held his hands out. "No, I just meant to ask if you were both all right."

"With money?" Lucy retorted, "We do not need that to be happy. We have no fancy furniture and we have three surviving children so far, so we are better off than many in the town."

"Lucy, I just care. How is he planning to make a life for you all?"

"How dare you cast aspersions from up high? My husband is up at six of the clock, to work on the land for six pence per day. He toils manually, casting a scythe around to cut crops for hours on end. Could you do that?"

Charles apologised and felt ashamed, despite the fact he had her welfare at heart. "Probably not now. I am too spoiled by comfort, though God is my witness, I try not to fall into that trap."

After they had stood for a few seconds, reeling from their own raw states, Charles realised he had played his own part in the family feud.

"Lucy, I know I have hated Will, nearly as much as Father, but today I saw a different person in him, the real man. For a

210

split second it was clear how much he adores you, and never before have I allowed myself to see this."

But William had entered now and broke them up, ordering Lucy away, Charles biting his tongue.

"God protect you," he shouted as Lucy and William made their way through the dispersing crowds, Lucy affording a last wave.

"What is happening to the place, Charles?" Anne demanded as he raised his hand while the coach left. She held his arm tight.

"It's all heated here; rumours fly with ease because of it, false stories of Catholics burning any Protestant bastion."

"Is it safe?" Anne probed, anxious for the truth, no matter how bad it was.

"Do not worry yourself, my darling, there was no fire when I went to Parliament," he said, side stepping the question somewhat.

"You would never want to be a father with London being so bad, I'll wager," she hinted.

"It is too distracted right now. To have my wife in a delicate condition amidst this entire furore would risk you and the child. I love you too much to do that."

She seemed to stoop, slightly doubled up, which prompted his care and curiosity. Asking about this, she responded with a faint smile, "I am just worried about things, it must be the food and the anxiety mixed."

"I wish things would be still, but this will not be until Strafford dies. After that we can talk of children, for believe me, I have no greater wish than for a child and an heir to the Berkeley name."

He now felt himself backing Strafford's demise for the sake of the peace of the kingdom, desperate to forget any contact or role he had with him. Pym's small organised bands of protesters had encouraged others to follow suit and now the success of this pressure had worked even on him, one who wished to remain neutral.

* * *

"Did you have any luck, sir?" Cotton asked.

"It was a stroke of good fortune that you spotted him outside and notified me. He is ideal for such a task, though no amount of flattery would break him," Digby scoffed, "I have never seen such a man with airs above his station. I will skewer him on a hanging jack and roast him over the fire. I have eaten true gentlemen and nobility alive, let alone such base fellows as him."

"Give me a room at the Tower of London for the night and two guards, and I shall change his mind."

"A room at the Tower? It is not an inn, man," Digby guffawed, prompting for his name again.

"Sir Arthur Cotton, you will become more familiar with me in time. If you wish to have this man's services, I can help you. You think up the charges and use connections to get me that prison cell and I will do the rest," Cotton suggested with a smile.

"You cannot bundle any man into the Tower for nothing, for everyone will notice him there. I helped the successful bidder for the post of Warden of the Fleet Prison; so that place would be more suitable, though I will need a few days to prepare the official to do my bidding. Do not go too far with Sir Charles though, and I know nothing of this," he warned with a nod.

"And if you get what you want?" Cotton hinted as he stood, the rugged chin raised as elegantly as any peer of the realm.

"Then you shall have what you desire in return," Digby said, the two men curiously aware that their personalities were like twins, seeming to communicate telepathically.

"My prize will be some proof that Berkeley delivered a letter to Strafford for the King."

Digby raised his eyebrows to question it.

"He is nothing, it will condemn him, with no danger to you," Cotton assured him.

"I may look surprised, but usually men ask for money or positions at court. You must really hate this fellow. But I do know the existence of such correspondence," Digby replied with a thoughtful expression.

"I will destroy him. My revenge is nearly two years overdue."

Digby nodded his head at him, still astounded. Cotton pictured the medal Berkeley wore. It had haunted him ever since he clapped eyes on it recently and each time he saw it his anger grew.

That is my damned medal, he thought as he worked himself into a fouler mood. He held his hand up and looked at the missing finger.

"He will pay for it," Cotton vowed as he bowed and walked away, footsteps getting harder and faster.

Chapter 22

Hurrying upstairs, he called out, "Anne, my love?"
Then he heard Louise shout back quickly and with alarm, "In here, sir."
Bursting into the bedroom, he saw his wife lying on the bed holding her stomach, the curtains round the four posts hanging as loosely as Anne's hair.

"She will not let me help, she won't even let me near her, sir," Louise said, with uncharacteristic panic.

Dismissing Louise, he ran over to Anne's side. "Tell me what is wrong, sweetheart?" he said, taking hold of her. She shook her head, eyes closed tight and screamed, wrapping her arms about her.

"My God, what is the matter?"

She seemed to indicate the pain was from her stomach.

"I have eaten something that has upset me," she told him between gasps.

"It cannot just be that," he dismissed sharply, his eyes stinging, infiltrated by sweat beads.

"I will be fine, Charles, do not fuss around."

At those words, she winced again. He remembered what

he had read and heard about Nicholas Culpepper, who had recently set up a practice in Spitalfields, as an astrologer and physician.

He provided many herbal remedies that might help.

Running downstairs, he yelled to Louise, "Get and find Nicholas Culpepper. Fetch him immediately."

He was in turmoil - what was wrong? Scores of things were passing through his mind; was it smallpox, fever, plague or even poisoning? He had no idea, but remembered how other loved ones had been snatched away; his daughter, brother and mother. Rushing back to Anne, he found her pain had alleviated.

"Charles, I am well now, be still I beg of you," she insisted unconvincingly.

"I will have it confirmed, Culpepper is on his way. This was far too serious," he said gruffly. Her face dropped as she digested what he had said.

"No, I will not have him examine me," she cried hysterically.

"What the hell is wrong with you? I am not going to deliberately let someone hurt you. I want to make sure you are safe, for I love you too dearly to leave this, can you not see that?"

Taking hold of as gently as possible considering his anxiety, he tried to quieten her.

It seemed like an age since Louise had set off.

"Where in Christ's name is she?" he cursed, turning to observe the now rosy streak of colour in Anne's cheeks, contrasting with the pale features.

A few minutes later, he heard the door slam shut before footsteps echoed up the stairs. Louise came into the room, Charles pulling her out of Culpepper's way. The physician stood panting and was evidently rushed as he tidied his hair, exclaiming that he had seen twenty people already.

"Sir Charles?"

Charles nodded and Culpepper walked towards the mistress of the house, who curled up at his approach.

"I am fine now, Mister Culpepper," she asserted desperately, watching apprehensively. The man looked at Charles, who shook his head to give the final say.

"I come and see people in person, rather than examine their piss - erm, urine - like all of the others do, as though it were the answer to everything. Do not give me a wasted journey, let me find out the cause of this, my Lady," he said as he gently moved the bedclothes back.

Charles was not bothered about the language the man was so apt to use, but despite the advice, Anne would not be swayed, staying huddled up tight. Charles saw her frown at him as she snatched the bedclothes back from the herbalist.

"My dear, I have never made a demand that you obey me as a lawful wife, but I feel I must now. Stop this strange behaviour, in the name of God," he pleaded.

Finally Anne relented, with tears in her eyes, lying straight as Culpepper felt her chest and examined her with greater detail.

She sobbed quietly as he did so, much to Charles's exasperation.

He shook his head, beginning to get annoyed, unable to understand her.

"My lady, please let me put your husband's mind at rest," the man gently persuaded. He was very calm and had a magnificent aura that could relax and soothe.

Culpepper's eyes soon told the story. As he slowly moved away from the patient, he lifted his head and Anne stopped, watching intently with a pale face. Charles waited on the physician's words, as though he were the last to know the cause of all this. Anne was shaking.

Charles felt his stomach churn and as his eyes got wider, a sickly sensation came over him. He did not know how he would cope if he lost Anne. Surely he would not be widowed?

Culpepper turned to him and breathed two words, "A baby."

He stood in disbelief and she started crying again. "But it cannot be a baby, it is impossible ... are you sure?" Charles questioned with disbelief.

Feeling Anne's stomach again, the curve became plainly obvious. When part of her stomach moved ever so slightly, Charles needed no more persuasion. He stood in silence, feeling his heart race, and then panicked. He walked to the window, leaning on the sill with both arms outstretched, Culpepper gathering his belongings again and chattering to him.

"See, Sir Charles, you did not need an insulting, insolent physician to diagnose that. They would have asked your wife to pass as much urine as would fill the Thames before they came to see her," the man told him discreetly, out of the ladies earshot.

Thanking Culpepper and telling Louise to see him out, Charles grabbed his leather purse, jingling with a few coins and handed it to the man.

"I am most grateful for your generosity, Sir Charles. This will help my poorer patients considerably."

"God be with you, sir and thank you for coming so speedily. I know you rarely take payment from the destitute, so I would like to reward that virtuous nature."

"You are to be parents, and judging by the movement of the little mite, everything is well. My congratulations and may the Lord look after them both, sir," Culpepper announced before leaving.

Charles sat on the bed and watched Anne. Tears were still rolling down her cheeks and she forced a smile. He felt unable to respond, now questioning how she had become pregnant.

"Charles, you wanted a family eventually, why are you upset?" she asked in between catching her own breath. They sat for a few minutes in silence.

"You did not say?" Charles said bitterly, "It is - I mean the baby is ..."

"Charles, it is *your* baby," she reaffirmed, raising her voice.

"Do not shout, do you hear? You lied to me all along, what else am I meant to think?" he bellowed.

His mind raced, wondering if it could be her dancing master's.

"As God is my witness. I had wanted to make sure it was safe for as long as possible before I said anything," she spluttered, finally giving the truth.

"Oh, Anne," he groaned, before embracing her. He felt numb and his mind simply could not cope with all the things going through it.

"I could not bear to have my hopes dashed again," she cried.

They held each other as they came to grips with the reality of the situation.

"I thought he was going to tell me I would lose you. How long gone are you?" Charles asked, clinging to her linen nightdress.

"I spoke to a wise woman when you were out, she thinks about two to three months. It must have been your birthday in February that did it."

"God's Wounds, I am to be a father and you a mother."

"It is good news, is it not?" she asked, clearly looking for reassurance. Charles was evidently silent for too long and she raised her hands in frustration.

"Yes, I am overjoyed, just so much has happened so very quickly," he said.

"Just leave it. You had to think about it - do you know how worried I have been since I knew? All this time it has been about you, I have thought endlessly about what you think and forgotten about my own person."

"I am sorry, but I was too petrified that I would lose you. Give me half the burden you have carried for so long then,

I beg you," he fussed.

Anne nodded and dried her eyes. "I am glad you accept the situation, for the Lord has blessed us, regardless of the state London is in."

"For months I have not realised you were carrying my child. This city will be at rest once more when Strafford is gone."

She smiled and took hold of his hand.

"I thought you'd drunk the water that we got channelled to us from the lead pipe, and it was causing you discomfort."

Anne laughed, chasing the remaining atmosphere away. How she would make fun of him - the water supply was a standing joke, for he would not get it taken out, despite the uncertain supply tasting funny.

"Nay, my love, I only worried that you may have been angry at my dishonesty in keeping it from you, but I did not know what else to do."

"Hush, I see why you did it. I will send Louise up to see you and you can break the news to her."

He walked downstairs, stumbling for a moment, but took nothing in when Louise asked if everything was all right.

Eventually with a smile, he encouraged her, "Go up and see them for yourself,

Lady Anne has some news,"

'Them' - he just realised what he had said as he walked into the study. Sitting at the desk, he took a paper from the drawer and cut a new quill. Dipping it in the ink, he proceeded to write to his father, to let him know the news. He had difficulty committing it to paper, still doubting the information himself and not daring to believe it. The writing made him realise he was to make his father a grandfather again. His full eyes narrowed as he smiled, wondering how the man would take the news.

He sat deathly quiet. Staring out of the window, he debated what he would have to do now and how he could safeguard his family. Questions ran through his thoughts - what will happen to us, will Anne survive, how will a child fit into the present troubles and how will our life be affected? Despite Anne's lack of concern about the state of affairs outside, he could not forget any of it. He had to plan ahead, think about how he could support his family. Lord Holland's ascent would help, as long as he was allied to the peer.

"A child," he muttered, beaming with pride, "Pray God that it lives this time and bless us with a healthy baby, Lord.

Please give my wife and child strength," he asked aloud, resting his hand on the large family bible.

Then he thought of Cotton's enmity and Digby's proposal and offer of patronage. As the night wore on, he wondered whether the prophesy of ruin would come true and feared it for the first time, now that he would have a family to protect.

A banging echoed through the house, waking him soon after. The rapping was louder than any knock he had ever heard, as though a giant demanded entry.

Irritated with this interruption and anticipating Louise answering the door, he tried to ignore it, feeling utterly exhausted. The racket continued and he decided to go himself to make sure it was safe. Louise was just at the entrance as he approached, two burly men pushing her to one side before Sir Arthur Cotton stepped past them.

"Sir Charles Berkeley?"

Charles stood for a moment, taking the scene in with disbelief.

"You belong in the theatre, Cotton, of course you know who I am," he shouted as he pointed furiously.

"Ah, but I am not acting," Cotton warned.

"Piss off out of my house," Charles demanded, storming forward.

"I cannot do that, I am on official business."

"You, official?" Charles said as he hurried towards the guards. "Do not touch my maid again."

They freed Louise and Cotton shook his head.

"You never learn; I have you cornered now. Repaying the favour you might say."

"What the hell are you chattering about?" Charles questioned, seething with outrage.

"Take him to the Fleet Prison."

The guards grabbed Charles, who struggled as hard as he could. "On whose orders? For what?" he yelled.

Cotton sniggered.

"You must have a warrant."

"I have, Berkeley, in these two men. Who will miss such an unimportant person as you? If they do happen to, I have backing from Digby or Parliament, whichever one I choose."

In a panic, he told Louise desperately, "Go to Anne and take care of her."

The guards dragged him outside. While he tugged, kicked and struggled, he heard Cotton behind him.

The door to the house slammed as Louise secured it, to prevent any of Cotton's men from entering again.

"Poor Lady Berkeley. Her husband is so lame and pathetic that he abandons her and is powerless."

Charles cried out, temper erupting like a volcano.

Chapter 23

He was manhandled through a dim, squalid corridor and past several cells in which people stood watching, shouting and reaching out in desperation. A scream pierced the dank atmosphere and the burly guards pushed Charles into the small, stone room. Some candles had been lit in preparation for his arrival. It was damp and cold, yet Charles was boiling with rage. Two men stood in the corner and a woman sat opposite, hunched up and holding her legs to her chest. Cotton sighed loudly from outside the door and Charles turned to his direction in an instant.

"You fool. All of this could have been avoided if you had just accepted Digby's patronage or declared support for King or Parliament. Now you are powerless and are watched warily by each side, while I am trusted by both."

Cotton's dark eyebrows looked strange against his grey hair, but nevertheless, he cut a tall, somewhat elegant figure, despite his arrogance and vindictiveness. Charles ignored him, determined not to respond to the mocking. He clenched his fists, but it was no good, for the taunts persisted like the water dripping down the walls, testing his already low tolerance levels to the limit.

"And now you have lost more than your pride. Your wife lies in with child. They say a lot of women die from childbirth," Cotton warned, the words shooting venomously from his mouth. As though Cotton had tapped Charles's reflexes, he responded immediately to this threat to his family.

He made a run for the door Cotton was peering through - the dog's eyes narrowly assessing Charles's every reaction as if he were a caged animal - and launched all his weight onto it with a crash. Now Cotton had disappeared and when he yelled at him and grabbed hold of the window bars, he saw him adjusting his clothes, the slit of a mouth open slightly, the upper lip looking even longer than normal. With a pale face, he walked away without looking back. Charles shook the door, kicked it and let out loud cries of frustration; his rage so high, that he felt like crying or destroying everything in sight.

Nobody came and nothing happened. In those few seconds of silent assessment, he noticed the other inmates watching intently; the woman trembled, the men glared with glazed, dense expressions. Now he knew what those lunatics in Bedlam were like when spectators came in to watch their strange, erratic antics. Was he the sane one here, he wondered, because Cotton and these prisoners all seemed to be fascinated with him.

An intense feeling of despair and panic washed over him.

He had never been so helpless before and this overtook his anger. He felt sick, so sat down.

Then dampness soaked through to his backside from the floor and he quickly got back up. The other incumbents of this grotty cell were silent; he must have been the first interesting diversion in years.

Following a period of pacing around, he leaned against the wall, waiting. He did not know what for, and that alone caused some of the maelstrom of feelings - what could happen to Anne created the rest. Her name kept ringing round his head like a bell pealing - soon he thought his head would explode like that huge culverin his men had named 'Roaring Meg' after the infamous prostitute. Thank God, he thought as the image of this twelve foot long cannon and its eighteen pound shot finally stabilised his mind from utter despair. With his thoughts randomly moving on, he shook his head as he noticed a broom in the corner. It was ironic that such an object had been left in a miserable and dirty hole as this and imagining it to be Cotton, he launched it the length of the room.

The bastard will be back soon enough, he must have further need of me, he guessed.

Then in true military style, he strode to the door and back every now and then, searching for signs of anyone outside.

He played with a coin in his hand, before bellowing until a small jailor appeared with messy hair and yellow and brown teeth. He grasped a lavish cloak about him tightly, despite his other shabby clothes.

What's all the noise about, man?" came the piercing voice.

"The noise? What the hell do you think? My confinement is illegal," Charles shouted.

"Just go to sleep," came the jailor's curt gem of advice.

"You ignorant whoremonger," he growled.

The man glared at him with hatred, wrinkles flashing out around the eyes and mouth as he screwed his face up in hatred, as if Charles had no right to complain. Behind him he felt the other inmates' eyes on him and it was like he had been cast into a mad underworld.

"You are bloody spoilt with your riches. Give me six pence and I can find you something to make life more amenable."

"How dare you, this is outrageous. Pay you for some comfort? I would rather die."

"I am trying to 'elp and if that's how you feel, sleep on the stone floor. I need my measly wage to be topped up. Strange 'ow roles change and you rely on a poor man now, eh?"

"Get a message to my wife for me and tell her I am all right."

The man raised his eyebrows. For the sake of contacting Anne, Charles flung six pence at him and the jailor left. He watched impatiently, wondering what the fellow was doing and whether he was taking the mission. Then the skinny man limped back and opened the door with a creak that echoed throughout the squalid dungeon, throwing in some straw.

Charles could not believe that the jailor had fleeced him and his pride took a battering.

"Oi, I gave you that money to send word to my wife, not for this damned stuff. I have more stamina and pride than to need suchlike," he bellowed.

"You ain't half a noisy pain in my backside. I did not hear you say anything about any errand."

"If you come in here again, I will show you where to stick your straw," he barked.

The woman scurried forward, gathering the tarnished strands like it was gold and asking him to spare further money.

Charles looked at her ragged dress, noticing that she had no ball and chain on her foot, whereas the men were both adorned with one each. Now they shuffled forward, intrigued with the possibility of money; indeed, they fed off the thought of it and for the first time, they came alive. It was as though they had been frozen, and the woman began singing a song as she happily made a soft base to sit on.

"A trooper lad came here last night, with riding he was weary, a trooper lad came here last night, when the moon shone bright and clearly."

"Why do you not have a chain?" Charles asked her, intrigued.

"He's taken off his big topcoat, likewise his hat and feather. He's taken the broadsword from his side, and now he's down beside her."

One of the men piped up, talking over her song and telling him that she might not have the shackle, but she has things the jailor needs that they did not. The woman lowered her head in shame, reacting to the voices for the first time. At that point, the blond man asked why he was here, guessing it was for debts.

"Nay, I do not know why. An enemy of mine has arrested me. What is wrong with her?"

"She is a gambler and up to her neck in debt. Opened the legs too often and got lumbered with a child an' all in the end; could not support herself, let alone another mouth, so they put 'er in 'ere until she manages to pay 'em all off. I myself dared to speak out against the archbishop and that was that," he explained with detail, continually speaking for the woman and now in acceptance of Charles as one of them.

Then they proceeded to explain about the freedoms he could buy if he paid the jailor, probing to see whether he had any money on him. For a fee, they could obtain bedding, coal or candles and even be let outside to beg for more money to go towards their debts. The other man showed him the bruising and gash he had received in a beating from the guard. Charles was aware that he looked wealthy, so they would know he carried money on him, and he gave six pence to each of them in pacification and sympathy. Truthfully, he had no sympathy whatsoever with debtors, for they caused their own misery, but he had enough enemies right now without an extra three.

Charles thought about the law and worried about what could happen to him and why he was here. If he were to face a trial, the only way he could appeal against any punishment ordered would be to ask the King to grant a royal pardon. In view of his neutral leanings and the fact that he was being framed, that would be as likely as King Charles and Pym becoming allies. It felt like an age had passed before he heard Cotton's usual cackle.

"Your arse is wet. You look like you have pissed yourself, Berkeley."

Charles walked to the door. "Why have I been brought here?" he petitioned, as he discreetly reached for the broom.

Slowly grasping the handle, he lifted it to the door beneath the bars. Cotton was still oblivious.

"You still do not know? By God you are stupid. You did not do Digby's bidding," he explained, leaning closer to the small window.

Without warning, Charles launched the broom through the bars and the end smacked into Cotton's face, round like a target butt. Charles glared at him, happy that his aim was as good as ever, and the others in the cell cheered and howled with laughter.

Cotton roared, his nose cut and bloodied, before clasping his hands over the middle of his face and swaying around in pain and resentment. Charles felt like a leader of some peasants revolt with them at his back, supporting his crusade against the tyrants holding them down in their pit of despair.

"You bastard, you will pay for that. I will visit your wife, tear your child out of her myself and leave them both to die," he screeched.

Charles's heart sank. He had succumbed to vengeance and it had given him no benefit other than a minute or so of gloating. How he should have taken note of the sermons he heard last Sunday about the sins of revenge and greed.

"Open this door, be a man for once in your life."

Charles watched him intently, which worked the man up further.

"How dare you assault me," Cotton said in a low voice, giving the impression physical violence had affected him before, touching the bloodied wound in disbelief. Then he started to scramble for the door in a frenzy. He could not carry out such a basic action, such was his indignation, so he shouted at the guards.

A burly sentry opened it and came in with him. At a nod from his impromptu master, the guard walked menacingly towards Charles - Cotton must have bribed him to do his bidding. The man's large frame and mean look seemed to fit in well with the place. Charles stepped back, but then stopped and waited, anticipating the coming onslaught and made a punch at the man, but it did nothing. He would not retreat further, so tensed himself. The brute let out a strike to Charles's stomach, causing him to fall to his knees, bent double.

Cotton then ran forward and kicked his ribcage, letting out a shriek of glee. Charles fell flat on the floor, straining to get some of the breath back that had been forced out of him. The air could no longer find a way into his lungs and he gasped and wheezed, desperate now for any of this stuffy, stale atmosphere.

"I have a meeting with Lord Digby tomorrow. I need to tell him you have *changed your mind* about helping with the Army Plot. If that happens, you get released, you see your wife, if she is alive, and it means I have finally dragged you off that damn fence of yours," Cotton whispered as he bent down close to Charles's head.

Charles stared at him, desperately pushing himself up, but unable to speak. The other prisoners simply watched, sinking back into the shadows and away from any danger.

"You think that was bad? It was nothing. Believe me, I know what a beating is, Berkeley. I was always told it would make me a man. I don't think any amount of thrashing would do that to you though."

"Is this what this is all about, that damned dirty work?" Charles panted, the outburst exhausting him again.

"All, all?" he asked, before shrieking with laughter.

"You arrest and torture me to get me to help in some poxy plot? I will discuss with Digby why he needs me first and only him. Now I demand you let me out."

"This is not all, Berkeley, my personal satisfaction and revenge is also addressed with it."

Charles stood up and grasped his ribcage. "Yes, just why in the name of God do you hate me so much?"

Cotton stepped forward, eyes blazing.

"Why do I despise you? You took something from me, made me have to learn how to handle a sword again, and made me feel like a child."

Charles frowned, frustrated at this nonsense, but Cotton's every quick inhale seethed with offence.

"Let me show you, perhaps this will help you remember."

Slowly Cotton brought his arm up and held his hand out, fingers rigid and extended, veins and muscles as exposed as the man's inner feelings, and Charles saw the first finger was missing. He was fixated at the crease of the lower knuckle of the stump, just under its misshaped end, and after a few seconds shot a glance to Cotton's horrified face. He looked like he was reliving the whole incident again.

"No? You cannot be him?"

Cotton nodded, grasping his hand and holding it to his body like a baby.

"Good God. I thought it was strange how you seemed to detest me. What I did was in war, and you lost, end of story," he stated simply, with disdain.

"To add insult to injury, this wound got you a bloody knighthood and patronage of Lord Holland. It galls me that I helped you achieve that. Now I am simply taking away from you what you do not deserve. I will oust you from your post in the Trained Bands and bring disgrace to you."

Before Charles could respond, Cotton left, leaving him to pace around, determined not to let them wear him down.

"Bloody plots, they are as common as the plague now and as deadly. In fact I have never come across a decision as deadly as King or Parliament," he cursed as he held his chest.

His mind was cast back to the Bishops War and his sword fight with Cotton. He raised his eyebrows with surprise that he had come face to face with the same man again. God knows what such intense hatred would produce next to secure revenge, but he was now clear about why the man seemed to revile him so much - and at least he knew what he was working against too.

Chapter 24

"Pilate would have saved Christ by using his privileges on his behalf, because that day, he could choose one prisoner to be spared. But he was forced to choose Barabbas; he would have saved Christ from death by satisfying their fury with inflicting other torments upon him, scourging and crowning with thorns and loading him with scornful and ignominious treatment, but the mob regarded him not. They pressed a crucifying."

As he listened to the sermon, the King of Great Britain, Ireland and France was impervious to the roaring and stampeding outside his palace. The most soothing act in his routine was his religion. He was devoted to the Church of England and loved the strict hierarchy of it, the ritual and rigid regime, which helped him cope. He took heart and strength from God, and right now, he was paying devotional service to the Almighty, the only one he personally had to answer to.

The King mused about the sermon and how it compared to that of his situation right now. As Pilate tried to save Christ, he was trying to save Strafford, but the mob showed no signs of being satisfied with anything but his death.

"Towards midday Pilate gave judgment, and they made such haste to execution as that by noon Christ was upon the cross. There now hangs that sacred body upon the cross, baptised in his own tears and sweat, and embalmed in his own blood alive. There are those bowels of compassion which are so conspicuous, so manifested, as that you may see them through his wounds. There those glorious eyes grew faint in their sight, so as the sun, ashamed to survive them, departed with his light too."

As his chaplain read on, the King again felt sorrow creep upon him. Both the House of Commons and now the House of Lords had voted to judiciously kill Strafford for the safety of the state. It would not be long before they would cast his minister's body onto the cross, unless the King stuck firm and refused to agree to the Bill of Attainder.

He sighed, straightening his back to maintain his discipline, thinking of the Queen and hoping she was calmer than this morning, sparing a quick prayer for her safety. He would never allow her to keep him away from his religion, but her Catholicism prevented her from worshipping alongside him. Despite the deep adoration, religion would always be a boundary, which the King crossed alone.

As the sermon finished, the monarch made an appreciative gesture to the chaplain, before casting his eyes to the cross and the altar. The service had given him a calming air and the chance to humbly consult God. He felt much more at peace again and remembering that the Lord was on his side gave him a boost of confidence.

The King knew in his heart that Strafford had been one of the main architects who had helped him build his rule during the eleven years he had governed without Parliament.

Would Strafford now have to pay for this loyal service with his life? He stood and filed out of the chapel in silence, the courtiers and attendants obediently following behind him.

The King seemed impervious to all as he went with his usual quick pace, leaving his followers struggling to keep up, no matter how much they tried to disguise the fact. It was even faster today in view of the pressure incessantly mounting on him, though nobody would notice any of the ravenous anxiety that ate him within like a tumour, the sudden feelings of despair and indignation, which had barred him from his slumbers. He turned and entered the Privy Gallery, providing access to his innermost rooms, the doors held open in time to prevent any change to his stride, not that he noticed this though, for it was normal. Hearing the din of men's voices from the streets for the first time since exiting the chapel, he stopped abruptly.

As he listened to the chanting sweeping over with the breeze, he closed his eyes. They stung for a few seconds, exhaustion creeping up on the five foot four figure as he stood in front of his army of attendants.

"The Queen, where is she?" he demanded of his cousin, the Duke of Richmond, with a rare flash of irritation.

"She is in her apartments, Your Majesty," the peer replied sympathetically.

The knowledge of her whereabouts reassured him, as did the tenderness and familiarity of his cousin's voice, which had a medicinal effect. Her safety was the one thing which caused most of his worry over this situation. Many of the courtiers had been left outside the Privy Gallery, not being of sufficient status to enter, and he looked again at the small crowd of survivors. For a second he imagined facing the gathering mob in the streets like this, before that stubbornness overtook him once more. This attribute had worked wonders for him time and time again, probably created when he conquered walking and talking, which had evaded him until past the age of three.

The brass boots they made him wear to build up his ankles joined forces with this new found grittiness, and before anyone knew it, this sick, rickety young Prince was careering himself onwards, devouring books and learning to ride, determined to live up to his older brother's sparkling personality. No sooner had he pictured Henry, than he extinguished such personal thoughts like a candle, still haunted by the boy's early death, his idol snatched away.

"Have you heard from the bishops?" he asked of Edward Nicholas, the man who had unofficially taken on the duties of the Secretary of State, who had fled the country to avoid imprisonment by Parliament.

"Yes, Your Majesty, following your command, Archbishop Ussher of Armagh and the Bishops of London and Lincoln have arrived."

The King smiled. "You know, Richmond, Ussher told me he would attend me once he had finished God's work. It amused me - I can do business with that man."

He continued on to his cabinet room; the inner sanctum.

On the way he glanced up at the magnificent portrait of the Holy Roman Emperor and felt instantly inadequate, which infuriated him. The Emperor's kingdom had no such Parliament and he was not questioned by his subjects in any manner. The King knew his realms had different customs, but he was angry at the demands made upon him following all of the concessions he had granted so far. He came to the same conclusion as he always did - the mob and a few vipers in Parliament were attacking him personally through Strafford and he would not stomach it. They were a small proportion of rotten traitors, spreading contamination to the rest of the populace.

He entered the cabinet room on his own, wishing for time to himself. As he sat in his chair, he breathed a sigh of relief at his solitude. His writing desk was in front of him and he unlocked the lacquered doors, revealing many drawers, slowly opening one of them and taking Strafford's latest letter. The cabinet was as furtive, intricate and layered as his own character.

Moving the gems and medals to one side of his desk, he laid it out and read it to himself in a whisper.

"To set Your Majesty's conscience at liberty, I do most humbly beseech your Majesty for prevention of evils, which may happen by your refusal to pass this bill ... Sir my consent shall more acquit you herein to God than all the world can do, besides, to a willing man there is no injury done."

King Charles shivered, suddenly naked, as though Charles Stuart, the man, had now come to the fore, leaving his role and the trappings of it to one side. He hung his head, resting his delicate moustached lip gently on his pale fist, deep in thought.

Could he sacrifice Strafford as the man himself advised? He was not particularly close to him it was true, but he was a brilliant minister and loyal servant and there was principle at stake. He could never as a decent Christian, let alone King, break the promise he had made to protect Strafford's life, honour and fortune, that had been delivered to the noble during the trial by Holland's man, whose name escaped him now. Also it would expose a gaping weakness in the royal ranks if Parliament managed to cajole him into signing the death warrant of someone he supported and who had successfully directed much of the royal policy.

He remembered his last minister and friend, who Parliament attacked over twelve years ago. Back then he had simply dissolved Parliament to stop them debating the Duke of Buckingham's impeachment, but now he had granted that power away, so Parliament could not be disposed of without their own consent. He realised the trap Pym had cunningly guided him into.

The King let out a muffled growl of frustration and anger.

The longer he sat thinking, the more tiredness caught up with him. He had not slept again last night - it seemed like every avenue he could take was blocked by another problem, so that he was powerless.

Since Buckingham had escaped Parliament, eventually

being assassinated by a madman, he had never allowed himself to be close to anyone but the Queen, but he also became oversensitive about his ministers being targeted. Indeed anyone that he held dear became off limits to any criticism whatsoever, which made him appear even more haughty and high handed than he was by nature. Henry would never have suffered this if he had survived and became King. His brother was loved by all and he called out his name, softly and respectfully, asking what he would have him do. The sibling would have squeezed them with a grip of iron, yet in contrast, here he was at forty years old, fighting desperately for survival. Weakness - he hated the word; his enemies probed for it and he struggled to prove that it was not a deficiency within him. Nobody, save his mother during her short life, had encouraged him and given him confidence until his father's minister, Buckingham, took him under his wing, and now his wife filled all their shoes. Even the old King had jibed that his youngest son would lose his crown in the end. He stood up, impatiently casting off his father's words and left the room, slamming the panelled door closed. He would never let himself lose his throne - his life would go first, that he vowed.

"Send word to the bishops that I am on my way," he ordered Nicholas.

As the man made his way down the corridor, the King followed, eventually reaching the Great Hall via a series of smaller rooms.

The archbishop and bishops bowed and the King sat at the head of the long table, while the clerics took their places at his invitation. The fire crackled like the sound of muskets going off, reminding him that this could become reality if the situation in the capital could not be resolved. Realising he had brought Strafford's letter, he placed it in front of him. The flames within the huge, stone fireplace that was crowned with two pointed spires at either side, cast warmth into his cold body.

"My lord bishops, I called you for advice and spiritual guidance. I bear a heavy burden, called upon by a throng of people to execute a loyal minister whom I promised to safeguard. He is innocent and to shed his blood would be murder. Yet I am mindful of my coronation and the oath I made to the Lord to protect my people. The mood outside threatens public safety. You see, my lords, how my duty, private feelings, conscience and the good of my family pull me in all directions?"

The clerics provided an air of serene tranquillity. Certainly Ussher's features gave the impression he was about to tell some humorous story; his small chin perched in between the large rosy cheeks accentuated the image. King Charles observed the perfectly arched eyebrows, with white hair curling out from under his black cap in rebellion.

"If you may permit me to say so, Your Majesty, I think this issue is black and white. You must follow your conscience," Ussher told him in melodious Irish tones, as he sat in his flowing white robe with long sleeves, and black clerical scarf, which hung around his neck and trailed down to his feet. A ruff separated his head from his body. Was Ussher making a joke when he said black and white, dressed as he was? The King frustrated himself by even thinking about it for that split second, so fragmented was his mind at this time.

"My conscience is not to sign," the King declared abruptly.

"Then do not sign, sir, refuse. Those people must realise they cannot bully you, for you are their anointed King," Ussher followed up.

William Juxon, the Bishop of London, added his level headed advice. The King was more than comfortable with this man too; for he had already held a number of important posts in his government; First Lord of the Admiralty and Lord High Treasurer, bringing the roles an unusually honest and dedicated incumbent.

"Your Majesty, I am responsible for this city's religious needs and should you follow your innermost desires and stand firm, you will do justice to those who fear the brutality of the mob outside, who are driven by ignorance. They are not evil, but have simply lost their way. Your resolve can put them back on course."

Inside, the monarch thought realistically whether the tempers he had heard of would dissolve. He was not so sure - some of his people were not thinking straight at the moment and were as unpredictable as the tides. He was worried by them.

"I have heard it bandied about Parliament that they will impeach the Queen and put her on trial if I refuse to let them have Lord Strafford," the King said with disgust, unable until now to even countenance the rumour with discussion.

"I say sign the attainder, Your Majesty. As a monarch you have two consciences, one public and one private. Sometimes in your role as God's anointed, you will have to commit acts you abhor, to ensure your people are safe," the Bishop of Lincoln asserted.

For once, the monarch took the man seriously. Ever since he had spoken out against the King's youthful travels to Spain to woo the Infanta, he had blotted his copybook and once he was crowned, King Charles had removed him from his office of Lord Chancellor, before the royal eventually had him cast into jail for several years after his continued course against the religious policy. Last year the House of Lords had forced the King to release him and the man had evidently learned some tact.

"Private and public conscience?" the sovereign pondered.

"Yes, sir, while you may personally hate what they demand of you, the public conscience should allow you to acquiesce on the grounds you are protecting your people from further riots. God will surely understand your actions."

The King went to speak, but hung back, sensing his stutter coming on. He thought his sentence through slowly, going through each difficult syllable.

"This morning the Privy Council urged m-me to sign the w-warrant. If only people realised how much more difficult my position is. In fact, does nobody spare a thought for the innocent man awaiting his f-fate?"

The King stood up. This meeting had been very useful, but he wanted to ponder the conscience argument Lincoln had used, for that would definitely mean Strafford's end and he felt his private conscience would never survive it. He quickly resolved - as he could well do when he put his mind to it - to see his wife right away.

"My lords, pray wait on me longer, for I may need your counsel again," he requested as the meeting ended.

This time he headed towards the Queen's apartments and passing a window, he took in the colourful array of this vast, sprawling palace, which had started life as Cardinal Wolsey's residence. It had timber framed buildings, red brick ones; part was of another lighter colour and then the new banqueting house of grey stone. Eventually approaching the Queen's rooms, he was met by several Catholics who he found rushing along like mice. There was an air of panic and their faces were full of fear, which worked the opposite with him and firmed his resolve. Then he noticed her Lord Chamberlain waiting outside. The man gave a full bow as he passed by.

He entered the Queen's bedroom to discover her huddled with a confessor. Her eyes were red and the two of them were whispering with a degree of despair.

"Your Majesty," they said, bowing, clearly taken aback at his sudden presence.

King Charles waved his hand for the confessor to leave them and no sooner had this happened than the Queen ran to him, clinging to him piteously. She looked up at him, her rounded features tapering to a smooth, delicate chin. She always asserted passionately that she lived only for him, and her lips quivered, struggling to contain her volatile emotions. He looked down on her beauty, never diminished through eight pregnancies so far, though only five had survived.

"Charles, we must leave this place," she sobbed, fresh tears streaming down her face.

He rested his hand on her head, aware now of just how strongly he was coping in comparison, at least outwardly. He held tightly onto the wooden post of the bed for stability, covering some of the carvings as he did so.

"Sweetheart, pull yourself together, I beg you," he urged as he took hold of her white hands, as delicate as that rare porcelain he had seen from China.

She put her head to his slim chest, hanging tightly onto him.

His wife was always the resilient one and the role reversal touched him to see her so broken. Yet strangely, it imbued him with more strength and determination to protect her and his children.

Inside, the decision over Strafford's fate rang around his head, pounding to escape. He steadied himself against the bedpost again as a dizzy sensation overcame him.

"Why do you not listen? We must go to France," she stressed, looking up at him with those big dark eyes, wiping her tears away. She waited eagerly for his response and the King struggled to catch up with the issue she had loaded onto him.

"France? Such a thing is unthinkable. We must face this, not run away, and all talk of that must cease."

She stared in disbelief, looking as upset at his chiding as she was at the answer. She screamed as she flung her rosary beads and ran to the door, yanking it open and calling for her chamberlain.

As the man entered, she commanded him imperiously, "Make my coach ready, I am leaving for France."

The King stood motionless, casting a disapproving expression at her - he was as unmoved as one of those carved marble pillars which held up the dinning room. He would continue to uphold the monarchy in the same way.

The chamberlain looked at the monarch, before addressing his mistress, "Your Majesty, I beg you to reconsider."

King Charles saw the Queen take hold of her head in both hands. He felt his stomach churn, knowing just how impulsive her emotions could be, and how much they affected her wellbeing. The passion clearly came from her mother's Italian Medici side of the family.

"Sweetheart, you must stop this - your health," he warned tenderly, now that he had made his displeasure known.

Her exhibition in front of a servant saddened him and he remembered how he had forcefully dragged her back from the broken window she was shouting out of, after one of the first arguments of their new marriage.

"Get my coach ready immediately," the Queen ordered again, this time fists clenched, face flushed and eyes wide.

The chamberlain dropped to his knees before her, looking equally as desperate, in a contest of mammoth proportion.

"Madam, I do not wish to disobey you, but I must advise you to reconsider. There are reasons not to go."

"Reasons? What could be more important than our safety? The people of this country have attacked the King to such an extent that they will not stop at Strafford's death, it will be me or our whole family afterwards," she yelled desperately. The Chamberlain remained tellingly silent.

"Well, what is your important reason? Are you not even going to grace me with a reply?" she probed further, composing herself somewhat. The King noted the chamberlain's hesitation and frowned inquisitively at him.

"Sir Henry Jermyn has already fled to France," the Queen's servant explained carefully.

"And he has the good sense I try to impart to you both," she snapped, ever adept at proving herself right.

"What of Jermyn?" the monarch explored.

"There are rumours, Your Majesty, vile and degraded tales from the basest people of this kingdom."

The King eyed the chamberlain warily, curiosity demanding to know more, but at the same time, hesitating at what he would unearth next, to add to the catalogue of hurtful lies.

"What of them?" the Queen demanded, as she folded her arms.

"Well, vicious rumour speaks of the Queen and Sir Henry being very close. Fleeing to France would indulge a scandal, no matter how vile and untrue it is," the man said as he braced himself.

"What rubbish. These rogues do hate me so, what have I done to them? I am Catholic, is that such a crime as to allow any slander of me to stick? Now get out, how dare you mouth such rot in front of His Majesty?" the Queen wailed.

She was standing near the four-poster bed. As she lost control again, she made a swipe at the velvet hangings, the gold embroidery that decorated it flashing as it spun around to reveal the satin lining. The tremor travelled up the hangings, and caused one of the plumes of ostrich feathers above to sway. He looked at the Queen, thinking of the nocturnal meetings she conducted in the dark corridors of the palace with Members of Parliament, in a bid to get them on their side. This sort of thing was bound to spark spurious gossip.

"I forbid you to abandon this palace," the King commanded firmly, leaving her in no doubt.

"Leave my carriage, I will stay with my husband," she hastily instructed the chamberlain, who had sheltered in the corridor, watching through the open door.

"Damn these people," the monarch said as he thrust his fist down onto her table, now that they were alone once more.

He felt the Queen's arms encircle his waist. She was hot from her outbursts, but now seemed anxious to make sure he remained calm, after working him up into the passion in the first place. She poured some wine and handed a goblet to him, creating the desired effect. He caressed its stem, focussing on the blue and white Delftware, decorated with cherubs and ribbons. Part of the gold stem showed one plump angel in the clouds blowing air from his mouth, symbolising the wind, and a small ship was being cast around in this turmoil. His father's constant advice in kingship came to his mind once more. Despite disagreeing with the man's slovenly behaviour, he had given some good advice that had formed his own rigid belief that he was appointed by God.

"They will say anything to discredit me; do you not understand my feelings? There are thousands of people wishing me dead," she explained, interrupting his concerns, with fresh upset.

Without replying, he began to focus on the death warrant.

"The Privy Council say I should sign, the bishops agree, the crowds out there demand it, both Houses of Parliament sanction it and even my Lord Strafford tells me to proceed," he summed up remorsefully, knowing it was one of those times when the decision was already made for him.

"This would never happen in France. The people here are so full of wickedness and hatred. They are beyond salvation," she said bitterly, as though as a Catholic, she was spiritually above them.

"I am going to have to sign, am I not?" the King asked, pouring his innermost feelings out.

She hugged him and he felt tears roll down his cheeks. He would have to betray his own conscience and intuition to save his country, people and family, castigated no matter what he did.

"Strafford will die and my self respect and conscience may as well perish with him," he said, despairing about the path laid out before him.

They stood together in the middle of the bedroom; it had turned into a rich, lavish prison cell for them over the past few days. He placed his hand over his mouth, raising his gaze to the ceiling. Weakness, his father's words taunted him once more, but this time he could not ignore them.

"May God forgive me," he humbly begged with complete devastation, "My Lord Strafford's condition will soon be better than mine."

"The fatal stroke which severed the wisest head in England from the shoulders of the Earl of Strafford, whose crimes coming under the cognizance of no human law, a new one was made."

John Evelyn, writing about Strafford's execution
MAY 1641

"The oppressing Earl of Strafford ... the twelfth of this month ... was beheaded on Tower Hill of London, as he well deserved."

The Earl of Cork writing in his diary
MAY 1641

Chapter 25

Now free, and his personal conversation with Digby over, he breathed a sigh of relief as he stepped gingerly into his house. He hesitated, wondering what to do, or say, before Anne filled his whole mind and he burst into a dash, through the long hall. He slid on the polished wood floor, grabbing one of the carved lions that looked on proudly from two mounts that provided an entranceway to the stairs. He ran up the steps, twisting around the square route of the staircase, past the large window.

Bursting through the bedroom door, he stopped abruptly, seeing Anne awake and splashing her face with water. She turned sharply.

"Charles," she shrieked, running into his arms.

He took tight hold of her, kisses pouring forth, relieved that he could embrace her once more, and that she was still here. His broad shoulder housed her head, her fingers pressing into his back, and there they remained locked together for some time, Charles stroking her silky hair.

"What did he do to you? Why were you arrested?"

She felt his face and body as though she believed he was

part of her imagination, hands resting on his rough cheeks with fingers spread apart like stars. Then she eased his doublet off. The soft sensations seemed to instil life into him by every touch with a magic that only the fairer sex could generate.

Every breath she took seemed to replace her worry with relief, passion and happiness.

"Did he come back here?" Charles demanded.

"No, thank the Lord. We locked the door and never ventured out. What was it all about, Charles?"

"Digby wanted me to do some errand for him. I have agreed now so that it keeps the peace. Cotton, the sly little shit, had me arrested until I agreed to this duty. Apparently I have to return to Newcastle, near where I was in the Bishops War, to sound out the officers and what they feel about the King. I am so suspicious about this though, for there seems more to it. And when I go, you and Louise will come with me, for I will not leave you here."

He wanted to share his thoughts about the shock of the pregnancy, and he winced as she took his hand to lead him to the bed, agitating a wound from his pounding. Anne grimaced at his pain, while they sat down together, his long legs extending out from the bed, and she began lifting the dirty, stained shirt, wishing to strip away the memory of it all.

"Will it be dangerous?" she asked, stroking his arm.

He had only one answer. "Well, I just need to gather information and give it to Digby. I am loath to do it, for I made a vow not to get involved in any scheme again, but

I am stuck."

"For our new addition, eh, is that why you made that promise?"

Charles agreed, feeling tears come to his eyes, not out of anger at Cotton or Digby, but for pride in Anne and their child she carried and he told her so, simply and plainly, the bare truth making the words more poignant than ever.

"I love you, Charles," she said as she looked up at him with nothing to adorn her but a nightdress, hair hanging loose about her. It was a tantalising sight.

"Even my shock at the pregnancy?" he whispered.

"I should have told you sooner. We are a pair, not individuals. I know how much you hate that Cotton, yet our baby and I are still your prime thought, not revenge."

She gripped him lovingly. He bore the pain of his ribs because the closeness was worth it.

"I could not sleep without you last night. I was frantic until Lou managed to calm me down."

He stroked her cheek and then looked at her stomach.

Anne said nothing and flattened her plain nightdress against her body. As he ran his hand over the curve that encompassed the very miracle of life, a shiver went through him. He smiled at her, trying to restrain his emotion, while goose bumps spread up his arms, and Anne beamed with pure happiness. He felt less burdened, nimbler and more awake.

"Who is this Cotton?" she asked quickly.

"Well I was in as much ignorance as you until yesterday. He is the Scot who I cut down up north, the one who owned the medal I wear."

"Well maybe he will calm down now he has got you back," Anne guessed as she assessed his wounds. At this, the second of her characteristically persistent attempts, he allowed her to tend his wounds, knowing she would not rest until she had done so.

Charles shook his head. "I cannot help feeling he is disturbed over his childhood. It is a vendetta. He will not stop, but I will not let him near us."

"Poor man, he is worth only pity, because he does not have what we do," she said as she went to fetch a towel.

While he stretched, he saw some old grey blankets at the foot of the bed and he froze, the lump of twisted and ruffled fabric standing out to him like the moon on a black sky.

As though being in a nightmare, he snatched his arm away from the object.

He wiped his face frantically with his hands.

The vision was of his stillborn daughter lying at the bottom of the bed, looking the same deathly, pale colour. This pile of cloth made him think of her, for she did not look human in her wrappings - cold, dark shadows around her eyes, arms and legs stick thin and under developed, causing her to look out of all proportion.

The sight petrified him and his heart pumped furiously as he leaped out of bed, smoothing the textile out quickly and erratically before Anne came back. Walking to the table opposite, he washed himself from a pewter bowl, the feeling of the water on his face keeping him sane. Life slowly drained back to his body, especially as he silently embraced a returning Anne. After finishing tending to his cuts, she took her nightdress off to change.

"Ah, that sight is well worth a beating," he whispered as he came up behind her smooth, curvaceous rear.

She smiled at him and allowed herself to be enclosed by his wandering hands and they kissed passionately.

"We are going to have to hold these thoughts for tonight, for I need to send Lou to market for some foodstuff. I know how hungry you get after any escapade in bed and if we have nothing cooked to satisfy you in that respect as well, then you will just have one of your grumpy moods," she told him with a final, quick kiss on the lips.

She rubbed some ointment onto her face and told him some clothes were laid out for him on the wooden chest.

"I have told you, you do not need apricot cream or orange flower water to improve your features, for they are perfect already."

He watched her pull her bodice over her petticoat and call for Louise.

"I will do it today," he announced, wishing to do even the smallest of acts for the person who was his world.

She stepped over to him, humoured at his offer. "I cannot wait to see you try."

He failed in his attempt, but redeemed himself after following the instructions she called out, quite pleased with the way he had tied up the back in the end. When she turned, he looked at her breasts, framed by her bodice, the sight of which added to his mounting ardour. The garment itself ended above Anne's waist.

As she pulled her skirt on, tucking it under her bodice, he put a shirt on himself and tied the strings of the collar. Then he sat eagerly watching while she put her leg on the chair, pulling the silk stockings right and making sure her knitted garter was level. She noticed him and playfully mocked the way he was tormenting himself. He was lost in passionate thoughts so much, that he did not realise that she was adjusting the stay which travelled down the middle of the bodice, resting - or should it be bearing down - just above her intimate area.

He turned, giving her some privacy and went to get his medal, leaving her to manoeuvre the vicious whalebone.

After a few minutes he returned. "Strafford is being executed today too, Anne, so all that worry about the political situation and bringing up our child in it will soon be over. Once he is gone, the King and Parliament can patch things up and we will all be back to normality."

"I hope you are right, for I want everything to be wonderful for us."

He decided to take a coach to the Tower, where Strafford was facing his end. Secretly he wanted to see whether he could meet anyone from court, to quiz them discreetly about this Army Plot, but it would also be good to actually make sure Strafford did die after all these months of tension. Most people had made their way there already, judging by how empty the streets were below.

"I am off to the Tower to see Strafford's execution, do you want to come and we can see those lions too, sweetheart? Be with me today, let Lou do the work herself," he asked.

After she hastily agreed, they went outside into the deserted street, finding a hackney carriage with ease. The iron wheels made such a noise as they clattered towards them and Charles groaned as the din echoed thorough his busy head.

"The Tower, coachman," he shouted as they got inside.

"Surely someone can come up with a more comfortable design. Straps holding this box to the frame of the wheels just make me feel like I am on the high seas," he complained.

Passing through The Strand, they saw the stripy Maypole, well over one hundred feet high, and like a ship's mast, giving the impression that the rest of the vessel lay below the cobbles.

A garland still adorned the top, like a crown of thorns, and the other woman in the carriage smiled, obviously recalling good memories of May Day. Indeed, the whole city had burst with excitement; dancing, drumming, singing and loving with the post being the centre of all celebrations.

It was right next to the main hackney rank outside Somerset House, one of the giant mansions that overlooked the Thames. This housed the famous Catholic chapel, built for the Queen, but a huge contingent found it loathsome to have such a place within the centre of London, and were offended by it. As they passed, three or four stood outside to shout off in protest at the papist monument that lay like a den of vipers within their midst.

"I hear they took charge of our church again?" Anne said with frustration, being reminded of religion.

"Who told you that?"

"Jane, wife of John Trumble. She said a fellow from that Society of Friends in Truth was giving his own special sermon once more."

"Aye, if you can call it that. I am told they just stay quiet and tell you to wait patiently for God to come to you and once he has, you can go home," he recalled mockingly.

"Why are some people starting to worship that way all of a sudden? The Book of Common Prayer is what they need," Anne stated.

"They refuse to take their hats off and stay covered in churches or other places. One of them got a right beating from a few people for not uncovering when the royal coach passed by last week," Charles added.

They progressed into Fleet Street and then Ludgate Hill, approaching Saint Paul's Cathedral, which lay nestled within the vast array of tiny houses, shadowing them with its immense size. But Saint Paul's was decaying fast, like the old man it was - four hundred years - after living through the dissolution of the monasteries, being robbed of its glory by King Henry the Eighth, even having shops and stalls trading in the graveyard and inside too. The final humiliation came nearly eighty years ago when God intervened, sending a lightning bolt to execute the spire. Yet for all this, the structure struggled stubbornly on, a focal point of London taken for granted.

Another hackney approached and Charles's stare was diverted from the mighty building to examine how close it was to get past the other carriage. Both drivers seemed to be playing a game with each other, seeing who would give way first. The street was only about fourteen feet wide and Charles shook his head as he heard their driver shout.

"You poxy fool, stand down and let me past."

The other coachman began his counter attack.

Charles leaned out of the window, unable to take any more of it. "Driver, for goodness sake, let him past. My wife is pregnant and such arguments are the least of our worries."

As he sat back down, nothing changed. He grew more annoyed at being ignored, until the other coach finally started to squeeze past, and they carried on their way again. The driver seemed to have taken offence, because the carriage swayed and jerked all over as it was driven round corners without any hint of finesse, which caused the other passenger to give Charles filthy looks of blame. Eventually they came into Thames Street and the river was visible, as busy as any street in the capital. The majority of crafts were ferries and ones involved in transporting goods, while a sturdy English frigate and a pear shaped Dutch fluyt looked over the small ships like parents.

"The other morning, I saw the women up at dawn to get those cloths they lay outside the night before. They wiped the dew all over their faces. Do you think that works?" Charles asked, the masts reminding him of the maypole and the day's traditions again.

"I have not done that for three years. It used to be so much fun."

"Ah well, you have no need of the May dew," Charles said with a wink.

She nudged him playfully and then took his hand, curling her fingers through his, in the same way as their marriage vows entwined them. They had to pass through the poor East End of the city to get to the Tower and Anne was fixated on the scenery.

As they passed by some shops, the apprentices shouted out about their master's wares within. Then they caught sight of a ragged man blowing a horn, wandering along the street.

"Whatever's wrong with him?" Charles pointed.

"He's a recovered lunatic. See the brass badge on his doublet? That tells you who he is. He's probably collecting money for the asylum," Anne said, bragging at her city knowledge, having lived here for years.

Renewed thoughts of the country's ills sent him into a trance, mulling over that and Sir Arthur Cotton. He knew he had to come to the Tower to make doubly sure that Strafford died - as long as he did, then he was convinced the turmoil would be buried with the man, and the effects of Cotton's threats would be eliminated. They came to the crossroads with Fish Hill Street and next to them, London Bridge stood out like a monument in its own right. The houses and shops built on either side created a tunnel of sorts across it.

Anne grimaced as she looked up. "In the name of God."

"You must have known about them, sweetheart, seeing as you are so knowledgeable about this place?" Charles teased, with a nod of his head.

She agreed, eyes still closed. "Yes, but I still get sickened to see the rotted heads of executed traitors."

Charles's eyes went back to the view on top of London Bridge, intrigued by the heads that were skewered on spikes, which seemed to be looking down on the city. It was a shame this grisly scene did not scare the protesters from their actions lately, he thought.

Finally coming to their destination, they left the coach and walked up to the huge white walls of the Tower of London. He presumed Cotton would be somewhere in the vicinity and also wondered who else he would see.

"You seem nervous?" she asked.

Charles shook his head. He noticed a leaflet pasted to the wall and upon further investigation found it displayed the names of the members of the House of Commons who voted to save Strafford. He scanned the list warily, anxious to know the identities of these people. She shook her arm, which he had hold of, thus getting his attention. She could be relentless when she wanted to be, he thought.

"This is important, I should know who stood in the way of peace," he explained, "And I am wondering if Cotton is here."

She could always get his thoughts out of him. A witch finder would have been a good profession for her, extracting confessions with this sort of resolve of purpose. He knew that it was their mutual love that was the secret key she held to his inner self.

"I will box his ears if he dares come near you," she threatened, her small body rigid with anger.

He smiled appreciatively as he eyed up her five foot four, slim frame. Sometimes she had as much fire in her as a man and this attracted him. She was not merely a little lady who would do her husband's bidding all the time. Anne seemed to relish his amusement and he observed the warm smile that lit up her pretty face.

While the Tower of London had held national enemies and weak traitors, it had also kept many a proud man in its years. Sir Walter Raleigh for example, whose adventures Charles's father used to tell him about as a boy.

Strolling arm in arm inside the gatehouse, they were directed to the menagerie where the lions lay, having just been fed. The great structure itself drew Charles's interest as he moved nearer each time to the centre it all, passing through another gatehouse, or layer of wall. Now amidst the defensive constructions, he spotted a timber framed, second floor building; the small panes of glass that made up the windows twinkled as it looked down upon him. It gave a gentler air to this military base, only possible if you could assess the whole sprawling area, rather than concentrating on the bloody history alone. Charles could sum up a place, person or situation in detail with his keen eye and curious mind, and the couple moved on towards the cell holding the lions.

One animal lay watching them intently, fair hair darkening to gold and then onto dark brown, forming a warm collar that framed the suspicious and regal face. Anne reluctantly walked towards them, but would not go as near as Charles.

"That one over there is called Crowley."

Anne raised her eyebrows.

"I surprise you with my knowledge, eh? Edward my tailor was telling me about them."

When one of them rose sharply to its feet, creating ideas

of just how speedy they were, she stepped back, bumping into one of the yeoman who was on guard.

"There are many of you around," he noted.

The yeoman answered in a gruff tone, "There be lots of trouble around too, with Strafford being 'ere and all. We have many men pounding the gates down, trying to get their own justice on him. He must be protected by the devil, for he shows no sign of being affected when I see him."

"So Strafford is meant to have told the King to attack Parliament?" Anne confirmed, as though realising she was about to see his execution without fully understanding.

"Not women's business, madam," the yeoman stated, his round face reaching the same shade as his scarlet uniform that was emblazoned with the King's initials.

"In short, he tried to overrun the country to impose the King's will," Charles added, in spite of the yeoman's words.

He looked at Anne and his stomach flipped over again with a strange sensation. For a few minutes he had actually forgotten she was pregnant and the realisation and excitement returned.

"Let's see the elephants that drink wine," Anne said, leading him through another archway, where one of them stood lethargically. Charles shouted out after her, joking that the trunk was as long as the list of crimes Strafford had committed.

Chapter 26

He sat in the middle of the plain, grey room, a coldness pervading the atmosphere, despite the fire that burned in the large fireplace. Everything was stone, the walls, arched door, window frames, the ceiling. Some said his own heart was as inhuman and hard as the cell. Gothic arches seemed to crown every opening, while the plain floorboards emitted a faint smell that can only be described as 'history'. This barren prison may have little furniture or beauty, but it possessed an identity of its own, created not only from its mediaeval beginnings, but from the dignified carvings etched into it. He had read some, taking heart from the religious words, the unfailing courage and belief in the Almighty. Only yesterday, at sunrise - it was irritating that only now in the midst of his downfall, when he could no longer sleep, did he find the beauty the world had to offer - he noticed the cross shaped slit in the wall light up as the rays passed over it, creating a glowing symbol of God's love.

"What is the time?" Strafford asked one of the chaplains with him; the question as simple as his now unpretentious outlook on life.

"It is nearly at eleven of the clock, my lord."

"Please, I will soon be the same status as any man, so forego the ceremonies and call me Thomas, the name I was christened into God's church with."

He saw the chaplain's face drop. Up until this point he was bearing up well and suddenly at the curate's speechless expression of sadness, he felt a pang of pain at leaving his own wife and children.

"Pray God that my family are cared for; remind the King of that," Strafford recapped as he touched the man's arm.

He walked to the window, staring out of it in silence and composing himself once more. For what seemed like weeks, he had stood here and heard the banging, as the scaffold he was to die on was constructed; the final insult of all that had been heaped upon him so far, though it had strangely helped him come to terms with the end.

But then he felt tears well up in his eyes.

He mulled over the power he had once held and his current helpless position. Then came thoughts about the King, and he hoped his own end would settle the kingdom to peace once more. Finally he pondered about God, his creator and he looked at the clear sky, and despite his strength and imperviousness to the trial, he now felt inferior and awestruck at the true trial he would have when he reached heaven. He knew God would judge on the truth, unlike his enemies here, who twist and mould information to suit themselves.

"Put your coat on, Thomas," the chaplain said, breaking his spiritual connection and hesitating with the informal address.

As he grappled with his cloak, he addressed the man. "Pray with me," he requested, whereas at one time he would have ordered.

The three men lifted their heads and Strafford extended his hands, as though reaching out for support and strength from heaven. He breathed deeply and they remained silent for a few minutes. He tried desperately to clear his mind of mortal things, thought of God, of peace, of the beauty of heaven.

"I regret nothing in my life. I do not fear my end, for I have laid the foundations for the King to conquer these few disaffected men in Parliament. I am confident that after my death, the backlash will awake all those people who have been led like sheep by the few. Yet I forgive them for their actions in my final hour."

Strafford seemed to regain the confidence that had always abounded in him, but assurance no longer in himself, but that he could sense unseen beings here to support his ascent from earth.

He was calmer, more serene, and his heartbeat had slowed. A knock echoed out from the door, but in comparison, the chaplains both seemed unnerved as the huge oak portal opened without a delay. Sir William Balfour the Lieutenant of the Tower entered and raised his hat briefly in greeting, a chilly draught rushing in with him, or was it Balfour's feelings for his prisoner?

"Everything is ready, sir. I strongly advise you to take a coach to the scaffold, for the crowds are thumping at the Tower gates, ravenous to be at you. There are near two hundred thousand gathered and I cannot vouch for your safety if you go on foot up Tower Hill," Balfour informed him bluntly.

Strafford smiled. He had accustomed himself to death but he found Balfour's bluntness amusing; it was the same characteristic which had often got him into scrapes during his own political career. Certainty of death added a superior perspective to everything, and he felt no worry, or indeed, any interest in the comment about his safety from the crowd.

"No, I dare look death in the face and I hope the people too. I care not how I die, whether by the hand of the executioner or by the madness and fury of the people. If that may give them better content, it is all one to me," Strafford announced.

He felt he needed to get away from this room immediately.

The chaplains' fidgeting and anxiety was clear and Balfour was speechless, although not out of any love for him, and it was all beginning to affect his concentration again. Strafford walked over to his brothers, happy to see them arrive at last. Then he bowed his head to Archbishop Ussher, ignoring the Constable of the Tower, Lord Newport, who had probably only come along out of morbid curiosity. Observing John Rushworth scribbling on some paper, he knew that Pym's henchman was here to try and capture any information or words that could be used against him.

"Well, gentlemen, shall we be away?" he prompted, as though going out for a stroll in the park.

He let his servants lead the way, walking behind and alongside his friends. Glancing back, he saw Newport and some soldiers follow at the rear. As they travelled, they neared the cell of the Archbishop of Canterbury, a close friend he had made while they had both served in the King's government.

Strafford cast his eyes to the window and saw the top of the primate's head, just high enough to peer over the opening and he instantly veered off to Laud's cell, kneeling down before him.

"Your prayers and your blessing," he asked of the primate, not being able to utter anything more.

Strafford watched as Laud extended his hands through the window, seeing how they shook. He looked to the floor, but heard some noise at that moment. The Archbishop had apparently fainted or fallen back according to his brother who whispered to him.

"Farewell, my lord and God protect your innocence," Strafford called out as he continued his progress.

The dignity and way a man conducted himself in his final hour was his last great epitaph, and a strange form of pride filled Strafford as he walked on, glancing down at his clothes, black as a night sky and broken by the rays of a star; the silver emblem of the Order of the Garter on his cloak. When Laud's turn came for death, he vowed to return in spiritual form for assistance.

He stepped outside his infamous prison and saw the intense crowd and stopped for a second or two. He was sure he would never get through now he had seen the sheer numbers. Sweat beads formed, showing how tested his meditations and preparation were right now, then the noise of those spectators around him ceased as quickly as he hoped his beheading would be. Faces stared at him, his very appearance causing a silence, and after a few seconds' delay, he forged onwards. A narrow pathway slowly opened up between the people, and he proceeded with clear cut direction, sharp enough even to carve open several hundred people like this. He entered the fray without further hesitation, determined to push on regardless, and then he removed his hat in politeness as he passed through the silent files of bodies. In the distance he heard continued chanting and shouts, but gradually, some expressions of those near him became warmer.

The atmosphere was positively tense, one of those knife-edged occasions in which nobody knew what would happen, the type he actually savoured. Then he saw a man salute him and he returned the gesture, appreciating the bravery, but deliberately not changing his direction or expression. Every now and then he simply bowed his head to the men on each side, maintaining his calm but solemn bearing as more people felt their hostility wane.

It soothed him to know that not all of the two hundred thousand gathered around the Tower of London hated him, as they stood lining the route up to Tower Hill, in the same way the curtain walls encircled the great White Tower.

Chapter 27

C harles and Anne had no sooner left the huge gatehouse than they saw a multitude of people who had congregated. They portrayed a wide variety of the city's populace - it was not only apprentices anymore. Charles put his arm around his wife's waist, resting his hand on the side of her stomach as though protecting the baby too.

The ripples of excitement, vocals and buzz of activity proved the traitor was on his way.

A group of spectators were murmuring to each other, grimly awaiting the fate of the man whose death they had demanded for so long. It was as though a fair had come to town, for some played games and sold wares, while food was passed around.

They all spoke to each other as if old friends, bringing their children along, telling them to see the evil 'Black Tom Strafford' get his just deserts. All were here for one common reason; to see the final demise of the man - but more so the detested regime he symbolised.

"Remember the twelfth of May, when England was saved from tyranny," one man shouted at the top of his voice.

This set the masses cheering.

Charles felt his throat dry, again unwillingly remembering Strafford's features. They walked over to a welcome but rickety shop, buying two cups of chocolate. The tankards were somewhat battered, but had to do. Anne frowned at hers, which had been scratched with, 'Priv of Parl.'

"Privileges of Parliament, I guess?"

"Aye, what all this fuss and distraction has been about," he confirmed.

Gulping his chocolate, they walked into the throng of spectators, joining some more wealthy looking people. Anne had caught sight of a game going on next to the pigpen.

"It's Aunt Sally," she observed.

"Who?" he said, taken aback.

She half smiled at him, continuing to watch two men throw balls at wooden figures of women in Elizabethan skirts, the cause of these celebrations taking the edge off her humour.

Charles, meanwhile, eyed the crowd warily, staggered by the amount of people here. Never in all his days in the Bishops War, with two whole armies facing each other, had he seen so many people concentrated together.

"You have played Aunt Sally, you must have done in that boring and sleepy village you grew up in?" she said, clearly trying to relax their minds somewhat. She adjusted her hold on his arm.

He paused for a few seconds thinking about what she had said. "Oh, James and I used to play that when we were young."

If he strained, he could see the small scaffold in the distance, with dark figures milling around it, literally a sea of heads in front of him, vying for a glimpse too. Men jockeyed for a place on top of stone slabs or rubbish, both of which had been piled up to hastily provide platforms. Special stands had even been constructed, hugging the base of the Tower and encircling the great building, acting like a wooden moat. They looked just like theatre boxes, here for the greatest performance of all. The Tower crowned this scene, sitting above historic events, as it had done since the time of William the Conqueror, its four turrets jutting into the London skyline. A coach drew up nearby. Sir Richard's grey hair fluttered like a flag in the breeze as he popped his head out.

"Berkeley, get in, otherwise we will miss the occasion."

They went carefully towards the coach, surprised at the offer.

"I am going to get close to the action; the Constable of the Tower is a cousin of mine," Sir Richard explained, before continuing, "Cotton said you would be grateful of the chance to see it close up as you had a brush with Strafford?"

"What?" Charles spluttered with an indignant laugh as he followed Anne inside, thankful she was now shielded from the mass of people, "I have never spoken to the man."

He sat pondering his enemy's motives, exercising an immense self control to stop himself punching the man in the face.

Then the coach stopped and they were escorted with difficulty, considering the packed lines of people, to the influential crowd on Tower Hill.

"Sir Richard does not realise what Cotton is like," Anne decided, as they waited for him.

"Nay," he said, anxious about what she would do following this statement.

She looked back at the colonel.

"You go on at me for losing my temper, so don't you go saying anything to him. If you get involved I will look weak," Charles warned, seeing her preparing to give the colonel a piece of her mind. The expression was unmistakeable.

Anne frowned at him.

"Oh, I will look like I cannot handle him myself and need a woman to do my fighting for me," he explained to her.

Charles pointed across the crowd, hoping his wife would lose interest in thoughts of Cotton. She was clearly not interested in the execution though, so he decided to forego any commentary. They were just in time, for a handful of people were making their way towards the scaffold. It was so quiet that he became aware of silly things he would normally dismiss from his hearing, like coughing, whispering, the noise of skirts swishing as women walked, and birds singing, all emphasising that life would go on after any death.

"I can see him," Charles gasped, feeling impelled to tell people.

"The devil himself, what does he look like?" Sir Richard asked with as much intrigue, straining for a view.

"He is a normal looking man," Anne observed with a look of surprise and disappointment, "I expected some evil and fearsome beast from what they say of him in the city. He looks like a simple *old* man."

He saw Strafford mount the steps to the scaffold, holding a hat and wearing black again, as he had done through the trial. He was speaking to the crowd now and Charles tilted his head, anxious to catch some words. As he did so, the peer's small, quite handsome face came to his mind again. The nose, petit chin, moustache and thin beard all as pointed and sharp as the man's supreme intelligence, wit and drive. And the eyes - dark as his hair used to be - able to penetrate any person, or so it seemed, when his gaze fell upon them. Sometimes people were under his spell in an instant, or were so scared of him that they hated him ever after.

Those eyes would have scanned that small letter which Charles had delivered. It had contained a promise to keep his life, fortune and honour intact; some promise, Charles reckoned, now thinking of the monarch's vow. Could the breaking of it cause civil war by a King now spoiling to get revenge, or would he continue as aimlessly as ever?

"I speak in the presence of Almighty God, before whom I stand, that there is not a displeasing thought that ariseth in me against any man. I thank God, I say truly, my conscience bears me witness, that in all the honour I had to serve His Majesty, I had not any intention in my heart but the joint and individual prosperity of the King and his people. I am not the first man that has suffered in this kind. It is a common portion that befalls men in this life, and righteous judgement shall be hereafter. Here we are subject to error and misjudging one another."

A few people jeered in derision of the words. One man even ran through them, encouraging protests and reminding them of the charges levelled against Strafford. Behind them from near the Tower came a wave of noise, the drone of thousands of people yelling, banging, and stamping their feet, getting louder, as though it would crash over them like the wave of a terrible storm. The uproar was so immense that it forced Anne to cuddle into him. Charles looked at one gentleman nearby who waved his fist erratically; it was as if he was possessed by evil and was totally fixated on the doomed peer. The distant figure continued the speech and Charles managed to hear some more.

"I wish that every man would lay his hand upon his heart and consider seriously whether the beginnings of the people's happiness should be written in letters of blood. I desire, Almighty God, that not one drop of my blood rise up in judgement against anyone. I desire heartily to be forgiven of every man, and so, my lords, farewell and also to all things of this world. God bless this kingdom and Jesus have mercy on my soul."

Charles watched, as if paralysed, while Strafford began talking to the people next to him. This man was to perish and England would return once more to the glorious old days.

He then averted his gaze to the ground as Strafford looked towards him. Charles was cold, and a shiver engulfed his body.

Thoughts of the good normality of life, which would surely return after this, were cast from his mind for a split second by a foreboding feeling.

* * *

Strafford examined the sheer volume of people, now thinking to sweep the whole crowd as best he could, wishing to observe as much as possible. He vaguely recognised one man, though he was not sure why, before losing sight of him and focussing on the relentless thoughts rushing through his mind. It put him off to see that some spectator boxes had even been built as close as a few feet away from him, their proximity into his private arena shocking him completely. One had even collapsed earlier, he had heard. He struggled on, with his inner peace and control of his mind and turned to his brothers, taking their hands one by one.

"Goodbye, William, tell my son to support his stepmother. Remind him of my last letter to him."

After speaking to everyone, he asked them to join him in a last prayer. He had focussed on his earthly thoughts long enough, and his full attention was to the Lord now. Along with his chaplain, they all prayed.

"O my God, I trust in thee. Let me not be ashamed, let not mine enemies triumph over me."

After a small pause, he continued.

"Turn thee unto me and have mercy upon me, for I am desolate and afflicted. Consider mine enemies, for they are many and they hate me with cruel hatred. Let integrity and uprightness preserve me, for I wait on thee."

Another brief, poignant silence followed.

"Redeem Israel, O God, out of all his troubles."

Strafford then kneeled down slowly and cast his head low in full prayer. He breathed deeply, fully and slowly, filling his thoughts with nothing but these final few minutes of devotion, cleansing his soul. Then he raised himself up for the last time, on seeing his other brother behind some men, and reached out to him, unable to depart without a last farewell.

"Brother, we must part. Remember me to my sister and my wife, and carry my blessing to my eldest son. Command him to be loyal to the King and our church and tell him to forgive my enemies and never to take up any employment in government."

George Wentworth nodded, closing his eyes in sorrow, unable to hold it back any longer.

"Carry my blessing also to my daughters Anne and Arabella and charge them to serve God and he will bless them. Not forgetting my little infant, that knows neither good nor evil and cannot speak for itself; God speak for it and bless it."

Strafford felt a coldness rise from the pit of his stomach.

His head felt dizzy and he knew he must hurry as his body untangled under the immense strain.

"I have nigh done, one stroke will make my wife husbandless, my dear children fatherless and my poor servants masterless and separate me from my brother and all my friends, but let God be to you and them all in that."

He removed his cloak, before unbuttoning his doublet. His heart pounded furiously as he put on a white woollen cap, hands trembling until he pressed it onto his head with firmness.

Impelled to speak again to allay the feelings of fear, and to ensure no such anxiety came across, Strafford added with a smile, "I do as cheerfully put off my doublet at this time as ever I did when I went to bed."

This was his final act in life and he was damned sure he would make it the noblest and greatest one, to be remembered for generations and make his children proud. In fact, in his hands he had the greatest glory of all; if he remained dignified, the shock of his death and realisation of his sacrifice would prevent further bloodshed, and reseal the bonds between King and Parliament. The executioner stepped forward and held a cloth out to him.

"Shall I fasten it over your eyes, sir?"

Strafford looked at him, the very question conjuring up determination. "Nay, for I will see it done."

He kneeled and prayed again, one of his chaplains lifting both hands up to the sky. Then Strafford was ready and he placed his head on the block. With his features now face down, so low they were out of sight, he began whispering a prayer, eyes wide with terror. The feeling of the wooden block on his neck scared him as he attempted to focus his energy once more, but it was no good at all. The end brought a strange sensation of helplessness, which froze his thoughts. The grain of the wood scaffolding of the floor seemed to jump out to him, before retreating back just as fast.

Over and over again it gave off this appearance, so fast that it began to make him feel faint.

He knew God was near to his body right now, waiting to receive his soul.

Those extraordinary eyes closed as tight as they could for the last time; waiting for the impact, praying it was swift and clean. His whispered words hissed out with the panic.

His head lay in the smooth curve of the large block of wood that had become his final pillow, as though he had merged with this dead part of Mother Nature.

Chapter 28

Strafford had now vanished from view as he laid his head down, as though proffering himself to his maker in the last act he would carry out on earth.

Charles tried to ignore the guilty sensation that came over him for wanting this man's death, as he observed the dark figure disappearing from view. As he stood, he wished for a moment that he had never come; Strafford seemed human, and was not a simple ogre anymore and this sobered him up to the full extent of today's event. It highlighted the mortality of man to a shocking degree.

One spectator cried with anger, "He still does not confess or pass regrets."

Charles watched the children present, who could not possibly appreciate the enormity of this death, while older ones cheered as loudly as their parents. Other adults had been carried along with the tide, as completely as these young ones, but now he wondered how far he had been conveyed too?

"That be the traitor there, my son. His head will soon roll," one man said as he pointed through the dense crowd, his finger shaking, as though casting his excitement and revenge out through the tip of it. The child seemed full of inquisitiveness and scorn.

Yet Charles remembered he had burned Strafford's reply about the escape plan - his own honour had indeed prevailed, and it salved some of his conscience.

"Strafford will get you if you misbehave," came a warning from one mother, to her misbehaving daughter, attempting to scare the child into better conduct.

Now Charles felt himself separate from the horde he had been fused with recently. The feelings of the people passed him by like a stream, his own outlook so changed. The communication through the spectators was amazing. Rumours and gossip spread that Archbishop Laud had watched Strafford from his own cell before collapsing out of guilt and fear of his own fate. Snippets of stories went around too, that Strafford had to be escorted into the crowd by two soldiers, as he had refused to leave the building.

"That popish coward Laud, he should be hung up with him," a man cried, "The accursed rogue would have sold us all to the Pope if he had not been found out too."

"Laud is our archbishop, Charles, he is not Catholic," Anne stated, as he silently put his arm around her.

He tried to catch sight of Strafford again, with bated breath and almost panic at losing sight of the momentous event.

"All the decorative icons, gold and paintings he put into the churches have brought this accusation that he is turning the Church of England back to Catholicism," he whispered in answer, realising that the display was practically over.

They both then concentrated on the scene, Anne with a horrified expression, as the axe rose slowly.

They could hear the distant drumbeat. The fast tune enhanced feelings within.

Sight of the long pointed axe rising slowly made a chilling sight. There was a few seconds of it hanging menacingly in the air, ramming home to Charles how dangerous politics was. Anne gripped him tighter and he could not stop himself imagining the impact, and anticipating it. The blow came down fast and Charles was jolted by the action as he observed, tensing at the final action. Everyone was quiet and nobody moved, until finally, the executioner stooped and held up the head by its hair.

That was it – Strafford was no more, though the crowd had one last chance to look at the late prisoner.

Shouts filled the warm air and got louder, forcing Anne to cover her ears.

The rejoicing spread through the ranks of people like a chorus of song and everyone chattered again, while some men made their way to the taverns to revel in the event. It was clear people saw this as their victory, saving the country. Bloodthirsty tales spread of the view from the front and many jostled for any sort of information. It seemed like everyone was in favour, but some near Charles still remained silent and forlorn, wary of the precedent this opened up, like a spectre hanging predatorily over the future.

Even though Charles had been exorcised of all bloodthirstiness, the execution still seemed a necessity to him, to curb the realm's fanaticism. He could not help but wonder whether other affluent people were worrying about their own safety, now that one of the most powerful peers of the realm had been wiped out as expertly as this. Men ran full speed to their horses, probably preparing to spread the news to the towns and villages.

"His head is off," a few repeatedly hooted.

It seemed like most of London had watched the scene - men and women could be seen in the distance on roofs or observing from upper storey windows and he overheard that one man had even paid a shilling for a tall crate to stand on.

Charles now felt a strange calmness, unwilling, or unable to talk. Inside he was tired, his heartbeat slowed and strangely enough, his armpits were wet.

Anne cuddled into him tightly, with her still eyes closed, upset at the sight. Strafford had faced his end courageously, much to the discomfort of his most vehement enemies in the crowd.

"God damn his soul," one shouted in an angry finale, "He has to be the devil's creature, for he showed no fear."

Anne screwed her face up. "Charles, they cheer so happily. Let us leave."

"They wish for peace and stability now like all of us," he explained, hastily acquiescing to her request. It was as though he had temporarily lost all sense of direction following the zenith of this political drama.

* * *

The ride home was a quiet, reflective affair, the execution seeming to be more than a culmination of national events; it stirred up every emotion within Charles. The death starkly highlighted how fragile life was, and once suppressed emotions about their stillborn girl began to rise, vulnerability over the way he had been cajoled into the mission for the King, the separation from practically all his blood family and friends and especially missing his mother.

Then eventually this turned to anger.

He needed Anne, the one who embodied his life, for he felt absolutely comfortable with her. He met her eyes and focussed on her tender lips, large, inviting eyes, and her delicate hand, the fingers casually resting on her cheek. The sight gave a positive account of the future, leading him away from past sadness, though not the family members themselves.

Then finally, the fact she was pregnant, carrying their second child, imbued him with pride, purpose, and hope.

The responsibility he had for them both spurred him on, determination galloping strongly within. In the long, drawn out journey, it felt he had explored his whole inner self, the wheel going full circle, before he returned to a fresh outlook.

Only now did he begin to notice details of other passengers.

Back home, he found a tatty, half crumpled letter lying on the formidable, oak table in the room they used for dining within. The writing was blotchy, but as flowing as the inlaid carvings in the chair he had just sat on, the correspondence having a rather pathetic air to it. He fussed over Anne as he eyed it. Rather than react terrifyingly to the small lumps missing out of the candles, signifying the presence of rats, or fall to ordering the house, she simply sat with him.

"I am tired from all that air and the journey."

"You will be, having to carry a little man around with you too," he told her as he pointed to her stomach.

"Him? How do you know?"

"Well your shape, of course. Like a half pear is a boy and that's you. Before I forget, I got some horse testicles and snails.

Culpepper says they are very good for pregnancies."

Anne screwed her face up. "You put so much stock in this Nicholas Culpepper. He is new to all of this, you know, and I do not think he will last long, especially with him catering for any commoner. He seems too false."

"He will go far, you'll see, for he knows his subject well and is not afraid of new things, or causing a stir with his views, even when they run counter to medical practice."

She shook her head, looking at him questioningly, letting out a chortle. "You seem to know a lot about pregnancies now too. Oh, if only you men could give birth, then you will see who the stronger sex is."

"Well if I could carry a child, I would go to Epsom and bathe in the waters. They say they have healing properties, but you will not listen to me, will you?" Charles commiserated.

"The three hour coach drive is terrible, it will shake me as though I were aboard ship in the worst of seas," she explained, excusing herself again.

Acknowledging her immovable resolve with a smile, he took the letter back to the study and breaking the seal, opened it up. Amongst the scrawl, he managed to analyse the badly written letter from Sir Richard. Crumpling the paper up at the instant he digested what it said, his face dropped and he slumped in his chair. He flung it as hard as he could and let out an almighty roar.

"The pompous bastard and that meddling little whoremonger."

He swiped a candlestick off the desk as he grabbed his cloak, snatched the paper back from the floor, before striding through the hall.

"Where are you going, my love, what is wrong? Charles."

"That old bugger has relieved me of my post," he shouted as he banged the main door and left.

The dry fact that Sir Richard had just been with him, inviting him into his own coach, created a tinderbox, radiating his anger.

On reaching his colonel's house, he pounded on the door, six raps booming out before he heaved a breath, full of indignation.

The maid showed him in, uneasy at his presence, and while she went to see her master, he paced up and down. As the woman reappeared, he barged past her, anxious to get to the heart of the issue. Sir Richard stood and stared at him, a telling blank look on his face. This made Charles tremble with outrage.

"What the hell is this?" he demanded, flinging the crumpled letter onto the desk and smacking his hand off it several times, rebounding as much as his disbelief.

"You are relieved of your post. I would have thought you were happy?"

"Happy? Why on God's earth would I be happy? I have a wife who is pregnant and I have lost my post," he growled.

"You have long disagreed with me over the running of

the regiment. Now you will not have that stress. Sir Arthur Cotton came with fine recommendations from Lord Digby and he will take your place. Cotton mentioned you had considered stepping down anyway, and I feel much more able to get on with that man."

Charles slammed the desk with his fist, this time harder. Sir Richard did not move an inch, watching him intently.

"That is another reason why you are no good, Berkeley, you will argue on the parade ground with a fellow officer and you frequently lose your temper. This behaviour is no use to me or my regiment."

Charles felt like throttling him, the calm chiding even set itself up as a comparison to his loss of control.

"For Christ's sake, are you a bigger fool than I thought?"

"How dare you. Get out, Berkeley, leave my house immediately," Sir Richard returned, standing with his hands behind his back.

"Nay, I will not. How long are you going to be a puppet to Cotton?"

"Puppet?" Sir Richard snorted.

"Aye, he drops hints and pulls the strings and you jump and do his bidding. I never thought I would see you, of all people, being such a pushover. This is your regiment; you should make the decisions, not Cotton."

"I make the decisions and that is why you are out. Now leave."

Charles felt a sober fear rush over him. He had visions of Anne and their child. What of their future now? His original worries swept back.

"I have connections at court," he threatened.

"Court, I do not need the King's cronies. It is Parliament who seem powerful to me, and Cotton and Holland are both well connected with that faction. You seem totally isolated, no influence with anyone."

Charles tugged the door and left it open, leaving the house without another word, in a bid to stop his feelings further exploding to his own detriment. He would waste no more time with Sir Richard - his connections with Lord Holland needed their mettle testing now, and in a flurry of haste, he resolved to visit the peer to call in a favour.

Passing down Westminster, he was surprised to see lots of apprentices speeding down the street, shouting and bawling.

They sounded in high excitement and ran frantically, as though their legs could not stop. He halted as they came closer - at first it was disbelief - but then he realised they were chasing a clergyman, shouting at the top of their voices, 'Abbeylubers,' and, 'Canterbury whelps.'

A group of women then emerged from the church, kicking sermon books and throwing crucifixes and candles around the churchyard, the final resting places of many being anything but peaceful. This was his church, a constant part of his life - his serene little world each Sunday - and he took it personally. The lack of manners and respect for such a holy place, never mind the fact that it was God's, provoked his indigenous outrage. The army of apprentices caught the parson and ripped the vestments from his back in a brutal fashion. Others then proceeded to throw the destroyed altar rail into the churchyard, making it appear the place was being cleared out for demolition. The King and Laud had introduced the rail to show the importance and holiness of the altar in churches and Puritans regarded it as a foreign, Catholic object within the church. Each frantic kick, tear, or curse at the item oozed pent up anger, over a decade's worth, at least.

He and others ran to the church and went inside, not knowing what to expect. Despite all this, a service was in progress, a plainly dressed man shrieking and howling, while the fabric of the interior was torn down around him, the scene carrying more poignancy than ever. A button maker he had seen only yesterday was the unknown preacher, at times making no sense at all, but the congregation were clearly happy to hear the rant.

Only a few people dared sit with expressions of disgust, talking to themselves about it all, while he joined the individuals that had followed him to investigate - he had a distinct feeling that their offence was in the minority here. Amazed, he felt like pulling the idiot from the pulpit by the ears, but refraining, summoned the parish constable from the streets. Leading him inside, the reluctant official ordered the man out, as Charles and the others gave gestures to strengthen his resolve.

A dozen or so of the congregation now responded to this fresh call from the official, ignoring the treasonous stirrings, though the bulk continued to go along like sheep.

"People who excel in serving the Lord are those who 'ave been chosen to be saved by 'im. T'is no worth trying to save thyself when the Almighty 'as already chosen those to be saved. All that 'appens 'as been planned out by the Lord, thy life and what 'appens to ye are already decided," the man said, speaking of the Puritan belief in predestination.

"This would have been unheard of until recently. This fellow blasphemes in God's own house," Charles cried, unable to comprehend it all.

Running down the aisle, he went to support the men who finally grabbed the button maker, pulling him down the steps with them. It had come to something when the massive institution of the church was being rescued by a handful of bystanders and one of the lowest legal representatives in the land; Charles summed it up in his head at that moment - civil war. This was people versus people, both backing a different form of Protestantism, yet strangely with the same principles. Some apprentices appeared to defend the man, though it was clear by the glee in their faces that they simply spoiled for a fight. The chance to attack the whole law and order which had kept many down was succinctly inviting as that same ruling stumbled.

The button maker struggled, still shouting, Charles put his arm around his mouth and gagged him, though he tried to bite like a mad dog. The apprentices surged forward, yelling and trying to release the commoner, causing general confusion as insults flew and tempers rose. The constable watched in bewilderment, before ordering the bells to be rung, to summon the flock, and hopefully troops, to their defence.

The official had finally begun to react in a fitting way, overcoming his reluctance, though understandable when he was picked to do the job for a term, whether he wanted to or not. The impostor of a preacher grabbed Charles's hair and then bellowed a muffled plea for help. The apprentices made towards him and Charles thumped the man in the chest, winding him. He fell to the floor, gripping himself, the sermon, ideology and body now being left behind. Fighting was on everyone's mind.

"At last that damned rubbish has stopped spouting from his mouth," one man cried in approval of the assault.

Fisticuffs broke out in the middle of the crowd and Charles saw some of them still throwing the religious paintings outside, sweeping the ornate candles and cross from the altar, condemning them as relics of Catholicism. He quickly shoved two crucifixes under a pew with his foot to save them from being totally destroyed.

"Our Church was reformed under Elizabeth the First. It has been beautified to the glory of God with gold and ornaments, and now you want to pull the whole foundation apart," Charles yelled, condemning the actions, but trying to explain the purpose of all the decorations they were tearing down.

Everyone scattered in their own directions. Charles and the people who disagreed with the Puritan views were in an ever dangerous position until some of the church's congregation began to arrive, responding to the unusually timed peals.

"The devil take you, for it's the likes of ye that try to move us to the Pope," a little man yelled, getting the attention of others. He ran at Charles with a dagger.

Adapting his stance, Charles made ready to receive him.

He grabbed the man's arm and pushed him backwards over a pew, eventually twisting the weapon free. The area round him was a shambles, with people running all over, some leaving, a few fighting, but almost all of them yelling. It had become chaotic. Charles and the others made for the door, realising this was rapidly spiralling out of control.

The jeopardy to his own life became apparent, and as the mob of people began to filter away, Charles decided to leave too. He soon found the exit barred by three men, swivelling round just in time to see a man coming for him. The fellow hit out and reeling from the impact, Charles felt another blow to his back. He squeezed his eyes together to focus, then swiping a piece of destroyed picture frame, he swung it erratically, determined to fight on. The enemy fell to the ground as one of Charles's newly formed accomplices got him and Charles seized the opportunity to join forces with his ally. Others had joined the pair, heartened by their fight, scaring off the other men who were barricading the doors.

And to think he had just thought that this anarchy would end with Strafford's death.

Chapter 29

Sir Arthur Cotton walked with his usual slow, outwardly confident pace, under the archway of the large, red brick gate - one of the two great entranceways, which interrupted the flow of King Street as it passed by Whitehall Palace. The entrance, its turreted walls crowned with cupolas, pediments, busts and signs of the zodiac, gave grand access to the palace area.

Turning left into Saint James's Park, his excitement rose as he took note of the wildlife here, being such a lover of nature.

It interested him to compare human life to the basic survival instinct in the animal kingdom. He eyed the small ponds, which were deliberately placed to attract birds including ducks, and was pleased to see they were free, for now at least, from the guns that would claim them for the royal kitchens.

Business was put aside for a minute to admire the majestic outline of Saint James's Palace at the far end of the park, and the larger feature called Rosamond's Pond. Old Henry the Eighth, who had reclaimed the monasteries' lands and riches from the Catholic Church, had similarly retrieved this former marsh from Mother Nature, turning it into the great park loved by so many.

Then leaving Whitehall Palace behind him, and pacing further into the abundant green energy that the area so exuded, he scoured the grounds for the peer. The place was busy today, with so many fine and smart people, that it made it hard to spot Digby. Some deer bounded away as he approached, causing groups to stop and watch, with one woman gasping in admiration. Then he saw his target chatting politely with some noblemen, and he set off in their direction, as anxious to catch his own prey, as the King was when he hunted these graceful animals. While making his way to Digby, another man joined him, walking alongside.

"Sir Arthur," the person greeted him, raising his hat, and displaying the exquisite manners that were required here amongst these distinguished people.

"Ah, Mister Belasis, are you away to see Digby?" Cotton probed.

The man nodded. "Aye, sir. I carry bad news about the enterprise he is involved in."

Cotton was puzzled for a split second, and then he realised that the man was talking about the Army Plot, which Sir Charles Berkeley was linked with, following his time in jail.

"Allow me to pass such unpleasant information on," Cotton practically ordered, raising his eyebrows.

"Oh no, I could not possibly."

As Cotton handed over a gold coin, the man quickly smiled and nodded.

"Actually, I do have other important work to do, so if you would not mind relaying it for me, sir?"

Cotton waved his hand, mockingly making out that it would be no trouble, and the fellow whispered that Pym had found out about the plot. Without further ado, the man raised his hat and bowed his head, leaving Cotton to approach Digby. Cotton sniggered, knowing that this could work to his advantage perfectly, and he looked at the peer, who was chatting to a group of wealthy men and women, standing around him as though he were an entertainer. Digby was talking about a courtier who had lost a fortune at cards and next day sported a bruise to the head, supposedly from his frustrated wife. He flicked a handkerchief in front of his face, attempting to get rid of a fly, as he finished the story and the people laughed along. Then he glanced at Cotton and sighed.

"What is it now, Sir Arthur? Honestly, I cannot get one ounce of peace; you bleed me dry," the peer expostulated loudly.

Cotton was about to speak when Digby's eyes lit up, and he addressed the others. "Bleed me dry. I hear that is the same thing his wife said to him when he returned, one hundred pounds short."

Digby snorted and then bowed his head, leading Cotton away. They strolled along the park towards the gilded birdcages that glinted in the sunlight. Each one housed a magnificent exotic bird and the noise of the chirping and singing made Cotton feel as close to nature as he would ever be in this huge city, and it seemed as though he had been walking in places more far flung than central London in the last ten minutes.

The array of the birds' colours was impressive and beautiful. One was every shade of blue, some parts so splendid that it made him imagine the crystal clear seas he had heard of, near the colonies in the New World.

"I am told that the enterprise is progressing well, my lord. You said you were to arrange for Berkeley to receive his map and instructions, detailing who to meet when he travels to the army in the north?" he recalled of the scheme.

"Yes, that is so. I have it all planned for tonight; Sir Charles is to be given the details at the Keg and Tankard alehouse," Digby confirmed.

"Excellent. I am sure the outcome will be very pleasing," Cotton predicted.

"I hope so, otherwise someone will end up as trapped as those birds. I am also relying on you communicating with your fellow Scots. Sir Charles has contacts in the English army, but also you have them in the Scottish one."

A man sauntered past them, looking over, before stopping and raising his hat. Digby responded and smiled, the crystal blue eyes sparkling, making Cotton realise just how persuasive and charming the peer could be when he wanted. Cotton observed the stranger with caution as he sauntered away.

"Son of Sir Edmund Verney," Digby answered, knowing the reason for Cotton's inquisitiveness.

Cotton knew the conspiracy was now doomed and would take one casualty with it when Parliament found out; the unwitting Sir Charles Berkeley. After this, Cotton could just tell Digby he had engineered it all so that sole blame lay squarely with Berkeley, exonerating the noble from any repercussions.

* * *

Charles was just about to leave, closing the door behind him, when he met Edmund Verney in the street. He belched, tasting the oysters he had just eaten for breakfast.

"Quickly, Charles, go back inside."

He smiled at Edmund, taking it to be a joke, but the man was serious and he went back into the hall as requested. Charles could perceive a man's character like a sixth sense and he knew Edmund to be an honest fellow, even without the genuine look in his eyes. They stood on the black and white tiles, the difference between the two colours as clear cut as Charles's outlook on life. He walked over to the long oak table in the middle of the hall and sat at one of the two wooden platforms, which were at either side.

"I bumped into Cotton and Digby earlier in Saint James's Park. They were talking about you."

Charles cursed. "They are as bad as each other and they both have no love for me, so it is not surprising. I am biding my time for wreaking revenge on Cotton; did you know that he bundled me off to jail?"

Edmund shook his head. "There is something afoot, so be careful, my friend."

As they were talking, a knock sounded at the door and Louise came through to answer it, stopping for a second in surprise to see him still here, more so that his routine had been interrupted. Now Charles could just see the man in the doorway asking for him, and Louise looked over for permission to show the fellow in. He nodded his agreement and the gentleman bowed his head as he entered the house.

"Sir Charles, Lord Digby asked me to pass a message on. You are to go to the Keg and Tankard tomorrow to collect details of your mission."

The man went to leave after a few seconds of hesitation, but Charles was having none of it, unsure and suspicious after his friend's warnings. He called him back with a command that made the man stand and turn.

"Tell Lord Digby that I will not undertake his mission until he sends me the fifty pounds I am to use to help pay a certain pair of gentleman for his services in this matter as well as a full list of meeting points and names of those aware of this enterprise. I wish for these tonight, otherwise I will not go ahead with the business."

The well built man gave a sharp nod of his head, seeming to be taken aback at the demands, before slipping away. Charles smiled at his friend, making his pleasure clear at causing such a stir. When enough was enough, he would stop at nothing to make his opinion known.

"What is all this bribery about?" Mun asked, unable to hold back his intrigue, as he assessed the situation through those perceptive, round eyes.

"It is all false. I am not meant to receive any money from Digby, nor any details. So if this messenger is genuine, he would know this. Do you follow me, Edmund?"

Charles nodded with a telling expression.

Edmund laughed, as flowing as his curled, fair locks. His outgoing and ambitious nature held nothing back and he told of his respect for such a quick thinking action, which would establish the truth.

"When I was in Utrecht, during the late wars, my colonel, Sir Thomas Culpepper, would discard his honour ten times in an hour to gain but sixpence. Men like Digby have no regard for anyone, so you are right to stand your ground."

"I am not going to any alehouse to receive such details. If they are in league against me, then they will surely have a trap planned. Where is it anyway?"

Edmund thought for a while. "Go down Church Street as far as the sign that displays a white goat, cut through the lane to Princess Street, and keep walking until you reach the sign of a sun. You need to turn left into a small alleyway and it opens out into a courtyard."

"Church Street? There are so many signposts hanging off the buildings there, that I shall be on all evening trying to find the goat. I wish they would damn well come up with a better way of identifying places."

"Never mind that, why do you wish to know if you are so set against going?"

"Whether my original task is planned to go ahead, or if this latest message is as false as Digby's character, they will wish they had never messed with me."

Daylight seemed to exit with Edmund Verney, as he took his leave, evening now drawing in. Charles stared down the table he sat at, noticing the way the fading shafts of light highlighted the cracks and texture of the old oak. Too heavy to move with each outgoing owner, it gave atmosphere to the room; an orphan of time, adding a consistency to the house.

Louise entered again to place a deep rush mat securely over the lower part of each window to stop draughts, before placing his foot warmer on the floor. A brazier of charcoal gave heat to the room, because the chimney in the hall always smoked too much when it was lit. Anne swept into the chamber and rested her arms around his neck, cuddling him from behind to complete the feeling of warmth. He placed his feet on the metal warmer, the hot coals inside heating them nicely. The past few days had been unusually cold and damp for May.

"There we are, sir. Was there anything else?" Louise asked.

"No, thank you. I will answer the door tonight - if anyone should want us, that is."

He slid the foot warmer over to Anne, who began to flick through his Shakespeare book. He was determined he would manage to read the whole thing, despite only studying it since he had left the army, and not having had the best of educations during his poorer childhood.

"I would love to have *Romeo and Juliet*. Maybe we can read it together?" she suggested.

He thought of the romantic story and of how he had courted Anne, after meeting her at a boring banquet he had initially been loath to attend.

"You remember I climbed up some ladders one Saint Valentine's morning soon after we met, determined to be the first one to see you so that I could be your Valentine?" He laughed, as he reminisced about his headstrong actions.

"I practically cried with laughter as I opened the window. Mother did not share my joy though, for your behaviour was most shocking, Sir Charles. Indeed, I should have shoved your ladders off the window ledge for fear of getting myself a reputation," Anne said, pushing his body to play out her last comment, with a teasing smile.

Finally, a knock echoed out from the door and Charles

jumped, not out of shock, but from sheer anticipation; he had been waiting to see whether the messenger returned and was sure this was him. As he opened the door and recognised the man, he ushered him in warily, limiting the fellow's entrance to the very perimeter of the room.

"This is half of the money you spoke of, sir, and the particulars. My master says that the rest of the gold will be sent to the inn tomorrow," the person explained, as he held out a small, leather purse and a sealed parchment.

"The document lists all the information you need. I stress it must only be opened at the inn though, for your own safety," the fellow warned.

Charles took the items in silence. He knew a plot was afoot, now that this courier and his 'master' had reacted to the earlier false statements. He would contact Digby immediately tomorrow to check the situation. As the man was speedily shown the door again, Charles bolted it securely and did not fully inhale until he had turned the iron key in the old lock. The clunk gave a temporary secure reassurance.

Chapter 30

Charles entered the Keg and Tankard alehouse and sought out the proprietor. The bustle and noise was immense, because today was a public holiday for Ascension Day, commemorating the ascension of Jesus Christ into heaven.

"Excuse me, sir, do you have a small room reserved for me under the name of Jones?"

The keeper nodded and shoved a tankard of ale to a customer, before grunting and gesturing Charles to follow.

They walked between the tables, while customers laughed and chattered, and he was shown to a small chamber that was railed off with a mucky green curtain. As he drew it aside, Charles wondered whether the movement would rip its rotten material, but it survived. He went inside and ordered some beer, sitting on the creaking bench and waiting for his contacts, though expecting something more from Cotton.

A small fire was burning behind him and he took his old cloak off. Today he had worn plain clothes more associated with a tradesman, and he undid his doublet. He examined the room again for something to do; the wooden beams seemed to be contorted with age, just like the keeper who returned with his drink. Charles stood at the opposite end, peering through the small window to see crowds gathering for the day's procession.

The view was coloured by the green tinted glass. He loved the sight of the celebrations and was irritated he had to miss them.

After a short while, the gentlemen who had visited him at home entered and closed the curtain behind him. He sat down on the bench, gulping at his beer, before he whispered.

"Sir Charles?"

He nodded.

"Have you brought the sealed information that was in your possession?"

Charles nodded his head, before patting the purse attached to his belt. He unbuttoned it and took out a document, putting it onto the table. The man gave a huge sigh of relief to see the paper. From behind the curtain, he was positive he could hear faint noises and a whisper, but continued talking to this companion.

"It should list who we need to speak to and where to go for our task."

He had not even finished speaking when Cotton ripped the drape aside, gleefully pointing at him. A particularly officious looking constable stood to the side.

"They spout treason and speak of a plot to threaten Parliament. Quickly, seize that document before they burn it," Cotton cried.

The constable raced to the table, while Cotton stood in front of the fire, and snatched it from Charles, practically growling with outrage. As the official read it, Cotton stood with his hands on his hips, a look of satisfaction on his face; he was practically pushing his crotch out at Charles, asserting his supposed superiority in the current situation. The constable glared at Cotton for a few seconds in silence.

"You bring me here, sir, reporting them for planning to buy a horse?" the constable bellowed.

"What, b-but…" Cotton stuttered, grabbing the parchment. As he read the names of those selling and hiring horses, together with the places the steeds were stabled, Cotton yelled.

The parish representative gave him a last minute frown and then left, while the messenger who had been liaising with Charles stood up to make an escape.

"You shit, did you really think I would be foolish enough to bring the incriminating letter that you clearly had delivered to me to a place like this? I just needed to lure you here by going along with your trap," Charles said quietly as he moved menacingly towards Cotton, anxious to appease the revenge that had been building up in him since the beating he had taken in prison.

Cotton flung the fabric aside, running out of the room. Charles chased after him, weaving through the customers and ripping the door open to pursue him outside. It was packed with spectators of the public event and he hunted for Cotton, eventually catching sight of him disappearing into the far crowd. Just then, the parish clergyman and his churchwardens came into sight behind the choirboys.

Cotton crossed over the street and their chase went largely unnoticed within the cheerful and noisy appreciation of the multitude and the procession.

As he tried to follow Cotton, the choirboys produced their sticks, a short sentence was read by the clergyman, and they began beating the walls of the small schoolhouse with enthusiasm. Charles went around them, carefully avoiding the ritual of beating the parish boundary, and sprinted on past more bystanders. Cotton vanished into an alleyway and he followed, narrowing the gap.

The passage tapered and grew more enclosed as they went between two large houses, whose upper storeys jutted out over their heads so much, that it cut out most of the daylight. As they came to the small exit that led into another street, Charles was close enough to grab Cotton, and he yanked the man by the collar. He fell against a timber framed wall and Charles went to hit him, but he managed to roll away.

Cotton seized some wood and plunged it at him. Charles grabbed hold, twisting it out of his enemy's hand and threw it away before hurling himself at Cotton. Grasping the rogue, he forced him to the ground, both of them writhing around. Cotton yelled and shouted as he was forced onto his back, Charles gaining the upper hand and striking a blow right in his face.

As he jumped to his feet, he kicked Cotton in the ribs, roaring that it was in return for the same honour he himself had received in prison. Finally, he dragged the dog to his feet and forced his head into a tub of old stagnant water, holding it there while he jerked and panicked. Eventually he drew Cotton's head out, gasping for air, before plunging it back again. This continued until Cotton stopped struggling so much and Charles pushed him against a wall, wet hair hanging limply down his pale face.

"Never cross me again," Charles warned.

Cotton wheezed for air, falling to his knees and coughing, as Charles walked slowly away, opening his old doublet to cool down. His body burned, especially his calves and head, which throbbed and ached from exhaustion. He had expelled so much anger and energy and revelled in his actions.

"Lest she should take the opportunity of making Papists of them"

Parliament's reason for asking the Queen to surrender her family into their care while the King was in Scotland.
AUGUST 1641

Chapter 31

King Charles the First had departed to Scotland in August, officially to oversee the final peace treaty following the Bishops Wars, but some Members of Parliament suggested it was to gain Scottish support to raise an army and invade England. Parliament had gone into recess while the King was away and a small committee of MPs was formed at Parliament's own initiative, chaired by Pym, to govern in his absence. The King had not left his own provision for Government, playing right into his enemies' hands. Overall since Strafford's demise, Parliament had now got some privileges and the King retained a little honour. Both the King and Parliament's horns were still locked together though.

As the monarch rode towards the remnants of his army in Newcastle, still stationed there from the Bishops War, his mood was nothing like as dark as the clouds that were swirling menacingly around the sky above him. The Scottish army was still there too and secretly he hoped his presence may entice the forces to his support, should he need them in future. Stretching long into the distance were the soldiers, interspersed with tents, horses and weapons, smoke winding up to the sky as fires warmed them, as well as cooking their meals. Every now and then a banner flapped in the breeze, mostly blue to highlight the colour of the covenant the Scottish had signed, bonding them together to defend their religion against the King. Despite the symbolism and cold shade of their pennants, King Charles still viewed them as his own troops, seeming to completely forget all the enmity that had passed. The flags slapped around, applauding the arrival of the approaching monarch.

While he passed by, with the usual huge entourage and standards following, the men cheered loudly, the English forces having already done so a little earlier. The cries were like energy to him and he sat straight, looking ahead, determined to exude dignity and majesty - his position was such a contradiction at times; they fought against his armies and now they applauded him, remembering he was still their King at the end of the day. This jubilation brought reflection about his wife in Oatlands Palace, just outside of London, where men did not seem to appreciate him quite as much. That was his only niggling worry right now and he thought about whether she would be safe from Parliament without him. He raised his hand to the troops as he passed, almost automatically, occasionally nodding his head.

He took deep breaths; the air drenched with excitement added vigour to his body, wiping years of premature age from him; already at forty, he had noticed his eyes more sunken and face drawn, only seeming to have occurred in the last year or so. Alongside his nephew, Prince Charles Louis, the Elector of Palatine, he felt exhilarated, a veritable conquering hero. He would restore peace to the land like a lynchpin to both nations, enhancing them with good rule.

"They are loyal," he whispered, almost with an air of relief.

"Yes, Your Majesty," came the tempered agreement, as though the boy could see events through the lens of a looking glass.

"I am at my best outdoors. It is as if I have cast myself free of the chains Parliament had wrapped around me. They tried to stop me leaving London, you know," he said with a wry smile.

"I am glad you held fast and went anyway, sir."

"They even sat in session on a Sabbath, discussing how to persuade me to stay. I am flattered by it all, for they must love me so," the monarch continued, mocking the assembly.

The royal eyes narrowed as they returned to observe the scene. He sensed he was in a strong position, but his nephew's expression left something to be desired. He felt some indecision creep into his mind. Why was Charles Louis not as confident as himself, he wondered. As the procession drew up at a nearby manor house, the monarch dismounted and went inside for some refreshments. His worry vanished as quickly as the bowing and scurrying of the owners, and he practically glided into the room, his short fast steps outpacing most who were not accustomed to it. Almost immediately, the King eyed up a painting hanging above the fireplace, his interests picking this object out. The amount of joy he took in studying it crowned his buoyant mood.

"What a wonderful little scene. See the landscape in the background, it is as perfect as any scene our country has to offer," he commented, sharing his interest with those assembled.

"You do the picture an honour, Your Majesty, with such a compliment by one so qualified and learned in the subject of art," the owner of the house stated, after a more relaxed great bow, now that he had managed to catch up with his monarch's speedy advance.

The King did a second sweep around the room with his gaze, catching sight of the owner out of the corner of his eye. As he did so, he took in everything from the shirt collar, which was not folded right and appeared to be shaking, probably from his nerves. The furniture was old and King Charles guessed the man's family were not as wealthy as they had once been.

Now he had discreetly assessed everything he wished, he glanced at the owner. "We are most grateful for the use of your home, Mister Gardener."

The man bowed his head again. "It is an honour to welcome my King into it. We would be overjoyed if you would accept that picture as a gift, if Your Majesty so desires it."

The sovereign nodded his thanks, carefully taking his cream, leather gloves off, and offering an equally delicate hand, which Gardener kneeled and kissed. The monarch leaned on the fireplace with one arm, the other holding the gold embroidered gloves, resting on his hip. The Elector Palatine and a group of his closest friends and confidants followed him over. There was his refined, dignified cousin, the Duke of Richmond and Lennox and another cousin, the Marquis of Hamilton, who lacked Richmond's intelligence and common sense. Unfortunately his suspicious Secretary of State, Sir Henry Vane, was here too, though the King knew he was a Parliament man at heart.

With one exception, he was surrounded by those immensely loyal to him and out of the public eye. He took his hat off, hanging it on the raised part of the chair back and ran his hand from his brow, through his long hair, leaving his auburn locks as free and glorious as he himself felt right now.

"I see Parliament has sent some bloodhounds after me to keep an eye, gentlemen," he told them. At first he saw the host hesitate, as if a joke from such an abstemious person took him aback. The company laughed along though, vocally melodious and smooth to echo their genuine regard for him, and also to leave Vane exposed as a runt of the gathering.

The King himself fluctuated back to being determined again, after hearing their merriness, probably more so than he had ever been for a year now, and especially since Parliament had got their teeth into his power. The handful of dour men they had sent after him tagged along behind, emphasising that he was now challenging Parliament to keep up with his actions, instead of waiting while they utilised their upper hand.

The monarch finally sat on a chair arranged by one of his footmen. He held his gloves out, anticipating a servant to take them, back as straight as his sobriety. King Charles the First had been adamant from his accession, to lift the monarchy away from his father's more licentious and lax manners; a role on behalf of God warranted respect and devotion.

"Such plain little fellows, sir. You know Parliament is in trouble now, for they have adjourned for a few weeks while you are in Scotland. The real truth is that most of its members are getting sick of spending time in London and wish to return home now, for a majority see their business done following your gracious concessions," one member of the intimate gathering announced.

"Aye, I hear there are but eighty members of the Commons and twelve of the Lords left, and the rest are scurrying away to look over their personal affairs," another added.

The King took some formality away from this cherished congregation, by a wave of his hand, inviting them to sit with him.

"A toast, gentlemen, to the Queen," he suggested, betraying his innermost thought, while a servant hurried to pour the white wine. The King noted with approval that it came from the Palatine, once his brother in law's lands, until he had challenged the might of the Catholic powers.

They drank the Queen's health, and King Charles twinkled with delight at talk of her. She instilled him with pride and he admired her strong will, even though occasionally it could be the cause of friction between them. It was the same sort of self confidence that he had recognised in his mother, brother, and a royal favourite, all now deceased.

"Her Majesty will deal with those rogues, I'll wager, such is her way. She will pull them out of the Parliament house by their ears," Hamilton joked in his Scottish accent.

The King smiled along, gently turning the small glass of wine round with his fingers. He could imagine this too; the small doll marching down there on her own, if needs be, to take revenge on her beloved husband's enemies. He continued to gaze into the gentle swirls of his wine, as rich as her lips that he adored to kiss, slowly, passionately, knowing that her love was what he lived for. The other devotion was to his country and its people, bound to him in marriage through the coronation oath, which brought his tender thoughts to a close, and back to the courtiers around him.

"Did your servant get his son's stammer resolved, Richmond?" the monarch asked.

"No, Your Majesty, nothing has proved successful so far."

"Tell him to stop using the pebbles. The doctors will instruct him to put them in his mouth when he speaks, but I found concentration helped. Advise him to think his sentence through before speaking it. Then he will conquer all."

The sensitivity of the comment and its referral to an intensely private matter echoed the calm, informal setting.

He was proud of how his own speech impediment had all but been overcome and felt little of the reserve which usually held back such personal comments. A servant then interrupted the gathering to announce that General Alexander Leslie was outside.

"Send him in," the King ordered, as the final curtain dropped on his carefree mood.

Standing up and letting a page put his sword and belt over his head, to lie diagonally across his chest in a flash of gold, sword at his left hip, the King walked over to the corner, distancing himself from everyone. Everything about him was perfection and order; the red scabbard matching his breeches, blue, silk Order of the Garter around his neck, re-enforcing an air of mediaeval honour and chivalry. He was quite anxious to see the general who had fought so well against his English army, and he was determined to exude the full aura of his personage. One foot stood further forwards, pointing outwards and adding a determination to his pose. In his younger years, he had felt terribly awkward standing up, lack of height making him feel conspicuous, but as King, his position put him head and shoulders above all.

"Your Majesty," Leslie said as he bowed his head, removing his hat. The sixty year old stepped forward and kissed the King's emerald ring, albeit in a soldierly and stiff fashion. The long, wiry, blond and silver hair fell low in greeting too, and King Charles was struck by the old soldier's similar height.

"General Leslie, we are pleased to be here to review your soldiers."

"And we are happy to welcome you, Your Majesty. Peace is the answer to all of our prayers and soon the men will be marching back home."

"Not before you have dined with us, sir. I insist you join us this evening," the King said, causing a moment's silence.

"I will be pleased to, sir," Leslie replied in his heavy Scottish tongue, reminding the King of his father's accent, which sometimes confused his Danish mother.

"General, do your troops regret fighting against their King's forces in the late wars? They cheer so heartily for him now," Hamilton jibed, unable to resist a taunt.

Annoyed at the insensitive comment and how indefensible it was, the King waved his hand dismissively at Hamilton and drew attention away from it. The very expression of the King's - no anger shown, but simple disdain - was enough to cast Hamilton aside like a thunder clap.

"Your men are a fine army. I hope to prove to them that their King is as dedicated to them as you are," the sovereign said, manoeuvring Leslie on side with a gush of that famous charisma.

There was a sharpness in Leslie's nose, moustache and beard, and the tight mouth seemed to echo the hero's tactful and discretionary attitude. Following a little more discussion about his military record and his men, the commander took his leave, but the King called after him, "I will think on you when I choose the honours, General Leslie."

The sovereign felt confident about Scottish support and he was brimming with self assurance, at best when left to his own devices and away from an army of courtiers giving so many differing opinions. Following the Scottish general's departure, Hamilton fell to a snigger.

"What is so funny, my lord?" Sir Henry Vane asked sourly.

"He commands the Scottish army fighting against the King's English forces and now he is to dine with us."

"And so it must be, Hamilton, for they are also my subjects. There may be four thousand men and General Leslie at my hand, should these riots and protests get out of control in London too. If you still find that amusing, then you should return to your home," the King explained firmly. He knew Hamilton and other peers would dislike Leslie for the pure fact that he was illegitimate, yet now leader of Scotland's armies and in line for a peerage. The King himself understood this, abhorring the sin of bastardy, but realised that his views had to take second place to necessity. One of the rare occasions he could make the differentiation.

As he examined the men around him, he saw their reaction seemed cool. Inside, he felt an anticlimax. It irritated him to have his opinions change so easily, but since his childhood years when he was not expected to live, he had needed other people's resolve to enthuse his own. From the earliest age he had fought and survived, overcome rickets, finally learned both speech and riding, and excelled at his study, despite the weak frame and isolation from family. Why were they not as positive as him, he helplessly found himself contemplating.

"What are your views, gentlemen?" the King asked, unable to bear it any longer.

"If I may say so, sir, you have negotiated with Parliament and Leslie's lot enough. You have abolished Ship Money tax, agreed they should meet every three years, discontinued your prerogative courts, offered posts in government to their leading members, and for the safety of your people, approved Strafford's murder. It is time to fight back, for as fast as you appease, they advance for more and more," Hamilton warned, though this time with some sense.

The King felt grave for the first time.

"Digby tells me it is but a waiting game and very shortly Parliament will call off the fight, as most members have become tired of the constant attack edging ever closer to my person," the monarch recalled, even now practically ditching Digby's fresh counsel in his absence.

"I am afraid I cannot see them simply backing down, Your Majesty, especially now they have achieved all of this," Richmond said with regret.

The royal plans and resolve blew away as fast as anything caught in the wind of change that engulfed his nation.

"I thank you for your advice. I am well aware … of how my enemies are abusing their positions to their own gain," he told them.

"They go too far in London, sir. I get angry at how much they scorn you. If I was asked for my opinion, it would be to arrest them or clear the rioters off the streets with force."

The King was deep in thought. He tended to listen to the last person he spoke to and Hamilton's advice was different – now he needed to weigh up in his own mind which counsel he felt was better. This was not going to be a quick process and he decided to do it when he was alone tonight.

"Do the rest of you gentlemen agree?" he checked again.

"Be cunning, Your Majesty, appease them in matters that

you know will cause them to fall out amongst themselves," one man advised.

The King nodded and sighed. Deep down, he thought about the army here and harboured the image of them backing up his true and just cause. He could envisage himself winning the Scots round and then building up support in England to counter Parliament and their treason, which people were tired of, and taking back his lost power. The Army Plot had been an earlier idea to do this; bringing his English force back down from Newcastle to free Strafford and purge Parliament, until its details leaked out and he realised it would never succeed. He had the whole ploy killed off by exclaiming that the plan was vain and foolish, ending all talk of Sir Charles Berkeley's journey to sound out the junior officers. The stench from this plotting was reaching Pym's bloodhounds though, so it would only be a matter of time before details fell into the public domain, to be chewed over by the mongrels.

"Yes, I see your points, gentlemen," the King agreed.

He still felt he could outmanoeuvre all his enemies, and Leslie and his Scottish men were now his primary focus. Then he would be able to reverse his fortunes - he was absolutely sure of it. In fact, he was positive God would not desert a King who He had appointed to rule.

Chapter 32

The King was riding again, this time through Edinburgh's Royal Mile and towards the Parliament House.

Wooden buildings, with each tier jutting out, lined both sides of the street, seeming to lean over inquisitively and hung with flags to welcome him. He sat in the royal carriage with General Leslie by his side, both men's ideologies now unified, in appearance at least.

Here he was in his spiritual home, land of his birth; a country more romantic, harsh and brutal - and in weather too - than rich, refined and elegant London. Yet at times, he felt like a visitor.

The sermon he had listened to this morning was still fresh in his mind and faith in God gave him an immense feeling of personal strength and righteousness. The fact that he had agreed to attend Presbyterian sermons in Scotland, at odds with the Church of England doctrine, did not figure in his mind. It was simply a necessity in the political climate. He was missing the Queen and his children greatly – alongside God, his family was the other founding pillar in life. In front was the Earl of Argyll - Pym's Scottish alter ego - holding the sceptre, and the

Earl of Hamilton with the crown, symbols of every power, land, entity, trust and honour his position engendered.

As the procession snaked its way through the streets, only a hint of frustration remained because of earlier news from London. The horses hooves and soldiers feet clattered along as a watery sun appeared to add brightness, and he hoped this was a sign from the Almighty. He eyed Argyll carefully, secretly detesting him, but outwardly fishing for his allegiance. Then he looked at the crown again and remembered his coronation oath, to uphold the laws, religion and to safeguard his people, as he saw fit. His stubborn nature added even more weight to the determination that he would never break it.

The carriage drove slowly through the crowds in Canongate and up the High Street, passing the Mercat Cross, where all official announcements were made. This was a different world to London, and the people were so dissimilar. Thousands lined the route, cheering at the rare sight of their King and in the distance; he could see tiny bits of Edinburgh Castle, majestically crowning the city from its rugged base. The procession approached the centre of government, Parliament Hall, which stood near Saint Giles Cathedral. It was so different and more intimate to be in a city which housed only twenty thousand, compared to the three hundred thousand in London.

He remained expressionless when a small scuffle broke out nearby, apparently between two people in his party. Once inside the Parliament building, the monarch headed straight for a small room, the gargoyles on the tall fireplace looked down upon him. The stone floor added to the chilly air.

"What the devil was happening back there, Hamilton?" he demanded with a rare flash of anger, now that he had the impromptu privacy.

"A quarrel betwixt two men, Your Majesty, the Laird of Langton I am told wished to have the place of usher from the Earl of Wigton."

"What an insult. Would they have their actions tarnish my appearance to my fellow countrymen?" he demanded,

"Especially as this is such an important occasion."

The King stood up and paced around restlessly, attempting to gather his emotions.

"Give me paper and ink," he ordered; a footman complying immediately, yet the King barely noticed the speedy reaction. It was as if most people were extra vigilant due to the rarity of having their ruler here. He then proceeded to write out a warrant for the arrest of the Laird of Langton.

"Get this put into action immediately," he told Hamilton with a resolution as steely as that of the lion rampant on the Scottish coat of arms, "I will not have my visit overshadowed by imbeciles."

The earl left the King alone with his Groom of the Bedchamber, who did not know how to respond to his master's uncommon anger. He was well experienced with shouldering the royal worries though - maybe it was the fact he did not aspire to high office, the mutual love of art, or the way he had been sent on embassies for the King, which brought him relatively close to such a distant master. At any rate, he understood both his King's qualities and faults.

"By God, what is happening to the laws of my land? I am told by the Queen that near a hundred people stormed Windsor to steal my deer. Michaelmas Day has just gone, and rather than follow the custom and pay debts, they fall to robbery instead."

He saw Porter give a remorseful expression to the news and knew he had a true servant in this man. He did not mind laying his frustration out in his presence. This act of theft struck close to his own person, showing distinct disrespect, and that bothered him slightly more than the perilous fact that Pym was setting up a committee to investigate the Army Plot that had recently been discovered.

After a few moments the monarch left to continue with his progression towards the chamber, anxious not to delay it further.

He carefully sat on the throne, under the hammer beam roof of Scandinavian oak, with a façade of renewed temperance. His nephew sat flanking him on a stool to his left.

He felt alien to the men who scrutinised him, whispering furiously and excitedly, but one thing did give him enjoyment and contentment; he was the one who had created this building especially for the Scottish Parliament, and this now being less than two years old, he could proudly appreciate his conception at first hand. He had honoured his Scottish hosts in more ways than this since his arrival, yet his own royal palace at Holyrood was run down in comparison to this new wonder. They had only just ordered some broken windows and threadbare rugs to be repaired, but still, he did not let this cloud the visit. He wanted these men more than a few old furnishings.

Though his concessions were great, and added a weakness to his cause that estranged some natural supporters, while doing little to bring any hostile Scots to his cause, the King did manage to gain something. Two loyal Scottish nobles were put on trial for their allegiance to him during the late Bishops Wars, but he was allowed to decide their fate, avoiding another Strafford scenario. He also submitted to allow the Scottish Parliament to advise him on his choice of ministers, though he had the final say. Such limits on royal power in Scotland were agreed cheerfully, as though their importance was minimal, and he implored the members to support his nephew in getting his lands in the Palatine back from the Catholic Holy Roman Empire. King Charles was sure they would rise to support the cause, it being a Protestant one. His own espousal of this would also distance him from the ridiculous rumours of his sympathy for Catholicism.

He looked at the men who represented Scotland, most of whom he did not know well. It was easy to feel they were unused to his person being in their chamber, some burning with resentment at the intrusion, but he was determined to remind them that four hundred miles away or not, he was their monarch and of their nationality. He would not have anyone forget this. Then Argyll was on his feet, glaring at the men close by and the King realised people paid more heed to this noble, a sea of heads switching focus to the fellow.

He warily observed Argyll's eyes and the way they were not aligned.

A prettier sight than Argyll was the great south window, beautifully illuminating the chamber and reminding everyone of a part of Scotland's history. King James the Fifth was portrayed in the stained glasswork, founding the College of Justice, and King Charles himself had been the main architect of the work, recalling minds to the fact that kings were the keystone to justice, as much as a father was to a family.

A man read out the monarch's proposal's for appointments to the great offices of state. King Charles was confident that by listing several of Argyll's family and known supporters, he could also slip a loyal peer into their number for the vital post of Chancellor. Once again, he hoped that by releasing some grants, and swallowing some of that intolerable pride, he could salvage a shred of his power. His cousin Richmond had spoken against compromise, when he pleaded with the King to be wary of such liberal actions.

"The Earl of Morton," was announced for the financial post.

Argyll stood and the King tightened his lips, astounded at the interruption, as the peer announced, "I must object. The Earl of Morton is debt ridden, old and is a suspect to other crimes."

The slandered Morton looked on, sad faced at the onslaught of his son in law, but nevertheless he rose wearily. "I am ignorant of what I have done to incur the displeasure of my Lord of Argyll. Indeed I have known him since he was a young boy and have brought him up to a certain degree."

Argyll's eyebrows dropped as he frowned, creases folding into his large forehead, while an expression of disgust swept over him, despite the sensitivity of the comment.

"And may I remind him that if it was not for me, this fellow would have been set upon by creditors as soon as he stepped foot inside the city gates for this Parliament's session," Argyll argued, without a hint of family ties.

Morton settled his doe like gaze on the King. "I graciously request you withdraw my name from the post of Chancellor, Your Majesty."

King Charles was incensed and shook his head, refusing the request; to him, Morton's easy submission was a disgrace.

When nobody moved or spoke up, the King felt obliged to back his demand up, looking at as many people as he could. He had to make a decision right now. Left to his own devices, he could exercise great skill.

"Gentlemen, I ask you to vote on this list of names not individually, but as a group. Either they are accepted together, or none at all."

During the continued silence after this wise offer, the King looked directly at Argyll, fully aware that he must keep his favour for the future.

The English and Scottish Parliaments needed to be kept apart, for he could not fight them both.

He stalled.

Morton pleaded again for his name to be removed. King Charles knew in his heart he would have to give way, but he would never show that his hand had been forced.

"I will consider your views, gentlemen, and respond at a later date, as I see fit," the sovereign tactlessly declared with little ceremony to the assembled members as he quickly stood.

Now the light, which entered via the huge window, was the only thing stopping a shadow from descending over the monarch. On departing, his cousin the Duke of Richmond came to him.

"I have some terrible news, Your Majesty," he whispered.

"More, my lord? I have had my fill of such intelligence," the King responded anxiously.

"The unofficial committee Parliament left in London while it adjourned, has decided to give itself authority to pass laws, without need for your approval. They simply approve them in their house and then pass them in the House of Lords and it is legal. This is in absence of any government in England, and so far they have ordered all church walls to be whitewashed and all crucifixes and beautification to be removed."

The monarch felt his face cool as the blood drained from it and he froze with intense anger for a few seconds - this was in total contradiction to his own policies and as such, a complete and direct attack on him.

Treason, it was foul treason.

He ordered Richmond to follow into a large hall, the King looking out of the window in silence for a few minutes.

He was watching the tradesmen going about their business and wishing they could see how he was trying to protect the laws of the land from such arbitrary acts, by a minority of rebels.

"They try to ruin the nation, while seducing my loyal subjects into supporting them," he said bitterly. The news anchored itself to his soul, dragging it into such a depth of unhappiness.

Richmond continued with further discouraging information, preferring to get it all out at once. "They have appointed a Lord General of the militia, for forces south of the River Trent, on their authority alone."

This infuriated the King and he could not help but cry out. "What treachery and sedition is this? Do they aim at my crown, or war? If my authority is taken by suffering such affronts, what hope does the common man have?"

He came out of his thoughts as sure as ever to continue with the plan of appeasement in his northern base - only this way could he lure Scotland away from such negative influences. Now he had to eat humble pie; the Scottish were more essential than ever.

"Get the orders written for honours. I wish to make Argyll a marquis and Hamilton a duke. And I want you to take the covenant, James. I will have the Scottish on my side against these traitors in London."

"Argyll? Sir, he is as much a wolf in sheep's clothing towards you. And the covenant is their bond of unity against your attempts to align the Scottish religion to that of the English."

"The man needs neutralising, I agree, but that will have to come in time. Right now, I need to prove to them I am as committed to this country as any man. Your taking the covenant will do just that because you are so close to me in blood and service."

He walked away, leaving Richmond to carry out his wishes without any further discussion. Back in the small room he had used earlier, he stood motionless as the door was closed behind him. He immediately felt his temper well up as he ripped his hat off. He slammed his fist down on the desk, the place blurring from his passion. Taking a swipe at the small bell, which he used to call for servants, he cast it onto the floor causing it to tinkle as it rolled around as adrift as his future. The noise did bring him back and he leaned on the furniture, breathing deeply. All he could imagine was Pym's head stuck on a spike on London Bridge, rotting like his disloyalty.

A tapping sounded at the door and he immediately stood up straight and snapped that the person enter. The door opened, and with a bow, a servant announced that he had heard his ringing, asking whether the monarch wished to see his Groom of the Bedchamber. He ordered him to send the man in, frustrated that he had lost his temper so badly.

"I wish to change for prayers, Porter. I will allow that ardent Presbyterian to preach a sermon before me, no matter that he mouths off against my bishops."

Porter discreetly retrieve the bell, anxious to remove any hint of his master's earlier outburst. The King noticed this as well as a look of frustration in the man's face at the news the King was offering himself up to such a preacher.

"How dare they do this treason in London? It is an utter disgrace, such an insult that no monarch has ever had to bear.

If they trouble my wife, I shall have their miserable heads," the King growled, unable to restrain his feelings in front of one of his most trusted and intimate staff. His heart pounded and his face burned with hatred.

"Sir," the groom said as he handed him a small drink of orange juice, knowing just what to do for his master.

"Do you know, Porter, Lord Holland and the Lieutenant of the Tower were at a dinner and he told Holland that my family should be secured as a ransom, depending on what I do in Scotland."

* * *

Tom 'Snipper' Lascelle held his impeccably clean linen sheet round Digby's neck. It was a usual routine for him now and he felt impervious to the peer's status, so close and personal a task it was to shave him.

"Damn weather is as grey as politics," Digby moaned.

"Aye, my lord," Tom agreed with a laugh as he began work on the double chin that betrayed extravagance.

"Did you hear how I made a speech in favour of saving Strafford? I certainly put a bit of colour back into the House of Commons that day. Fancy coming out in support of him in face of all the opposition," Digby continued, indulging in his favourite subject - himself.

"You are much closer to the Royal Family since then, my lord?"

"I am, the Queen knows me personally. I must say, Lascelles, you are a damn good barber. How many other clients do you have?"

"I have a modest amount, sir. There are some senior staff in the Earl or Arundel's household too."

"By heaven, you will need to shave Lady Arundel next time then, for I hear that old thing has growth beyond a man's."

The Puritan Tom grunted a fake laugh, keeping his face static and out of his customer's view, offended by the nastiness of the comment.

A loud rap at the door echoed through the large room.

"Enter," Digby snapped.

A footman announced that Sir Arthur Cotton wanted an audience.

"Send him in," he ordered with an impatient sigh.

Cotton sauntered through slowly, before stopping in the centre of the room that was jammed with glittering, colourful objects of beauty and show. At Dibgy's instruction, Cotton's eyes wandered to observe the painting of himself and Lord Russell, and the tapestry of Sherborne Castle, the family home in Dorset.

The barber was finishing his work now.

"Well, Sir Arthur?"

"My lord, you remember our bargain? Berkeley agreed to do your bidding in the Army Plot, so do you have my reward?"

At the mention of Charles's name, Tom's gaze shifted quickly from Digby's jaw line to the new arrival.

"That tatty letter in his hand? What a damn fool you are, but you can have it. My secretary has the wretched thing at his house with my papers. I have no need for such a scrappy item."

"Oh, it is far from a wretched old thing, my lord, for it is proof that will condemn him," Cotton said, cackling so much he started a coughing fit.

"Get out, sir, before you infect my whole household."

"I can still be of further service to you, my lord. You will need me again."

"Sir Arthur, I think 'may' is the best word and if I do require you, I will call on you. A man of my standing never *needs* anyone."

"Thank you, my lord," Cotton said as he bowed.

"And do not go pestering my secretary today; he is busy with my business. See him tomorrow."

Chapter 33

As Charles sat on the bed, foot tapping the wooden chest at the foot of it, he felt anxious. Nothing about his thoughts was as smooth as the curls and circlets of the flowers, serpents and grapes that were professionally carved into the trunk, yet his mind absently explored every part of this pattern in a bid to avert his inner worry. Anne shuffled into the bedroom, startling him in this moment of reflection.

She playfully tickled him, evidently sensing something was wrong, her brown curls merging with the rich, oak walls that made the room feel so cosy.

"What is it, Charles? You look ill."

He cursed as she sat looking into his eyes on the thick blanket, nature adorning that too, in the form of leaves with red and pink roses. Her very skin was as lovely as these delicate flowers.

"I am summoned to appear before the Parliamentary Committee investigating the Army Plot," he felt impelled to explain, handing over the letter he had so imperiously dismissed when it came, late last night. He had only opened it when he had got up this morning.

Anne frowned at the message written on it, 'Haste, post, haste for thy life' and the drawing of a man hanging on the gallows reinforced the order, probably for those post boys who could not read, to emphasise the urgency of the official correspondence.

"Come and have some breakfast and tell me about it," she said.

He got up and walked after her, as slowly as the glum mood he was in, prompting Anne to turn with a reassuring smile. She nipped into the crimson chamber to get her embroidery. He stood at the door, examining the red walls, remembering that she was desperate to redecorate the room and change the colour she hated so much; she hardly used the room because of it, despite him setting it aside as a closet for her to sew, entertain her friends and house her prized ornaments.

After she returned, they went into a little room that they used for meals or breakfasting, and Louise had already laid some food out.

He slouched into the chair, adjusting the cushion on the seat, and Anne poured some beer, cutting a turkey pie in half for him, before taking some bread for herself. A breeze that floated through the small window was soothing, and he began to relax a little. The mellow green walls reminded him of fields, and with an open window, the noise of birds and sight of the blue sky made it idyllic.

"You remember I told you Digby had me arrested and he wanted me to write to the officers in the north and return there to sound out what they thought of the King?"

"Yes," she agreed, awaiting enlightenment.

"Well, the King apparently cancelled the plan when he was told about it, but I have since found out that my role was not just about probing the officers - the army was going to march on London and secure the capital, freeing Strafford. I have been as used as the whores in Cheapside, yet I knew there would be more to it," he said with anger.

"Charles," she replied at the comparison, with humour, but feigning shock.

"Now Pym's lot are questioning everyone they can find who was involved. Pym is going to reform our churches to appeal to the Scots. A few others and I will be in the middle of this, getting questioned about the plot, to allow him to push this religious policy through while everyone's attention is distracted by the investigation of such a huge conspiracy."

"Well just tell the truth. You knew nothing about the full scheme and were forced to agree to being involved, you had no choice at all. Honesty is the best path," she told him.

Charles could not help but react with a short laugh, showing her advice to be unrealistic. "Anne, I wish it was so simple. If I do tell the truth, I will implicate Digby and the King and then they will certainly never trust me again. Parliament already hates me now I am linked with this plot, so I will find both against me more than ever. I will face ruin, for I have no family connections to rely on, being of such lowly birth, as they constantly like to whisper."

"Politics; I am glad it is left to you men."

"Sweetheart, this is serious. I could find myself in prison again, or torn to pieces by the mob, never able to get patronage, and without any income but from my lands, if they do not take them too."

Anne's face changed, her emerald eyes washing over with emotion. He held both her hands and gently rubbed them. He regretted being so brutally honest with her, but after a while she stood up somewhat abruptly and tidied his clothes.

"What are you doing?" he asked.

"You must look your best. You will be fine I am sure," she said confidently.

The fussing made his nerves worse as he stood up and pulled his doublet on, fastening the discreet buttons under the waist to his breeches.

"I have to go. If I am late they will probably say I have fled," Charles said as he took her fidgeting hand, stopping its nervous caressing of the shirt which he had pulled through the slits of the arms of his black doublet. Following a tender kiss, Charles went to open the door. While stepping out of the house, he saw two men walking towards him, as though desperate to catch him, one of them with a face that instantly made him think of a bird.

"Why the hell have they sent you? I can make my own way to Westminster Hall, you know," he said with frustration, which was ever increasing at the haughty look of the lead man.

The two frowned at each other, the one closest narrowing his eyes, the mouth so tightly closed that it seemed to form a small beak. "I am sure you can, sir, but you should arrive there with less money than you have now."

He looked at them, wondering whether they meant to rob him, and noticing the large book one carried. The fellow that grated upon Charles made fleeting movements with his head.

"Sir Charles Brakely?"

"No, it is Berkeley," he corrected with a glare. The man had instantly gone further down in Charles's estimations, so low that only a miracle would earn a pardon from that depth.

"Well we need your pole money, sir. Fifteen pounds it is," the secondary henchman demanded.

"Damn taxes," Charles muttered as he reached for his purse.

After he had handed some coins over, the man removed his name out of the list with some charcoal, allowing him to continue his journey. He pondered his sister Lucy's pole tax of six pence - her husband was always refusing to pay it, ever since a corrupt Justice of the Peace was sworn into office there. The difference in taxes made him feel slightly guilty for the disparity in wealth of the two; he did not mind that the levy depended on status. He saw a hackney pass by and let it go. Like every bit of nature that sprung up in summer, the plague had also returned to the hot, dirty streets of London - all of this acting as a fertiliser for it, and a hackney was too confined to sit with other people during such danger. Crossing through a side street, he gasped and stopped, a sickly feeling coming over him.

The door had a red cross daubed on it and he read the words with panic. "May God have mercy upon us."

Ever since he was a child and had seen one of the houses in the village smeared with the blood coloured paint, the family locked inside to prevent it spreading, he had been terrified of the disease. The sign on the house would strike fear - which he rarely felt in its purest form - as the symbol of this horrific affliction. For a few seconds he recalled the old plague house being opened after days of silence, to find a child cowering in the corner, traumatised, hungry and now an orphan. He quickly walked on, terrified that the Grim Reaper was only a few streets away from him, his scythe as busy as any harvest time. The deadly menace penetrated into any area, no matter how rich or poor, invisibly stalking the streets looking for victims and Charles made a mental note to have a bible reading each night until it was vanquished. They must also put some scented roses around the house to keep the pestilence out.

Finally, in Westminster Hall, he waited apprehensively, watching the people walking round the makeshift shopping stalls, stacked full of books of all kinds. Like a wild and unrestrained plant, the wooden book cabinets stretched up the walls of the vast hall, masking the glory and beauty that the naked chamber would offer. The lesser wares included hats, beer and hosiery. He looked over to the other side of the expanse of space and examined the wooden partitions, which formed rickety, makeshift areas, acting as courts and suchlike for official business. It had been transformed back to this normality once Strafford's trial had finished. A tatty bill of mortality was stuck on the wall and even now he could not get away from the plague. He hesitated before examining the causes of death for the previous week; the scourge was catching up to the usual high numbers of convulsion, fever, stillbirth, teeth and old age. The black skull and crossed bones stood out to him, as though embossed, seeming to stare through the eerie, eye sockets.

Instructions in the summons he had received were to await a page who would conduct him to the committee. He stood near one of the law courts and looked above it at the immense window, examining the ornate shape, and then even further up at the old wooden beamed roof.

He wondered what that pioneering oak construction had seen, guessing it must be several hundred years old by now.

Then in the midst of the beauty, he examined again the old timber shacks holding officials and judges above the shoppers, symbolising their superiority in status and legal matters over the laymen below. Some courts had benches, with spectator boxes stacked upon each other like a tower, and he overheard a session regarding a case of manslaughter. Curiosity of the trial made him contemplate the usual punishment of imprisonment, as well as being branded with a hot poker, and he listened further, until eventually someone argued that the charge should include robbery.

"I plead for benefit of clergy, my lord," the terrified voice said, clearly that of the accused.

Charles felt calmer as he eavesdropped, getting interested in the proceedings.

"Very well, I request you read to me psalm fifty two to prove you are of the clergy, and as such, protected from full punishment for certain crimes."

Charles listened with bated breath, moving his foot to get rid of a dog that had begun sniffing his shoe.

"H-have mercy on me, G-god, after Thy great goodness, according to the multitude of Thy m-mercies do away with my offences."

After a short silence a voice boomed in final judgement, "Very well, we will reduce sentence to whipping and a spell in the stocks for both crimes."

Charles raised his eyebrows. The judicial system had always interested him, and he remembered how a man from his village had been declared a criminal for committing suicide. His estate and possessions were forfeited as punishment for ending a sacred life and passed to the state, rather than his family. This had ignited questions in his young mind, although his parents refused to listen to him, or give answers of any detail to the scandalous event.

A plain man approached him as he waded deep in his reminiscences. As the page went to speak, Charles noted how his bottom set of teeth seemed too high for his mouth, visible throughout his oration, giving his speech an air of soft muffling.

"Are you next to enter the law courts or are you just waiting, sir?"

"My God, I have no wish to be in there. I am expecting the committee investigating the Army Plot to call me," Charles snapped.

"Oh, so you are looking for the committee?"

"Well, I think they are looking for me, sir," he said with a hint of sarcasm.

The man signalled for Charles to follow. "I am clerk of the committee, come with me please. Any interesting cases in the law courts today?"

Looking down at the balding head and resenting being escorted by anyone, Charles wondered about whether to reply.

Then he realised he was being rude to the clerk, who after all, he had no quarrel with.

"Yes, he pleaded benefit of clergy."

Without a second to listen to his words, the man mumbled on, one finger moving, pointing and thrusting along with a new tale. "Well there was one man up for counterfeiting money the other day. Death it was, the Judge recapping that counterfeiting was treason, until they finally commuted it to transportation to the colonies in the New World. Not heard anyone get the death sentence and keep it yet. Although one man did plead judgement of God in a murder case and so was executed, but spared the guilty verdict, so that his family would be allowed to have his poxy possessions."

Charles sighed at the incessant talking about death and punishment. He was thinking only of his own trial now and then it crossed his mind as to whether this idiot was deliberately bringing up such subjects. Eventually he stopped outside a door that the man entered. He politely asked a rigid Charles, arms folded, to wait.

"For the love of God," Charles muttered as he paused. Two men stood by the door making sure he did not escape.

"You may go inside, they are ready for you, sir," the man instructed.

Charles's heart was pounding fast and his body sweated beneath his shirt as he stepped gingerly forward - the uncertainty of what he would be asked, how many people would be there played as much havoc with his mind as a body of skirmishers.

The door clashed behind him and he was left feeling as though he had been pushed into an arena, just like an ancient gladiator in the colosseum - he was quite used to standing firm, since he was the eldest child of the family. This position had brought a double dose of heavy burden, due to the fact that he piled responsibility on himself in a bid to match the heroic and colourful life of his seafaring Uncle Tom.

The committee men glared at him suspiciously, which did not change one bit, and were as dull as the room with its deep brown wooden panelling. The place was sparse, like the members humours, containing only a long oak table that looked like it had not moved an inch in centuries.

The committee sat on plain chairs, ready for business, and he guessed he was destined for the only empty seat at the end of the table.

"Sir Charles Berkeley?"

He nodded. At least this lot had got his name right.

"No, sir, we need your affirmation that you are this man."

He tutted with annoyance. When his father was joining some of the customers playing games in their inn, the man had always said that Charles would never be a good card player with such easily recognisable emotions.

"I am he."

He played with his wedding ring.

"Pray be seated," a man said pointing at the lone chair.

As he sat down, he remembered Strafford isolated in Westminster Hall for his immense court session. He actually started to feel a little respect for how the man had dealt with that, along with embarrassment at his own reactions to this small examination today. He fidgeted with his hands under the table, trying to maintain his dignity.

"Why am I here?" he queried, the sharpness of his demand falling like a thunderclap into the drab surroundings, similarly signalling the start of a barrage of questions, frowns and coughs.

"You are here to be questioned, Sir Charles, so we ask you to leave that to us from now on."

At this slighting, his irritation welled up, while a tight lipped older man, who seemed to be the central figure, made ready to speak. Wrinkles spread across his forehead and mouth as he made a slurping noise, like he was tasting an invisible delicacy.

"We, the committee for investigating the Army Plot, have met for near two months now, but some fresh news has arrived about this conspiracy, just when we thought we had finished interviewing all those involved. A secret informer has told us that there is documentary evidence to highlight the plotting."

Who was the mystery person, Charles wondered. As this went on, he focussed, breathing deeply, but imagining the air to be as foul and tainted as some of these hardened Puritan hearts.

Anne had recommended deep inhales and he realised how much he relied on her; even now in her absence, she still lay entwined with his spirit, as constant as the sun and as equally warming in these cool times. He saw a carved wooden box in the middle of the table, the kind that normally held bibles, and he suspected that it had been placed to add some moral authority and gravity to the meeting. Eventually his gaze came to rest on a small picture at the other side of the room with religious overtones.

"Let me remind the committee that so far we have found that the Governor of Portsmouth was ready to secure that place, for purposes not fully known, though surely to receive a French invasion force. We discover that Lord Strafford cowardly attempted to bribe the Lieutenant of the Tower of London with twenty thousand pounds for his freedom, and now less than six weeks ago, we find a treasure trove of further information.

The Lord High Admiral, the Duke of Northumberland, gave us a letter from his brother detailing this. The correspondence told us that the King was informed that his northern army was still loyal, but crucially that the Governor of Portsmouth and some other evil people had then thrust upon the King a plan for occupying the Tower, and London itself. The leading men in Parliament were to be arrested, Strafford freed and the people of this country would be overrun by tyranny."

The speaker paused, bulging eyes burning at as many people as possible.

Charles was astounded to hear these details spoken officially and realised just how much of a pawn he had been in it all.

The complete scene became apparent, as if Van Dyck had just painted it himself right now, and the result was as outstanding as the canvasses themselves. No wonder Parliament was worried by all this - just what had he got himself into by speaking to Digby, he panicked.

"We believe that this man was involved too. Sir Charles Berkeley, did you know of this dangerous plot?"

Charles sat up straight. He was as mortified as they were about the totality of the scheme.

"No, sir," he answered simply, subdued with the revelations, and desperately hanging onto the notion that all this could be trumped up propaganda. But this managed to sweep away his usually grounded mindset and he began to get engulfed by it all.

"No? You knew nothing of it, sir, yet we have been told you were about to travel north to speak to the officers in this army," one man probed with outrage.

"I knew nothing of the detail," he insisted.

The man gave a hearty laugh, much to Charles's chagrin.

"Ah, now we see, gentlemen. He is changing his tune as easily as a morning bird. I must warn you, sir, I will get my worm in the end."

"I was not told of what you have just mentioned, sir," he asserted with a fixed look as he paused, half reticent about speaking his mind, "Seeing as you insist of speaking of the animal kingdom, then remember there is always someone bigger than you up the food chain."

One or two men coughed, or covered their mouths delicately, hiding their amusement - clearly those who did not like their colleague - and took great pleasure from Charles's comment.

The divisions his retort had exposed gave him some hope.

"So just what was explained to you?" another committee member demanded, putting the group back on track.

He did not reply, unsure of what to say.

"Sir Charles, answer the question or we will assume you know a lot more than you tell us."

Charles thought of Cotton and he realised he could

overshadow his own implication by turning it on that man and with his last verbal victory under his belt, he began to lose restraint.

"God damn it, answer, sir," the fellow insisted, slapping his hand on the desk.

Charles bit on his lip in anger, tilting his head, about ready to stand up at the impertinence. Following a few seconds of realisation that his temper was being taunted, he resumed his dignified posture.

"I was imprisoned by Sir Arthur Cotton. He said I would only be freed if I consented to correspond with the army in the north," he explained, smug in the knowledge that his opponent had been dragged in.

"Sir Arthur Cotton is a friend of Parliament, I hardly think he would have done that if what you say is fact, sir. But tell me, correspond in what way?"

That name was synonymous with any hot water Charles was in, and in an instant, he suspected. The remark made him sure that Cotton was the unknown person who had tipped them off about his involvement. As soon as it was uttered, it was like a clue that linked up with everything. But where did this whole matter now spring from, in view of their earlier comments about the existence of apparent documentary evidence?

"Well, to see what the army thought of the King," he told them, reeling with indignation at the fact that his enemy was certainly not loyal to Parliament, being under the patronage of Lord Digby, a decidedly royal supporter.

"And was the King aware of this?" the furrowed, old man asked, proving he had not died during his inactivity, leaning forward on the table.

"I was told he was not. It went no further, apparently, because the King did not want it to," Charles recollected. "So if he did not know of it, how could he say it should go no further?" he retorted quickly.

Charles shook his head. "The King knew nothing initially and when he was told, he refused to countenance it. That is when the whole thing ended."

The man smiled again. "This is twice now that he has amended his words, gentlemen."

"Sir Arthur Cotton imprisoned me. I was forced to agree to correspond. I waited for a while and was eventually told the King had rejected the idea when it was explained to him. That is everything I know," Charles summarised impatiently.

"Gentlemen, let me remind you what Harry Percy's letter told us. He said that the King had rejected the Governor of Portsmouth's plans for the army too, but a plot did exist, and today we have seen more proof of it. No matter whether the King was involved or not, his friends, ministers and courtiers were definitely architects of it. He is still surrounded by evil men trying to galvanise him into unlawful action. Sir Charles, on whose authority were you imprisoned?"

It was a question he was dreading and he hesitated.

"I am not aware, sir. I was not given this information. All I was told is that I had to agree to sound out the army officers. When you are snatched from your home, leaving your pregnant wife, that is the least of your worries."

Hoping that this satisfied the men, he waited, cornered in the trap he had wished to avoid. It was like a fox being chased by the huntsmen and this was not a feeling he thought a knight of the realm should experience.

"Again, this mysterious person who ordered your arrest sounds very much like they are linked to the King's court. Nobody could authorise such a thing unless they were well connected or privileged themselves. Behold, gentlemen, just how insecure our Parliament is at this moment, despite all of our gains," he concluded.

This is just like a play, he thought. He assumed their aim was not to impeach him, but to use him to raise the spectre of this conspiracy and scaremonger all and sundry back into the fold. At least he had managed to implicate Cotton, though leaving Digby and the King out of it, but crucially, he had shown himself as being forced into this and not through any detestation of Parliament. He would say no more. The dogged man was still gunning for Charles though, and he advised his colleagues that the evidence was only half a story, threatening to imprison him again until he told the full truth.

"I move to hold the witness, until we have reviewed his evidence."

Charles looked wide eyed, the comment immediately causing him to turn to the only location he could hope for support. He had put forward a name for the position of major, the lad's father asking for Charles's support. Now the father sat as a member of the committee and he looked on with a heavy expression.

Each member began to assess the call, blank expressions of contemplation causing Charles to panic, for they were just about to end the session before this interloper spoke up.

The file of men began to break, some conversing with neighbours, until at last, the man Charles knew held his hand up.

"I for one am satisfied by Sir Charles's honesty with us. He was used as a pawn, so he will not know any of the more intimate details, such as those the brother of the Earl of Northumberland spouts. I move we adjourn the meeting for now, as I see little need for keeping him further."

Thankfully, this view was echoed, but it was only an adjournment, and the knives were still drawn. He was about to speak, to demand why they did not want to call Sir Arthur Cotton to give evidence, but the sympathetic man widened his eyes, warning him off.

Digby's position was just as precarious. The peer had even published his own speech in defence of Strafford's life, without the permission of Parliament, and the members had gone mad demanding his imprisonment. He was only saved when the King ennobled him as Baron Digby of Sherborne, therefore warding his foes off. Pym was in a strong position, but to arrest a member of the House of Lords would create a breach with that house, which he could ill afford. It would upset the balance of the national scales, between the King, House of Commons, House of Lords and the Scottish.

Chapter 34

Charles was in New Palace Yard, waiting for James. A shoeblack was polishing his friend's footwear with an old wig. Charles stood bored and irritated, looking around at the buildings. He had already been approached by all and sundry selling their street wares and being stationary made him a prime target. As a woman neared, he grumbled inwardly instead of doing something about the problem.

"Care for a merry song, written by my own hand, sir?"

"No, madam."

He looked at her crooked flat hat and stained white apron. She massaged the song sheets in her pocket as if wishing them away.

"Oh … what are they called?" he asked, deciding to get some conversation to pass the time.

"Mister Pym's Jig, or My Sweetheart's Love."

"Give me the love one."

The oysterman pushed his laden wooden barrow past while Charles paid her. Now all that was left was to look at the hackney carriages drawn up in a line outside Westminster Hall, then at the small wooden shops which had been built onto the front of that huge building, clinging to it like barnacles. The entrance, which rose to a point, and was crowned with a weathercock, was flanked by two turreted towers. Streets of houses enclosed the yard he stood in, with a huge gatehouse at the opposite end, Westminster Abbey's spires and towers reaching out to God well above all of these structures. Lastly he observed the various groups of people milling around, with the occasional horseman trotting past. The rain earlier had washed the muck and horse dung into the crevices of the cobbles. He felt his purse, making sure the list of midwifes was safe for Anne - he had been checking they had licences from the Bishop of London.

He then moved towards James, who was chattering with the cleaner.

"Aye, sir, you can say you had thy shoes polished by some French earl's wig."

"Get ye gone, such a man wouldn't hand you his wig," James scoffed.

"I tell you straight, his valet got it when he finished with it, then he gave it to his servant who threw it out it the other day. I thought it best not to let it waste."

James slapped the man's arm with a loud laugh - he was always touching, cuddling or patting - and they left after paying him, with a tip too. Sauntering along, the two men passed a narrow alleyway and James joined another person in the corner, relieving himself on the building, elaborately spraying what seemed to be a pattern.

Charles rolled his eyes at the publicity of the whole thing.

"For the love of God, you dally as much as a woman of quality. Get your backside moving," Charles playfully teased, "And why do that on a street corner, you are not a dog."

"I do not see woman of quality pissing on street corners, Charles, but I wish I did," James sniggered as he shook his manhood.

Charles had to chortle at his comment.

"Get an eyeful of this; many a woman would beg me for it," James said as he thrust his manhood out.

Shaking his head, Charles shouted jovially for him to fit a lock to his trousers, continuing on and leaving his friend. James soon caught up, and as they strolled along the street, they were stopped by a pedlar selling chapbooks.

James interrupted her discussion with another man, as was his custom on most occasions. "Have you got *Long Meg of Westminster*, madam?"

The peddler handed him the book and he gave two pence.

"God save you, sweet mistress," James said happily, as he left her.

Next came the obligatory explanation; the story was about a girl of eighteen, who came to London to get employment.

Marching around the City at night disguised as a male, she would challenge men to duels and win them. Eventually marrying a soldier and deciding to be an obedient wife, the story encouraged all women to be the same. James was still the boy he knew, so at ease with life.

"Sir Charles, sir, it is me, Tom."

He turned round to see his barber with a red face.

"Bad news, sir, I was with Lord Digby today."

"That is terrible, Tom," he joked, infected with some of James's casual humour.

"Sir Arthur Cotton arrived and said he wanted some letter you had written. Something about his reward for doing Digby's bidding."

"Letter? Gods wounds, I have only written one," he remembered with a gasp.

The letter about Strafford's trial - it must have found its way to Digby. How could he have been so stupid to put anything in writing at all? Charles cursed.

The committee investigating the Army Plot. Documentary

evidence. It all added up now, and his hunches during the questioning had been spot on.

"Why did you write to Digby?" James asked, jumping on the point like a hound.

"Never mind, I need it back," Charles retorted bluntly. But James's excited expression warned him he still had his teeth in this bone of intrigue.

"Digby said it was with his secretary. He lives near the sign of the compass just up the road."

"Thank you, Tom, I owe you for this," he said. He passed over a couple of shillings in gratitude.

"One more thing, Sir Charles, Digby said he would have his man fish it out of his cabinet, for the secretary was very organised, one of the best, he bragged. Apparently he is so good, that each drawer in his cabinet is labelled alphabetically, according to the sender's surname."

Charles seized this piece of information, shaking Tom's hand several times.

"That man is worth his weight in gold," Charles told his friend. James simply stared at him though, waiting to find out what was going on.

"I must get that correspondence, for Cotton will have me if I do not. Will you help me?"

"What is in this note? You are not normally as furtive as this...have you been a naughty boy, Charles? That is unlike you - my parents were always telling me I should be as honest as you, God bless them."

"I have incriminated myself. James, I am ruined if he gets this. We need to break into that house and get it before Cotton."

"Now hang on a minute, you are having one of your moments," James said, sensing that Charles's determination and immediate reactions would lead to a risky situation.

"James, my own and my family's lives can depend on this, for pity's sake."

"He won't declare for King or Parliament, yet he will rob a secretary to a lord," James whispered, eyes to the sky.

Charles stormed back towards the clock tower to get a glimpse of the time, cursing and muttering, telling his friend he would do it all on his own in that case.

"All right, all right. Meet me here at two and I will help you, but just because I value you so much. You are like a brother to me - of course I would not see you suffer."

Charles looked at him in surprise, before returning to the matter at hand, warning him to come dressed in old clothes, for already he had a perfect plan for the time of the meeting.

* * *

The alleys were dark and menacing and Charles pulled his cloak around him, tapping his foot impatiently. He had tied his hair back and put it under his hat. A figure approached but he could not see who it was yet and he stayed put, finally shooting a glance over - it was not James.

He panicked and cursed as the individual neared him.

The shadowy scene unnerved him a little more; it was as if the figure was staring at him. He could do nothing now but stand firm, or leave. He felt the steel dagger he carried sometimes, normally for use during his lunch at the inn, but now to cut different meat if the visitor was hostile.

"Are you lost, sir?" Charles demanded.

"You don't know me?" the person asked.

Charles stepped closer, taking hold of the handle discreetly. Then he recognised it was James.

"You buffoon, why have you shaved your moustache off?"

"So nobody knows me, of course, and it evidently worked."

"But if they see you tomorrow you shall still have no moustache, so they will know it is you."

James complained under his breath.

"Come on, I have just seen the night soil men go down here, we need to catch them," Charles said, grabbing his arm.

They walked speedily up the road, keeping to the walls and the dimness, and then cut across the street to a narrow back alley. The night watchman shouted from a few streets away; it was two of the clock exactly, and for once, James had been on time. As they emerged into another street, they saw the dung cart just passing the sign that hung out from a shop - even it creaked a little in protest at the smell. They sped up and Charles noticed the notice portrayed a compass and he realised now that they were in Norfolk Street.

The signboards extended right down the lane, the majority of properties sporting one to identify them. Trade notice boards interspersed them and they passed by a row of coffins - the carpenter, a goat - the leatherman, a bag of nails - the ironmonger. The night soil men and their slow horse and cart were just ahead now.

"Can we cover part of your shift, gentlemen?" Charles asked as he approached the two men, but rummaging in his purse to add weight to the request.

The stench of their basic clothes, covered in excrement, caused James to step back as it hit his nostrils.

"What are you talkin' about, mister?"

"We need to empty a house, so want to borrow your cart, no questions asked. Here's a shilling each, so just wait nearby and return in an hour," Charles instructed.

They took the coins without hesitation, then one of them held out for another coin. James groaned and whined about the smell as they finally left. Charles examined the horse and wooden cart piled with dirt and the leather buckets hanging on the side of it.

"I'll lead this mare," Charles decided, taking hold of the reins and commencing the short journey, insisting that James stop moaning, lest he give them away.

After about fifteen minutes, they stopped outside a house.

The odour was gradually losing its edge as he became used to it, but James was still frowning deeply.

"I am sure this is it, I remember the windows and the crooked panes in this one," he said, recalling the one time he had visited on behalf of Holland.

"Pah, you remember the stupidest of things. I'm not breaking into a house that could be the wrong one, just because you are sure of the windows," James mocked.

"Now listen, from now on take this seriously or you can piss off."

James widened his eyes, before peering through the leaded window. "How are you going to get the letter when our business is in the cellar?" he queried.

"Ah, well, I prepared a plan earlier. The secretary meets with Digby for business each Tuesday, so just the old servant is left in the house. You will have to keep him busy while I slip away."

Charles knocked on the door before James could comment.

It seemed like an age before glowing candlelight illuminated the upstairs window. After another long delay the door opened, and an old man stood there in a nightshirt with a shawl wrapped around him.

"About time too; you have left us for four days, and things are getting unbearable," the elderly servant chided.

"People seem to be shitting much more lately - it must be the fear of what the King is going to do next with his powers," James interrupted, causing the servant to glare at him.

"Shut up and come on. We need to get the place cleared for this poor fellow," Charles barked.

He picked up the main, larger wooden pale, and a pole, carrying them into the house, both holding a lantern in their other hands. He noticed on passing, that the study was just ahead, the door open and desk visible. They awkwardly descended the stairs and were greeted with an even more overpowering stench than earlier. James stomped his foot down without noticing the extent of the excretion, splashing some all over.

"What have these two been eating? This shit stinks to high heaven," James grumbled bitterly, going on to demand that the letter be worth all of this.

Charles screwed his face up, looking at the mountain of filth and wondering where to begin. He set the lanterns down and sent James back for the shovels, to be met with a cry from the old man, who insisted he wipe his feet clean. When he returned, reluctantly wading through the dirt as delicately as possible, Charles began collecting the muck up in an instant. If they did not start, it would never go.

"What next then?" James pressed, as a pretext to beginning his own efforts.

"He will not venture down here while we work, so I'll have to sneak upstairs and get in that study. You'll have to do something that will cause him to go to another room for a time, instead of standing guard in the hall like a damned sentry."

They filled the first bucket full and slotted the pole through the holes at either end of it, carrying it back up the steps and into the passage, sweating profusely from the awkward work and the secrecy of the mission. The servant stood well back and Charles deliberately dropped his end of the pole, the bucket falling, before he caught at it again. As planned, some of the contents had tipped over the floor, though splashing James right up his breeches.

"Good God, man, you arse. Can you not hold it properly?"

James howled, as the old man tottered around in disbelief at the smearing.

"My back has gone off," Charles said, pretending to be in pain.

"You will clean this up immediately," the man instructed, as he headed for the kitchen. It was hard to tell who was more annoyed; James or the servant.

Charles pulled his shoes off, picked them up, and wiped his hands on his clothes, bounding into the study, and leaving James to curse and lift his hands to the sky in frustration. It contained an ornate writing desk surrounded by enough paper to light a bonfire, and he rummaged through several loads of recent correspondence, before finding the older pieces arranged in date order. He stood well back from the work, anxious that it should not get stained.

"Thank God he is so organised."

He wiped the sweat from his head, noticing at the last minute that he had spread some muck all over his brow, leaving traces on the back of his hand. He wiped that on his clothes too, before taking some leather gloves from his belt and putting them on to fumble with the sheets.

"God damn it, get a grip," he cursed, shaking his head, before handling them less impulsively.

"Ah, April, we're here."

Then he heard James practically squeal at the servant, "No, we need more rags than that. I will help you get some water, come on."

For an instant he thought he was going to be discovered as he heard the servant asking where he was, before James seemed to usher him away, claiming his friend had gone for air. To Charles's immense relief, he saw his small note lying at the front of the pile, and snatched it, before his eye caught another that lay on its own.

"Your humble servant, Sir Arthur Cotton," Charles muttered as he read the end of the letter.

He scanned the rest of it.

"I really can serve your Lordship and the King's cause now I have Sir Charles's position. Soon I should be able to secure the whole regiment for your use, if the need arises," he whispered as he digested the information.

He was just about to open the door fully when he saw the two men return.

"Where is your cursed colleague who caused all this?" the man continued, flabbergasted and outraged at the situation, before swearing that he would fetch the constable if his partner did not turn up.

Charles saw James make an angry expression at him and he pointed to the door, trying to signal to James to get the old man out of the hall again. James was not getting the message though, or was being obstructive, and both men's irritation was growing fast.

"Has he gone outside? You might be prepared to clean this on your own, but my master will be back soon and I will not suffer any blame," the servant continued, on and on, as he peeked into the night to search for Charles.

As the old man had his back to him, Charles took his shoes out from under his clothes, unconcerned at the mess within, and sneaked out of the study and down the cellar, putting them back on as he stood on the stone steps.

"Oi, James, I have filled another bucket now, so we will have to get that mess sorted," Charles shouted, before emerging into the hall again.

"I have never seen such fools as you two, now I want this cleared. You, sir, you will pull your weight."

"Aye, for it is your fault we are in this mess," James growled poignantly.

The two men did their best for the floor, washing it down and scrubbing it, before they were chased back down the cellar to remove the rest of the excrement, leaving the old man to inspect the result. After what seemed like an age, they gave up and left a quarter of the muck, assuring the man that they had finished and knowing he would not be going to check tonight.

Charles was careful to keep up the pretext of his backache too.

"Well, I suppose you two sorted it in the end and your back looks like it is giving you some aches. I have a recipe that would help, but I'll have to try to remember … now what was it … wax, resin, galbanum, litharge, white lead, beat to powder, add neats foot oil and heat it, then slap it on."

"Thank you, I shall remember that," Charles said, rubbing the affected area with one hand as he walked to the door.

As the fossil thankfully closed it behind them, Charles gripped his fists and punched the air with joy.

"You swine, talk about being up to our necks in shit; I thought you were going to get found out. If only you had mentioned about your back being bad before we did this, then I could have thought of a different plan than carting heavy buckets all over. I have a better cure for your aches than that anyway," James let loose, releasing all he had kept pent up.

"My back is not bad; I had to pretend, didn't I? Good God, I sometimes wonder how Elizabeth puts up with you."

"You mean you tipped that dirt all over me on purpose?" James said, puffing his chest out with indignation, horrified that it could have been deliberate.

Charles ignored him and James continued his foul mood.

"Anyway, don't mention Elizabeth; she is suffering from her regular womanly way."

"Oh."

"I don't know how many times I have to tell her to keep away from my casks of wine; she is determined to turn it all sour. She knows full well she will if she goes near them at these times, but she still does so," James bleated on.

"James, I don't want to know. Anyway, everyone knows that its sugar they turn black. Now, more importantly, I got the letter and I found another gift waiting for me too; a letter from Cotton to Digby. I cannot wait to show this to Holland or Sir Richard."

‘[The king's allies] "Will repent that ever they showed themselves for the king, for the public applause opposes monarchy and I fear this island before it be long will be a theatre of distractions."

Endymion Porter, the king's Groom of the Bedchamber commenting on the king's many concessions to his opponents in Scotland.

Chapter 35

J ohn Pym sat amongst a great gathering of Members of the House of Commons, chatting wildly around the whole perimeter of the sixty foot by thirty foot chamber. The centre of the room was like an island, with two stranded clerks sitting at the table, in front of the speaker, quills ready to record and take notes, while a man progressed around the end of the room, holding the golden mace over his shoulder.

"Those bishops would have been long gone by now, if the Queen had not summoned her gang of loyal, young, aristocratic fops to the House of Lords," William Strode complained to Pym, about the fact that the bishops' fates had been given two weeks' grace by the Lords, while the matter was discussed by them in more detail.

"Well the main issue is what we will discuss today," Pym said, shifting priorities, and highlighting the importance of the coming debate, though not many knew of it yet.

The speaker's chair back rose like a tall grandfather clock; the royal arms adorning it may as well have been ticking, for time was certainly on the monarch's side. Less than a week ago, with the opening of the new Parliamentary session, the several hundred men, still under strength from absent members, had sworn the usual opening oath that King Charles the First was the only supreme governor of this realm, and that they would be true and faithful to the King and his heirs, as well as not to know or hear of any ill or damage intended to him, without defending him.

Pym watched with amusement as the speaker stood up, anxious to begin the session, though men were far more interested in catching up with their colleagues, and the din continued to race up and down the many ranks. Eventually, out of pity, some men stopped, while one or two others interceded on the speaker's behalf, until it was subdued enough for him to take over his role in full.

The usual Privy Councillors and important members had taken their all but reserved seats near the speaker's great chair, and gossip about the King's activities in Scotland, along with the stunted attempt to remove the bishops from voting in the House of Lords, occupied most of the conversations.

A man called Robert Goodwyn stood in one of the farthest rows. "Gentlemen, I propose the desperate need to follow in Scotland's footsteps, and advocate the desire for Parliament to appoint all the great officers of government, to prevent any further evil councillors being unwittingly employed by His Majesty."

Pym observed Strode, a Devon man, from the same part of the country as he was. They exchanged a look of knowing anticipation, before Strode nodded his confidence in his coming part.

"If we do not secure this point, then all we have achieved in this Parliament will come to nothing and our hard won privileges will be seized back," Goodwyn continued, warning of the dangers.

As soon as the virgin speaker sat down, for he had rarely been heard to talk in debates before, Strode stood up, lifting a hand, as though vigorously clinging onto the argument that Goodwyn had just unleashed.

"By God, the man is right. Everything we have accomplished thus far will be cast into the fires of hell and destroyed, unless we have a veto over the choice of the great officers of the nation, by whom His Majesty has so recently been deceived and our nations threatened."

Strode's roaring, like he was preaching a sermon written by one of the fire and brimstone Puritans that Pym so enjoyed, caused a great silence to descend upon the house. Pym could count on the honest and brave bearing of the man, for he had spent near eleven years in prison, even in the Tower itself, for opposing the King. It was allies like this which Pym needed; those with the same skills as his.

"Let the Scots' bravery inspire us. They now approve the men who are chosen to lead them."

Pym shuffled through his notes, meticulous details of any precedent he could find from history, about Parliamentary control of ministerial appointments. During the recess, with time on his hands for once, he had filtered through ancient scrolls and documents in the Parliamentary archives, stretching from Saxon times, to the reign of Richard the Second.

He stood to echo Strode, attempting to inject some legality into the argument, based on past history. "Gentlemen, we simply seek that which our forebears have requested. We have precedent on our side; during the reign of King Richard the Second, we see the Lord Admiral, Lord Treasurer and the Lord Chancellor, all being appointed by Parliament."

As Pym stood, searching for signs of opinion, he sensed that this was going to be another close divide. Unlike the issue of bishops, which unified the house, this matter would be debated right down to the last man. Sure enough, Edward Hyde, who Pym knew to be in touch with the King recently, rose to comment.

"This is one reform too far, in my mind. The great officers of the crown are to be appointed by the King alone, for this is an hereditary flower of the monarch. Parliament has so far abolished the royal courts, illegal taxes, secured the duration of Parliament, so that it can only be dissolved with its own consent, though it must be called again every three years, and I believe this has done very much for the good of the subjects of this country. I am positive that all particulars of the balance of power in this land are in a good condition, and we should but preserve them now as they stand."

Pym had expected a rocky ride, but without being able to shout Hyde down, because of the great support and willing listeners, he had to endure the argument. As Hyde stood, one man after another got to his feet; Viscount Falkland, that respectable and good mannered man, Mister Strangeways, Mister Waller and Mister Holbourne. This four pronged, follow up attack whipped the chamber into such a frenzy, with great cries in support of them.

"The late King James, of blessed memory, had once commented that true monarchy was only possible with the authority to decide which persons were to serve him in positions of trust, as ministers of state. We will upset the balance of power too far by aiming at this prerogative."

Strode stepped up, removing his hat and brushing his sweaty hair back with his hand, in one fell swoop. His passion and determination with this matter was of such mammoth proportions, that he felt the fatigue of a battle.

"I beg you all, do not lose sight of the intense threat we still face. All of those gains Mister Hyde so gloriously listed will be swept away in an instant, should another Strafford be appointed, deceitfully encouraging the King down a dark path of rule. To ignore this would be folly," Strode cried, with forceful, sweeping hand gestures.

As he was finishing his display of emotion, about to launch

into another reasoned essay, he was faced with several men on their feet, seizing the debate from him.

"If we are to be concerned by such a future prospect, then I motion that we petition His Majesty and tell him of our fear. That way, he can be mindful of our thoughts and this will encourage him to seek our advice in future appointments, whereas dictating to him, about a right which is lawfully his, will simply enrage and distance him from us," came another voice of opposition, the moderate course immediately attracting calls of support.

Pym was about to get up, but another voice cried out.

"Precisely. We have secured ourselves and rid the King of his evil minister, Lord Strafford. Let us not forget that both King and Parliament share power in England's government. To grasp at the choice of ministers of state is to make an attempt at a power which lies solely with the King. We will endanger ourselves more by doing that, than by anything Mister Strode spoke of. We are here for the people's safety, not to constantly demand more and more, until the nation reaches breaking point."

Pym remained seated, seeing the matter was hopeless. With a shake of his head, and a glance of exasperation to Strode, he realised that the King's supporters had used reasoned argument to muster the house in their favour. They had blocked a main measure that Pym had aimed to get through, and exposed a severe weakness in his ranks - the first time this had happened so far.

"So let us draw up a petition to discuss future appointments, laying bare the fear we have over potential candidates. We should implore him to choose only those who are truly committed to a joint and happy settlement between the King and Parliament,"

Hyde summarised, closing the session, his great belly enlarged even more by pride in his achievement.

Strode sat still, flabbergasted and paralysed, his gaze fixed to the floor. Pym was not as low as his colleague, though it was a blow to suffer a first major defeat in a home area, the normally safe arena of the House of Commons. He had expected the bulk of the opposition to come from the House of Lords, whose members were usually the ones taking up those great positions of government.

Finally, snapping out of his hypnotic state, Strode predicted with an air of depression, "And now, he is still free to bribe and solicit men with handing out these important roles within government."

Chapter 36

A t the end of October, as the King was preparing to return to London, Parliament reassembled in preparation.

Charles was returning from Westminster where he had picked up the christening gown, as Anne was not feeling well enough to come. He would have used his own gown that had been passed through the generations, but the moths had destroyed the fabric. His attention was caught by the fencing master who regularly challenged all comers to sparring matches.

He looked on as the expert finished his current game, slicing the opponent's weapon out of his hands and into the air. As the master searched for other contenders, Charles moved on.

While he was sauntering into the market square, he saw a group of people enjoying a performance by some travelling players. They acted on a wooden stage, while the spectators ate and drank, throwing things and shouting boisterously.

They reluctantly parted to let a carriage through, and Charles recognised the crest on the door as the Earl of Warwick's and he progressed easily, in the wake of the traffic. The city men and women, sailors, apprentices, merchants and servants then fused back together after it had driven on and he marvelled at how the city contained every part of the hierarchy, but so completely mixed together. Thinking again of the power struggle, he compared the gulf between King and Parliament, as gaping as when the Red Sea parted for Moses.

A woman approached him. "Do ye want some oranges, sir?"

He raised his eyebrows, it was an age since he had had some and he paid the six pence. But then an almighty quarrel broke out as the players mimicked the King and Pym. The area got invaded and the fake mob was attacked by a real one of idle apprentices, who were gathering in preparation for the recall of Parliament, bored with their inactivity. He shook his head and cast the remains of his orange away, turning for home. His family were uppermost in his mind and he had no inclination at all to get involved in more scuffles this time. Not long after this, though, someone grabbed his purse, taking advantage of the confusion and he felt it snap from his belt. Instantly running after the thief, the outrage at wrongdoing coming naturally to the fire, he chased him down a side street. The man was fast and he was losing pace, until the felon crashed into a woman who stepped out of a small doorway.

"What the 'ell are you doin', you little poltroon?" she squealed as the crook fell to the ground, bearing face down onto the dirt and grit of the filthy, narrow lane. The daylight had been repelled by the way the houses were built over half the alleyway, enclosing it. The scum would be sorry, Charles thought as he towered over the flat body.

He grabbed the scrawny neck, lifting him to his feet and slamming him against the wall. It turned out to be a mere lad, looking no older than eleven.

"But you are only a child," he panted in surprise.

"Aye an' you are rich. I 'ave seen you come out of the palace. You can afford to lose thy purse, Mister. I 'ave my family to feed and get beaten if I ain't got any spoils," the boy said with a look of hate, the eyes deep and opaque - certainly no mirror into his young soul.

He grabbed the wretch and tugged him sharply. "If you expect any sympathy from me, son, then you are sorely mistaken. There is about six shillings in that purse and you know as well as I do that thefts over twelve pence carry the death penalty."

He snatched his purse back and also another one the boy had, which he threw towards the old woman standing in her rags. Accountability was something Charles lived and breathed; for himself and his family, future, actions and wellbeing, and he determined to teach this lad a harsh lesson.

Just as he was about to drag the villain to a constable, he stopped abruptly, hearing a word chanted on everyone's lips.

"Rebellion? God's wounds I never thought the King and Parliament would come to war," he said as he felt his body chill over.

A few men raced up the alley and other routes to spread the news, in the same way as shock dashed through their bodies.

"We are all lost. Is it really civil war?" he asked aloud with despair.

The boy wriggled free and ran away, but Charles was too alarmed to give chase. Instead he made his way out and stared at the people in the street, eager for information. Groups of apprentices and common folk stood around gossiping, tensely telling the stories they had heard, prompting shrieks and cursing as the news meandered its way around the city. People ran around stricken with panic, not knowing what to do.

"Who is rebelling?" he bellowed to some people speeding past him. He had to grab them to get a response.

"The Irish, the papist bastards, and they murder all in their sight. They are near London now. Save thy family."

This hit home as though he had been slapped across the face. He must protect Anne and Henry from the murder, rape and pillaging that the Catholics would bring.

He ran down the street.

Shops began closing again and one man was barricading his windows, frantically nailing wood over them. Women screamed and wailed as they tried to find their children and apprentices grabbed anything they could get their hands on, which would double as a weapon. In other narrow lanes he watched the public jostle and push each other out of the way, trying to get through and thinking only of their own safety.

"T'is true, my friends, they murder, rape and burn our fellow Protestants. They skewer children on hooks," one man shouted to a group of mesmerised people.

Charles overheard these stories, feeling so much anxiety that he stopped to learn more. He pieced together the picture in his mind - a rebellion had broken out in Ulster, now that Ireland was removed from the firm grip of Strafford's rule. The native Irish Catholics had risen against the Protestant settlers and massacred between twenty and forty thousand, depending on which rumour he chose to believe.

"I knew it, the Queen is behind this. Mister Pym told us all and he is right," another cried.

Charles sped down the street as fast as he could. His legs felt rigid and running seemed harder than normal. Pym had obviously been at it again with his propaganda about the royals - that part Charles was sceptical about - but the apprentices took hold of this latest excuse for unrest. The whole matter was still of mammoth proportions.

"The Queen, the Catholic whore, has a lot to answer for," someone yelled with shocking treason, which nobody would have imagined possible until recently.

The personal words about the wife of their anointed sovereign seemed to shock most people into silence, along with fear of retribution from the authorities.

Charles shook his head. He could not believe that she was

involved in something like this and for someone to shout it out in the street was outrageous. He remembered a time only a year or two ago when some men were branded or had an ear cut off. This was all for their view that women - hinting at the Queen - were harlots for acting parts on stage, a comment made just when the Queen was taking part in a court masque.

Only men were allowed on the stage and not even the Queen could overrule that in their eyes.

He raced away again, desperate to get home.

"Forty thousand barbaric Catholics in arms, they will soon have eyes to invade the mainland," another warned.

"Mainland? They are already at Reading, a couple of days' march from here. We will all be slaughtered if we do not leave now," a woman shrieked. She tugged at her hair, shaking like a lunatic.

Charles was out of breath, both through worry and running.

He stopped once more for a few minutes, heart pounding as much as the streets with the stampedes. Two children stood bewildered, watching all the panic and a woman constantly cried near him. A horseman galloped past, brushing his arm, forcing him to jump back and more shops closed rapidly, as people gathered their belongings together for a quick flight.

The news created images in his mind. He was sure forty thousand was excessive, for there would be no way they could get from Ireland so fast. He had no idea about the truth, but it was bound to be less.

Crates and chests stood outside buildings and men waited along the street, ready to defend their families and property. He saw various Members of Parliament heading to Westminster, probably for a hastily reconvened session. This normal sight sealed the truth of the matter for most, who looked for anything to confirm the rumour.

"God's wounds, what can we do?" he cursed, formulating plans for the future.

It was easy to be overawed by all this during his brief pause, caught amongst it as he had been. A group of men drew their swords, stopping suspects. He slowed again for a desperate break. He was as cold as Strafford's corpse would be - wasn't the peer's last words about hoping not one bit of blood rise up in retribution for his death?

Moving off faster, he sweated profusely, some resorting to pushing others out of the way, behaving as though everyone else in their path was invisible.

The harder he tried to run, the more his nerves frayed out of control. He slid on the dirt that had built up in the street, but continued on, ignoring the horse dung, which had blocked the drain, as well as the filth sloshing over the cobbles. Then a commotion forced him to slow down. The groups were silent and this was unusual considering the news, so he stopped to investigate. A man sat on an old stool telling the people what seemed like a shocking story by the expressions.

"The government in Ireland is as much use as the carcasses of all their dead soldiers. The Catholics decided to strike and terrible it was too. Even as we speak, regiments of men are mutinying from the Irish army to join the rebels. The papist dogs roam the country, taking whatever they want and the government cannot restore order – all the commander can say is that they are a company of naked rogues."

The crowd reacted with anger.

"Naked rogues, eh? Well they are certainly giving the government a pounding. They are made up of native Irish and Catholic settlers. Us Protestants are being beaten to a pulp and not one hand is raised in this country to help us. Parliament sidesteps the issues and the King calls for an army to be raised but is weak or unwilling to do more."

Charles shook his head, feeling the desperation of this man and his fellow people.

"They declare they are loyal to the King, these Catholic

murderers," one woman shouted.

"Aye, they will have a commission from Queen Mary, I'll wager."

"They are loyal to nobody – claiming to have royal backing is an attempt to get some justification behind their slaughter. I was told they feared that extreme Protestants in Parliament were ready to wipe out the Catholic religion and that is why they decided to act," one man asserted.

The crowd surged towards this fellow and he fled, followed closely by several others, yelling threats and baying for his blood.

"How dare he excuse those murderers," another stunned observer howled.

Charles, however, saw the common sense in the words of the fellow they had instantly decided was wrong.

The story of Ireland continued, "Aye, I saw them breaking into the farms in the village next to mine, burning it all, thieving, driving cattle away. I was so horrified, I could not move for hours. Town after town falls to them, people butchered in cold blood no matter what age or sex. If they are not stopped, then we will suffer the same. Are you all prepared to see your family end up this way?"

The crowd was fired up and chanted, most heading off towards Westminster to protest and spread these stories.

"When did you arrive here then if you have seen these atrocities, sir?" he asked the speaker.

"That is of no importance when lives are at stake."

Slowly, Charles's own sense was returning - this man did not speak in a different tongue, he seemed no different. And how come he fled his home so fast, yet sat here calm as can be, when apparently those same rebels were close by? Realisation did not add up to the momentous illusions of the stories.

Nevertheless, he continued home and burst through the door, reeling the news out to Anne, but excluding the parts he disbelieved. He regained his breath and composure and Anne watched him for a few seconds, digesting what he said.

"Oh, Charles, are we in danger, what do they want?" she asked as she grasped him tightly.

"They want the right to exercise their bloody dangerous religion, to hell with us. It may be rubbish, but I'd rather be on the safe side, so bring my sword down here, Louise, and make sure Henry is kept upstairs. Lock the doors and keep them secured. Give me all the keys. Anne, gather your jewels in one place."

As master of the house, he took immediate action. Looking in each direction, thoughts crowded his head. The table needed to be pushed over the door and Anne and Henry should go into the safest part of the building.

"Even after Strafford's death this has not ceased," he growled despondently.

This was the final straw. It was now past the line of protests and high tension - bloodshed and civil strife was involved. If the Irish did not arrive, then the mob could cause just as much destruction.

He ran to the study, tearing open the drawer of his desk and unlocking the secret compartment, gathering all his gold together. If a hasty flight were needed, then they would have to prepare now. At that moment a knock sounded at the door.

He grabbed a candlestick and snatched at the handle, yanking it open quickly. James stood in front of him and he lowered the weapon.

"I came to see Henry. I guess that you are as foolish as most of these out here, Charles?" he asked, pushing him out of the way.

"Why, do you not believe any of it?" Charles questioned impatiently, grabbing his arm.

"They are all going berserk about the Irish and they live hundreds of miles away. You need to improve your geography," he said with a snort.

"Be serious for once, you damn fool," Charles shouted, his voice going hoarse for a moment.

"Calm down, just think straight. Christ, they are nowhere near us, I know a Member of Parliament…"

Charles cut him off, "Oh yes, I forgot that *you know a Member of Parliament*. I know just how much they are being manipulated out there, but there must be some truth in it? Even if it is all a lie, those crowds are out for blood."

James tutted and whispered, "Parliament are making use of the situation to turn it to their favour, before the King gets there first. The papists are nowhere near us. Unfortunately, without any patronage from either side, I see you are in the dark as much as those poor souls out there, and as easy to worry because of it too."

"What? I have heard so many details that it cannot be a complete lie. You are not a Parliamentary leader."

James raised one eyebrow. "No, maybe not, but I am a damn sight more in the know than you. Now let me in, I have a present for your child when it arrives."

Charles calmed down a little and Anne appeared, still upset, until James produced his gift, lifting it into the house. The baby walker lit Anne's face up and she clasped her hands together in surprise. The frame would hold the baby upright and allow him to move around with the help of the wheels on the base.

Anne flung her arms around James and Charles thanked him, before pushing it along the floor to try it out. Anne was happy to have anything to distract her from the bad news, but Charles was more confrontational with it all, preferring to get to the bottom of the issues outside.

He stood watching James and Anne; the noise was immense with the contraption rattling and bumping over the wooden floor, and he guessed that the novelty would soon wear thin after an hour or so.

"Tell me exactly what is happening then?" he demanded, returning to the main topic.

"Nothing."

"What do you mean by that, and how do you know? Something obviously is afoot, because you say Parliament is exploiting a situation?" he asked with astonishment.

"I supply this Member of Parliament with most wares that he wants, but every now and then I will give reduced rates. In return, I get close to the gossip."

"Even so ..." Charles dismissed.

"You know what I am like; it takes a lot to worry me. Come to Parliament and find out. I'm going there later this afternoon. I can tell you are coming round to our view."

Charles was adamant. "I will not. Anne is heavily pregnant and my trooping off there will not help one bit," he said, holding his hand out in her direction.

"Very well, then I will tell you what I was told today," James continued unabated, "Ireland has rebelled, granted. An army would need to be raised to reinstate English authority there though, but Parliament does not feel the King should have control. Nay, because he will use it to subdue Ireland and then us in England, just like Strafford had advised him," exclaimed James.

"But he would be the lawful commander of such a force," Charles stated in blunt acknowledgement of the law as it stood.

"Right. So what better way than to stir this up and play on people's fears. I am sure that after the Queen is so closely linked to the rumours, everyone will be happy to give Parliament control of the army in the end, no matter what the lawful position is."

James continued the chance to pump his views. "The King tries to turn us into a Catholic nation again, just like Bloody Mary Tudor."

"Catholic, pah. Then why did he sell his own jewels to raise a fleet to save the Protestants in La Rochelle, when Parliament would not vote money to that cause?" Charles asked, thriving on playing devil's advocate.

"There you go, appearing like a royalist through and through," he warned impatiently.

The argument both men had their teeth into monopolised their attention, so that they failed to notice Anne wince and take hold of the doorframe.

"You make me go that way though - you would think you were getting a commission for working on me. I feel Parliament has lost most of my sympathy, with what tactics they are using, James. Maybe it is time for both sides to recognise they have a joint share of government now, otherwise they will cast us into oblivion."

"Charles, this is going to lead to civil war, for God's sake, you must have more urgency in deciding which side to back," James yelled, causing a cold silence.

Chapter 37

Anne let out a scream as she grasped her stomach, wincing at the onset of fresh pains. Charles cursed and ran to her, taking her weight and urging her on, towards a chair.

Louise appeared, wiping her hands on her apron and confirming that she would boil some water and bring clean linen sheets in abundance. Anne nodded, showing how well she had planned this moment. She groaned and her breathing became erratic, with short, fast gasps and Charles signalled to James.

"Will you help us up?" he asked of his friend, forgetting all they had spoken of.

Anne placed her arm around Charles's neck and he eased her forward, slowly mounting each step, anxious to let her lie in bed. This was it, childbirth had started – he was galvanised into action, although now it was here, just what could he do?

Panic set in, at the severely limited speed, as much as the nervous apprehension for the labour.

"I will call on Madam Arrowsmith, across the street," Louise called out.

"Arrowsmith?" Charles asked, questioning everything, to be at the forefront of such a crucial moment as this.

"The wise woman. She has six children already," Anne panted.

This soothed him, knowing someone would be here who had experienced everything. Plus she was an intelligent lady, and he remembered how James's mother had acted in the same capacity for his own mother.

Then as Louise went to leave, he reminded her of another task. "Go, find a midwife," then he added, "I think Mistress Clarke is out of the country, so you will have to get Sharp, Jane Sharp."

Scurrying towards the stairs, Louise made all haste as though her life depended upon it, encouraged by the force of his emotion and commands.

"No, I don't want a midwife, Charles," Anne protested, going on to remind him that the one who attended Lucy had been so vicious that the child had died.

"I want as many people here as possible to help. Besides you did not have one last time," he told her, anxious to explain his view.

"Will everything be all right outside, for I worry I am laid up while chaos descends?" she asked, betraying the root of her worry that had initiated the onset of labour.

"They are mad at the best of times, so this is nothing unexpected, my darling."

Anne yelled with pain again, stepping up his stream of adrenaline. He gently reassured her as they finally reached the top of the stairs and went into the bedroom. Now she was sitting on the bed, James lifting her legs onto it, while Charles fetched some cold water from the washing bowl. Soon her brow was soaked with sweat, so he laid the damp cloth over it, but Nicholas Culpepper's herbal book of advice for pregnancies stayed on the shelf.

"I will stay with you, my sweet," he promised her. They had no time now to prepare a herbal bath like it was suggested to give birth in. In any case, it was far too complicated an affair, consisting of hollyhocks, betony, mint, chamomile, marjoram, linseed and parsley all boiled. He could not remember the day it was at the moment, never mind arranging all that. Complaining under his breath and cursing the delay, he hoped everything would be all right.

It seemed like hours had passed, but James was a Godsend, talking about his and Charles's childhood, which both distracted Charles and calmed Anne, even causing an occasional chuckle when the spasms and pains abated a little.

Despite intense fretting, he felt privileged to be so close to Anne, for James had never been with Elizabeth through her many pregnancies, but he wanted to be different to most men.

Anne at least had a comfortable setting in the fabric covered bed, hangings all embroidered by her own hand, hiding any trace of wooden posts. She had created scenes from her life, the main one of their marriage and this seemed to comfort her as she pointed to it. Charles, by contrast, was apprehensive and overawed at the pretty needlework, for it reminded him of the happiest time in his memory and how delicate this moment now was.

Charles stepped back with James and his friend patted his arm, assuring him before he left that she was a fighter and would give him a healthy boy. Louise eventually ran into the room, bursting through the door, before stopping and apologising.

"Oh I have no time for that, get the midwife up here," he snapped.

Jane Sharp strode briskly in and approached Charles, telling him she had just abandoned a different birth because of his call, leaving that one to her assistant. Without any hesitation, but more confidence than most men, she asked how much extra he would give her to keep her solely with Anne. He offered ten shillings, which she accepted, though it never changed the haughty expression below her white headscarf.

A knock came at the door and Madam Arrowsmith entered, handing Anne a hare's foot to put around her neck, explaining she swore by it. After a few seconds of observing the midwife, the neighbour retreated to the window, ready to be on hand after the birth.

Immediately Jane Sharp wiped her hands on the apron, which had every bodily colour on it, and examined his wife quietly and patiently, checking the advancement of the pregnancy. She closed some of the bed curtains a little and lifted the sheets above Anne to assess the situation, announcing that the membrane had not broken yet and told him it must be done now.

"Sir Charles, I never had my membrane broken in all my pregnancies," Arrowsmith interjected, resting her hand on his arm.

"Stop, I do not want that," he shouted to Jane, causing her to frown.

He grasped his fists together with frustration, uncertain, powerless, but eaten up with worry for his wife's safety. He did not want to lose her.

"What would you do?" he eventually asked of the midwife.

"I need to burst that membrane and allow the baby to move down," Jane told him, eyes burning at him for questioning her work.

He was in a predicament, relying on a professional woman and in no place to contradict her, even with their neighbour's advice.

"Can there be no other way?" he asked distraughtly, raising his hands in the air, while the sweat rolled down his face, stinging as some of it touched his eyes.

"No," she answered sharply as she took a coin to do her

work, regardless of his thoughts.

"You had better be correct or you will be sorry," he whispered under his breath and he watched her like a hawk.

He guessed Jane simply wished to get the birth over and done with, to move onto a new patient and this impelled him to take the midwife's arm.

As if to solve the impasse, Anne gave one loud scream and took hold of the bed at either side. They had no need for the coin; nature had kicked into action. Jane had clearly lost patience with Charles, and he was sure she was about to leave had the pregnancy not advanced. With the baby on its way, she encouraged Anne to push, occasionally easing things with her hands if it slowed. Anne's expression was such that Charles held her hand and kneeled on the floor to be close to her. He watched his wife with horror as it progressed, the excruciating pain and torment coming through in her shouts and expressions.

Jane appeared to be prodding and poking and he cursed himself for putting Anne through such horror so soon.

The midwife coolly announced that a limb had appeared.

Charles had never felt so many emotions running through him at once, nervously commentating to Anne, "It's here, not far to go, my darling."

He felt light headed and on fire, an emotional wreck.

Looking for something he could to do to help, he fumbled around, constantly being approached and calmed by Madam Arrowsmith. The desire to shout as loud as he could came over him, one minute petrified, the other of exhilaration after She took hold of the limb and bent forward, obviously physically easing the baby out. He undid his nightshirt, brushing a dollop of sweat from his head and shuddered at what the midwife was doing, reciting the Lord's Prayer in his mind.

"It is a breech birth," Jane murmured, without looking up.

Anne screamed, louder and more final than the rest and

Jane began to lift the child from the bed. Finally, Charles could see their offspring.

The image was as clear and cold as the Thames when it froze over. He stood riveted, the unnaturally light pink baby had a covering of white film.

Its wrinkled face, eyes still tightly shut, was covered in membrane and blood, as was the delicate body, arms pressed tightly against the little one's chest. He had seen wounds of every degree in his soldiering, but this was nothing like any of them and the sight of the blood still made him wonder whether it was alive, despite Jane behaving as if everything was fine. The effect it had on his senses was more intense than anything he had seen in war. Taking the child to be dead, tears rolled down his cheeks and he shook violently. Mucus ran from his nose with the devastation.

Yet another stillborn child. God forgive me for what I have done to deserve this, he thought, forlorn emptiness swiping his own life to the bare limit. How would Anne cope with what he had caused? Was it because he was not sure about the pregnancy that God had decided to take the child? In an instant, Anne wept and he took her in his arms. Finally they glanced over to see the blood covered baby, which Jane had wrapped up tightly in linen, wiping the immediate mess from it. She handed it to Anne and the child began screaming in a piercing rhythm.

"It is alive?" Charles whispered, barely registering the fact.

Then it occurred to him, a bolt of pure joy; this image was so different to the last child - this leg moved, a warm feel emanated from it. Gone was that haunting image of pale, almost grey, twisted limbs.

Jane nodded, wiping her hands, as though the issue was never in doubt. It was a boy, and Anne's tears mingled with her sweat and blood. As he kissed her, his messy hair covered her face.

Jane wanted to pull the afterbirth out of her now. Anne had spoken to Elizabeth and Madam Arrowsmith with regards to childbirth and apparently this would come out naturally. He remembered their discussion and pounced in.

"Leave it, she is exhausted enough," he barked.

The bed was soiled and the sooner they took the sheets the better. Louise scurried off with the old linen and returned with a cloth to further clean the child. After Jane had left with her hard earned money, Louise brought both clean and sodden linen and Arrowsmith showed the women how to swathe the newborn, proving her valuable presence. She left out the wooden supports though, which were so often put into the layers of wrapping, designed to help a baby with rickets.

"It's called swaddling," Anne told him tenderly, her voice faint, as this work was carried out in front of him.

He smiled at her, still gripping her hand. Louise hugged Anne and they cried together, before she wrapped her arms round Charles too. He lifted Louise up and laughed out loud, inadvertently making the baby cry. The piercing sound filled his whole body, his life and veins with happiness and pride.

"Assure all my servants there that I am constant for the doctrine and discipline of the Church of England as established by Queen Elizabeth and my father and resolve (by the Grace of God) to live and die in the maintenance of it."

King Charles I
OCTOBER 1641

"And what may be expected from such zealous and fiery professors of an adverse religion but the ruin and extirpation of ours?"

Viscount Gormanston, an Irish Catholic peer commenting on the uniting of the Scottish Presbyterians and the English Puritans and their success over limiting royal power.
OCTOBER 1641

Chapter 38

Travel was the usual slow pace between Westminster and Whitehall, especially with the ever present gangs outside Parliament. The hackney Charles was travelling in had stopped due to these obstructions, as men scuffled and howled at the members of both Commons and Lords. His endless thoughts about employment were not interrupted for long, for he had got used to the commotion. He was finally struck though by what he saw of the lords and bishops making their way to Parliament.

Watching the multitude now that his attention was gained, he heard them shouting, "No popery, no popish lords and no bishops."

"Move on," he shouted to the driver as he thumped the roof, eager to leave them to it.

Within this melting pot of discontent, the arrival of a peer and a bishop thrown into it all was enough to spice up the flavour as tempers were brought to the boil.

He remembered the personal vow he had made at the christening to stay out of the dispute. This determination was severely tested as a mob brought his carriage to a halt.

Some of them took hold of the coach door, wrenched it open and started to search the interior.

He was furious, words escaping in a reflex action to the intrusion. "Scoundrels, get out!"

Looking right at him, they proceeded to enter, more determined to do so by his order.

"Out, you dogs, or I shall have your heads!" he bellowed as he stood, stooping against the roof.

The rogues stopped for a second and then dragged him from the carriage by his clothes, yelling as they proceeded to question him about his views and religion. Flabbergasted that this had happened, he shouted for help from some guards, while intending to draw his sword. He thought twice and left it, unwilling to cause bloodshed and start something he could not end, without leaving his child fatherless.

Instead, he roared with indignation, while lashing out and smashing his fist into an assailant. The sheer strength in his actions and the cry he let out forced the men back, and he swung again at the man closest to him, casting the fellow back into the others. The comrades rose in uproar, yet undeterred by any of their anger, Charles stood his ground and stared back, yelling at them that he was Protestant and had no interest in government, demanding they leave him.

Now he was silent, but adamant they would not get near him.

Then at long last, the Earl of Dorset's mounted halberdiers thundered towards the group from the distance, causing the scum to scurry away quickly like cornered rats. He seized his opportunity to jump back into the hackney, while Dorset's horsemen quietened the area. Ironically, it was the King who had installed these horsemen around Parliament. If the monarch had not ordered Dorset to clear the rioting apprentices out of the vicinity of Westminster, to stop pressure on the Members of Parliament, then he may have been ripped to pieces by those rogues. But the move was stark; the King seemed to have halted his political retreat, now standing firm. Charles also realised that having the approaches to Parliament permanently covered by troops loyal to the monarch, was another additional advantage to the King, veiled as an attempt to protect Parliament. He pondered the King's recent actions – they all hinted of a fight back. It was about time someone curbed the dogs, no matter which side.

Watching revengefully as the group was eventually assaulted by the horsemen, he undid some buttons of his doublet whilst he calmed down. He was outraged that he should have been manhandled and until recently it would have been unthinkable.

For the rest of the journey home he continued to bathe in a black mood.

"It seems like every damn villain, layabout or those with grudges will use this climate of fear to do whatever they please to everyone else. The rule of law has been suspended," he complained aloud.

When he arrived home, he jumped out, handing the driver some money. His jaw felt almost locked from the way he clenched it from frustration.

At home the place was still as bustling as ever a washing day was. Striding into the kitchen, he saw Anne and another maid putting the linen into the wooden buck tub.

"Arabella, pour some water and lye into it and then get this laundry in dirtiest first," Anne ordered.

Charles could smell the pungent odour of the urine and wood ashes which made up the lye.

"Anne," he said, trying to catch her attention.

"Right, now leave it and I always like to run the water and lye off and pour it back in again three times. That usually gets rid of the stains. Then wash it with cold water," Anne instructed as she brushed her hair back with a wet hand. Arabella was getting a full training session on her mistress's preferences'.

Charles sighed impatiently. "Did you succeed with my ink stain?" he interrupted again.

Anne looked up. "It is soaking now in some urine."

He walked back to the study muttering about how she never listened to him, then sat down and took a sheet of paper from the drawer, ready to catch up on some work to distract his mind from the disrespectful mobs. He dipped his quill into the ink and proceeded to tally up a list of the equipment he had purchased for his regiment, and which he had not been fully reimbursed for yet. Each pikeman had cost a whopping one pound and two shillings to kit out. The ink flowed badly, just like Sir Richard's monetary conscience, leaving blotches on the paper at times and he constantly had to dip it after every few words. He then did the same for the musketeers. The price he had paid for each of their equipment was one pound, three shillings and four pence. Their weekly wage of just around four shillings was often late too, never mind his own personal arrears.

Thinking of money, he put a further three pounds aside for the two tons of coal he had bought from James. Sickened by the missing funds, he left the papers for now; they were minor irritations that gnawed at his festering outrage at being held up in his coach by a bunch of brutes.

"My dear, what has annoyed you?" Anne guessed with concern as he walked into the dining room. She seemed to have the knack of sensing his feelings simply by glancing at him.

"If things continue to be violent here, I would prefer it if you and Henry were somewhere safer," he told her.

The expression changed, that fixed look of willpower coming to the fore, which both excited him and reassured him - at least she was coping with events.

"It cannot be that bad?"

"Some rogues have just tried to pull me out of a hackney," he told her, still astounded at their audacity.

"But I could never leave unless we all went."

He laid an arm gently across her shoulders. "Maybe I am making things more ill than they are, but if I am right, it would reassure me you were safe if you go to the country. God knows what could happen here."

Anne stroked his chest, both thriving on their closeness.

He smiled at her - his maxim on life was to start the day with a stolen kiss from her. Sometimes she would escape playfully, seeing how long she could hold him off for.

"Why are they protesting now?" she queried.

"Today Parliament will vote on the bill to remove the King's right to command the armed forces. They demand all power, even that to which they have never been entitled," he sighed, unable to defend such a foray into that slice of royal prerogative.

The anger began to melt away and he felt better for discussing events with her, no matter how brief. Anne gave him one of those looks – the type that made his heart race and he remembered his little present he had bought her today.

He led her into the main room where Louise had prepared the flowers.

"Oh, Charles, they are gorgeous."

He could not understand how women got so excited over flowers, but he did not care about that, as long as she was happy with them.

"I tried to get yellow ones, your favourite colour, but the nurseryman laughed at me," he said, raising his eyebrows.

Anne giggled at him now, prompting him to lift his hands in the air in mock bewilderment.

"You will not find yellow roses in England," she told him with a grin, "Red, white, or red and white striped maybe, but yellow ones are not popular in this country."

Charles nodded, acknowledging his ignorance of the subject.

"Come on, I have something which will make you content," she announced, taking his hand and leading him away.

As she led him to the stairs, he smiled, feeling his heart pound. Passion seemed to have fizzled out lately - well, in the last week or two - and he felt excited. Ascending the stairs he lapped up the view of Anne; he liked nothing better than her curvaceous figure, slim waist and fulsome breasts, and those slender legs. He aimed at the bedroom door, but Anne led him a different way.

"Eh?"

"See Henry, he is sleeping. What is wrong, you seem bewildered?" she guessed.

"Oh right. I thought … never mind," he said, realising his mistake, and he adjusted his direction, happy to see his son.

He put his arm around her small waist, holding her to him.

They watched little Henry sleep peacefully, feeling a settled atmosphere descend over them.

"I thank God every day for him and how healthy he is," Anne told him.

"Aye, he completes our life. No treasure even compares to what we have here in this little room. I know I was reluctant to have a child in the present climate, my sweet, but I would never turn back time. You have both made me so proud."

She embraced him warmly.

"Complete, yes. Now as for satisfied, my love, then we still have tonight. I did notice you going for the bedroom door," she whispered close to him, breath tickling his ear and exciting his senses at once.

He laughed because she had realised his thoughts, but glad she had, if the truth be known. As she relaxed in his arms, he was shocked to hear her scream and shout all of a sudden, the noise piercing because of their closeness.

"Mother."

"What?" Charles countered with a frown.

He turned round to see his mother in law standing in the doorway. Anne left him and hugged her, the women holding hands and practically dancing round the room. Then the inevitable gossiping started as soon as the surprise wore off.

"Wait a minute, what is going on?" he asked.

Nobody replied. Charles watched them chattering to each other.

"Erm, madam, why are we graced with a visit?" he queried, raising his voice, dubious as to the sincerity of the occasion.

"Must I have a reason for seeing my daughter, sir? Things were getting a little heated back home, plenty of ignorant louts taking me for a Catholic murderer," she said in her Irish accent.

His eyes widened and he cursed, remembering her nationality.

"Charles, ladies present," Anne reminded, now giving off a mature air that made him aggravated.

"Ladies present?" he scoffed, before addressing the visitor, "So they thought you were Catholic Irish in Oxford?"

"I am sure I have just told you that?" she said with a loud shriek of laughter, which made him cringe.

"Madam, am I right in thinking that you left your husband and the countryside because they thought you were a bloody papist rebel, and in your utter wisdom, you thought London of all places would be safer?"

"That is right, as I expected my son in law could protect me in his home for a while."

Charles rubbed his eyes, groaning, to avoid letting his irritation come out.

"I see your husband is as happy as ever. He even cries because he is so overwhelmed to see me," she joked sarcastically. Anne's stepmother had the qualities of a great courtier - one who could cut another down with the tongue, never mind a sword.

"This place is like a tinder box ready to light up, for Christ's sake. If one apprentice hears your accent, they will burn our house down without asking a question. What of your husband – did he not give any sane counsel to you?"

"My husband is not my master, despite any vow of marriage. I take it I am not welcome here?"

"Did you not understand what I just said? You have travelled to the most dangerous part of this kingdom, in the worst political struggle in near two hundred years. You could be easily mistaken as part of the most hated and feared religion, and nationality."

"Charles, sorry, Sir Charles, I am no Catholic," she snapped.

"You are Irish. People will assume that you are Catholic. How can you be so foolish? You cannot stay, you will endanger us all and we have your grandson to consider above all."

"I have some say in this, Charles, she is my mother," Anne said, breaking into the dispute, adamant to push her opinion.

Now Charles seemed like the miserable man Anne's stepmother had painted, while she took the role of wronged victim.

"This is my house and I am head of it. I will not have our family endangered because of her," he told Anne.

Charles had the ladies' safety in mind when he argued with them, but his ruthlessly sober, realistic and honest views sometimes came across in the harshest of terms. Anne aligned with her stepmother to protest against his tone, while their visitor played upon this rift. Charles could see what was happening, but could not translate his words and argument into the humorous, vulnerable, alluring array of colours that Anne's stepmother managed. She had always been expert at making people feel sorry for her - Anne had always told him this - but absence must have wiped the slate clean of past experiences.

"Sir Charles," his she interrupted, turning to the attack in true fashion, "Remember this house was bought from the dowry my daughter brought you, and the lands you have in the countryside came from her too. Considering this, I should have a say in staying in this house, for I paid for it."

He felt anger rise in him like a fountain.

"How dare you, madam. You have nobody's care in mind but your own," Charles shouted, before being interrupted by a knock on the open door behind him.

"Charles, you will wake Henry," Anne warned with a disapproving glare.

"Shouldn't you answer that, it may be someone coming to kill us," his mother in law warned.

Anne strained to keep her smile back, but failed, which bothered him more than anything that had been said.

"Yes, yes, it is all funny," he growled as he looked at the door, irritated at the fresh tapping.

Louise rapped on the door again and called softly for him. He tugged it fully open, taking a piece of paper from her with a sigh.

It was in James's handwriting and simply said, 'See the King lose the most crucial vote so far - Parliament, fifteen minutes.'

He crumpled it and threw it on the floor.

"What is that?" Anne asked.

"From you know who, asking me to go to Parliament to see the coming vote."

"Then go, Charles, you need to keep up to date so that you can make sure we are all in the know, especially after what you told me earlier."

He watched her in silence, astounded at her concern for events, considering the circumstances of their new guest. Anne made a gesture with her head, pointing to the door. He felt like a dog taking orders.

"Safety?" Charles spluttered, "I am going to go to Parliament after all, for that will be better than being here. If I do not, I will explode at the ignorance of you both."

"Now, get me a glass of wine while I relax after my

horrendous journey, girl," Anne's mother demanded of Louise, with a haughty flick of her hand, as lazy and carefree as her own character.

When Louise did not respond immediately, she gave a sermon on her lax behaviour. Charles regarded her manners with disbelief. He remembered her drinking habits at the wedding and dreaded her presence. Then he wondered whether she had brought finance with her to fuel her alcohol and extravagant lifestyle.

"One moment, do you have any money with you, madam?" She looked him up and down.

"Ladies do not carry money, Sir Charles; it is for their gentlemen to provide that. I hope there are some generous men in this city to look after me while my husband is not here?" she said, the last part uttered as Anne hurried to Henry's room to get him.

Charles got a thought of how much this sounded like a whore speaking but he just managed to hold his tongue.

"I chastise or praise the servants in this household. And if you think it is for the men to provide money, you should get Anne's sister a decent husband, instead of imprisoning her with you to do your bidding, frittering her years away as a lackey to your ego," he lectured.

"And my family affairs are nothing to do with you. Do you enjoy chastising your that serving girl then, eh?" she asked softly so that Anne could not hear.

Charles moved to within a few inches of her face, warning the woman that he knew her tricks, before he stormed out into the hall with Anne calling after him. She followed and tugged his arm, so he stopped as she put her hands to each of his cheeks and kissed him.

"I do love you."

Charles sighed, although he would not admit it, this relieved him of a great deal of frustration and niggling worry.

"Anne, she makes me so angry for she has no regard for us at all."

"She means well, please consider this. It will only be for a few nights," she whispered tenderly.

He kissed her, knowing the ultimate decision would have no bearing on his thoughts, and stepped outside, pushing through the throng.

Chapter 39

"**I** am glad you have come here to support reason," James said in greeting.

"Reason? What would that be?" Charles asked, still angered by Anne's stepmother. He half knew what James was getting at, but wanted him to admit it himself.

"Recapping in official debate every wrongful act the King and his government have committed," he said, wallowing in excitement.

"I come here to know whether my family are safe, not to accuse and attack. I support neither of the two, but by God I see that should I be forced, then the King is the one who is protecting the laws now."

"You may as well have claimed that all along. It is clear you have transferred your allegiance as cheaply as a whore," James joked, "If push comes to shove, I know you will back the right side despite these words though."

Charles felt stronger in his leanings towards the King - he was so stubborn that proving James's comment wrong could even add weight to the opposite view. At his friend's mocking, he flew into a rage.

"Aye, I care only for the side that is going to make sure my family are allowed to live in peace and to keep the rule of law established. I see you care not about anyone. How long is it since you spent time with your wife and family, instead of being tied to this place? We need to restore the balance of power, for Parliament is going too far now, and that is why I have changed my mind," he growled.

James grinned, as though he had said something hilarious. Charles knew the man was playing up to his colleagues to gain their favour. Whenever he pushed anyone too much, James would always cave in and try to ignore the backlash, or play it down.

"My friend, I had supported Parliament, maybe not as obsessively as you, but I have decided that they no longer hold my respect. I am not on the same side as you, for they aim to overturn ancient laws."

He knew he would say more, so walked away.

"That damn fellow drank to the reduction of the King's power, rather than my new son," he muttered as he left. He had bottled this particular incident up for months and now felt this day was a time for releasing all the words, thoughts and feelings he had kept hidden.

As the Members of Parliament arrived for the vote, mumbling filled the air. The great round window of Westminster Abbey was visible above the rooftops like a giant eye peering warily at the stampedes of people. A strange and eerie sense hung over the area and a group of men formed near the steps. They seemed to grow fast as more people flooded into the area, like spectres, ushered in by the faint haze from the Thames nearby.

"There is one, he is an enemy of the nation," a man cried.

As though this was a planned act, which maybe it was. Another added, "Stop him going in, he will betray us with his vote; he sides with tyranny."

The group seemed to launch like a mass of human cannon balls towards the individual. Some other MPs ran to their colleague's rescue, but Dorset's horsemen were nowhere to be seen, and they were forced to retreat. Charles frantically scoured the area for the guards, but to no avail. People jostled around and men bellowed out as chaos descended, all too easily, in the darkness of the early evening. It was impossible to move.

"Let him in, keep our protest peaceful," was a lesser plea.

A couple of men came together and linked arms defensively round the MP, but it appeared hopeless. Others defended the makeshift wall with their fists and various weapons as it was pummelled and manoeuvred.

"If you support the laws of the land, let him in. This is tyranny if we prevent elected members from voting. Do we want a coup?" was another warning.

Charles was pushed and shoved, stumbling, at any moment likely to be trampled. He knew he could help the few men, who to be honest he admired for their perseverance in the face of such odds.

A fire in the Palace of Westminster had allowed King Henry the Eighth to search for another home. The area had not seen anything as heated since, until now, when several hundred fanatical people came in droves, as though someone, or some rumour had herded them here. A dangerous core appeared idle, with grudges, eager to cause trouble and rebel against authority of any kind.

His heart pounded and he wanted to run to support the Member of Parliament in the midst of it, but his feet stayed put. The lone man was descended upon, and the defenders around him paid the price for their minority loyalty. Charles did not want to get injured or killed, which would inevitably leave Anne and Henry in an untenable position. But the event was disgraceful and honour was at stake - what kind of father was a man who had no honour?

Edward the Third's great clock tower chimed out, a peal of panic at the events at its base. The noise only seemed to propel the fighting.

The faces of those leading the barrage were screwed up, eyes burning with hatred. They were fixated on the Member of Parliament, as though he had committed some heinous crime.

Scuffles continued between both sides as the few daring supporters of the man bellowed threats and insults in return. Charles felt impelled and surged forward, practically swimming through the bodies of protestors. The individual's guardians began to waver.

"Stop, let him be. Are we Englishmen? Stopping Parliament functioning is worse than anything that the King has done," Charles bellowed, to halt the attack as he approached.

Shoving some men away, he secured the small band of people round the Member of Parliament with his fresh reserves of energy, while his outburst momentarily caused a brief respite from those immediately surrounding the small band.

"He is a traitor," one man shouted, pointing at Charles.

"A Catholic," was the instant and unfounded slur.

"If you want to settle this matter in peace for the safety of your families, let members in. If you persist, then you are the traitors, you are the ones who overturn our laws and you should pay for that. I beg anyone who is honourable to help me. I want to see the people who were elected to give the commoner a voice being allowed to do that."

Charles hastily linked arms with the small band, which gained more recruits. With each courageous addition, came another, heartened by the last. The multitude moved round them like a tidal wave growing with ferocity, jolting them from one way to another with each roar.

People came forward nonetheless, further thickening the party as it slowly moved its man towards the entranceway. Small scuffles broke out, some vicious onslaughts too, and one man was trampled on as Charles tried not to fall over him. For a second he wondered what he was doing with these people, protecting but one man, yet he quickly realised again that it was the principle and the moral cause which was at stake, enshrined in that single being. His own honour made it impossible for him to let this issue lie.

The noise had escalated now to an immense din, making it impossible to think clearly or hear anymore. Action was the only thing available.

Some men began tearing at their foe, punching, kicking and drawing swords. One man was slashed on the arm, his scream barely piercing the commotion and his fall to the ground going largely unnoticed. Other men supporting the MP refrained from linking arms, so that they could fight off any attack, while their colleagues nudged and forced a way through for him.

Charles saw the horror, hatred and the ferocity, and was cast back for a few moments to images of the Bishops War. It was easy to think in an instant that these men were going to kill each other - simple to hate them and want to kill them first - but they were English, his own countrymen, not some foreign foe.

Then finally Dorset's horsemen trotted into the square, drawing their swords, and the sight of the weapons being unsheathed sobered many. The metal had a shine of its own in the approaching darkness, making a terrifying scene, as if ready to rain down, the slightest drop or wave of the blades ready to cause a massacre.

Yet still some brawling went on in pockets, the main bodies of men staying put, rather than running away, showing the strength of conviction from both sides. Men punched at Charles, dragged him and ripped his shirt, trying to get him out of the scrum surrounding the member. He hit back, being careful not to fall or allow their group to be infiltrated, and he was defended by his other comrade. He felt a blow to his ribs and turning to lash out, he found himself looking James in the eye.

He stopped dead. The eyes of his friend were unrecognisable and Charles felt tingling disbelief and sorrow.

James shook his head. "Get hold of him, lads."

"Wait, what are you doing?" Charles demanded.

James shook his head remorsefully. "Friendship will have to take second place whilst you ally with enemies of the state. I will never lose my affection, but by God, I never thought you would do this."

He grabbed his friend to try and talk some sense into him, losing sight of his mission, but James was under a spell.

"If you cannot appreciate others may hold different views, then our friendship is truly nothing," he barked.

James still did not reply.

Then lunging forward, he smacked James in the stomach, with tears in his eyes. James reached out, desperately trying to pull him away from his group, now bellowing that he was wanting to help Charles get away from his mistake. The men to Charles's left held onto him, keeping him steady, as his friend was lost in the crowd. Behind him, horses neighed, men screamed and shouted, heralding Dorset's onslaught.

"Come on, fight through them and get him into Parliament," he roared, taking up the reins of this cause and riding it onwards. His passion was controlled purely by his head, for his heart was suspended after the anguish with James.

A trooper trotted right in close to him, slashing at a protestor opposite and cutting his arm. The fellow grabbed the wound with a deep cry and let go of Charles's accomplice. The horse's nostrils flared, small clouds of air expelled from them and Charles fought as hard alongside the steed. Looking up at the magnificent beast was an awesome sight, the rider's head and upper body crowning the top, towering above like a floating apparition. It made him feel small and insignificant.

"Bloody Dorset does the Pope's work, he will massacre us all," someone protested loudly.

The resolve and desperation was beginning to give way to fear and clear judgement as the sea of people broke into clusters, the horsemen dividing them like they were carving up lunch.

With the horde dispersing, the Member of Parliament managed to get up the steps and run into Westminster, towards the House of Commons. Some faces peered out above, observing the desperate events, and Charles saw Digby watching from the summit, looking directly at him. The peer nodded with a grave face, before turning away. The mob calmed, now ready to sit before the Parliament buildings like a besieging army, awaiting the coming vote.

"Friends, we are all as good as dead men, for the Irish rebels are coming. They are come as far as Rochdale and will be at Halifax and Bradford shortly!"

The cry of a man interrupting the church service
in Pudsey, Yorkshire
LATE 1641

"I thought we had all sat in the valley of the shadow of death, ready to catch each other's locks and sheath our swords in each other's bowels."

Memoirs of one of the members of the House of Commons after the all night sitting over the Grand Remonstrance
NOVEMBER 1641

Chapter 40

I nside the Parliament chamber, formerly Saint Stephen's Chapel, John Pym and his close supporters huddled together, as members continued to mill around and arrive.

The former use of the chamber was apt, for despite the change of occupancy, the building was still being used for God's glory in their eyes. The noise outside was noticeable, but for now, only some stray gossip told most MPs about the commotion, closeted as they were behind Westminster Hall and the various royal courts. Within their sixty by thirty foot headquarters, with seating running right around the chamber, Pym and his most important colleagues sat near the speaker's chair. With such a vital coming vote, the place was packed, many standing, or up in the viewing gallery, and there was much grumbling about seating.

Only the King's councillors and leaders of Parliament could sit near the speaker, though Pym's party were seizing these places, ousting most who politically decided not to argue.

"We need to pass this, otherwise all is lost. We have achieved so much, but we must make men realise that it is just the tip of the iceberg. The most dangerous thing is resting on our laurels.

We cannot be caught by surprise. They are swinging to the King, gentlemen, so we must grasp the pendulum and force it onwards, otherwise we will never have security for the people, or freedom of conscience in religion, and our lives will go back in time," Pym told them with as much passion as a Puritan preacher.

The man was as sturdy in appearance and sense of purpose as the strapping oak trees that surrounded his childhood home of Brymore House in Somerset. Like most of the ancient trunks, the Pym family had been established there for centuries and John Pym could flourish as continually as them.

"The demand for us to approve his choice of ministers has set a lot of these moderates against us, John."

"We will have to ride this storm then, for men want calm to return, but it will not occur yet. In Ireland an army will soon be needed to restore order. We cannot trust the King's ruthlessly influential advisors while their master wields such a power, for they could easily work on him to employ it against us."

"Such a motion would cause chaos though," one warned.

"Great things cannot be ushered in if they only have a tranquil tide to travel upon. As I have said before, we must reopen all the wounds the King has managed to close with his appeasement.

Only then can we remind the people about the worry and mistrust that we all so justly feel, to enable such a bill to pass through our house. Remember we are not against the King, but we need satisfaction that his power over the army will be used for the good of the country - pruning the royal prerogative back so that it does not overgrow," he explained.

"You are a shrewd man, John Pym, if it was not for you, we would be lost."

The compliment passed Pym by, like a faint breeze gliding over some treetops.

"They say the rebel Irishman leading the Catholics over there has a commission from King Charles. Perhaps the mob would be interested in knowing this rumour," another leading member hinted.

"A wise thought, but first we need to win this battle. Go, persuade these men that for the safety of Parliament's privileges, we need to pass this remonstrance. They have got quite a number together to oppose us in the form of Edward Hyde, that fat lawyer over there," Pym announced anxiously.

"Mister Hyde, Lord Falkland and Sir John Culpepper have all left our fold recently, stop them from herding others away," another member ordered, echoing Pym and aligning himself with the leader.

Tension hovered above the heads of about three hundred or more members of the House of Commons like a swirling tempest; even the three large windows at the far end of the chamber merged into the darkness of the night. Then Pym was informed that Edward Hyde had sent a messenger to call the members who were outside, or in the corridors, back into the chamber. A quick scan of the benches - that reminded him of pews - told him that most men were crowded inside.

"The sly dog," he muttered with a smile.

It was as if he had found the King and his advisors easy pickings, and now the quality of his opponents had risen, he both worried and thrived upon it. As the speaker of the house took his seat, a lot of the men prepared and sat down, for the officials' arrival signified the legality of the gathering by his representation of the King. Edward Hyde and Lord Falkland got to their feet immediately to start the crucial debate, barely after the golden mace, with an end shaped into a crown, had been laid on the speaker's table. Some men looked at Pym, worried at how Hyde had managed to grab centre stage in this sea of shadows, the black clothes of most of them adding to the mystique. An official was sent off to scour around for some candles, such an unusual request from a house used to a strict daytime schedule.

"Let them get it off their chests, for men will remember the last word, not the first," Pym dismissed, calming his colleagues.

The man beside him tapped his foot, while the sea of faces around the chamber looked sombre and desperate. This was make or break for each side.

"The King has told his supporters to stop this remonstrance at all costs," one man whispered to Pym from behind, anxious to get in with his thoughts.

Pym took his arm, easing the man forward. "If you were as knowledgeable about our own cause as you are of the King's, you might be of more help."

The house eventually quietened down at Speaker Lenthall's timid requests, gathering slightly more force with each repetition, until politeness decided the issue, and Hyde could begin his speech.

"Gentlemen, we are come to discuss the issue of a remonstrance."

"Aye, aye," roared out again and again as confusion arose once more, before the speaker eventually managed to take control, but only after his urges had been backed up by several others.

"He is utterly useless, he could not control a lapdog," one man said of Lenthall.

Hyde raised his hand, signalling he was continuing and the noise eventually abated. This must have been one of the rowdiest sessions so far, some guessed, enough to waken the souls of Edward the First and the other Plantagenet kings who brought the building into being as a marvellous, glittering chapel, paintings and stained glass celebrating their victories, dynasty and crown. The monarchs would probably shun the place now, their decorations masked by wood panelling, as though the beautification offended the majority of sober commoners now filling the chamber.

"I do not oppose a passage which sets out the work of the present Parliament, but what is currently being discussed is a whole list of every complaint and injustice since the beginning of the King's reign, seventeen years ago. To date, he has made several notable concessions and has listened to our concerns, but such an immense list would be a provocation beyond any other to him and it will not serve us well. We will only cause a negative response to be put back to us from both the King and the House of Peers, which will certainly not support such a remonstrance as is being proposed at the minute."

The House of Commons rang with yells and cries, so that nothing could be understood out of it all. Hyde looked hot and sweaty and his friend, Lord Falkland, stood to take the mantle. He began despite the rumpus, and curiosity prompted many to start to listen to this delicate, handsome man, before he repeated himself for the benefit of all. If Hyde was the intelligent manager, then Falkland was the public front, better known, respected and connected.

"How will people view us in this house if we continue to stir up the past, resurrect it and wheel it through the streets again? Such things should now be left to rest in peace, for a new understanding with the King has since been born. Mister Hyde is right; the King has come a long way to meet us since we set out and he has approved everything we have asked of him so far. He will soon return from his other kingdom and if he is met with such a protestation as what is proposed, it will do us and the cause of Parliament an injustice."

Pym disagreed and shook his head, waving some papers.

Others near him stamped their feet or waved their hats. As Falkland resumed his seat, Sir John Culpepper stepped up relentlessly, his sharp nature launching into the attack, the third and more uncertain part of the trio.

"If we were to get this current proposal through this house, gentlemen, the House of Lords will surely toss it right out.

By making ordinances about the church and ordering communion tables to be moved without any consent of that house, or the King, we have alienated them already. They will reject this as a protest against us."

A deluge of pandemonium began at this statement, which incited more affront over rivalry with the House of Lords, than the nature in which it was intended. It risked pushing members into supporting the remonstrance, if simply to prove that they did not care about what the Lords thought.

Pym smirked, displaying disdain. "The fool. He has surely turned people against him because it sounds like he thinks of our house as a servant to the Lords."

Culpepper continued unabated, "Gentlemen, more crucial than this, such a remonstrance is unprecedented in our history.

It is put over as a document for the King's attention, but in reality it is a statement of disgraceful accusations made to the people, about the sovereign."

This time the protesting did not stop.

Sir Edward Dering stood up to endorse the points. "When I first heard of a remonstrance, I presently imagined that like faithful councillors we should hold up a glass to His Majesty. I did not dream that we should remonstrate downward and tell stories to the people."

By now, Pym was sitting bolt upright, fixed on Hyde's expression, which to his disappointment, had not changed. The round face, betraying unashamed plumpness, firmly fleshed out his cheeks and jaw, the tiny chin set within it all, made to look even smaller by a minute beard. He could also hear a lot of shouts to the support of Hyde and these men. They were doing what he feared most and uniting with other moderates, presenting this as a wholehearted attack on the King, nothing more.

"Enough is enough, this charade must end," Pym said to those close by as he rose.

He felt his bulk under him, the nature of his nickname 'the ox' but he knew he had more political agility than Hyde. They needed two people just to match up to him, firming his hesitating resolve in the face of the newly efficient opposition.

The racket died down somewhat. Pym's confidence soared once more in anticipation now, and he felt sure he could undo Hyde's gains by picking them off one by one with an assassin's precision.

"Gentlemen, I hear so many worries and questions. I hear so many men scared to seal our position. I answer you all with one statement; this is simply a necessity of the present times. A lot of evil councillors still surround the King and could persuade him to attack us at any minute and we must neutralise this potential threat. We have seen many plots recently that you all seem to have forgotten about. The Army Plot, then countless others, and all have been traced home to the King's court. While he receives such advice to encourage conspiracies and rumours, we in Parliament, our people and our religion, cannot be safe. It is time to speak plain English, lest posterity claim that England was lost because no man dared speak truthfully. I urge you all to support this remonstrance; there is no question about its importance. I accept the wording may need amending in small parts, but it must go through in principle as it is."

The arguments and rages continued with no end in sight, the cheap tallow candles - all they could find at such short notice - were burning lower, further circulating a stink of the fat that made them. The whole issue rumbled on, looking like both sides were adamant they would have the final say. Never had he seen such a session.

At midnight, Pym observed Hyde stand up, stretching slowly and wearily. He spoke to Falkland and gradually made his way out of the chamber with a hobble.

Pym shook his head.

"If it is so important, why does he fly home like a pigeon?"

he asked of a colleague, making a mock flapping action with his hands, linked by the thumbs.

Then he nudged someone awake who sat two seats down from him. Inside, Pym honestly did not know which way the coming vote would go, for a solid core of people still opposed it. He fought off fatigue with this uncertainty.

By one o'clock in the morning, the order finally came to divide, for the debates looked as endless as the King's guilt over Strafford's execution. The length of the sitting was unprecedented and many men were getting highly frustrated by the continuation of the arguments, but fearing more dangerous results if the tempers were left to grow like a fire, until it consumed them all in the chamber.

A show of hands was ordered, though that soon proved to be problematic with the dense lines of members, so those in favour of the Grand Remonstrance were ordered to stand, and raise their hands. For the first time there seemed to be two distinct parties. Pym was one of the first to raise himself, as quick as his old body could manage, mopping his brow as he waited.

Maybe it would be better to stand, than punish oneself on these hard old pews? The small chamber was hot from the bodies crammed into it and the strength of feelings being thrashed out. After what seemed like an age, the speaker stood up to announce the result, the robes of office highlighting his central role. The smooth, encircling, brown cloak was rich, with a vast array of golden horizontal lines stretching one by one down the middle, to the hem and also along most of the arms. The small sheet of paper, with the final tally, was held close to this sumptuous dress, creating a pause of anticipation.

As it was raised to his gaze, the document appeared to climb the ladder of his golden embroidery and Lenthall prepared to announce the vote.

Pym held his breath.

"Those in favour of the remonstrance are one hundred and fifty nine."

The supporters cheered loudly. Pym was sure about three hundred were left in the chamber, so this was going to be a dangerously close ballot. If it failed, then their cause would not go any further and would be defeated with it.

"Those against - one hundred and forty eight."

A sigh of relief escaped his tired body. Those around him jubilantly shook hands, losing sight of the miniscule margin.

Cheering and protests combined to further exacerbate the atmosphere of this severely divided house. Parliament had never known such scenes, nor such a long debate stretching into the early hours, coming near to blows. Victory it was, though it was clear that the King had managed to attract an array of men to his side. Members then hastily left the chamber, piling through the doors in a crush. After about one third had flooded out, a solitary figure rose in one of the furthest benches.

"The minority wish to enter a protest against this remonstrance. We wish to vote on whether to enter this protest or not."

"Who in God's name is that?" Pym demanded.

"Geoffrey Palmer, member for Stamford and a known King's man," he was told.

A lot of royalists started shouting and bellowing in sympathy and before Pym knew it, the remonstrance was in jeopardy once more. His friend hastily and resourcefully organised jeering to oppose Palmer. Because more than forty members were left, then the sitting was still legal.

The house was in turmoil for the second time that night. A candle went out in a wisp of smoke as Pym watched the speaker.

The timing made it appear that the house would extinguish all the achievements as fast as this, a free Parliament independent of any interference by the King, as burnt out as that.

The place was claustrophobic to Pym, who was anxious to leave, and for the session to close before any more business could undo his work. The three great windows in the far wall were like dark gravestones, as black as the night sky outside.

Men began getting to their feet, rattling their swords and banging the scabbards on the wooden floor, the echoes of all this creating a reminder of the early sixteen twenties, when the speaker was forcibly stopped from dissolving Parliament and held in his chair. A few men could not hold themselves back and assaulted each other, tugging hair, while others grabbed at collars. It was so close to outright violence that shortly it seemed there would be a riot. The speaker rose to try and restore order but he was completely drowned out as the storm blew up. Pym was speechless for once and another of his supporters stood up beside him on the bench, holding his hands in the air.

"Enough, enough."

The house paused long enough for him to be able to command everyone's attention with his booming voice.

"No further business shall be done tonight. Many members have left. No further business, I say."

The speaker took the opportunity to adjourn the house and scurried from his chair, meaning that anything that was discussed would be unauthorised. The rest of the hundred or so men filed out of the chamber in a mixture of spirits, but everyone shared a common anxiety.

As Pym left, he managed a weary piece of sarcasm to his friend, "Can you believe that the idea of a remonstrance was suggested by Digby last year, before he ran to the King's side with his tail between his legs?"

* * *

In a calmer atmosphere outside of Parliament, yet still with regiments of people around them, waiting for news of the vote,

Cotton seized Charles's arm. The sensation was as gripping as the action, as he wondered whether it was the fingerless hand, or not. Before he could look, the man had begun shouting.

"Just wait till these bloodthirsty bastards hear what you did. I will tell them now - this is perfect for such news," he said in a gruff, low voice. It was so different from the loud way he usually relished revenge, that it gave the man a totally different air; more dignified and ruthless.

Charles panicked, reeling with shock at what he meant.

"They will tear you apart."

The disparity of Cotton's behaviour was most worrying, as if he was now fully satisfying this hunger for revenge, the victory finally exorcising his soul of the jealousy and high feelings.

Charles let out a roar, while the members filing out of Westminster reignited the passions of the spectators, and the mob fused back together and began their demonstrations again. Snippets of news, contradictions and repetitions of the speeches sailed through the night air, sending ructions through the whole yard.

Charles pounded his fist straight into Cotton's face, losing any restraint. The force knocked the man to the ground and Charles began kicking him repeatedly. Cotton shouted, squirmed around and desperately tried to cover himself with his arms, curling up like a baby.

"You bastard … I have had enough of your threats."

Then one of Dorset's men rode over and held his sword up.

Charles stopped and glared up at the slender blade. The trooper paused for a split second as Charles cried out, "I am not a rebel. I am for the King and the laws of the land."

He was furious that the trooper should dare to threaten him, especially after what he had done earlier, clearly declaring his support. But as he edged backwards, the blade was lifted in preparation to slash him anyway, and he gasped, frozen out of simple disbelief. As the horseman put his weight down onto the stirrups to cast his weapon, another trooper galloped over and yelled out, dragging the reins of his colleague before the two of them looked behind Charles and rode away.

"The vote is carried, the Remonstrance is through," it was announced with a reverberating yell, sending the crowd into jubilant chanting.

Cotton continued to lie on the floor to enhance Charles's appearance as a menace, and also to keep low, away from the trouble, while Charles took a deep breath. As he swivelled round quickly to counter any threat behind him, judging by the troopers' previous glares, he caught sight of Digby standing on the top of the steps once more with a guard accompanying him.

Like a tide, the remainder of the crowd ebbed and flowed now that their mission had been accomplished, surging around at a loose end to enjoy the victory, before finally drifting back and thinning out as more and more seeped away. Charles panted. His hair was strewn all over, clothes messed up and dirty, while small bits of blood, both dried and fresh, stained his hands and face. Digby was as immaculate as ever amidst all this physical, mental and social mess. As the peer descended the steps, Charles walked over to him automatically, without any thought.

"Sir Charles. Well done, you surprise me all the time. I have just heard of your deeds before the session," he called out.

"I did nothing but stand up for my family, my principles … and the laws, my lord. I sincerely hope the King will honour the concessions he has made so far, for they should prove the basis for a decent settlement."

Then came the realisation that Digby must have ordered the trooper off, but he could not bring himself to thank the arrogant peer all the same, no matter how important manners were to him. He would not show weakness to this man by acknowledging his role in that escape.

"Well, Sir Arthur's power will never be the same again with the King," Digby predicted, "Two men declared their true colours tonight and he joined with the mob. He surprised me with his duplicity as much as you with your loyalty."

"The debate?" Charles said, between the maelstrom of images and worries flooding around him.

"Is lost," Digby confirmed, adding his answer.

There was silence for a while, both seeming too engrossed for words, while Cotton struggled to his feet after hearing his name mentioned.

"Sir Charles, I am determined to get you a post in the King's Guards after the way you commanded this rabble. I will see to it and you will hear from me, for your skill needs to be utilised to beneficial ends," the peer told him, before leaving.

Perhaps Digby wanted to strike a blow at Holland by becoming his patron. The court was full of petty squabbles, despite the King's orders that nobody should scorn each other - Holland was often challenging other courtiers to duels. Charles was taken aback by this blunt offer, more like a command, but it was one haughty action that he would go along with. Finally he nodded his thanks. Cotton warned him with a low, deep voice that despite having no proof, he knew about Charles's involvement in a plot with Strafford.

"I know you got that letter back somehow, too. No matter though, for nobody is interested in evidence these days. The mere story of you and that evil man will suffice."

As Cotton left, he felt well and truly alone and sat on the steps in silence, thinking and worrying, planning and wondering. The position Digby offered was lost on him at the minute, for he needed to get to grips with the sheer amount of change that had happened today.

He could concentrate on nothing else but James. He thumped his leg, cursing the loss of friendship - for every success, there seemed to be a downside. Then he cried like his baby, head in arms, unable and unwilling to stop the urge, but retaining some privacy this way. Wiping his eyes on his arm, he ran his fingers through his hair and stared to the sky. The impartiality he had struggled with for eight months had finally been forcefully cast aside. Employment, and new political prospects would dawn with tomorrow's sunrise, ushering in a fresh, brighter future.

He felt utter relief.

Then after this, he thought again of James. Guilt, betrayal, sorrow and memories filled him now. Was he wrong to hit him and would their friendship be lost, or was it simply heat of the moment? Would Cotton tell his secret and endanger his family? His family - he thought of Anne and Henry.

"I love you, my darling," he whispered, in tribute to the pair he had fought for. Not the King, nor Digby, but his wife and child, and a stable city for them both.

Chapter 41

Two days later a cavalcade of carriages and more than five hundred horsemen clattered up before a platform, some fairytale spectacle that elaborately adorned the King as the central character. Like the rays of the sun, the royal party lit up the city as it passed by, in a dramatic reminder that the King's favour could cast rewarding light onto those loyal subjects, while traitors would face the cold shade. Considering the monarch and the hundreds of courtiers that followed him had been away for months, London trade and business had felt that dim shadow for long enough. The royal coach appeared to be packed out, with the King, Queen, children and the Elector Palatine filling it. At last he had returned to London after the Scottish visit and overjoyed crowds welcomed him - absence had made their hearts grow fonder.

The new Lord Mayor and Recorder of London made a speech of loyal welcome, overflowing with gestures and elaborate words, like the fountains that cascaded wine for the occasion. People cheered and the King reluctantly drew himself away from his wife's side for a while, and got out of the coach to stand with the Lord Mayor. The twenty eight golden 's' figures that joined to make his chain of office, hanging around his neck, sparkled as much as his extremely loyal stance. Indeed his very occupancy of the post within the cities government confirmed the changing sympathies of London towards the monarch.

King Charles told everyone, "It is our determination to m-maintain the liberties and true religion of this country and rest assured, we will restore the estates some of you have l-lost in Ulster, after the rebellion there has been crushed. The recent unhappy scenes in this city have been down to the meaner sort of people, for I can see that most of the populace are true and l-loyal subjects."

The royal then drew his sword and knighted the Lord Mayor, who kneeled before him, followed by the Recorder of London. Many had urged him to reward loyal supporters, and not only his enemies, as he had done in Scotland lately.

King Charles then mounted up, sitting on the saddle of gold and silver thread, his white steed beginning to ride into the middle of the ranks of his royal officers. He personally had deliberately chosen mostly Protestant nobles for the procession, and also ones who were not necessarily his most loyal, to reinforce to the population that he was not closeted with dangerous Catholic magnates. In front of him he had placed the Earl of Manchester and Lord Lyttelton, both Officers of State, flanking the Prince of Wales and the Lord Mayor. Directly in front of the King was the Earl of Hertford, carrying the gleaming Sword of State. He observed the Earl of Lindsey to his left and the Earl of Arundel to his right. Behind him was the royal coach, followed up by the Earls of Hamilton, Salisbury and Holland.

The London Trained Bands had turned out to line the route and the people cheered as though the dispute was at an end, rather than the pinnacle. It was spellbinding to observe this jubilation and the King sensed the strength his position had generated. The Lord Mayor was favourable and that man commanded these bands of London militia; it was easy to get drunk on the image, without realising how fickle opinion was, or so his cousin the Duke of Richmond had delicately advised. Yet he felt Richmond was simply pessimistic - he was clearly master of the city now and should be able to deal with Pym once and for all.

King Charles spared a wry smile for Holland in particular, for he knew the man would not like having to take part in the pomp. The peer was part of the group who lent support to those opposing the crown, but while still holding a government post. The position meant that Holland had to attend today, the divided allegiance being a source of amusement to the sovereign. The King was damned sure he was going to make it as awkward as possible for men like this; his feelings of compromise and conciliation were fading fast with each new indication of support for his cause.

As they meandered through the narrow streets of the capital, the King lapped up the huzzahs. Tapestries hung from windows in welcome, bells pealed out, practically calling his name, and he followed the Roman wall on his way to the Guildhall for a luscious banquet. The people on the route seemed to be dazzled by the beauty of the parade, as well as by the veneer of power that it oozed.

At nightfall, supportive crowds of people were now escorting their sovereign back to his home, passing by celebratory bonfires. Despite the formal meal, he was still hungry for the demonstrations of loyalty. The flaming torches surrounding him stretched way ahead, and exhilarated from his welcome, the sight imbued him with a burning determination to stand up to his enemies. A King united with his people's love was unstoppable, and he confidently predicted the end of their problems to Queen Henrietta. The delicate runaway chin accentuated those luscious lips, which were never far from his thoughts.

The monarch's jubilant mood was sustained as he entered the palace, despite the remonstrance vote slipping through his fingers. His tanned leather riding boots and their spurs clinked as he walked, his happiness to be back overtaking his rule that boots should not be worn in the palace.

"With God's help, this interminable quarrel with Parliament will be dead. I am confident I have won over the Scots and now London welcomes us tumultuously. Mister Pym has shot his bolt too far with this remonstrance. By God I will not answer the impertinent document when I get it, for no King has been treated as outrageously as I," he told the Queen.

"You are Lord General of the forces south of the River Trent. Parliament's stuffy Lord Essex, has been cast aside by your return too," she reminded him with glee, the peer being Parliament's temporary appointee until the sovereign's return.

"Parliament were fully expecting me to formalise his appointment, and all this after they selected him without any recourse to me. Such an action is unprecedented and now let them see how much I disapprove. I will no longer assign anyone to the role, for I will keep command personally."

She looked at him lovingly, desire swirling around in her doe eyes, heightened by his rare strength of opinion, which she always advocated.

"I have missed you, sweetheart."

"And I you, my dear," he confirmed, taking her hand and kissing it. Then with a glance, he amorously planted several more, on her arm, then lips, cultivating the passion of their reunion.

The ovations were drowned out as his whole interest was absorbed by her, stroking the dark ringlets of hair that hung over her right shoulder. The couple entered the Privy Gallery and he felt like a conquering hero as he stopped her and tugged her gently towards him. He was truly happy.

"While you were away, I fought like a demon for you. I wrote to every sympathetic peer and ordered them to come to the House of Lords for the votes. We have a loyal Lord Mayor, so we are now in the ascent at last," Queen Henrietta told him, proud of her part in struggling for her husband, and always anxious to promote her hard work as proof.

They were so lost that they failed to notice the Queen's sparkling, witty and cunning lady of the bedchamber, Lucy, Countess of Carlisle, watching them intently from the distance.

Queen Henrietta interceded for Lord Holland, begging her husband to give him command of the armed forced north of the River Trent. Charles nodded this title away, giving the peer one last chance to prove his loyalty. The King stroked his wife's cheek tenderly and her dark lashes flicked, practically pointing to the royal apartments

"If I cause the House of Lords and House of Commons to fall out, the loyal people and Members of Parliament will surely rise against the vicious minority. Parliament's bastions fall one by one. I have but to wait a short while for it all," the King said, sure of himself.

"Wait?" The Queen frowned, her whole bearing swaying as wildly as the forest of lace that adorned her gold dress. A silver heart brooch clipped a lace collar together. Her real heart was always worn on display too.

"Yes, my dearest. It will not be long now. We can see from this remonstrance's narrow victory that Parliament is torn right down the middle."

"A mighty King does not *wait* for his subjects to do the work. You must go and pull them out of Parliament like naughty schoolchildren. Do you think a school in this country would function well if it did not cane its unruly pupils, or show them the difference between right and wrong? Fight back, I beg you; the time is right and you have such great support now, that it would be foolish to sit idle for it to evaporate. For the love of me, do this, darling, or we will all be lost. Do not delay and give these traitors time to grow once more."

The King went quiet and stroked his immaculate beard.

He was thrown upside down at this confrontational advice, though the pair were now alone, Lady Carlisle having discreetly left, following the Queen's comment.

"For goodness sake, they have got a measure through Parliament requiring you to let them approve your ministers, they question the upbringing of our children, demanding they cater for their education, and now they threaten me daily. While you were away, Lady Carlisle informed me of many things; they were going to attempt to take the Prince's from me, and are plotting to imprison me for starting these Irish massacres," she insisted with tears in her eyes.

Inside, the King quivered with fury at such a contemptuous demand, instantly desiring to take action against those traitors in Parliament. He had a ruthless defence mechanism when it came to his wife, never mind the fact that she was nine years younger than him too.

Chapter 42

harles read the proclamation by the King, that the Book of Common Prayer be used throughout the kingdom again, all other preaching being illegal. This would gag those illiterate, jumped up men who had recently begun to take over churches, spouting their own rubbish, he thought.

He also noticed that this set the King out as the protector of the traditional form of church and worship, still supported by the vast majority, judging by the petitions on the subject.

It was during the lunch that a letter arrived interrupting the meal, and the newssheet he was reading, Louise bringing it in and commenting on the royal crest. The official packet also carried the ominous picture of a hanging man, a warning that the post boy should speedily deliver it, or else. Since the riot outside Parliament, Charles had found complete comfort in Anne, as if all uncertainty had fallen away. Their love survived all turmoil, and a delay ensued before he took his eyes off her to examine the message, ignoring Anne's troublesome stepmother. Putting his wine down, he pulled the paper apart, breaking the wax seal.

"What does it say?" she queried calmly.

His dark eyebrows rose. "God's wounds, what will be next?"

"What is it?" she asked again, now with frustration.

"Things are getting desperate. The bill for removing control of the armed forces from the King passed in the House of Commons by thirty three votes, so Pym is still maintaining a slim majority. No wonder the King has ordered all members to return to Parliament immediately," he explained to her.

While speaking, he picked at the pieces of lamb. He put the letter down and took some salmon, placing it on his plate with the vegetables he had left.

"Yet Ireland is left to rot by them both. I notice that despite your pessimism about my presence, we have not suffered one bit," his mother in law piped up.

Charles ignored her as he had done for the majority of the meal, and instead asked Louise to pass the chicken pie. She scooped some filling out of the pastry casing that was used to cook the ingredients in, and he reminded her to leave all the pastry for the birds, rather than throwing it away like they normally did.

"Does that mean you will be under Parliament's control soon?" Anne asked.

"Nay, the Royal Guard is the King's own. There is no fear of me being used by Parliament to further their thrust into his power, but he does order us all to wear swords when at Whitehall," he explained.

Digby's word outside Parliament had been kept and not long afterwards he had been summoned to take up an officer's position within the King's Guard. Ironically, this employment had brought security, but the force was beginning to be isolated as monarch and parliament grew further apart. The men of the band were segregated because of their direct loyalty to King Charles, and this had begun to add a peril of its own.

"We have to drill this afternoon too and it sounds like our friendly mob have returned again. I will face them with a tidy moustache; I am going to get ready for Snipper Lassell."

As he stood up, he swiped two cakes, unable to resist them.

"What are these?"

"Sugar cakes," Anne said.

"Nonsense, Anne, they are called jumbles. I should know, I baked them," her stepmother corrected.

Charles stopped for a second and put them back when he realised who the creator was. The old battleaxe scowled, as if this annoyed her more than anything he had ever said to her.

"Watch out, that barber might get the urge to cut your throat. He could be an Irish Catholic in disguise," Anne's mother screeched after him, taking a swig of her wine. Anne nudged her, frowning at her open hostility. Charles had learned that to say nothing brought out the worst in the woman as she would keep following up her successes.

Inevitably, the arguments were beginning to eat into Anne's enthusiasm for her stepmother's stay.

"The only thing around my house which is cutting, madam, is your tongue," he calmly retorted.

He heard the glass slam down and Anne remonstrating with her about the remarks as he left them both to it. After a few minutes, Anne left to look round the stalls in the exchange, and Tom, his barber, arrived and was shown to the bedroom where Charles was.

"Good morrow, Sir Charles," the man said as he bowed on arrival, his son, and apprentice, handing him the bowl of steaming water.

He sat in the chair by the window while Tom wrapped his white cloth around his neck. The barber placed his dish next to Charles and produced the sharp razor, before wiping his hands on his apron.

"That rabble wanted me to hand over my blade, so they

could slit some Papist in two. My lad nearly spilled the water trying to keep up with me as we hurried through the street," he recollected with shock, while starting his work.

Charles looked at the bowl the boy held under his chin, decorated in a novel fashion with pictures of the instruments Tom would use.

"Bloody scum, why don't they get back to work and do something decent for a living," Charles observed, sick of talk about papists being sliced to shreds.

"They held my old hackney up too. The coachman couldn't pass by, there were that many of 'em," Tom continued. He chattered like an old woman, as though it focussed his mind when he was delicately manoeuvring the instrument.

"Damn apprentices. I think it is leaving their family so young that causes them to lose control. Flying the nest at twelve and living with their masters for the next decade must do it. Their masters need to be a damn sight stricter with them," Charles complained, as the barber kept pausing while he spoke.

"I hear a mad dog attacked a man near the sign of the Cork and Bottle in Princess Street yesterday. They threw the fellow in the lake, hoping that it stopped the bite affecting him, but he just took too much water in and drowned. All those protesters could do was stone the dog," Tom commiserated about the gossip.

He began to snip Charles's moustache with some small scissors, with his son wiping the razor and watching, learning his future trade.

"Well my new post in the King's Guards means I will soon be coming face to face with mad dogs of a different sort to that canine," he told Tom as he moved his head to the side.

As the barber finished, he wiped the face and neck. Charles got up and reached towards the large over mantle of the fireplace, taking the coins he had left there between the vases which adorned it.

"Thank you, Mister Lassell, if you see Louise, my maid, she will prepare some wine for you before you travel back. I have given you a tip for the good work."

After relieving himself in the chamber pot, he followed Tom downstairs and heard murmuring from the hall, followed by giggles and then more furtive chatter. Opening the door, he envisaged Arabella messing around once again, ready to chastise her and deciding to dock her wages immediately. Instead, he found Cotton of all people at the front door, close to his mother in law who was giggling like a girl. Charles slammed the interior portal and yelled for Louise to get Tom some wine, shocked and irate at what he had just witnessed. The two were cavorting on his doorstep where anyone could see them and this astounded him. But on the other hand, at least his enemy had not been invited into Charles's house, his inner sanctum.

After a minute he went back to the pair, who had a lot in common, but this time they were more subdued. Cotton's presence infuriated him and the continued closeness of the two, especially with one being family, was offensive. Storming over, he tugged Cotton's arm so hard that the fellow stumbled. The smile went from his face and he grabbed Charles's doublet, pushing him to the wall.

Charles got a surprise at the force. "Good God, you have found some balls; fighting back now, Arthur?"

He grabbed hold of Cotton's firm jaw, pushing him back with this vice grip and then went over to Anne's mother to demand answers.

"Really, one cannot have an ounce of privacy," she whined, the thin eyebrows arching with scorn. If it were not for her rude nature and greed, the woman would probably have a beauty about her, though her foul expressions held any of this back.

"How dare you, this is my home and you are a guest. Not only do you abuse my hospitality, but you talk to men on

413

the doorstep like a common slut, and not just any man, but the biggest double dealing whoremonger in London. In fact, man is not a term I would use for him. I will have you both away from my house."

"Language, son in law, please," she hissed, her black ringlets as dark as her resentment of him.

Charles almost immediately gave a low, firm order, "Shut up and get inside. I will deal with you later."

Seeing she had pushed him too far, the woman stepped away, obeying the gruff demand. He gave his enemy a helping hand to leave, but all he could do was cackle.

"Leave him alone. He is more exciting and mysterious to a woman than you will ever be," his mother in law screeched, embarrassingly loud.

He paused and Cotton smiled firmly, toying with his bamboo cane, as though proud the manhood issue had settled on him for once. The lazy look on his face casually asserted his easiness in the perimeter of Charles's house.

"I have found out what that letter contained, that you took back from Digby's secretary. I know all about your close links to Strafford," Cotton said with a wink.

As he forced him further into the street, the man eyed him down his long nose, without saying a word.

"Get away from my door, unless you want another beating," Charles threatened.

"Ah yes, very clever to put it around that I got my wounds from the mob, rather than your hand, in that riot. And now we both have settled our political judgement on opposite sides. Mark my words I will ruin you, as easily as tackling a baby."

Charles laughed at him, loudly as he could. Some people looked round from the street.

"Why do you not have children, Sir Arthur? Could you not satisfy your wife?" he queried.

Cotton stepped back, as though devastated at the

comment, almost tripping over the loose black lace that had tied his shoes up.

The insult did more to finally get him out of the doorway than any manhandling. His eyes glared, face glowing red.

"It is not just a family I have, but also more fingers than you too," Charles snorted, before slamming the door on him, making Cotton snatch his fist away before further damage was done to his hand.

Going into his study to watch from the window, he brushed past Anne's stepmother. Cotton was standing across the street, observing the house like a hawk. He then went back to the main chamber to deal with the other thorn in his side.

"I want you packed and out by this evening, madam. I will have a coach pick you up."

She shook her head, sitting bolt upright and continuing to embroider, the small, fulsome lips pouting with concentration. Grabbing her hand to stop her artistry, he threw the work across the room, provoking an intense glare from her.

"I am afraid my daughter will not be happy with any of this," she told him firmly, flicking her hair behind her shoulder.

"In the name of God, are all Irish as ignorant as you? I do not want to see you again. If you insist on staying here, I will be forced to tell Anne about your cavorting."

He stared at her, hatred easily visible. She disgusted him.

"You would not, it would devastate her. I would never forgive you if you did," she warned, now acting as Anne's protector.

He took hold of her wrist, unwittingly pressing the bracelet into her thin arm, and dragged her upstairs as she shrieked, like a naughty child.

"Pack your rubbish immediately, I command you, and by God, I will ensure you do it," he cried, though the cloud did not clear around him.

She burst into tears and he heard Anne returning. Thinking

415

of Cotton outside and Anne at the door, he fled down the stairs, making sure she got inside.

"Your mother is going to have to go tonight."

She stood still, mouth open in shock at the words. He stroked the hair that framed her face, pearl earring moving as she shook her head.

"You have never liked her, but you said you would give her a chance," she reminded him.

"I have, darling, plenty of them, but I caught her talking to Cotton. She will ruin us all."

"Is it all about that damned man?" she snapped, losing her patience.

"Anne, she must go and that has to be final. If Cotton tells the mob she is Catholic, they will storm this house to get her. He is capable of anything and you know what he is like after all that has been done."

"No, that is not fair. She does not know the situation between you both."

"He has assaulted me, Anne. I fear for you because he is so handy with his fists. Look at his temper," Anne's stepmother shouted, looking down on them from the landing.

Anne's eyes filled up and she went upstairs to talk to her, while he went back to the window. He spied Cotton walking down the street, but in the opposite direction to the parade ground, where Charles's old regiment had been going every other Tuesday. This intrigued him and he watched closely.

He decided on the spur of the moment to follow, and he ran out of the house, leaving some distance between them both.

* * *

Cotton tugged on his cloak, tucking it around his neck. He was cold and vulnerable and having it around him made him a little more secure. The snow crunched beneath his feet as he passed by a blacksmith's, feeling warm heat for a few seconds and hearing clangs, as metal was hammered against an anvil.

As Cotton walked, he found satisfaction from crushing the snow harder beneath his steps. He was sure he had just seen someone disappear round an alleyway, but a passing lady magnetised his attention. The black mourning clothes of dull silk, black shawl and gloves cut a distinct sight in the white world of snowy London. Her blond hair was even subdued beneath her hood, the bright and vibrant colour being far too rich to show in such a sad period. The plainness of her apparel, and lack of all jewellery and anything with a shiny surface, made her basic beauty all the more attractive. Her maid was similarly dressed and as the mistress approached, Cotton bowed his head.

"My condolences on your loss, madam," he said, placing his cane over an icy puddle, to warn her about its proximity.

The lady continued her neutral look, though nodding her thanks. This was enough for Cotton, who felt excitement gush through his body, enough to melt the white blanket on the street. As she drifted away, a dog's barking and deep snarling broke out behind him, so he focussed on the sound.

Eventually he sought out the noise and watched as two dogs fought, some children cheering and throwing snow and stones at them. He shook his head.

"Godforsaken children, I am glad I did not have any after all."

Remembering what Charles had said about offspring, he let out a quick breath through his teeth, jetting a stream of air into the distance.

"The bastard has angered me. I will see my day soon."

He stomped on, nearing a house.

"Cannot satisfy my wife," he growled.

A man sat on a barrel outside, one leg casually hanging down as he smoked a clay pipe as Cotton approached. He greeted him and he entered the building, feeling more settled inside. In the doorway he shook his cloak free of snow and stamped his feet, the temper dispersing too. Walking through the corridor, being careful not to slip on the stone floor, then into another room, he leaned on the fireplace, warming his hands. Wooden beams travelled up the walls like veins, giving a life of its own to this sanctuary.

A shadow sped past the window and made him jump. It was bigger than the others and he tugged the curtains closed, the metal rings screeching like a warning as he did so.

After lighting some candles he walked to a bookshelf, fumbling around the side of it, until he pulled the shelf away from the wall. It opened up and inside was a picture of the Virgin Mary, looking down upon him. He lit the small candles next to it and made the sign of the cross, bowing his head and took hold of some rosary beads. As he knelt down on a cushion, heart full of devotion, he mumbled a prayer, fondling the beads as though his life depended on it.

Following his devotion, he remained in silence, thinking. A noise near the window made him glare over once more, so suspicious and irritated that it broke his meditation. He leapt to his feet and blew the candles out, slamming the bookcase shut. There was someone peering through, he was sure of it.

"Probably heathens, none of them faithful to our true church," he spat, as he left in a hurry, to investigate.

Chapter 43

C harles could not move, his body felt numb. He watched
as Cotton threw his cloak back on inside the room,
shrouding his Catholicism. Five window mullions
divided the opening, and in the far end, through a gap in
the curtain, it was just possible to see him, before he stormed
out of view. Goose bumps chilled his body. Cotton was no
longer a simple enemy, he was bonded to the Catholic church,
dangerous and severely underhand. Charles ran, without
hesitating, towards a back lane. He turned back for a second,
catching sight of Cotton's thin frame. He kept on sprinting,
past animals and people, squeezing by carts and through
another narrow alleyway, all the objects and beings becoming
a blur. As he approached a market square, he slowed.

Cotton was no longer to be seen now.

He knew Sir Richard was due to parade the Red Regiment
today, and he pondered reporting what he had seen to the
old colonel. Worry sparked his imagination, which was vivid
once engaged, and he was sure now that Cotton wished to use
his military post to his religious ends. He felt fear of Cotton
for the first time, because of this new fact, panicking over

whether he had been seen earlier. He hurried on, still without any direction.

Children ran around trying to skate on some icy patches, while traders and the public strolled past, well clad against the biting wind, which shrieked and howled in his ears. He stopped on the pavement, watching people huddled together while they chattered and gossiped. With his mind running ahead of him still, he stayed idle, distracted now by what their attention was fixed upon. A cart was being pulled slowly through the streets with a man at the back of it, naked from the waist up.

His wrists had been tied to the vehicle and someone was making ready to flog him. As the cart trundled by, rattling over the cobbles, people jeered, flinging rubbish. The escort drew his whip back, before casting it across the prisoner's back, the sound like a storm tide had clashed upon a vessel, causing the fellow to scream out. Lines of people formed to watch now, children scurrying curiously to the front through narrow gaps.

The hangman, who was carrying out the work, handled his weapon with experience, the three strands of rope now bobbing loosely as they waited for the next occasion.

"This man has refused to work and insists on begging in the streets, bleeding the parish dry. Let everyone know that this parish will not allow idle men to abide here. The bible tells us that Jesus himself associates laziness with wickedness," the hangman yelled in warning.

The pink and purple lines on the offender's back resembled long fingers; with the hand of Jesus now across his back, the fellow was sure to find impetus to secure employment. The hangman was as relaxed with this minor punishment, the legs of his breeches casually flapping open at the knees without any cord. The sight had calmed Charles, seeing punishment being doled out gave a confidence that the state and laws had not altogether collapsed, which reassured him that the Protestant government was still ruling. Cotton and his Catholics had every right to be furtive.

He now walked to a coach and getting inside, sat down opposite an old man as it moved off, passing the procession. As he drew level with the flogged man, Charles shouted his dislike of those who would not work.

"This weather be most unsuited to my soul," the stranger said.

"Aye," Charles agreed, a deep sigh blowing out some of the tension he had felt earlier. He sat back in the wooden seat, pressing his spine straight, and he pushed his shoulders back too, stretching and maintaining the position for a while.

"You be in the army then?" the man queried, a stubby finger pointing in the direction of his medal.

"Well, between posts at the minute," he muttered, now thinking calmly about Cotton's secret.

Sir Arthur Cotton had changed in his eyes now and he felt differently towards him. After all, Catholics were capable of all sorts and he worried about the threats that had been made in the past. Then he grunted and shook his head, determined to fight the man to the end, no matter whether he was Pagan, Catholic, or Puritan.

"Then why in our Lord's name do you not shift those Puritan dogs, which protest daily around Westminster, or drive off those accursed troops of Lord Dorset's who also threaten the peace of this country?" the man asked, interrupting him again. Charles liked nothing more than peace when he travelled in a coach.

He noted the plain appearance, a strange looking fellow with creases stretching down from the each side of his mouth and bushy eyebrows giving a very dour air. The eyes, hidden slightly by drooping lids, were narrow and to Charles, all of this gave his comment quite an arrogant touch.

"Do you really think one armed force trying to eject another would solve matters? If that is what you advocate, then thank the Lord you are not a commander."

The man sat silent for some seconds, a smile crossing his old face, before replying, "You are wise, my son."

Charles was put off by the interest the man was showing in him, but it was easier to be anxious about any slight thing now. He looked out of the window as they passed the public gallows. The hangman's apprentice was there burning papers.

It was a long time since he had seen him destroying news sheets, those that condemned the royal policy. Before the Archbishop of Canterbury's incarceration, he remembered how the King's prerogative courts were used by the cleric to punish all those who published anything criticising the government. Since the courts were abolished, the printing presses had gone mad.

The man in the carriage brought his attention back.

"Probably sheets reporting all of the proceedings in Parliament, published without their consent. I doubt very much whether Parliament truly minds them though, as they just spread their propaganda. Today must be a feeble show."

Charles looked at him, wondering where this tirade came from and resenting the way he seemed to know everything. Just who was he?

The stranger was grey haired, with silver streaks shining out as audaciously as his opinions, though balding on top. His eyebrows accentuated every expression and his stubble suggested he had not shaved for quite some time.

"You are not from London? Your accent is not local," Charles queried, now determined to quiz him in return.

"Nay, I travel a lot," he said, eyes turning away.

Charles debated whether to enjoy the quiet, or persist in searching out the man's background, a niggling voice causing him to choose the latter. The carriage slowed as it altered course, turning into a narrow street. He saw another in the distance, tilting over because one of the wheels had come off.

The passengers were standing outside, bemused, while the coachman hastily gathered his hat and belongings from the roadside. Then he thought he saw Cotton in the crowd, but when he checked, it was not him after all.

His heart beat faster.

In an instant, the carriage jerked violently, thrusting the older man across the seat. Charles quickly steadied himself on the side of the coach, glancing around to check the window and the sights outside, to see if everything was as normal.

"Blessed Virgin protect me," the stranger cried in a panic as he clung on desperately, trying to pull himself up.

Charles's eyes widened at the religious exclamation and he realised then that the man was a Catholic.

"Thou art a Papist. I knew you were too insolent to be normal," he yelled.

"My son, I am here because our flock in this country needs us."

He frantically cut him off, panicking that his suspicion had been confirmed, "I have heard enough and *nobody* needs thee. You are murderers; how many of you are here? I know you are infiltrating London, I have seen none but your type today."

Slamming the roof with his fist, he growled beneath his breath, "I will be hung if I am caught with you. How dare you jeopardise my life."

The priests held a hand out, fingers tense with his pleas, mouth open as he glared. Charles stood up, and the hand came forward to bless him, though he quickly swept it away. As the coach stopped, he fumbled with the door and jumped out.

"How dare you," he cried again in disbelief.

As the carriage set off again, he speedily paced down another street. It was a short walk to the Artillery grounds now, for he was determined to go to confront Cotton, sure a plot was afoot.

They are like vermin, slipping into the country without anyone noticing, or caring, until there are so many of them, that it will be too late for us all, he thought.

Walking out of the street, he saw the men sitting on fences and standing talking. A group of officers were conversing at the side, while Sir Richard sat nearby, his boy helping him with his boots. Charles felt safer and more secure seeing the soldiers, as they could be needed soon. Cotton might know of the letter Charles had written about his mission to Strafford, but like a gift from the gods, he realised he had checkmated his enemy.

Strafford was hated, still, but Papists were the antichrist, and Cotton's secret was much more explosive than his own.

Heading towards them, he viewed the servant fumbling with Sir Richard's footwear. Slapping the boy's head, the colonel pushed him away, tugging the boot on himself. Sir Richard stood up, mopping his brow and then he strode towards the group of officers, separating them with his baton.

Charles approached and greeted them. "Good afternoon, gentlemen."

"What are you doing here?" Sir Richard bluntly questioned, before yelling an order to a nearby captain.

The officers marched away, as Charles tried to get more civil conversation.

"I need to speak to Lieutenant Colonel Cotton," Charles said with an upbeat smile, now grasping the enormity of his enemy's weakness.

"Never mind that, he is a serving officer in this regiment, so has important work to do."

Then Cotton raced over and Charles stopped speaking. He eyed him to assess the reactions, but apart from looking rushed and having less arrogance than usual, he seemed no different.

Charles was loath to go near him. Over near the men he saw Captain Johnson raise his hand in greeting. He saluted him in return, walking to the side of the grounds to watch the training, leaning against a post.

Cotton was deep in conversation with the colonel now.

He wondered if Sir Richard was also a papist? His legs were jumpy and prickly, as though impatient at being idle. As the officers got the men into line, he felt impelled to holler the instructions that he was used to, and seeing Cotton parading, while he stood on his own, now fanned the smouldering hatred.

The insolent drummer boy turned his nose up at Charles as he walked past, and then he saw Ensign Wilkinson who frowned at him. He ignored their reactions, before sauntering towards Sir Richard. As he passed, most of the men lined up still nodded their heads in respect, some confidence returning from their reactions alone. Common soldiers they may be, but their loyalty was worth more to him than any other.

"How are your wounds, Sir Arthur?" Charles asked provocatively, reminding him of the thrashing he had inflicted upon the man during the riot, adamant he would show no nerves.

"Damned mobs beat him up, a disgrace they are. What in God's name is this city coming to? It is a good job we parade to cap their unruly behaviour," Sir Richard announced.

The pikemen stood with their pikes straight, while the captain bellowed to the musketeers. Cotton barked at one individual who was lax about his manoeuvres, grabbing the weapon, pushing it into position, though he forced it too far back and the man had to adjust it when Cotton had gone. This caused Charles to smirk.

"What is wrong with you?" Sir Richard growled at the man, giving a double onslaught.

The soldier muttered an apology, yet still the colonel placed his baton to the man's head. He kept pushing, until the soldier was forced to stumble backwards, pushing him down to the ground for fifty press ups.

"Sir Richard, I really must speak to Sir Arthur," Charles urged.

"Get off this parade ground, man, what are you still doing here? He will see you afterwards if it is that urgent."

Charles strode away and watched the men move off at a slow pace. The drummers beat their tune and the standard flew in the breeze at the front of the regiment.

"Right, catch up, get moving and keep formation," the sergeant shouted and cajoled.

Sir Richard scowled along the lines as they passed him, then he hit a man on the back of the neck with the baton, which had now turned into a weapon in its own right.

"Get in line I said, wretch."

Others were manhandled forward to catch up, before the colonel joined the rear to pester the drummer boys, easy pickings for him. Charles heard him scolding them about their beat. After they had marched around the grounds several times and played out all their various postures from the drill book, they got the long awaited order to stop. As he was inactive, Charles constantly thought of the old priest and Cotton. He beamed a smile to the sky with realisation that the Lord had exposed two enemies of the state to him of all people. He needed to eliminate them both now and he resolved to inform the constable of the old priest's actions after he had dealt with Cotton. After the drill, the order was given to end the parade and he felt a hand slam his shoulder.

"Now do not detain him long, for we have a regimental dinner this evening," Sir Richard warned, as Cotton joined them.

"It is not I who keeps Sir Arthur Cotton, but the Virgin Mary."

Sir Richard frowned and then let out a roaring guffaw.

Charles laughed along, leaving Cotton silent with bewilderment.

The comment was too much for Sir Richard, who began coughing, and he withdrew to his coach and his serving boy.

"What do you mean? Do not underestimate me, Berkeley," Cotton said slowly, emphasising his words.

"Sir Arthur, what if I do underestimate you?"

"Your wife and child will see."

"I want you to stop preaching to me," Charles said with a knowing glare.

"I do not preach, I warn," he snapped through his tight lips.

Charles started to walk away. "Oh yes, that's right, you don't preach. You leave that to a priest. You and your bookshelf, eh?"

Charles continued his walk, turning once to observe him, relishing the ashen face that stared back with a hollow expression.

"You," he cried.

Cotton stormed up to him, his gaunt face burning as bright as the candles he used for Mass.

"Me?" he asked, mimicking surprise.

"Do not play with me."

"More threats? Are you going to get the Pope to excommunicate me?" he asked with a chortle.

Cotton's eyes widened. As he rested his hand on his sword, Charles felt on top of the world. His enemy's nostrils flared like a horse that had galloped out of hell, and Charles continued his journey, ready to draw the weapon if needed. He felt Cotton take hold of his arm, pulling him close, the warm breath fouling his nostrils.

"You will wish you had not seen, for I will watch your every move. I will ... I will kill you, Berkeley."

"Now you see what it is like to have the dearest thing to you threatened. You destroyed my position in this regiment, and by God, I will smash you in return, if you dare threaten my family again," Charles growled.

The desperation positively oozed from the man.

Chapter 44

As they sat around the sturdy, plain oak table, most of the members of the Providence Island Company were too distracted to realise that the table had the same qualities as John Pym, secretary of the company, and also leading member of the House of Commons. Pym was taking a withdrawn approach in this meeting, unusual though it was.

The seasoned Earl of Warwick, Lord Holland's naval brother, was being particularly vociferous, for he was the one most involved in the founding of colonies in the America. Apart from their political sympathies, the men were linked in their private and business affairs.

"Damn those Spaniards, Drake should have burned the King of Spain altogether, never mind singeing his beard all those years ago. If I had but one first rate ship, I would sail out and pound their colonies to pieces in return for this."

"Our dream is gone. A settlement where men could exercise religious freedom, too far away from England to be prevented. And now simply rubble," Lord Brooke commiserated.

Pym sat back and listened, as heartbroken as they were he could see this was of lesser significance to the work he was doing in Parliament. The news was months old, but they could not help speaking of it with fresh emotion each time.

"For as shareholders in this company, we could discuss our plans for Parliament amongst company business too. Now we are all out of pocket and to a tidy sum. I have lost most of my savings; the King must be laughing at us," John Hampden said angrily.

Pym coughed, continuing to sit back in his chair. Some of the men turned to him with expectant looks on their faces.

"Gentlemen, we undertook this enterprise of our colony as a place to get away from persecution. Now it is gone, perhaps it is a sign that we need to be bolder. We need to free England from this tyranny, so that we can have that religious freedom here, and not in some small island in a far flung part of the world." he said with his gruff south western vocals.

Most people agreed, all in varying forms with this country man, who had fermented in Somerset, eventually leaving the apple orchards and rolling hills behind, to lead the House of Commons. His great ability and management skills far too metropolitan to be wasted in his quiet region.

"You are right, Mister Pym. We have more important things to do here and Providence Island served its purpose by uniting us to do God's work in reforming England," Warwick thundered, like the cannons on board the ships he commanded. Even Pym was taken aback by the earl's intense response. With a similar barrage he had launched the Bill for Strafford's death to the House of Lords, working alongside Pym in the House of Commons.

"It is a good job we are still Members of Parliament, currently within a sitting session. As long as this is so, we cannot be imprisoned for debt," Hampden said sarcastically.

"Hold thy tongue, John, we do not want anyone to smear our reputations by accusing us of benefiting from that," Warwick chided, marshalling them into line, in the same manner he did with his captains.

Pym noticed Lord Brooke's eyes twinkle, as though he had just cottoned onto the benefit.

"The King is gaining an ascent over us. People sleepwalk into supporting him," another peer proclaimed as he slapped a sheet of paper onto the table.

The gathering focussed on this proclamation, headed with a huge image of the royal coat of arms, the first letter of the King's title 'His Most Excellent Majesty' enlarged. Pym was drawn to the letter 'H' and the backdrop behind it, which portrayed Hercules about to slice the Hydra, more commonly used as a depiction of the triumph over rebellion.

The decoration behind the letter often changed, depending on the meaning of the proclamation, and this stark warning betrayed the King's increasing power and wrath.

"His royal will and pleasure to be that all the members of both Houses of Parliament do repair to the Parliament at Westminster, at or before the twelfth of January next, and give their due and diligent attendance," Brook read aloud.

"And what pray tell happens on the twelfth of January next?" Warwick grunted.

"Yes, yes, it is obvious. He is trying to get all of his supporters back into the chamber for a counter attack, for then he will have the majority," Hampden surmised.

Pym nodded. "We must get the King to launch prematurely, before he is at full strength."

When a knock came at the door, the men stopped talking. Brooke jumped to his feet and stood by the fireplace while Warwick's servant answered it. As the door opened they saw Lord Holland standing there. The relief was evident, for now they had no colony discussion to give them cover to talk about politics, and would be wide open to accusations of treason and conspiracy.

"You are damn late, my lord," Warwick pointed out to his carefree younger brother.

"Chide me another time. Sir Harry Vane and I have been dismissed from our posts at court. The King is done with us," Holland said sadly.

"That is two less informers we have now in the den of thieves," Hampden cursed.

"So how can we force the King to attack us before January?" Warwick asked aloud, as he laid his arm over the back of his chair, returning the group to their original issue.

This seemed to alienate Holland, who sullenly stayed on the outskirts of the gathering, and beside the fire, more interested in getting warm. Pym could not help but smile when he saw how Holland solemnly stroked his lace cuffs into place. The man looked positively distraught.

"The Grand Remonstrance was supposed to goad him to attack us, but so far he has simply ignored it," Hampden said with exacerbation.

"He is to create new Bishops too," Holland casually remarked, not even lifting his head.

"We do not care about Bishops, Henry," Warwick snapped back in response.

"They get seats in the House of Lords and more Bishops means more votes for him," Pym warned, raising his gaze to the roof, feeling that the King was leaving him behind in the tactics race.

"He will soon secure both houses. We need to get the voting rights of these Bishops removed once and for all, especially because they are remnants of Catholicism," Hampden told them all, though the long standing issue had been attempted several times, and met with fierce resistance from the people.

"Now hang fire, Mister Hampden. They sit in our house and the House of Lords will not thank you for interfering with our makeup," Holland replied, finally facing them all.

"This is just what the King wants, both houses to fall out amongst themselves," Brooke said as he tried to restore calm.

"And there have been petitions sailing in from all over the kingdom in support of these wretched clerics," Hampden conceded reluctantly, clamping his hand across his mouth, and under his hook nose. His oval face and fine features were incensed, and with his hand, he stopped further comment, descending into thought.

"The King has made a few mistakes so far we can capitalise on. Up to now, he has not declared the Irish rebels as traitors. Yet when the Scottish rose up, he denounced them immediately. To even the most ignorant of men, this could suggest that he is in league with them. Maybe people should be aware of this possibility," Pym suggested, as he was cut off by a renewed Hampden.

"He is so short sighted. He forgets the most basic of things, which let him down in the end."

"Be wary of him," Holland warned, "I have seen his newfound backlash personally, and when he is angered, he will be swift."

"And me too, my lord, for I was imprisoned for daring to stand up to him and refusing to pay his illegal taxes," Hampden countered, leaving Holland's prominent jaw tensing.

Warwick nodded, before cursing. Pym felt unnerved that such a stalwart as this man should feel so negative. It was hard to believe Warwick was born in a former priory, for the man was far from peaceful, yet he was devout in his plain, Puritan beliefs. Holland, meanwhile, was still licking his wounded pride and Brooke got up to leave; Pym hoped that the whole reform would not melt away so easily at the crux of the struggle.

"I must be away, I have much to attend to," Brooke explained as he bowed to them.

Warwick swivelled his chair round to face Holland, while Pym pushed himself up and took his pewter goblet of wine. The talking, and although he would never admit it, the anxiety, had made his mouth dry. He observed his maid tightening the press in the kitchen, squeezing his wet linen shirt into place, ready for his next appearance in Parliament. She left it jammed inside to flatten it and began to scrub the stone floor. Hampden joined him, as though introducing a hierarchy into the room, as it was in life. The peers by the fire and the commoners by the kitchen.

"My wife wants to change her hair colour."

He smiled at Hampden's breaking news, after such setbacks that they had just experienced, lifting his head and letting out a short burst of laughter.

"It is good to see you do not forget your family in all this mess," Pym said, "I know not why women want to mess around with their hair anyway," Pym admitted as he stroked his grey, wiry locks into place.

"She has instructed me to purchase lime ceruse and powder of gold. Apparently this will change her red hair."

"It will be a transformation - it will drop out." Pym laughed.

He took the wooden mirror from the wall and held his plump hands round the ornate carved frame. He rubbed a thumb over the cherubs and the sculptured fish and lobsters.

"You are not normally so admiring of intricate objects," Hampden stated.

"It is a present," he excused himself furtively, eyes narrowing further, as he used the mirror to check his moustache.

"From Lucy?"

"Really, John, it is the Countess of Carlisle. You must use her full title when men like those are present," Pym whispered in jest, pointing to the two noble brothers.

"Going back to our great work, you must meet my first cousin, Oliver Cromwell. He is most supportive of what we do and I'll wager he will turn into as great a statesman as you," Hampden told him.

Pym shook his head at the praise, though inside a flutter

of pride filled him as he thought about his crusading part in history. With comments turning personal, he led Hampden to the door. They bowed their heads to the peers as they strolled out into the grounds. The gardener was pushing a stone roller over the grass to flatten it and they avoided him, searching for somewhere more private. The two men walked down the gravel path and past some small rectangular lawns. Flowers had not yet been planted at their boundaries, but hedges hemmed each lawn in, shaping the whole thing into a diamond.

"Well, when the Grim Reaper takes his own weapon up, who knows which men he will have next," Pym muttered, pointing to a scythe, that lay discarded.

"Do you know what someone was telling me the other day? They said that the King had received several presents from the pope himself in years gone by, paintings and marbles," Hampden announced.

Pym did not bother to look up. "He has been bought by them. They try to convert him I am sure."

"They say he is the only Protestant Prince that Bernini the sculptor has created a bust of," Hampden continued unabated.

"Keep your voice down for now," Pym warned.

Hampden was adamant and his strong character refused to put his concerns aside.

"You said in there that he has not condemned the Irish rebels. I will point this out to Parliament in the next sitting, for I have no qualms about revealing the truth, whether he is our King, or not."

"We both know he can be persuasive and tactical, but sooner or later he will need guidance. The only advisors he has left are fools. Suffice to say, mind you, we still should not underestimate him, and you are right, he is still our King," Pym warned.

Chapter 45

K ing Charles the First stood looking out of the Gothic, arched window, in a long chamber that was once the living quarters of the monarchs of England, when they lived within the Palace of Westminster. A page adjusted the flowing waves of blue cloak, folding it back to reveal an expanse of ermine lining.

"This will blast Pym's goals apart, shifting focus from his attacks on Your Majesty's right of appointing ministers of the crown, and of controlling the armed forces. Let them all see that you are the one trying to send aid to your subjects in Ireland, while Parliament greedily continues to claw at your lawful power," Digby gloated, with eyes as wide as a frog's.

The King absorbed the confidence exuding from the peer and nodded his agreement as he admired the blue, red and greens of the murals, which portrayed virtuous figures treading vices under their feet. He had come to like Digby, who was always quite charming, with the right word to say at all times, and had conveniently forgotten that the father had been a thorn in his side during his early years on the throne. With Digby, he always felt as though he was doing well, and he admired the peer's self belief, which had the strange effect of shoring up his own.

Colonel Hadleigh and Lieutenant Colonel Berkeley of his guard entered the hall from the opposite end, the colonel bowing and announcing that Viscount Falkland, and an Edward Hyde were outside. Into the empty expanse of this abandoned, but still lovely place came a plump lawyer with a delicate and graceful member of the nobility, but both were Members of the House of Commons.

"Lord Falkland and Mister Hyde," the King said in greeting, casually resting an arm on his sword, hand dangling over the end. He nodded to the officers of his guard, who promptly secured the portals once more, ensuring complete privacy for this conference.

"Your Majesty."

Both men paused before turning to the papers on the table.

The monarch moved slowly, his robe gently swaying to reveal a golden sword hilt and belt lying across the royal waist.

"Be seated," the monarch commanded as he manoeuvred elegantly towards them with the help of a pageboy.

The King felt his chair being pushed in by another servant as he sat down, bolt upright, at the head of the table, cloak stretching away to where he had once stood. Now with an anointed sovereign here once more, the painted chamber seemed to come alive again, and it was easy to imagine the old fireplace with a blaze warming every inch, right up to the wooden roof that was interspersed with shields and coats of arms. Indeed, as Hyde bowed, the blood rushed to his face; either it was nerves, or his unsteady balance that fired his cheeks. King Charles understood he had not been in his presence many times before, so excused the silence that now descended.

"Lord Falkland, my Lord Digby tells me about this statement Mister Hyde has drawn up in an unofficial capacity. He insists it reads very well and would be such a good response to Parliament's impertinent Grand Remonstrance, which up until now, I have ignored. Silence has taken the wind out of their blustering document."

The King observed Falkland, instinctively struck by a sense of the man's honesty - the noble had volunteered to fight in the King's army against the Scots in the Bishops War, yet recently he had voted for Strafford's death and for the changes Parliament pursued. But now, this moderate and deep man had morally felt that the right balance had been achieved. He was not with his sovereign again for titles or favour, but for a sense of righteousness, which King Charles recognised, and that flattered his cause. The slight frame and delicate face, together with his timid tone made the monarch feel comfortable. Pure, uncut wisdom and talent practically cried out for a royal patron who could polish and mould some glittering career for him. Hyde was the less well connected man who had also left Pym's ranks.

"I shall summarise it, sir, if you wish?" Falkland suggested, subtly bringing the royal mind back to the matter at hand.

"Do we need to reply?" the King asked, with little mood for appeasing gestures, still less to acknowledge the disgraceful details within the Remonstrance.

"I feel that I would not be serving you if I did not reveal my true thoughts, sir. I believe a reply does not have to give countenance to the paper, moreover your words can equally acknowledge the document, and discredit it at the same time. If you care to give me leave, I shall explain?" Hyde said with a nervous deference and respect.

The sovereign consented, interested to hear Hyde's words.

Even in this short time, his legal mind and intelligence was clear. Falkland arranged the papers, in the same manner as if he were exploring a hand of cards. King Charles nodded at Digby, who was beaming with delight upon the scene, obviously anticipating the information, as though his discovery of the pair's work would solve every problem the King faced.

"Firstly, sir, we summarise the action you have taken to try and resolve Parliament's grievances and list your compromising, and acts of generous favour. We also go on to outline a policy for the future, so that all moderate men can see that there can be no benefits to persisting with the current Parliamentary demands. We hope you do not mind that we have taken the liberty of reinforcing your loyalty to the Church of England."

At that point, clapping was heard in the distance, echoing from the House of Lords, only a few rooms away.

"Read some of it, Mister Hyde," the King commanded, dubious about the wording, and notoriously reluctant to give trust.

Hyde held the paper close. "Should you agree to use my humble words, Your Majesty, it says that in your view, the Church of England is the most pure and agreeable to the Sacred Word of God, of any religion now practised in the Christian World. It also says that you would be willing to defend that view with your own blood and that you wish only for a peaceful settlement with Parliament, so that you may reign as a great and glorious King over a free and happy people."

The monarch felt emboldened by the words and he related to them instantly. Such astute men as these were a glorious jewel in his crown, and if he could attract this calibre, Parliament would quickly fall behind.

"Perfect, gentlemen, this sounds like a very good manuscript that will remind men just how much I have laboured for an agreement. I have my coronation oath to the Almighty to uphold our laws, and I am the only one left to stand against these desperate men, who wish to pull the same edicts down," he reminded them.

"I knew it would be an asset to your cause, sir," Digby announced, after he had made sure the King approved of the draft.

King Charles stroked his small, exquisitely trimmed beard, deep in thought. "Is it firm enough? I wish to pacify, but also to rigorously defend myself, my ministers and servants. I have seen no benefit to simple appeasement with these people, and especially the rabble that yell and protest."

Hyde was cast into action, thriving on the management of the declaration.

"Sir, what if it were to say you feel that none of your servants adhere to a wicked or malignant party and then go on to declare your support for the bishops retaining their right to vote in the House of Lords?"

The King felt it was appropriate and acquiesced. He sensed he was personally in control and at last was retaliating against the small group of rebels, who had seized the reigns of Parliament for their own ends.

Digby jumped in to stop the show disappearing without him. "It needs to assert that it is the undoubted right of the Crown of England to call people to the service of the monarch and the public, as the King alone sees fit."

"This is all good. Please be kind enough to finalise it and publish it as my official response," was the royal order.

Hyde and Falkland tenderly gathered their writings up, betraying pride in their work, and then left the room. Colonel Hadleigh entered once more.

"Your Majesty, Sir Edward Nicholas and Sir John Culpepper are outside."

King Charles replied by nodding and moving his hand. As the two men entered, the King gestured for them to sit down.

"Your Majesty, are you ready to address their Lordships?" Nicholas queried.

The monarch felt a tugging at his nerves. He was outraged at the recent discussion in Parliament about his control over the armed forces, and deciding time, and the city, were on his side, he had come to chide and warn them off, whilst seizing attention with a call to hasten a relieving army to ravished Ireland. The timing of his counter attacks were vital, just like when he would race roughshod over field and hedge to stalk a stag. The King had grown up with hunting, for its exertions strengthened his young, vulnerable physique; increased his stamina, fortified his nerve, muscles and co-ordination. The passion had definitely been inherited from his father though, for his mother had once shot one of the old King's favourite hounds in her attempts at the sport.

The King hooked his thumb around the blue ribbon of the Order of the Garter, which hung around his neck, regaining his concentration. A mounted Saint George adorned the end of it and his mind moved to this, the greatest mark of distinction in the land. Just over six months ago he had consented to Lord Strafford's execution, and all thought of honour was still tainted by what he saw as a personal betrayal of a loyal minister. His own conscience would never allow him to forgive himself and as if wishing to honour his minister's memory, he addressed the men around him.

"I wonder how the young Earl of Strafford does?" he asked, in a moment of deep thought, casting his coming speech aside for one moment.

"The poor boy accepted his father's title with pride, sir. It was a gracious and brave act to bestow it on his son, especially in such a heated atmosphere," Digby told the King.

"It may have stirred up the passions of Parliament to see you do it though, sir, just after they had pulled the father down," Culpepper told him bluntly.

"I will go head to head with any who disagree with it, for his father was innocent. I shall see the Members of Parliament in the House of Lords now," the King announced, sending his black clad usher to the House of Commons to escort them to his presence.

Efficient Nicholas waited patiently, filling his time by

arranging the speech papers, living and breathing service to the crown. His large eyes flicked around as he ensured everything was prepared, grey hair with tiny wisps of brown fluffed up at the sides, but thin on top. Nicholas gave a bow of his head to delicately remind the monarch he was due to leave now, the plain features and friendly eyes were warm and almost fatherly, for his looks and behaviour seemed so much older than his actual age.

"Let us remind them of their duty then," the King said as he stood, two pageboys fluttering around him like butterflies, as they assisted with his appearance. The velvet swirls of his apparel were stroked into place, while one lad took hold of the train of the cloak to ease its passage.

The sovereign looked straight ahead and took a breath.

Nicholas handed him his notes from behind, and he stepped through into a narrow hall that travelled down the side of the Lords chamber, allowing him to enter the place at the other end, near the throne. His presence was heralded by a fanfare of trumpets. Saluting the peers he was most friendly with, and haughtily eyeing the ones that were hostile, he mounted the red carpeted dais, ascending above everyone else.

The King sat down and held his head high, placing his own arms on the chair arms and resting his fingers on the wooden engraving at the end of each one; lions' heads that practically roared with the resentment the King now felt. He sat still, full of grace and majesty, watching the members of both houses. It was times like this that he truly felt the hand of God on his shoulder, reminding him of his obligation to rule this part of the world on the Lord's behalf, answerable to him alone.

* * *

"I demand to address the King on his return," a man stubbornly demanded, which secured Charles's attention, being the most senior officer in the corridor. His senses were already so finely tuned from the tense duty.

"That will not be possible. Who are you, sir?" Charles questioned, facing the man full on and blocking his progress.

"I am not budging," the man announced firmly; his eyebrows had risen, just like Charles's temper at this comment.

As Charles stepped closer, ready to move him on, the man began to turn, as though ready to leave, though this subjugation did not last long. He soon stopped still again, and Charles took his arm, ordering Major Fanshaw to take over, while he escorted the man out of the area.

"You will regret your high handedness, sir," the man warned.

Charles ignored him, leaving his capable men behind to guard the King's route, sure he could deal with this man alone.

Once the two men had reached the end of the corridor, the argumentative bearing left the fellow and he looked back.

"Sir Charles," he whispered.

Charles flicked a stare to the man, examining his features and relatively short hair that was brushed back. He did not recognise him. The large eyes glared back, ornately curled moustache moving as he spoke again.

"Lord Holland has mentioned your interest in the sea. His brother, the Earl of Warwick could secure you a post as captain of a good rate of warship."

Charles could not help himself express short, initial amusement at the surprise comment, before glancing around to check they were out of all earshot.

"If you were to send onto me any details of orders that the King's Guard receives, then Parliament would be most grateful, and as such, Warwick could arrange everything."

Charles stepped back, flabbergasted at the offer, realising it was serious. He was beginning to see the full face of politics and was actually quite proud that some Parliamentarians had felt the need to make approaches to him.

"No, it is a kind gesture, but I hold the King's commission. Besides, I am loyal, and not to be bought like that," he said, with a polite wave of his hand, lost for further words.

Charles turned away, anxious to see the King again, for his order was to follow him and guard the door he had just gone through, into the House of Lords.

"Take this then, sir, and should you change your mind, there will be forty pounds for each order that you convey. You will find me in Westminster Hall most mornings. Do not spurn such an offer, for Parliament will soon appoint all army officers," the man persisted, thrusting a small bag into Charles's hand, before heading away without further ado.

He glared down and unfastened the bag, pouring the contents onto his hand. Several golden unite coins - worth twenty shillings each - fell out and the beauty dazzled him, though beneath this appearance it felt like they had burned into his palm.

The visages of the present King, and that of his father on an older coin, seemed to eye him warily, uneasy with the manner they had been passed over. He looked up, but the fellow was long gone and he hastily put the coins away again. Charles went slowly back to Major Fanshaw, though too amazed and aware of the sensitivity of the explosive offer, to report it.

The grand chamber he could see into was packed out, with crimson lines of robed peers, highlighting the varying dress of the House of Common's men, standing out like sore thumbs in comparison.

"My Lords, and Gentlemen," he heard the King announce, beginning his speech. Charles turned to watch the royal through the doorway, drawn by his words, and keeping the green, leather bag tight in his hand.

"The l-last time I was in this place, and the l-last thing that I recommended unto you, was the b-business of Ireland, whereby I was in good hope that I should not have needed again to have put you in mind of that business. But still seeing your slow p-proceedings, and the d-daily dispatches that I have out of Ireland of the lamentable state of my Protestant subjects there, I cannot but again earnestly recommend the dispatch of an expedition for their relief."

The monarch stopped, eyes seemingly assessing the reactions and scouring the chamber, though Charles had heard and observed him enough to realise that this was simply a break to gather his thoughts and words to master that stutter.

"I might now take up some of your time in expressing my detestation of rebellions in general, and of this in particular. I do here in a word offer you whatsoever my power, pains, or industry can contribute to r-reducing the Irish nation to their true and wonted obedience."

Some supportive men clapped politely and a great murmur of agreement dully echoed out, though Pym and his party stood mesmerised by this seizure of the political agenda, and especially on such a pivotal issue that affected so many people of both nations.

"And further, seeing there is a dispute raised concerning the bounds of my ancient and undoubted prerogative to appoint the officers of such a relieving army, I propose we avoid further d-debate on the argument at this time. I offer that the Bill for raising of men may pass, with a salvo jure both for King and people, leaving the question of officer appointments to a time that may better bear it. If this be not accepted, the fault of further delay to Ireland is not m-mine, but those that refuse so fair an offer."

With that, he stood up while a few bowed, some more reverently than others. He stepped slowly down the dais and glided majestically out of the door.

The King's speech became starkly personal, as Charles remembered the phrasing of the subtle warning from that earlier stranger, hinting that his future as an officer lay with Parliament.

Now the King was coming out fighting, defending his powers, and setting the time for a coming battle with Parliament over the matter, once Ireland had been tackled. In such a drawing up of arguments, Charles felt like a column of reinforcements, and this final decision of King or Parliament, really did mean the success or failure of him and his family. Should he take an offer of Parliament's as a captain, or retain his place with the King?

Loyalty overrode such a question. The monarch was always going to be King, no matter what, whereas Parliament would come and go, with different leaders eventually. It was clear that his current post within the guards would be safe in the long term, despite any rocky moments from Parliament's barrage.

He would weather the storm with the King.

Now Hadleigh was approaching, with a furrow in his brow, giving the impression he was looking right at Charles's fist that clutched the coins. The realisation came that he had accepted a bribe. After a few seconds of worry, he walked towards Major Fanshaw. He was adamant that his position would not be jeopardised.

"Be wary, major. I am suspicious of any Parliament man after that fellow demanded access to the King. Follow His Majesty and do not admit anyone anywhere near him. I must speak to Colonel Hadleigh."

As Fanshaw nodded and strode away, Hadleigh approached.

Charles saluted and Hadleigh betrayed the cause of his agitated expression.

"Sir Charles, I heard one of the men say some madman attempted to break through to the King?"

"Yes, sir, but I escorted him out," Charles said, irritated that some common soldier had chattered about the matter before he had managed to convey it to his superior.

"Why did you not get me?"

"With respect, sir, I do not think I need to bother my

colonel to remove some idiot."

Hadleigh grunted an agreement, before smiling. "Aye, I see your point. We cannot afford any problems when we are in the heart of a building full of so many traitors."

"I can well understand it. In fact, let me say I have experienced their double dealing first hand," Charles said as he moved closer and held his hand out.

Hadleigh watched as he opened it and poured the money back out of the pouch.

"These coins were given to me as a bribe. I felt it best to make you aware right away, for they were wanting details of our orders."

"What? Very good, Sir Charles, I am pleased you sent the fool packing. I will take half for the regiment, and you keep the rest, but take my advice and burn that purse. Now, keep your eyes open and tell me if you see this man again."

"I could dupe him, and give over some fake orders. What do you think, perhaps we could discover why they want to know about our orders?" Charles suggested.

"I am not so sure. Let us discuss this further on parade," Hadleigh responded cautiously, as they walked together.

Chapter 46

W ith bookshelves covering the small shop, a smell of both freshly printed volumes, and old works mixed in the intimate room. John Pym faced his full frame towards an alluring and smart lady. Unlike Saint Thomas, whose day it was today, this female always had confidence in her future. For her part, she stood side on to him, eyes scanning an open book, but every now and then, flitting back to him as he spoke. The occasional glances were the only indication that she even knew he was there. The difference from being sought after in Parliament almost every day, to his own pursuing of this lady, caused a rush of excitement through the fifty seven year old. Maybe it was because she was a beautiful, wealthy widow of forty two that did it, courted and written of in poems.

But then the shopkeeper left his premises at the haughty command of the lady who did not need verse to be aware of her celebrated features or her powerful position. She suddenly dropped a bombshell.

"You are to be arrested, Master Pym, with several colleagues. The plans are being laid now."

Pym watched her flick the page over casually, his heart sinking at her apparent lack of concern. His secondary thought was about the tactics behind his coming incarceration, which he had foreseen for some time. Strangely, he regarded the news as positive, for he had been goading the King to act for a long time, anxious that the monarch's wrath should be loosed prematurely.

"You speak of it with such a carefree nature, my lady?"

She looked at him, amused, for that delicate mouth was always a shade away from a smile, whether the situation was grave, or not. The round face, high eyebrows, framed as they were with an abundance of dark ringlets, could deliver any message to him, no matter how bad. Pym smiled too, releasing himself for a moment from his serious minded politics.

"I know that it will take more than his order to seize you. They call you King Pym, and that tag does not get applied for nothing. I know you too well," she said, before returning to browsing her book.

"I am glad you summoned me here. It is always a pleasure to cast my eyes upon you."

She was still smiling down at those damned pages.

"What is it that attracts such attention, for it makes me jealous?"

She looked and slammed the book shut, holding it up.

"Love Lies a-Bleeding. It is so humorous, and so apt."

"Ah, the play about Philaster, the rightful King of Sicily, until it was conquered," Pym remembered.

She nodded, moving nearer to him, the very action he saw as a compliment. "So you know it? The new, interloping King cannot kill the troublesome, Philaster because the people still support him with their hearts," she added, allowing her hand to come to rest near his, fingers slowly touching and sending a spark through his body, such that he had not felt for years.

"Forgive me, my lady, but there are several gentlemen

looking for Mister Pym here," the bookseller said, bowing his head low as he poked it into his own establishment. She snatched her hand away and Pym wondered if the man meant that the visitors were guards.

"Adieu, Philaster, until our next meeting," the lady said quietly as she passed him, causing him to smile at the comparison between himself and the book's hero.

Pym watched the lady depart, attendants ready to flank her as she exited, and he saw some familiar faces of his Parliamentary colleagues. Now that the identities of those searching for him were no longer mysterious and threatening, he shook off all thoughts but the great matter of Parliament. The owner stepped inside, staring at him with worshipful, wide eyes and instead of leaving, he stopped, picked up the book about Philaster and handed the man five shillings.

Armed with the publication in his firm grip, he met the two men, descending the staircase in silence, until they came out onto the quadrangle arcade of shops. The four cloister-like passageways led out onto the open square in the centre, which was teeming with merchants conducting business. It was the centre of London's commercial life, straddling the junction of Cornhill and Threadneedle Street, ever since Queen Elizabeth the First opened it in fifteen seventy three.

The huge Corinthian column pinpointed the place, mounted with a giant copper, gilt grasshopper, the symbol of Sir Thomas Gresham who founded the place.

"What did the Countess of Carlisle want, John?" gruff William Strode asked, with a bluntness that was sharpened by a past eleven year imprisonment by the King's orders. During that long period, he had refused freedom, because it carried a clause for his good behaviour, eventually released to appease Pym and his rising tide of reform.

Before Pym could reply, Hampden was pointing out the odd looking fashions of the foreigners who provided a melting

449

pot of nationalities within this trading haven. A Russian of giant proportions, like a bear in his black fur hat and robes, was particularly interesting, or more so than talk of Strafford's former mistress.

Pym covered the book title discreetly, knowing of Hampden's dislike of his lady friend. "She warns me that the Tower is to be making some of us welcome soon."

"Well if she is to be believed, then we three are sure to be on the list, Will and I have already been accommodated at His Majesty's pleasure in the past. My cousin, Oliver Cromwell, always said we needed control of the militia to prevent such a coup," John Hampden lectured.

"This final attack has been too long in coming," Pym said simply, as the group moved aside for some ladies and their maids.

"He is full of himself lately, is he not? First he removes Lord Newport from his post as Constable of the Tower, putting a loyal lapdog in his place. Well, he has shot his bolt too far this time," Strode said, trying to restrain his grim satisfaction.

"Ah, but it all links back to one thing. Newport spoke of arresting the Queen, in his little tête-à-tête with Lord Holland. If you want a reaction from the King, then throw anything at his wife, and he loses all reason. A good way to do this, is to have William Jephson accuse her in Parliament, of causing the Irish revolt," Pym tellingly advised.

The bell in the tower that crowned one side of the quadrangle rang out, signalling noon. By the time it would ring again, at six of the clock this evening, Pym hoped to have another rendezvous with Lady Carlisle planned.

"Ah, I see, get him to react in his old arbitrary way now, before his loyal Members of Parliament obey his summons to return next month, to give him a majority over us," Hampden caught on.

As they passed milliners, apothecaries and armourers shops,

Pym issued them with a warning - they must play ignorant of his plans, and escape the royal clutches at the very last moment, leaving the King looking like the tyrant he was. If this failed, royal power would be unrestrained once more. Even if Pym were to survive the Tyburn gallows in that event, Lucy Carlisle could never have any affection for someone without power. He sighed with frustration at thinking of her again.

*   *   *

Opening his eyes, Charles shivered with the chill, having not slept well. It was the coldest winter he had experienced for several years; hopefully the Thames might freeze over so they could skate on it, although that had not happened for a long time. A few minutes after he had closed his eyes again, he heard little Henry crying in the other room. He groaned, rubbing his face. If only they had employed a wet-nurse to look after him, like everyone else, they would be able to leave this to her. But Anne had refused and wished to go against the norm of their social group.

She stirred instinctively, and he reassured her that he would go. She had been under the weather lately, as Henry was having a lot of restless nights. Pulling his cloak on top of his long, white nightgown, he quickly ran through the hall to the baby, before the cries completely woke her. He reached down, scooping him into his arms, but keeping some of the blankets around the baby, should the cruel air affect him.

"Shhh, you shall wake your poor mother," he said as he gently rocked Henry, kissing his forehead.

This was one of the few times he had got up to soothe Henry himself and they had been occasions that left their mark on his heart and gave him such tender feelings that he had never experienced in his twenty seven years. It was only recently that he had felt fully confident in holding the delicate bundle, knowing how to manoeuvre the baby to keep him safely snug, in spite of any wriggling. Until now, Charles had only scratched the surface of life, and this realisation had dawned with the birth of his child.

"It is Christmas Eve - you can help me put up the branches later," he whispered.

The child's arms writhed around as he tried to cover them, foiled in his every attempt and the baby even managed to reach out to Charles's nightcap, coming close to the pretty colours of the trees and flowers that adorned it. As Henry was rocked and comforted, he calmed, eventually resting his little body, much to Charles's relief. He watched his son's dark eyes looking back, examining the world he was growing up in. When Henry smiled at him, that sense that he would do absolutely anything to protect his child rushed over him. The feeling was of a strong bond and Charles's eyes welled up, hoping that his mother could see them now. Contentment ran through his veins and the early hour made no difference. He kissed the child again and sat with him for what seemed like hours, trying to fight off sleep until Henry had dozed off. What a contest it was too and he found it humorous as he hummed the military tunes he had long been used to. He wondered whether all children were so averse to sleep, or if his son had simply been granted some of the family stubbornness.

Not long after, he heard noises and he looked out of the window. The clattering and dull thuds got louder, until he saw people marching solemnly along the street. Next some horses clip clopped along and he counted six, all with black dressage, pulling a small carriage, holding a coffin. Plumes of dark feathers decorated each corner of the vehicle, waving farewell in the night breeze to the body below, and he bowed his head in respect for the deceased. As it left, another coach came into view, with more male mourners and some children.

"Ah, Thomas Abbot's funeral, who donated to the orphanage," Charles recalled aloud.

He stood for an age observing coaches pass by and a string of around fifty people following it all up on foot, emerging out of the night as if it was all a ghostly vision, before he felt tired again. The cortege had finally gone past and he wondered about the cost of the fashionable nocturnal funeral. He had paid eighteen shillings for his daughter's burial in the church aisle, though money was no object when loved ones were concerned, he thought.

He took the family bible and turned the huge pages, past the image of the apostles gathered around with their books, crosses and writings. Inside he saw marks of his grandfather's highlighting passages and this gave some indication of the sermons he had read to the family. It amazed him to be able to ponder the same parts as he flicked through the pages of the heirloom, searching for a suitable reading to give to the family and servants over Christmas. He took pleasure in deciding what to preach to them, recognising the important part he had to play in their spiritual lives.

Yawning after making his choice, he went to the kitchen and took a drink of beer. Walking somewhat sleepily back to his chair, he continued with his reading before drifting into a deep slumber. The next thing he could hear was the distant sound of voices, laughing and chattering. He felt his body awakening, albeit rather reluctantly and was startled as his nose was fondled.

Opening his eyes, he saw it was Henry and Anne and he yawned and stretched.

"What time is it?"

"Eight of the clock," she answered, her rosy, fresh cheeks beaming a radiance of happiness.

He groaned at the answer, but took delight in her features. "You slept well?"

"I did, but I see our son did not though," she commented.

"Aye, he woke, but soon went back. I never thought I

would see the day that I should comfort my own child at night to get him back to sleep."

Then unable to resist her any longer, he jumped to his feet and kissed her, relishing the soft connection with her lips.

Following several more short bursts of kisses, he smiled down at his son. "Hello, young man. Your father is going to decorate our house shortly."

It prompted a giggle and flurry of movement from the baby, until he stroked his tender, little cheek. Seeing his large, rough hand next to this delicate nose added to his sense of protection over his little boy, though he had far from forgotten the sister the child would never know. Those inquisitive, large eyes were from Charles's father, while the nose and delicate chin and mouth were Anne's. And when he smiled again, Charles was reminded of himself. He winked at Anne and went upstairs to the bedroom to get dressed. With a cloth he rubbed his body down, the perfumed water cleansing his skin and leaving the sweet smell behind. The scent of roses made him think of Anne, for she would drip it on the bedclothes at times and loved nothing more than pink ones in the house. Tapping his foot to the tune of the drums he marched to, he put on a white linen shirt, with black breeches, stockings, shoes and doublet, before going back down with a box of holly and foliage that he had purchased yesterday.

Everyone was in the kitchen, helping the cook maid to make the cake for Twelfth Night, the main day of the Christmas celebrations in thirteen days time. Anne became involved in the cooking, guiding and giving orders for how she wanted the cake to be made, while Louise brought the baby out to the main room. Charles took and fixed evergreen branches around the chamber. A cluster of them were interspersed along the beams of the roof and he laid some on the mantle of the fireplace, creating a natural feel, which he loved so much, to this city dwelling. During the arrangement, he would pause and run up to Henry, playing peek-a-boo with the branches and making strange noises, causing the baby reach out playfully.

"You can get the food and wine sorted I hope, Lou?" he queried, as he hung a thick array above the portrait of him and Anne. The green was a welcome colourful splash on the dark oak interior.

"Yes, sir, the wine will be ordered exactly as you wished."

"Excellent," he summed up, and walked to the kitchen to see his wife.

"And we can play Blind Man's Buff when we have to take these back down on Twelfth Night. Your mother can sing," he told Henry aloud, so that Anne could hear.

She laughed at him, because he seemed to forget just how young Henry was at times.

"Louise says everything is getting ready," he interfered.

"Yes, Charles, it is just the guest list which needs confirming now," she said ominously.

He sighed deeply. "Aye, I know you mean James."

Until now, he had forgotten about the raw feelings over his former friend. Now it all came flooding back, with more guilt than anything else. He thought about what had happened and wondered just how he was since the riots last month. He cringed, closing his eyes tight.

"Charles, you should invite them still, you have not spoken properly to him in months," she said, almost chiding him.

"I know, I know, but we cannot invite them until this trouble is done with, we both understood our positions when we last saw each other," he explained, eating some of the cake mix.

"You men. Honestly, can't just be mature, and you are the ones in government. No wonder it is in turmoil; maybe we should try female ministers and bishops."

Charles burst out laughing, unable to stop for a good few minutes, and she ignored him.

"That will never happen; I mean can you imagine giving such important posts to a woman? Anyway it is not immaturity that is James's problem, it is just we are on opposite sides and being seen together may jeopardise us both."

He walked to the window again to peer through. It was quiet outside and picturing a female Secretary of State, he let out a chortle. He tried to imagine how she would handle ambitious men like Digby, and thought that judging by his wife's spending, the country would be bankrupt within a year.

"Can you imagine a female bishop? The whole teaching of the church means this is impossible. How could she wear a mitre on top of her curls anyway?" He guffawed, as a smile eventually cross Anne's face.

He returned to his festive duties, taking the Holy Bough and hanging it on the ancient, rusty hook that had served the purpose probably since the house was built. He twisted the red ribbon into place, admiring the spherical object and the evergreens and holly that made it, with the tiny model of the baby Jesus in the middle.

As Anne came in, eager to see it, he asked, "I wonder who will be first through our door this Christmas to be embraced by us, under our bough."

"Aye, it is such a warm, loving time of year. I do not know why we cannot embrace all of our visitors throughout the year?"

"Because I do not fancy being so personal with the tax collectors, Sir Richard, or your stepmother. I'd much rather we keep it for the holy festivities, when we invite only close friends here."

He groaned. It was a sin to mention that dreadful woman who he had only just got rid of back to Oxford.

Then he began thinking of the country at the minute; things were coming to a crossroads now that the King had adapted a similarly determined path to Parliament. But this certainly looked like it had resolved the matter, for the mobs had gone away for Christmas - the King had kept the upper hand now for the last two months or so, leaving a happy balance of power between the two institutions and stopping Parliament's encroaches for more.

He was feeling so healthy today; it was good to experience silence and relax at home. There was only the maids' wages to sort, so he took a purse from the drawer, emptying the contents onto the desk. The coins fell out and he examined them before collecting up the amounts due. He observed that the edges of most of the gold coins had been filed ruthlessly, so that they were nowhere near the size they should be, disgusted at the remains of one of them in particular. The silver ones were only a little better. Then there were the irritating, tiny little farthings.

Louise received the largest salary because of her more trusted and close ties. She also did more than the others, living in with them. Arabella got two pounds per year and both their clothes were made and paid for, on top of the salary. A short while later Henry was in good voice again. He left the coins and went to the other room and waved in distraction as Louise changed him.

"Oh, my son, there is no need to be upset. Just look at that gorgeous cake your mother is baking for us," Charles joked.

"I am so glad that events outside seem to have improved. It is three months until sixteen forty two, and I do sense that the King and his Parliament will enter the New Year hand in hand, I am sure of it," Anne said with a prediction of relief.

"Well, I don't quite think it will be hand in hand …"

"It is a phrase, Charles. They seem to have accepted one another though, and our son can be brought up in a safe environment, that is the main thing."

Charles hesitated about whether to voice his true feelings; he was hopeful that both sides would simmer down after meeting each other at the pinnacle of their propaganda race, but he was sure it was nowhere near as simple as Anne's vision. She tilted her head, reading his thoughts and impatiently waiting for his inevitable comment.

"Aye, you may be right, darling," he concurred, releasing a long sigh as he forced a smile.

He took his picture of her, which he was working on for their anniversary, breaking the uneasy silence and sharing his progress with her. Using a small piece of charcoal, he finished sketching the shoulders and upper body, smoothing the intense lines out with his little finger. The resulting smudging gave instant tone and structure to the form and he became immersed in the work, easing the stresses of the year so far. The curls and waves of her hair were a joy to work on and he was pleased with the lifelike imagery of her flowing locks, which he thought complemented her so very much. Indeed, they transformed her appearance when she cultivated them with the glue and hot tongs, making her irresistible in every sense. Next he drew the outline of her dress, hugging her curvaceous figure, before choosing which colours he needed. Ultramarine, the most expensive colour, would have to come from a colour man though and he had chosen this to show how much she meant to him.

The image drew on his love well enough to pause his art while he kissed her longingly, relishing the physical reality of this beauty.

Then he looked at the ivory paintbrush with the squirrel hair, still in good condition, his French grandfather's on his mother's side, or so he was told. As he ran the smooth bristles over his hand, he wished that he could have painted the man whose skills he had inherited, or his late mother, for all he had to remember them by was his memory.

How did it feel to flee to England, leaving your country to escape persecution from fellow countrymen, he wondered, knowing his grandfather's ultra Protestantism in that Catholic hub. Then he breathed deeply, savouring the quiet, relishing the time to think and remember such things - maybe Anne was right, England would enjoy the peace of the Lord once more with the season of goodwill ushering it in.

"God forbid that the House of Commons should proceed in any way to dishearten people to obtain their just desires in such a way."

Pym replying to the House of Lords, who had called
for a joint declaration condemning the mobs and
rioting in London
DECEMBER 1641

Chapter 47

On the twenty eighth of December, Charles stood outside Parliament at the head of the company of the Royal Guards. Colonel Hadleigh had received orders to be wary of increasing civil unrest. The King's offensive was still in full swing and they had been ordered to 'guard' Parliament by royal decree, to stop the mobs influencing the democratic process.

"Lieutenant, sir," an intrigued voice prompted.

"Yes, captain?"

"There are waves of people coming into the square."

"I am not blind, man. Parliament's reassembly has brought them out from under their stones again," Charles told him curtly.

He saw Sir Thomas Lunsford, commander of the King's Guards, ride over to Colonel Hadleigh and exchange words. A messenger soon ran to Charles, following the juncture of the two; the older colonel acted as a sanity check to gung ho Lunsford.

"The colonel's compliments, sir. He wants all officers to understand that the protesters are made up of mariners and dock hands today."

As he nodded, he watched warily while the area quickly filled up, and one man handed leaflets out to all and sundry, the prints causing initial laughter, which developed into determined frustration.

"No bishops."

"Devilish bishops, and popish lords, no good for anything but our swords," another howled, with people repeating the rhyme.

In the approaching bustle, one of those intriguing newssheets blew over and Charles ordered the sergeant to catch it. It was an invitation to a funeral, and he frowned, examining the images of a man and a woman standing at either side of a box containing information about the event. Above them were a skeleton and a strange man with a long beard and an hourglass, exclaiming that the time had come. Below all of this was an image of a funeral, coffin and clergyman leading the congregation into a church. Nothing unusual there, though the details of the funeral revealed all; 'You are invited to accompany the corpse of The Bishops and Catholic Peers. From Westminster, to the parish church of Saint Margaret. Please bring this ticket with you.'

Charles handed it to Major Fanshaw with a sarcastic expression.

Within the swirling mass of apprentices and other men were seamen with their blue breeches. The dirty white jackets had as many buttons stretching from their neck to the navel, though many seemed to leave most of them open, flapping around at the chest and cuffs, like the tongues of these protestors. Charles kept a close eye on any man in this outfit, for sailors had much more knowledge and experience than an unruly apprentice.

Eventually some ran over and started pushing and taunting Charles's troops, one man's face as screwed up as his old apron that was wrapped around his waist.

"Hold your positions, men, do not rise to their behaviour," he demanded firmly.

A din filled the air once more, just like the time he found himself opposing James in this same place last month. Tension mounted as some guards began to curse and hurl insults in return. Hackney carriages at their stands were swamped, and all he could see was their upper frames in the distance, such were the numbers milling around them, while other coaches that drove past were stopped and searched. His eyes darted around, for he was anxious to keep abreast of all developments, observing even the most minor of activities, like a dock hand stumbling and being overtaken by the swell of people around him. Next he heard a whole host of yelling coming from where Lunsford was. The rioters were surging around the troops near the commander, attempting to get to him because he was such a figure of hatred.

Then Lunsford drew his sword.

The sight of the knight on horseback, sitting high, as though he were riding the crowds and his guards, made a chilling sight. Charles remembered the tale about how, as a young man of twenty two, the commander had tried to shoot a neighbour as he was leaving church. This whole incident resulted in Lunsford's exile from England for years, and all because the neighbour had successfully prosecuted Lunsford for poaching his deer. This really did put the quick temper into perspective, faced as they were by a fired and offensive crowd. The flashing blade was as cold as the air.

One of Charles's own officers copied the commander and the men edged forward into the sea of faces. Charles howled at them to resume position, tugging some back by the collars.

He hastily examined Lunsford again, to see the guards there preparing to assault the protesters.

He froze.

A guardsman knocked someone to the ground and put

his sword to the throat, bawling threats. Charles searched the scuffle out in the gathering, the noise ringing in his ears and his heart pumping furiously.

He had to act fast - defend or attack?

"Get that away, soldier, do you want to start a war?" he bellowed, before clashing the sword with his own. The man on the ground was James.

"Good God," he whispered with sheer astonishment.

James grabbed him by the doublet and pulled him closer. "If he had slit me, I would never have been able to tell you what a true friend you are. Now go, lest they realise you know me," James whispered quickly.

Charles pushed his friend away, aware of James's meaning, and thankful that he had been given the chance to speak to him for the first time since their dispute. Things were getting worse though and his men had moved in, thinking he was being attacked. Scuffles were breaking out all over the place like a plague epidemic. Chanting and shouting cranked up to a new level, and the volume simply kept increasing, as though it were a competition.

Next, a whole row of men started to stamp their feet.

Charles knew order would not survive for long. A large group of rioters broke away from the main huddle and moved towards his ranks, Charles gripped his sword and stepped forward to lead his small band. Then the offenders began picking up speed - this was going to be a big clash.

"Close formation and get as tightly together as you can," he bellowed, pulling some soldiers closer to him.

Standing in the middle of his men, he remained stoic as their enemies narrowed the distance, loosely formed, waving fists and throwing things. The group of demonstrators stopped suddenly, to continue this tirade of abuse, waiting for all their missiles to be launched. Stones and wood made up the armaments and Charles stopped a lump of wood that nearly hit him, rebounding from his arm.

"Everyone mount the steps behind us," he howled, as a hail of stones began raining down.

He edged backwards, up a few steps to Westminster Abbey, and they again stood firm, securing the butts of their poleaxes against the stone blocks, aiming the points out towards the spirited rabble. The crowd approached the lower steps, like a wave encroaching upon a beach, jubilant that they had forced the guards back. At the foot of the soldiers though, some seemed to realise their folly as they began to falter, and the crush of people behind them forced the bodies onwards.

Some soldiers punched and kicked out at a few of the leading opponents and scuffled with them, knocking them down.

As the struggle went on, Charles instructed the men without pikes to draw their swords and threaten the rioters with the blades from their superior elevated position, now that this was unavoidable.

A dockhand ran forward to him, drawing a sword and thrusting it at him. Charles responded, smashing it out of its journey in one swoop of his own weapon. The adversary quickly recovered his position and came back in for a second go, slashing at Charles. He met the blade with a clash, but the stranger's energy and speed was surprising. Charles observed the assailant, and tried to work out what his next move would be.

His foe pushed forward once more, cutting diagonally, but Charles barred the move. To his surprise the man ripped his hat off and held it in his other hand, swinging it erratically, before bringing the sword down towards Charles's head. Again he dodged it, before following it up with a strike of his own, pushing the opponent back. As the man's arm was temporarily forced away, Charles sliced across his body. The fellow jumped, but it was too late, and Charles managed to cut the shoulder and upper chest.

He was only afforded a few seconds to look round to his

men, who had met the other protestors and were forcing them into a retreat.

Another one of the mob wielded a long pole at Charles, holding the centre with both hands and swinging each end at him in a fierce and relentless attack. Charles took a swipe at it, and his sword stuck fast in the wood for a second, only getting free when the man smacked Charles with the end of the shaft. It was a blessing he had managed to keep his grip on the sword, and this movement dislodged it. He was sweating profusely now as he swung his blade against the adversary for a second time and they locked together in combat. Both men eyed one another as they struggled to push the other's weapon out of the way, in order to launch a blow to the resulting undefended body. Feeling his arm weaken, Charles swiftly grabbed the end of the pole and tugged it with all his might.

By now another antagonist stepped into the fray to outnumber him two to one. Charles swept the pole away with strenuous effort and then thrust his sword at the resultant gap in defences. It stabbed the man and he withdrew, eventually leaving with a cry of pain, just in time. Seeing Charles victorious, the other remaining foe veered towards him.

Charles stepped back, desperately inhaling some welcome breaths, and then lunged his blade forward. As both weapons met, each man tried to force the other's weapon to one side.

With his blade being uppermost, Charles quickly took a risk, and withdrew, to slice in from the side. The opponent dropped his weapon as he leaped away, eyes bulging with fear. The sharp edge had already cut him lightly, for Charles did not take any risks, and wanted to make sure the man had ample reason to surrender.

Stepping forward, Charles advanced until eventually the opponent stumbled and Charles felt content to leave him, picking up the other sword and handing it to one of his men for the arsenal. No sooner had he rejoined the ranks to recover, than he saw a smartly dressed trouble maker in the crowd screaming, "Storm the hall, storm it."

Exhausted, but determined to see each of these rogues off, he ordered his guards forward and they advanced onto the mob in good spirits, attacking them effectively until the screaming man disappeared. Immediately the confused mass of bodies dispersed and fled, just at the point when he became worried about the sheer numbers in their path. He saw the ringleader lying on the ground, blood pouring from his head. Colonel Hadleigh arrived with some guardsmen, joining their flank.

"Sir Charles, are your men all right?"

"Aye, sir, but I am not sure about him. We did not kill him though," he panted, gloved hand wiping sweat and hair away from his eyes.

"It is Sir Richard Wiseman; the King imprisoned him for non payment of taxes years ago. Looks like a tile has fallen from the abbey and killed him, what a sign from heaven," Hadleigh joked, ordering the body to be taken to a church.

Charles laughed, more out of relief, than anything else. He felt tired after all the fighting and his last bits of energy had been sapped, so he happily sheathed his sword for a break.

Standing watching the scene of the square, he had expected the confrontation to resume again. But to his surprise, Wiseman's death seemed to cool their tempers and a lot of people had left completely.

"Oh, before I forget, Sir Charles, you will need to get to the tailors to be fitted for some clothes," Hadleigh casually remarked, as he pointed a letter at him.

As Charles took it, the colonel drew him away to one side.

"These orders have been sent to every officer. The regiment is to make itself ready on the morning of January the fourth at the palace. More details are inside," Hadleigh explained furtively, only whispering the date.

Charles nodded his head as the colonel left, and feeling

curious, he ripped the letter open and learned that all officers were to report to the colonel, the date written simply as 'that given verbally'.

"How vague? It sounds very ominous to me," he murmured.

He read on to find that Sir Thomas Lunsford and his officers had also been invited to the palace on the twenty ninth of December for a Christmas meal. Charles now found himself with an invitation to socialise with the monarch himself. He put the paper away and stood deep in thought at what was afoot – this was more evidence of the King digging his feet in. Both sides were in such entrenched positions now, that he failed to see how this could get resolved, especially when the King was openly sabre rattling his approval of a military man like Lunsford. What's more, this event would galvanise his own loyalty to that of the monarch, come what may.

Chapter 48

"**C**uddle me, I am nervous," he joked to Anne, as he crowned himself with a hat sporting red ostrich feathers that matched the new pair of smooth, silky stockings.

She came over, telling him she would do more than cuddle him, seeing him as smart as this. Then she embraced him, the pair laughing.

"Eating with the King, who would have thought? I think you chose to support the right side, darling. I can see a peerage soon."

"Do you think I look good enough?" he asked.

"You look perfect. Red suits you, Lord Berkeley," she reassured.

He felt excited, nervous and proud all at the same time.

"The Countess Berkeley looks ravishing tonight, I must say," he said, playfully kissing Anne's hand.

"Well, hold that thought and come to my chamber on your return, my lord," she said provocatively, gently tracing her casual fingers down to her chest. Charles beamed at her, looking forward to tonight's gathering, but now also eager to rejoin Anne after it. Then she finished his lovelock, curling this stray, longer piece of hair separately from the rest, tying the end with a white ribbon. This was one of the few times he had sported such a fashionable hairstyle.

"You know, despite all these troubles, Parliament does not attack the King directly. There's something magical about him and his position, which holds our entire nation together. I cannot imagine England without a monarch. Even the church binds us all. If ever any of them were to fall, God forbid, I think this country would be finished, no respect or care for anything."

Louise followed him with a lantern and hung it on a hook on the outer wall of the house, wiping the glass with her long, white apron.

"Glad to see we are still following the regulations for lighting this damn street, even if most people flout it," he told her, raising his voice at the last part, trying to wind a neighbour up.

Thomas laughed as he told him his own maid was on her way to do the same task, and it had become a standing joke after they both complained to each other about the general lapse of this rule across the city. Then with a friendly salute, Thomas went back inside his house.

Louise smiled, adjusting the white headpiece which covered the back half of her head, "It should be still on when you return, sir."

He waited outside for Major Fanshaw who was meeting him with a carriage, but instead, he saw the officer approach on foot, recognising the strut of 'Major Peacock' anywhere.

"Good evening, sir."

"Evening, major, where is the transport?" he queried.

"There is a vast mob and a fire blocking the road ahead, so I thought we could go by barge. I have a boatman waiting for us."

"Good crisis planning, Fanshaw," he joked.

The pair marched down the street, avoiding the pig, which was snorting around the base of the houses. The firm strides were refreshing, Charles realising just how fast they were going when they passed the tailor's shop, in what seemed like a minute.

They winced as the animal was covered in excrement, poured out of a window from one of the rickety houses above them.

"I see our commander has a new record to add to the one the people have given him about eating children," Major Fanshaw commented, continuing the easy informality of banter off duty. The man had a calm, genuine air and a good humour, qualities that Charles appreciated.

"Sir Thomas Lunsford, what now?" he asked with intrigue, having worked on the finances and documents to do with his land all day, never leaving the house.

"The person to hold the post of Lieutenant of the Tower of London for the shortest time. Less than two weeks."

"Yes, I heard about that one a few days ago. Lunsford was at least better than the one before him though, who was sympathetic to Parliament."

"And have you heard who Lunsford's successor is?" the officer asked.

"Sir John Byron, who is just as loyal," Charles told him.

"And so the Tower of London and all it's arsenal are still safe," Fanshaw concluded.

They walked down a narrow alley a touch wider than both of them standing shoulder to shoulder. It was pitch black. A light appeared behind, and a young boy ran down towards them with a lantern on a long pole. It lit the passage up a treat.

"What a saviour," Fanshaw exclaimed.

On catching sight of the two of them, the boy stopped and began whistling. A man appeared at the end of the alleyway and signalled for the boy to return faster.

"For the love of God, we are lucky. That damned boy was about to lead us to a thief," Fanshaw growled now, in an abrupt change of tune.

"Aye, *what a saviour*," Charles said, slapping him on the shoulder.

The man and the boy had vanished now, probably looking for easier pickings. Fanshaw laid his hand on a fine sword, hanging by his side on a brown, leather belt. The hilt was silver, decorated with his family's coat of arms, reminding Charles of the officer's heritage; younger son of Sir John Fanshaw, baronet.

Sometimes Charles felt out of place in a highly prized regiment of patronage, though he never dwelled on it for long, it still amazed him that he was there by Digby's machinations, of all people. Approaching the old stone steps, they saw the ferryman sitting in a small rowing boat, looking as worn as the ancient stairs. They descended and walked cautiously across the wooden jetty, stinking mud smearing it from the comings and goings, before stepping into the craft.

"Whitehall Steps please, boatman," Charles ordered as they carefully sat down, eyeing the five inches of freeboard that separated them from the murky river.

The vessel set off, gliding gracefully across the Thames, and he examined what looked like London Bridge in the gloomy distance. The shops and houses that were built on each side, converted the bridge into practically its own little enclave within London, and the flickers of light from some windows were one of the only ways you could make it out in this weather.

Every now and then, another vessel would pass by, both sets of passengers acknowledging each other cheerfully and politely.

The air was cold, especially now, being on the water. His leather gloves, woollen doublet and breeches kept him warm though, and his face was the only part of his body to suffer the chill. Silk stockings were fashionable, but less attractive in this weather, but he had gone for them to make the effort for this special occasion. Thinking of fashion made him look down at his shoes, which had red heels and were fastened with red ribbons. He searched for the scuff mark he had incurred yesterday but could not see it on the shoe on his right foot.

Puzzled as to its whereabouts, seeing as both shoes were straight and could be worn on either foot, he eventually discovered it and wiped it.

The boatman slowed as he neared the jetty of Whitehall Palace, having passed by the more elaborate, enclosed walkway that was for ministers, giving direct access to the King's lodgings.

The vessel slipped towards them and the fellow took hold of the blocks, steadying the boat. It was clear the man had done this all his life, judging by the skill and ease at which he worked.

"Thank you, that was very quick and easy. I have a mind to travel by water more often," Charles said as he handed some coins over.

"Goodnight, gentlemen," the ferryman said, tugging the front of his hat in respect, before he lit a candle, signifying his availability.

They climbed the stairs and walked up a narrow alleyway leading to a back entrance of the sprawling palace, which must have been a huge security risk with so many entry points. Indeed, the father of his friend Edmund Verney, who was Knight Marshall, responsible for policing the King's court, would frequently have to clear the place of prostitutes or beggars and make sure all people around the monarch behaved themselves.

The chapel lay ahead, the black and white chequered battlements giving a fortified tone, quite symbolic of the attack the church was under right now. A small tower raised the roof slightly higher than that of the Banqueting House beyond.

Inside, the guards saluted them on receipt of the invitations and a page welcomed them. Fanshaw made him laugh when he expressed surprise that the boatman did not gossip so much as they normally did, positive that news is discovered on the river ferries. They walked through several corridors, passing a room which housed several golden maces.

"Colonel Hadleigh waits for you in here, gentlemen," he announced, pointing at a doorway, the top surrounded by tulips.

Charles felt goosebumps on his arms and tingling on his neck, with a complete sense of pride and awe to be back in Whitehall, this time at the King's personal invitation - well, if not personal invitation, it was because he was in the direct service of the Head of State. It had been a complete circle he had gone through since he was last here. His heart thumped and he moved his shoulders back as he began to head to the door. The page opened it and announced them.

"Lieutenant Colonel Sir Charles Berkeley and Major Jacob Fanshaw."

Colonel Hadleigh sat with a group of officers, puffing on a pipe. The cloud of smoke hung above them, like the fog that clung to London.

"Gentlemen, we are awaiting Sir Thomas. Please sit down," Hadleigh told them, pointing at some drinks.

The fire roared and the room was very warm, giving a subdued air of welcome. The ceiling provided a hint of what was to come by venturing further into this maze of rooms; a tromp l'oeil effect gave an impression of ornate flowering plasterwork, though at this stage of the perimeter, it was simply a painted illusion. He laid his cloak on the oak table and took a glass of wine, offered by one of the captains. Then not long afterwards, the door flew open with a crash, and Sir Thomas Lunsford made his spectacular entry, similar to the way he had come bounding back into the country two years ago, following a long exile.

"It is as cold as a whore's heart out there," he bellowed.

He flung his hat onto the table and tugged his cloak, swinging it from his shoulders in a great swoop.

"Right, men, shall we go to the chamber now? We do not want to be late for the King, for someone needs to keep the respect for his person, seeing as Parliament and these bloody apprentices do not," he announced.

They all stood and followed him out, the sparkling colour of his silver doublet and breeches illuminating the way, though the burgundy stockings with this outfit made it all somewhat garish. In fact, it appeared as though he had waded through a stream of blood - a credible possibility judging by his reputation with people, and his nickname of 'Roaring Lunsford'.

"I have not made your acquaintance, sir," Lunsford noted of Charles, before looking to Hadleigh for an introduction.

"Sir Charles Berkeley, our new lieutenant colonel," Hadleigh said. Charles felt awkward, unable to bow to the commander as they continued on, though Lunsford only turned every now and then, settling for throwing his comments and conversation over his shoulder.

"Ah, it is an honour, Sir Charles," Lunsford said between his swaggering journey up the corridor.

"This is the fellow who has divine sponsorship, Sir Thomas," Hadleigh jested, "The Lord blew a roof tile onto Wiseman, the leader of the men who stormed Westminster Abbey. Sir Charles's men were the ones facing the brunt of it at the time."

Lunsford let out a deep laugh and Charles felt good about the compliment, while they eventually arrived in the long gallery. He gasped at the splendour, Hadleigh commenting that this roof was the real thing; stone, with gold patterned into it. As he continued in wonder, he was struck by the huge picture at the end of the hall, depicting the King, Queen and their children.

It was near ten feet high and showed them as a perfect family, a boast about the fact the King had secured the succession. He felt so proud now, knowing he had also secured the Berkeley name through his son. With little more time for sightseeing, Lunsford led them out of the corridor and through several smaller and more menial rooms, until they came to the great hall. He was astounded by it all, dazzling and awe inspiring as it was.

"It is so vast," Fanshaw said, trying to sum it up.

Charles nodded and Lunsford watched them, his great shoulders blanketed fully in rich, white lace, as was his wrists and forearms. A sword belt crossed his chest like a golden streak of evening sun.

"Vast? One thousand, one hundred rooms in this place. And do you know the good thing?"

The pair looked at him expectantly, awaiting more details.

"There are seventy five garrets for our pissing, so we will be well served by them after all the wine."

Everyone burst out laughing at the quip, Lunsford holding his hands up in the air as he paced away. The hall was magnificent, with a breathtaking pitched roof. He looked at the inlaid wooden walls and then at the tapestries and the biblical scenes they displayed so vividly. The great windows and the coloured glass scattered reflections of coats of arms and heraldry onto the proceedings, as though history was reaching out and touching those present.

"This one was made in England at Mortlake around thirty years ago," Fanshaw told him, explaining his father had been in the trade when King James the First tried to set up an English tapestry industry.

Two servants stood by after emerging from behind the screens, which covered the small passageways to the buttery and kitchens, one making a start in pouring wine after seeing them arrive. Sitting down next to Fanshaw, Charles saw he was opposite Lunsford and Hadleigh, so he should be in for an enjoyable night.

"Sir Charles Berkeley. I have heard the name. Was it from Lord Holland, sir?" Lunsford asked aloud.

"Lord Holland was a patron at one time, Sir Thomas," he confirmed.

"I am damn glad he is still not then," Lunsford guffawed, "He was dismissed from his post at court last month by the King. What a foolish, indulgent man; knew more about fashion and manners than soldiering, and I am glad the King got wise to his political sympathies."

He raised an eyebrow at the news of Holland's discharge.

The King had indeed been flexing his muscles, he thought, as he weighed up all the information he had heard lately.

"What other commander than our glorious Holland, would write to the Scottish in the Bishops War to apologise that his men crossed the border into Scotland without permission?" Lunsford joked.

Charles felt a little guilty for finding the remark funny, though he could not restrain his humour. Holland himself must have realised he was no Mars.

"On yet another occasion, our Lord Holland led a retreat, insisting that they faced a mammoth army. This horde turned out to be nothing more than a herd of cattle the Scots had drawn across the plain with them, adding to the dust from their march, but haunting our cavalry commander to the bone. The only attack he made in his career was to accept a challenge from the Earl of Newcastle over the fact that he had placed the man's men in the rear of their army," Lunsford howled.

"And even then, the King arrested Holland to stop the duel going ahead," Hadleigh added, not be outdone.

Charles was weeping at the humour, as were most men. As he wiped his eyes, the door at the other end of the room opened, and the King entered. The men stood up and Charles quickly put his wine glass down, anxious to make sure he did not spill any. He looked at Fanshaw and some of the others and most seemed to share his nervousness. All except Lunsford, who did not fear God, let alone any mortal.

"Please, gentlemen, be seated. You have all served me well and I thank you for that," the monarch said as he took his place.

"We are proud to serve you, Your Majesty," Lunsford said as he lifted his glass, "To the King," he toasted enthusiastically.

They all drank the royal health. This looked to be the start of a long flood of alcohol.

"Thank you, Sir Thomas. Despite having to take command of the Tower away from you, I still retain you within my trust, and let Parliament see this by my invitation tonight," the King said, with only a slight hint of the stammer which Charles had heard during public occasions.

Perhaps it was down to being amongst a small gathering of loyal soldiers, relaxing the monarch and making him more confident, Charles perceived.

"How is Her Majesty, sir?" Hadleigh asked, prompting the royal to turn his head, though the posture was stiff.

"The Queen is in good humour and would devour these men in Parliament. I am confident we shall soon have an end to all troubles though. I have the backing of Scotland, following my visit, and of my people here, now they see that these men wish to lay their hands upon my crown and alter our religion. I will suffer their assaults no longer."

"Damned rogues, none of them with an ounce of intelligence, otherwise they would see the folly of their actions. Pardon my phrase, sir," Lunsford asserted, characteristically excusing his words after they had been said, with no real regrets.

This bravado and hostile talk seemed to change the monarch, as he sat back in his seat, one elbow now resting on his chair arm. Charles spotted that his royal namesake - probably deliberately done, knowing his father's ultra loyal core - now looked at most of the men directly, no longer as if he could see through them, like they were ghosts.

The warmth of the fire eased Charles as he listened to the sovereign. He was in the heart of this huge palace; the nerve centre of Great Britain, housing all activity about the King, who was now sitting a matter of twelve feet away from him. The King had the magical effect of making him believe all was well in the country.

He took another quick peek at the royal visage, intrigued, overawed and wishing to remember the sight, despite it being impolite to look for long.

The monarch was the picture of what he had imagined, after only seeing him this close once before. Even though a knight himself, it was the Earl of Arundel as commander of the army during the Bishops War, who had knighted him on the King's behalf. Being in such proximity was a privilege that few men of his relatively low status would ever have - and he was worlds away from the image on coinage. A sad air, despite the faint tinge of an informality to the dinner, hung in the King's eyes. He was smaller, though extremely elegant, masked as it was with this aura of dignity. This also gave an effect of arrogance at times.

After impulsively dismissing another thought from his mind, he found himself drawn back to it. He actually felt closer to God being with the King, who was divinely appointed to rule.

Was he not indirectly in the service of the Lord by being in the King's guards? He pondered.

He was woken from these theological thoughts by Lunsford chortling again as he drank more wine. The King sipped slowly at his, and he noted that careful moderation seemed to be the key to his whole lifestyle. The sovereign and Lunsford began to converse about hunting, of which both were particularly fond, or at least Lunsford claimed to be. Charles heard Hadleigh discussing the pepper trade, telling a man that it turns over forty eight thousand pounds per year through supplying London alone. Charles felt poor. That was more than thirty times his annual income.

The servants brought some soup and tender pieces of beef out and laid them on the table, along with some mince pies and more wine. Other plates were placed amongst this and with the conversations, splendour and royalty, he was distracted from the food. Then Charles glanced up to see the King looking directly at him.

He froze, averting his eyes for a second, as his spirit seemed to rise out of his body with the shock. He chilled over with this sensation, until after a split second, he returned his attention to the King and bowed his head, mouthing the words, 'Your Majesty.'

King Charles nodded back, a final sign of recognition.

"Sir Thomas, I am concerned at how Sir Charles Berkeley manages to get into as many scrapes with the mobs as he has done of late," the King said unexpectedly.

Without knowing what to say, he felt mortified at the royal displeasure, having only just secured an acknowledgement that his missions and struggles had not passed without any gratitude.

The monarch then smiled and Lunsford and Hadleigh echoed this joviality. Charles felt life return to him - he was totally shocked that the King knew his name, and flabbergasted that he should make a cheery comment about his service.

"Aye, anyone would think he feasted on human flesh like me to get such an appetite for fighting these dogs," Lunsford jested.

Charles smiled, trying to keep up with the repertoire.

"Sir Charles and our men did well controlling that mob on both occasions," Hadleigh commented.

"No doubt Lord Digby will insist he deserves praise for recommending Sir Charles for the post in my guards."

Charles did not want to contradict the King by telling him he had really been adamantly neutral, until accepting the post, and now he tripped over himself to speak, leaving those ancient feelings and worries far behind. He was anxious to show how enamoured he was by the monarch's compliment and how wholeheartedly he supported him, especially now. He actually felt that he would willingly do absolutely anything for him.

"I am very grateful for the trust you place in me, Your Majesty, for it is not misplaced. As for the rioters, I simply told them of a rumour that Sir Thomas and I had run out of meat for our lunch, and their attack faltered. I'll wager they did not want to be the next roast on our plate," he said with bated breath.

The King smiled again, though it was soon eclipsed as he took a sip of wine, and Lunsford guffawed, clinking his glass against Charles's, before slapping the table.

Bringing his commander into the comment seemed to form a mutual banter. By this time, the candles had burned low and Charles felt drunk on the wine, company, excitement and adrenaline. He slowed down on the alcohol and reached for a mince pie, determined not to lose his senses. His eyes widened, as he tasted it.

"Delicious," he said, passing verdict to Fanshaw.

"The mutton is superbly done within them," the major agreed.

"You sound experienced in culinary techniques, sir," Charles noted.

"I have flicked through, 'The English Housewife', because the wife insisted I pass on her shopping list of ingredients to the maid yesterday," Fanshaw admitted, "Mutton, pepper, cloves, mace, currants, raisins, prunes, dates and orange peel. She has got the stuff etched onto my mind."

Charles shook his head. "I shall watch you on parade, a soldier should not know such things," he said playfully.

The King then placed his napkin down and the table went quiet, the silence heralding a culmination of emotions from all present, somehow feeling like a new age would dawn with the approach of Christmas. Gone would be the disturbances, tension and worry, both in the city and in men's souls, tormented as they were with the uprooting of the tree of stability.

"Good health, gentlemen, and may God bless you and your families over the Christmas period. You have the greatest of services to perform for me soon, and with the Lord's help, we will give the greatest gift back to my people and this land; peace. Sir Thomas will acquaint you with more details nearer the time and until then, I bid you all goodnight."

The King rose to the rigorous applause of all present and Charles felt jubilant. After seeing the King in this setting, he became irrepressibly furious at Parliament for encroaching onto the lawful royal prerogative further and further. He began to take the insults against the monarch quite personally, for they were overturning the laws of his land. They drank off the rest of their wine before getting ready to leave, gulping it down in their thirst for action.

"Right, lads, we can exit by the palace gate. I have some spaces in my coach for those who may need a ride home," Lunsford offered.

The group walked through the inner chambers and corridors, respectfully keeping quiet. They strolled through some long hallways, which in turn brought them to the odd small, outdoor square, before leading back indoors again. Eventually they found themselves in the main courtyard, which was opposite the great banqueting house and palace gate. It was like a rabbit warren.

"I bet the King had to leave because the Queen wants her Christmas present," Lunsford suggested.

"For a man who is so averse to showing personal feelings in public, I bet he doesn't hold the same restraint in private," Hadleigh added.

"Where he lacks confidence and is precise, she provides the opposite, sometimes to his downfall, mind you. Remember when she stood scowling at the people on a progress through London? She does not endear herself at all," another judged, with more reasoned comments.

They chattered like woman as they exited, Charles in the middle of them. Outside, a group of apprentices were still loitering around the vicinity, coming into view as they left the portico gate and entered the area separated from the street with balustrades. With the emergence of the soldiers, the louts began shouting and yelling as though in pain, hooting louder than the market traders who were here most of the time.

"No bishops."

"Down with the popish pigs."

Lunsford growled like a mad dog. "The bastards will not leave off. For sixpence they would shout that their master, Pym, was a whoremonger," he announced.

As Charles neared the protesters, the cries got louder until a few started throwing stones. Lunsford lost his temper and Charles watched him rip his sword out of its sheath, holding the impressive blade as though it were some small dagger. He stared, motionless for a while with a blank look of anger on his face, suggesting he could cut every man down without one thought for them. The apprentices closed in on the group of officers and Charles quickly drew his weapon too, though for defence, rather than attack.

"This lot uphold the bloody bishops," onlookers cried out about them.

A man dodged Charles, ignoring his warnings to stay away, and punched him, but Charles was prepared, and grabbed the ruffian's fist.

The man scowled and caught hold of Charles's doublet, tugging him close. He responded by smacking the handle of his sword into the fellow's face. He did not want to draw any serious blood or cause this quarrel to be escalated to extreme violence.

Besides, the man was clearly out of his depth, pitted as he was against a professional officer. His foe soon retreated fast.

Then Charles saw Lunsford was not of the same mind, as he slashed and thrust out with his sword, quite ruthlessly and violently, wounding a few men. Major Fanshaw was set upon and kicked to the ground, as the gang realised that sheer numbers could overwhelm one professional. With a few others, Charles ran to help him. As he got Fanshaw to his feet, a man smacked his head with a stick, instantly boiling Charles into a rage - the slightest touch, or proximity of another to his head made him defensive and he slashed his sword at him. At the final moment, the fellow leaped out of the way and scurried away.

The rest of the apprentices made off and ran down the street in realisation that they would be killed if they persisted, yelling and hollering about a supposed massacre. The wounded limped after them, and Lunsford jabbed his sword up one of their backsides, much to everyone's delight. At least there had been no deaths Charles thought, trying to excuse the violence. After five or ten minutes of talking amongst themselves, he saw a lot of flaming torches appear from the direction of Westminster - it looked like they had alerted their associates. Lunsford, Hadleigh, Charles and Fanshaw leaped into the commander's coach, without further hesitation.

They sped through the streets in silence, Hadleigh looking a little perturbed. Not even Lunsford could let out a wisecrack to break the atmosphere, realising they had gone too far. The country only needed the major players in the dispute to lose their temper like this, to cause civil war.

Charles jumped out when they arrived at his house, after taking leave of them. The lantern had gone out long ago and inside, after lighting the charcoal in the brazier, he heard the night watchman cry the time and weather report and rushed out to catch him.

Opening the door he asked impatiently, "Have you been near Westminster?"

"Aye, sir," he replied with a puzzled expression.

"Was anything afoot, for I saw hundreds of torches?" he asked with bated breath.

"As normal, they threaten to break into the Lord Mayor's house over some incident outside the palace. I hear they descended on a prison and broke into it, freeing the inmates."

Charles groaned. Christmas was anything but quiet, as he thought it would be. London was simply simmering away, ready to erupt once more, but the question was, when and how?

Chapter 49

A s they sat in the upper chamber, the House of Lords was in turmoil. The aristocracy within swirled around, as though churned up by the strength of opinion outside, chattering tensely to each other. Another bishop, who had managed to break through the ranks of gangs outside, struggled in, adjusting his clothes. Over half of the clerics were missing, probably being prevented from arriving. Lord Digby sat observing the Archbishop of York. He had been pestering the clergyman to gather his bishops together in support of the monarch, for the small band of clerics were key voters in the sparse house.

Recently Digby had tried to get the House of Lords to agree that, because of the threatening behaviour towards members from the multitudes, the subsequent votes were invalid due to this intimidation. The peers had rejected it, but Digby was sure that with today's concerns, he could escort the measure through in another vote. By pressurising the archbishop to lead the debate, the motion would receive more justice, because the pressure exerted on the churchmen was clear. He observed the prelate get to his feet, with colleagues gathered around him.

The same proposal that failed before, was now dressed up in a bishop's lawn sleeves and rochet, petitioning that the whole of Parliament's actions were invalid, without the presence of all bishops. Archbishop Williams, once an opponent of the King, had been greeted with bells pealing all over London on his release from prison last year. Now it was not bells that rang in his ears, but the screaming of the populace against his kind, and especially his new royalist sympathies, which had earned him a promotion to the see of York.

Digby addressed the Earl of Newcastle, until recently, Governor of the young Prince of Wales. "My lord, we must be ready to stop a dictatorship by the hordes outside - let us pray we turn the tables on the House of Commons and fight against such coercion."

Newcastle gave him a disdainful look.

"How violent the rabble is to the venerable bishops. No votes in the house should be classed as valid, especially when we are under duress," Digby explained, attempting to woo the peer, notwithstanding the earlier snub.

Newcastle spoke to an earl beside him. "The archbishop boxed the ears of some protestors only the other day. How can he say that the fellow is threatened by them? That is not the behaviour of a venerable person."

Digby squirmed at the slight and began to search for someone more worthy of his conversation, for Newcastle obviously seemed to shun anything he proposed – whether he was inclined to support it, or not. Then the Lord Keeper of the King's seal stood up and attracted the attention of the calmer members. Sitting on the edge of his seat like a schoolchild, Digby was eager to hear him. He knew exactly what the man was announcing, for it was the work he had been centrally involved in. Like a new play that the peer enjoyed writing, the Lord Keeper stood to narrate the introduction, Digby casting himself into the main part for disarming Pym, who he believed he was more than a match for.

"My lords, a petition has been moved by the noble Archbishop of York and his colleagues, and I put to this house, their assertion that while bishops are forcibly excluded from sitting due to pressure and intimidation, that all laws, orders and resolutions are null, and of no effect."

The Lord Keeper was shouted down before he had finished, the plump, red cheeks lighting up further, while the peers howled with anger. Alongside the din, a surge of antipathy towards the issue grew as more of them cottoned onto what Archbishop Williams was trying to do. The imperious statement from the clerics had inflamed what should have been a sympathetic crowd of nobility. The fury surprised Digby, for he had expected unrestrained support for the issue.

"We have already discussed this issue when Lord Digby raised it. Why bring it forward again?" one earl shouted.

Digby waved his papers, unable to understand that his plan seemed doomed. "We have seen the riotous behaviour of those beasts who clamour for rebellion. Surely their actions have a bearing on our decisions, and how can Parliament function when it is controlled by this mob of unruly, common people."

It was no good and Digby was drowned out. Like a child, he withdrew from the fracas immediately, sitting back with his arms folded, piqued at his treatment and the ignorance of everyone who did not show support.

In the face of such continued opposition, he now dropped his role, though failure would never be his reason. His sanguine nature was quick to explore other ways to advance the royal cause and by default, his own prospects. One day he would propel the King forward and be the driving force behind eventual success, he thought, aiming to be remembered down the generations as a great Parliamentarian. His gaze became fixed to the arched roof and the painted illusion, which gave the impression it being adorned with sunken square panels for decoration. The effect was as deceptive as Digby's own façade, as he thought about more schemes.

Like a desert island in this sea of privileged people, the Lord Keeper remained standing in desperate silence, his own reactions left high and dry. Wave upon wave of anger and outrage lapped up against him, causing the man to focus one way, looking at Digby, and then the next, observing Archbishop Williams.

Amidst this carnage, the royal plans for tearing down anything discussed in the absence of the bishops, collapsed; hostility to them grew from within the chamber, combining with the outright hatred of the mobs outside. Williams desperately defended the matter, as though he sensed the downfall of his bishops hinged upon it.

Digby, meanwhile, thought about why nearly all men called Edward, were fat. The Lord Keeper's bulk caused his golden chain of office to positively stretch as it hung around his neck, while the small strands of receding hairline stuck together from sweat.

Then Holland's brother, the seafaring Earl of Warwick, spoke to a page, until the servant eventually left the chamber. The reason why the old warship had despatched a small craft out intrigued Digby, and he pondered over the man's destination. By now, he was too bored to be particularly bothered by it - the archbishop's motion would clearly founder; it was no longer his own idea. The churchman, in comparison, was bravely holding onto the view, arguing with those around him to the bitter end.

"Anything agreed through force cannot be valid. What is the point of a Parliament if we are cajoled and beaten into submission by a pack of base men, instructed by Master Pym in the House of Commons?"

This serious allegation, which nobody had dared voice publicly, seemed to force Lord Keeper Littleton to fall back into his seat, the small circular window in the top of the far wall lighting up from a winter sun, like a warning flare.

"How dare you all list the same complaint again? You should ask yourself if it is right to continue proposing the same motion, until it is finally agreed. Surely this is intimidating the members just as much as the rabble?" one peer stated, pointing at the band of clerics.

Every now and then, Digby shook his head, and then glared at Archbishop Williams with contempt. He felt ridicule for how the cleric had conducted the matter, for he had wrecked the whole plan to put Pym in checkmate.

"The Welsh fool, too used to living in the hills, than in this city," he jested to a peer sitting by him.

After what seemed like an age of dispute, in which nobody could restore order, Warwick's messenger entered the house and spoke to the Lord Keeper. The official struggled to his feet, shouting to the nobles in a voice as deep as thunder, imploring them to allow him to relay some important details.

"The House of Commons has speedily approved a motion to impeach the twelve bishops who have put their names to this protest," he announced, showing the lightning bolt speed of the counter attack. Digby began to grasp that Warwick had tipped Pym off via the servant and they had seized upon the outrage caused by the topic.

Shouts rang out.

"Aye, aye."

"Impeach them, and then let them complain about their absence from our house. Bishops are not senior to us," a member of the aristocracy cried out.

Digby's body cooled, as though he had abandoned ship into some hostile, cold sea. Finally, he realised the dangerous situation, but it was far too late.

This had gone drastically wrong, and within half an hour it looked like Pym was gaining more strength, blasting the King's recent gains into oblivion. If the bishops were removed, then this chamber would easily fall to Pym's control, the only bastion that the King currently had a narrow control over.

"My lords, can we vote on the issue of the impeachment?" the Lord Keeper asked obediently.

Williams had stopped airing his views and sat quietly with the clerics, now facing trial with grave dignity. Their futures were as black as the armless cloaks they wore, though every inch of their white robes, with the small ruff and great sleeves, highlighted their assertions of innocence.

It was around quarter to eight in the evening when the Lord Keeper called out that his colleagues had cast their votes with Pym's call for impeachment. The tall grandfather clock next to the door chimed out into the disarray, booming an end to the royal come back. Time was rapidly running out for the country now.

"Can you not see we allow ourselves to do the House of Common's bidding? They play on your bruised pride at having this protest presented again, and as you steer away from it, you run right into the arms of a greater storm," Archbishop Williams bellowed as a guard came to arrest him. Then he lifted his black, diamond shaped headpiece, politely taking his leave, without knowing how long for.

Digby closed his eyes, dreading the King's reaction. Watching with dismay, he observed the twelve bishops being led out of the chamber by armed escort, off to prison. All this was in the middle of a chamber that was surrounded by huge tapestries depicting the glory of the Spanish Armada, the full length of the walls. The naval images did nothing to insulate the peers from the growing pandemonium outside, though by hanging over the doors, they accentuated the realisation that there was no way out for the country, and the road it seemed to be on.

Some of the lords here today would have been born at the time when England was saved from Catholic Spain, and now it seemed they were unwittingly plunging their country into chaos. With the absence of any threat from Spain, England had begun to find new enemies within its own people.

But Digby would find a way out of this for everyone - he was adamant this would only be a short interruption to his master's success. Next time he would pick a more able man than the archbishop to help though.

Chapter 50

Less than a week later, Charles received an order to appear at the palace. It was the day he had been waiting for, since he got the suspicious details regarding an arrest they had to make. The King had not expanded on this mystery at the Christmas dinner, and Lunsford was keeping the secret.

He arrived at the palace courtyard, and seeing the guards milling around, he made his way to the colonel, who stood with the officers around him in a crescent shape.

"Sir Charles Berkeley," the page formally announced.

Feeling accepted within the regiment, he was content. The title stood him in good stead, as the officers were all rich and well connected in court. Colonel Hadleigh called for a small glass of sherry, before commenting about the recent proclamation from the King, declaring the Irish rebels as traitors.

"To me, it is long overdue, but better late than never.

You know he also offered Pym the post of Chancellor of the Exchequer?" Hadleigh asked with a snort of surprise. Despite thinning on top, the colonel maintained his long hair, which lay flat against his head until it bushed out at his ears, in recognition of his earlier, flamboyant days.

"And it was refused, I presume?" Charles guessed.

"Aye. It had to be, but it is a gesture nonetheless, which proves he is trying to negotiate even at this late stage."

Another officer sauntered over, seemingly after observing Charles occupying the sole attention of their commander, factional rivalry being rife around important figures.

"Lieutenant Colonel, which regiment were you in before this, then?" Captain Rossiter probed with narrowed eyes.

Charles felt little inclination to indulge, simply wanting to find out more about this mission, and what they were doing standing around idle for hours on end. The cold was wearing his patience thin.

"The red regiment, London Trained Bands, and before that, in Lord Holland's regiments of horse in the Bishops War."

"Ah, now you will truly see a great band of men, and a greater leader. Colonel Hadleigh and ourselves are the elite, for we guard the King himself," Rossiter bragged.

"The King," the colonel toasted, before leading all the officers to a table in the corner of the court, set out as though it were for a picnic. Ladies strolled under the covered walkway that split the great courtyard in two, while servants and household staff loitered around the opposite end, nearby the spicery, pantry, kitchens and buttery.

"We, in the guard, will play a key role in bringing these tumultuous events to a close. We must arrest several men. I cannot say more, as details are strictly limited, but we need to march to Parliament, so get the guardsmen lined up, for we escort our monarch."

"But we have been waiting here for an age, sir," an officer stated.

"The King will come," Hadleigh said, a thoughtful look transforming the words into a veritable prayer.

The colonel's rather friendly face made sure all had understood the importance as he observed every officer in turn. While Charles returned to the troops, he studied the information and the finality of the phrasing, sure that Pym would be the intended recipient of their social call. Colonel Hadleigh stopped him and handed him a document.

"Sir Charles Berkeley, I present your commission in the name of His Majesty the King," Hadleigh announced, beaming with importance when he uttered the last part of it.

Charles bowed his head and read the parchment.

'Charles, by the Grace of God, King of Great Britain, France and Ireland, Defender of the Faith ... to our trusty and well beloved Sir Charles Berkeley, greeting. We do hereby constitute and appoint you to be lieutenant colonel of a company of foot, under the regiment of royal guards, commanded by our trusty and well beloved colonel, Sir George Hadleigh.'

A gush of pride filled every vein, pumping unashamedly to his core - it was a source of security being in the direct service of the sovereign and he thought about passing this manuscript down through his family. As he held the document, the royal carriage was driven away; even when empty, it was a dazzling spectacle and everyone moved closer to it or studied it as though it were a holy relic. A servant accompanied it, while the coachman adjusted his tunic with the royal coat of arms on, now seeming redundant for the day. The carriage roof had carved crowns at each corner and the while thing glittered with colour; the horses had golden reigns, while red ribbons decorated their manes and tails, the saddles covered with rich red and gold material that hung low on either side of the animals. Again, the royal arms decorated the doors and all this colour was emphasized by the fine white mares themselves.

"Get the guards into two lines," the colonel commanded, with a demanding look. The large array of tassels that fastened his shirt together may well have been indicative of his military campaigns, the eyes now beadily examining every movement.

As he mounted, his leather boots, unfolded to stretch right up to his thighs, highlighted the strength of those thick, muscular legs.

Charles relayed the orders and saw that they were neat. The men cut an awesome sight, dashing and smart, certainly standing out in their red uniforms. The guards wore black hats, with tunics which ended at their knees, followed by white stockings and black shoes. They had immaculate white collars, swords and pole axes. The crowning detail of the whole layout though was the King's arms emblazoned in gold on their chests; that of a rose with a crown above it placed in between the letters 'CR', for Charles Rex.

A young ensign ran up to Charles. "The King comes," the lad squeaked with excitement and relief.

Then as the men stamped their feet, or blew into their hands, the monarch and his young nephew appeared in the courtyard, as if by magic. They strode firmly, as fast as any surprise attack, and the King stopped briefly to scour the area. Something told Charles that the royal was looking for the carriage, though the march soon began, uncle and nephew heading now for the palace gate. They were going to go on foot.

Hadleigh was barking like a mad dog, with such a rare outburst of urgent passion as he cajoled the men and officers alike, signalling bluntly for Charles to rejoin him.

Lunsford went with the King, who had begun to pick up stray followers with each foot that he travelled. There were so many old officers from his northern army here now, disbanded and without service, yet anxious to serve him, that they seemed to outnumber the men at times.

Charles hurried over to Hadleigh, who had soon abandoned his positions to chase the King, leaving a drummer to pass on the command to follow him. As he rushed to the gate, the royal Party were now out of it, and in the main street. Intrigued, anxious to see what was happening because of the

King's resolute actions, Charles ran to catch up. He was just in time to see Lunsford stopping a carriage that was passing by, while the King stepped forward to get inside. With wide eyes, he observed this private, strange coach turn about, ready to catapult them to Parliament.

"Follow me, my most loyal liege men and soldiers," one man was ordering, repeating the King's instructions that he had uttered as he burst into the courtyard earlier.

Charles quickly joined the soldiers at the side of the carriage and they set off, in a magnificent cavalcade, with the man God had appointed in the centre of their ranks. It was three o'clock; the journey should take around twenty minutes. He prayed no mob would set upon the King, for this time they would all have no option but to kill, and there were several hundred guardsmen on this excursion.

While moving frustratingly slowly, a man broke through the ranks, running up to the carriage and bowing his head. Until he made the gesture, there was a panic, but the King instructed the troops to leave the fellow alone and held his hand out of the coach as the ragged man kneeled at the now open door.

The monarch laid both of his own hands upon the cheeks of the fellow and said, "He put his hands upon them and he healed them."

People watched in wonder. King Charles remained within the coach, a serious look upon his features, seeming to stay closeted within as much as he could. As the visitor continued to kneel, a flurry of activity ensued while a guard hurried around those assembled, until someone was found with a golden angel coin for the diseased man, in order to finish the ritual.

Charles stood speechless during the improvised ceremony, astounded to see the awesome spectacle, and it served only to heighten his awareness of the King's powers and nearness to God. At that, the man stood, looking ecstatic, shouting loyal proclamations in his wild, unrestrained joy. Charles noticed the abscesses and a tinge of blue colouring on the man's neck; no wonder he was happy, for he had managed to get the King to touch him and this would cure the scrofula.

Resuming their journey, they wound their sluggish way through the streets, people mostly being silent, puzzled at the royal trip. As it progressed, some men shouted their suspicions of the military band, and a lot followed behind them, anxious to see where the end of the journey would lie.

On reaching Westminster, the monarch and his nephew eventually alighted and made their way up the steps. Hadleigh ordered the guards to follow, and Charles frowned with disbelief as they headed for the House of Commons, his earlier hunch confirmed. The progress had taken an age, the journey betraying nothing of the original urgency.

He followed Hadleigh to the front and had a good view of the King, who betrayed no worry, and calmly walked as though he were going to open Parliament, not to make arrests. His overbearing and ruthless stance was a reminder of his early days as King, times which most thought would never surface again. The pages cast open the huge doors into the chamber and Charles used his advanced position to see the many faces of members looking out in bewilderment, some pale, some shaking their heads. Almost all, though, were united in a telling silence that this visit was completely unwelcome.

The King entered nevertheless with his nephew, and Charles watched as the young Lord Roxborough held the doors fully open for the soldiers to see inside, and for the members to observe this. He caught sight of some of the guards lifting their pistols, as though ready to fire into the chamber.

"Lower those weapons, you fools," Charles snapped, though Hadleigh cut him off from continuing the rest of the scolding.

"Nay, let them have their fun. There are none but rogues inside who could do with a lesson about loyalty," Hadleigh said with a wave of his hand.

Chapter 51

The King removed his hat in respect as he entered the chamber, his gaze falling immediately upon the three huge windows at the opposite end, and then dropping to the high back of the Speaker's chair, mounted with the royal arms. Walking into the chamber and seeing the sight before him was unique, for it was always the monarch who summoned Parliament to them. He felt silently confident that he had the advantage in public support, strength and moral right; strong because of this dramatic action that would remove the main catalysts behind the riotous behaviour in his capital.

Undoubtedly, this would end everything. The radical steps that Parliament were taking bolstered his view that *he* was the last hope for saving the ancient laws, the church and his people, from the insolent few he was about to seize.

He nodded to some of the members he recognised, careful to make sure he was as graceful as possible with such an unprecedented visit. Most stood with hats off, so quiet that you could only hear the King's footsteps echo in tune with his nephew's.

The royal eyes darted to the right of the chamber. He saw an empty seat and his heart sank.

Pym had gone.

Doubts played havoc with his confidence after such an unexpected result. Who had tipped the rogue off? Where was the man and what would he do next? For a few crucial seconds he stood still. He was determined to show none of his true feelings, and resumed his journey to the speaker, nodding at other familiar characters, though so many were packed into this space, that he found it hard to focus clearly on any individual.

"Mister Speaker, I must for a time make bold with your chair," the sovereign told his personally chosen representative in the House of Commons.

Speaker Lenthall quickly stood, the prominent bone structure and features as washed out as his ability to keep control of the house. Nevertheless, the hesitating, fifty year old stepped down for his master.

The King mounted the steps, taking centre stage near the chair.

He leaned his walking cane forward, before addressing all the members, "Gentlemen, I am sorry to have this occasion to come unto you."

As he tried to make eye contact with as many as he could, he searched out another of his targets, Sir Arthur Haselrig. The man was not here either.

"Gentlemen, you must know that in cases of t-treason no man hath a p-privilege and therefore I am come to know if any of those p-persons accused are here."

The chamber remained silent and King Charles felt anger well up inside. This was openly scorning him and he would not have it - he had stomached such insolence for too long.

He addressed the Speaker, whom he had promoted last year, an unassuming man from Henley on Thames, who crucially would not try to seek glory.

"Are any of these persons in the house? Mister Pym, Sir Arthur Haselrig and the rest?"

Lenthall dropped to his knees before him, the question finally sapping all of his resolve. The very action took King Charles aback.

"I humbly beg Your Majesty's pardon, but I have neither eyes to see nor tongue to speak in this place, but as this house is pleased to direct me, whose servant I am here."

Feeling irate, as he always did when his authority was challenged, he was impelled to correct Lenthall, and remind him he was the monarch's own representative, but he held his tongue, mastering his emotions even now. Three hundred little kings were here, compared to a single lawful one; To cowardly bow down to the majority was nothing surprising from this little worm. All too late he realised it had been a great mistake to choose Lenthall for the post.

"T'is no matter, I t-think my eyes are as g-good as any others," the King announced, as he cast his glare along the rows of wooden benches, examining member after member.

His eyes darted to the gallery above the door through which he had entered, hoping the men were up there. It was not to be, so he sat down in the chair, anxious not to be seen to flee, though the faces that now peered back at him in wonder of his next actions, were changing to reflect anger. Realisation had settled with the dust from his soldier's short march.

"By the word of a King, I never did intend any force, but shall proceed against them in a legal and fair way, for I do not mean any other."

Digby had advocated apprehending them from their beds during the night, but he had refused such desperate, unceremonious action. Then the Queen's words rang out in his head, warning him she would leave him if he did not come here today to drag them out of Parliament. If only he had stayed firm and listened to his own mind.

Instead, all of the targets had escaped, and he was left in the garb of a tyrant, who had attempted to subvert Parliament.

After what seemed like an age, he dismissed thoughts of Pym and started thinking out his sentence. "I see all my birds have flown. I trust you will send them unto me on their return, for their treason is foul."

With his nephew in tow, the King stood and made for the exit as tempers began to rise behind him. Some shouted after him and as he walked past the golden mace, the symbol representing the monarch in the house, he experienced a deep humiliation.

"Privileges, privileges," a mounting chant began.

The King could not restrain his anger and frustration any further and his pace grew even faster than normal.

Chapter 52

Charles opened his eyes. They stung. He was glad to get back into the house last night after the attempted arrest of Pym and his henchmen. He could still not believe that the King had made such a public and poorly planned venture, which had the danger of losing all. In the cobbled streets it sounded like uproar and not on the normal scale, but much more intense. He grunted, swung his legs out of bed and quickly wrapped himself in his cloak. People rampaged round below. He gasped, for he had never seen as much intensity in the protests as the thousands that had merged together overnight. He felt this was the climax.

"God damn it. Why did the King have to do that?" he whispered to himself, in disbelief. It was everything the opposition could have wanted and enough to completely destroy the monarch's case - indeed, whoever advised it, must have been in the pay of Pym.

The mob outside held weapons of all sorts such as clubs, swords, old bits of furniture, and anything that could be wielded, with nothing but lust for blood and violence in their minds. They stopped everyone who passed by and the road was blocked completely with rubbish and chains. Large stones had been gathered and were taken into houses, creating makeshift fortresses, and Charles guessed they would later be launched via the upper windows. This was England, which until recently had enjoyed nearly a decade of peace - the actions now could have fooled anyone, so warlike were they.

He hurried downstairs, nearly tripping over himself, and took the wooden chest, putting the valuables and necessities inside, before shouting for Louise.

She rushed inside from the kitchen, panicking. "Sir Charles, I am here."

"Pack Anne and Henry's things for me, they are to leave tonight," he snapped.

"But, sir ..."

"I have instructed you, Louise, I am your master."

Obediently but somewhat reluctantly, she gathered clothes from the cupboard, while he went to speak to Anne, who held her hand out as she lay in bed.

"I must ask you to do something for me; I dearly wish I did not have to ..."

She interrupted him, "Come over here."

He sat down and she eased his cloak off.

"Come back to bed."

He caught the cloak falling from his shoulders, and though he wished to oblige, the very fact he put his cloak back on alerted her sharp senses.

"I think it would be better now that you and Henry leave the City, for things have deteriorated."

More noise and commotion came from outside and he got up and went to the window, Anne following with a sheet wrapped around her.

"God's wounds."

"What, my love? You know what they are like; this has

happened before," she reminded as she put her arms around his neck.

The hundreds of people outside were hurriedly pulling benches across the roads, or tightening the chains that spanned the street, like they were throttling someone. They looked fired up and united. Anger radiated off each one of them, and it was abundantly clear to him that these men and women were taking matters into their own hands with one subtle difference - they felt they had a superior moral authority now, and all the allegations and slurs had been instantly proved by the King's latest action.

"That is why I need to know you are safe in the country."

She gasped. "Are there armies?"

"There would be if they had their way. I believe this alone will cause them to rise up in revolt. You know what someone called me the other day?"

Watching fixatedly at the mass panic below, he waited for her reply.

"Cavalier, they called me a cavalier," he said indignantly.

"What is that?" she asked with a slight hint of humour.

"It is not a compliment, you know. It is means a longhaired, marauding Spanish horseman, who is attracted to the ways of Catholics."

The frown told him she did not fully see the significance.

"They call those who support Parliament, Roundheads, because they say they are mostly Puritans, who wear their hair cut short and look ridiculous. The names are no importance, but it shows that the country is brutally dividing down the middle. Now that is dangerous and there will be no turning back - I think we are heading for civil war."

"No, Charles. It is near two hundred years since such a conflict. That is impossible," she replied unconvinced.

Outside, women were even helping take large cauldrons of boiling water to the roofs and upper storeys of houses, ready to pour on the anticipated Catholic army they howled about, which it was claimed would be headed by the King and Queen.

"I am insistent, please, my dear."

She took tightly hold of him. "I cannot leave you, Charles. Why should I be forced to part from you, just because of your paranoia?"

"I have never seen them like this since all the trouble broke out. I can tell in their faces that they are baying for blood. It is but a matter of time before this city erupts into terrible violence," he bluntly warned her.

"I beg you, I would suffer more in the country worrying for you," she pleaded, shaking him in an attempt to change his mind.

He kissed her and gently stroked her cheek. "I adore you. My nerves are shattered with worry for you and Henry. London is going to implode."

With tears ready to spill over from her eyes, they embraced again. He felt himself relenting. Perhaps they could get through this together?

"Well Henry has to go, and he needs you to take him, so there is no alternative."

She paused, finding some room in this statement. "Then I shall, but I will return afterwards and we will both stick with each other. That is our strength," she reassured him.

Charles stood still as he continued to watch, mesmerised by the reactions and pondering the predictions about civil war.

The very words felt as though they had travelled to every nerve ending, tensing each muscle in his body with terror. Then he asked himself the inevitable question; whether he was still for his King? Parliament constantly went too far and he was adamant that he would put his wholehearted support behind the monarch. This was the only way to even the imbalance and restore normality, he was sure, weighing up all the appeasements the monarch had made so far.

Then a flash shone out as a huge bonfire was lit to keep the crowds warm, finally showing signs of being subjugated to basic human needs. The flames that engulfed the wood and burned high into the air all but mimicked the tense city that, no doubt, would shortly be set alight too. A muffled bang pealed out and he scoured the area for the source, catching sight of a man with a musket, who had fired it through a window. The lunatics were piling inside the house and some dragged a person out along the ground, shouting and cheering as they did so.

Next an impatient rapping sounded at the door and he went to answer it - he had forbidden Louise to do so. With a pistol in the hand hidden behind the door, he snatched it open, to see a handful of men looking at him and the house.

"Yes?" he snapped, without any mask to his thoughts.

"Which church do you go to, sir?"

He frowned at the question. "The same damn church as him," Charles said, pointing at one of the men who he recognised from Sunday services.

The men eyed the individual as though questioning the answer, and he nodded his agreement to Charles's assertion.

Behind them, other groups were finding ways to cause trouble, making more fires in the middle of streets, or guarding the water conduit and only letting certain people get supplies for their households.

"And will you protect the glorious Parliament, who safeguard our liberties?"

Before he could reply, and anxious to pacify them while Anne and Henry were still in the house, someone screamed out from behind him, "The King is at tyrant, the devil take him."

Amazed at the comment, he saw Arabella being calmed by Louise. As he looked back at the men, they beamed smiles of satisfaction and went towards another house. He slammed the door as Louise bustled Arabella into the eating room, while Anne called him to the window to point out a scuffle outside.

Worst of all - it was the sixth of January, Twelfth Night, but the Christmas celebrations and traditional parties were a world away. Louise had found buying food a challenge, as most of the shops had closed. As he observed the situation with Anne, a howl pierced the biting air; a dog was being stoned.

"His owner attends Mass, I have seen him," a faint cry could be heard from outside.

"The Catholics are little more civilised than this scrawny animal."

He eyed the sight with sorrow for the animal and frustration for the reasoning behind the violence, holding his head deep in thought. Arabella the maid entered and caught his attention.

"What is it?" he asked gruffly, still surprised by her opinions.

"Well we were wondering if you still wanted ye cakes an' things for tonight, sir?"

He laughed sarcastically. "Nay, we will have the cake, but you may take the rest for yourself. Though I am sure you will not want it, my dear, for the King paid for it through my wage from being in his guards," he commented stingingly.

Arabella was just about to hurry to the kitchen to tell Louise of their good inheritance, not at all bothered by what he thought of her, but he called her back.

"What were you ranting about back there?" he demanded, coming to the point.

She glared at him and Anne stepped over, making him suspect something more was going on.

"I spoke the truth. I have no reverence for a King who wishes to butcher all the true Protestants of this country," she replied impertinently.

"How dare you speak to me like that," he yelled, as Anne took his arm, stopping him from approaching her.

"Arabella, go and see to my packing with Louise," Anne ordered, taking a clearer approach.

As the maid left, she muttered rudely and he was sure he

heard her tell him what he could do with his food, but as usual, Anne was a calming influence as she held him.

"If I had not got better things on my mind, girl, you would be out of that door without a penny to your name."

Anne picked their son out of the cradle, holding him to her breast.

"Oh, Charles, stop worrying about her damned opinion. I care nothing for the King either when I think of our son; taking him to your sisters will tear me apart."

The child began crying too, absorbing his mother's anguish over the forthcoming journey to Lucy's. Charles grimaced and held them both, realising the complete truth of her heartache.

Her breathing was erratic, as though she had shed every tear in her body, and every so often she would make a noise as she inhaled sharply. He whispered to her to get ready to leave, because the coach would soon be here, but her grip on the child remained strong.

"Please?" he asked.

"You may as well kill me, do you want that?" she cried, shooting her words to his heart. The red eyes and tears that sped down her face got lost within the sorrowful expression, making his own distress come to the fore. Rubbing his head, he felt as though the combined upset of his wife, son, two servants and his extended family and friends were all bearing down upon his soul.

"I will take him to Lucy's, see he gets there safely but I will return here tomorrow, and you will not stop me," she vowed, wounding him with the defiant words.

"I wrote days ago telling her to expect you, ever since I received those mysterious orders from Hadleigh, but I did not explain why, for I do not want the clergyman knowing my sympathies when he reads the letter out to her."

Anne ignored him and left the room, so he hurried after her. Louise had warned that the carriage was here. Then he spotted it further up the road, the blockades proving effective, and he felt completely barred from Anne too. She was quickly making towards it, glaring at the coach, ignoring everything around her.

Gone were the rainfall of tears, now replaced with an expression of warning to those who may try to interrupt her course.

Stopping beside the larger back wheels, they finally glanced at each other.

For some time their gazes locked together, opening up a silent communication channel, with Anne's pupils dilating and softening the intensity of the situation. Then without a word, they embraced each other, a passionate kiss betraying an eventual realisation that their reactions to one another simply served to highlight the love.

Then standing as though round a graveside, he stroked Henry's cheek, who looked at the sights the street had to offer. Charles kissed him and whispered a prayer.

"Protect him, Mother, please watch over our child for us," he begged as he passed him over.

"Come on, sir, we need to leave now," the coachman called.

"Our hands and hearts with one consent hath tied this bond till death prevent," he uttered, repeating the words engraved within the band of her wedding ring, before taking hold of her for one last time.

Tugging her gently back to him, he told her, "I will ever love you with all my heart. No violence would change that."

She was shaking slightly as he let her go, but with a gritty determination about her presence, and this reassured him.

Before delay could jeopardise this journey, or his own resolve gave out, he thumped the carriage and it drove away. Her hand was raised, and he watched until every bit of it, both sight and sound, disappeared out of view.

"I will lay my life down to protect you both," he said, as tears ran down his cheeks and he spun around, heading back home.

Chapter 53

Back inside the house, Charles tugged at the brass handle of the oak chest of drawers, taking a small box from it, before slumping into a chair. As he lifted the lid, the candlelight created an alluring sparkle with the contents, reacting with the rich metal of a gold ring. It was emblazoned with a red ruby, so beautiful that it held his attention for some time. This was meant to be a special present for Anne at Christmas, which he would have given in front of all their guests for Twelfth Night. Now, he realised the devastating effects of the country's descent down the slope of anarchy. He struggled with his decision to send them away, but thought that at least they were safe, and resolved to send a speedy message after Anne, instructing her to stay with Lucy too.

Louise brought through the fruitcake and he groaned sorrowfully at the appetising creation.

"You have not eaten, sir, we feel you should at least have a slice of this."

"We?" he questioned, disbelieving the gesture was associated with Arabella.

"Sir, she did not mean to offend you; she is headstrong.

510

I have no such opposition to your employment in the King's Guard, or your sympathies with him. But then I am not being courted by a man who is firmly in favour of the Parliament."

A faint smile of appreciation crossed his face and he nodded at Louise, taking a piece of cake. Biting into it, he spat something out.

"It is a bean, which means I am King for the night. How ironic, it is the hardest time to be in such a position too," he commented, finding some distraction out of the old tradition.

Then he remembered how James had once got the clove, meaning he was the villain.

Louise glanced at him, and he instantly knew the ideal way to exercise his regal powers.

"I order you enjoy this cake with Arabella and then retire for the night. God bless you, Louise."

With the heart shaped handles, he moved the brazier closer. It was smouldering like his resolute feelings, and he formulated the defence of the house, now that this was his sole concern.

The atmosphere continued to be interrupted by the multitude outside, much to his immense frustration. Earlier, he had ordered Arabella and Louise to fix the wooden shutters over the insides of the windows. They normally used them to keep out the cold draughts at night, but they had the added attraction of blocking out some of the noise from the desperate multitude outside.

He pulled up a floorboard near the corner of the room and put the ring into the small hole under it, along with the other gold and jewellery. Then he laid two flintlock pistols on the table, close at hand, before hanging his sword over the chair back. The guns were state of the art, the mechanism just over ten years old, and there was something ornate and fine about the polished wood and crafted brass barrel, pointing out like a small cannon. After a while, both servants tapped at the open door again.

"Thank you for the cake, sir. Forgive us for taking the liberty to ask, but what will happen?" Arabella said boldly, forgetting his earlier displeasure as she was always wont to do.

"Civil war is the only result, but that all depends on the actions of those out there. Shops close, people cannot travel around with the barricades in the street. All we can do is wait and hope."

The two females looked at each other; Arabella hankering for more detail, and a different answer, while Louise's expression of 'didn't I tell you so' confirmed her more mature grasp of the situation.

Charles sighed sadly. "I will do my best for you both while this crisis ensues though, be sure of that. But mark my words, Arabella, you will not repeat your earlier disrespectful behaviour if you wish to remain here."

As they curtseyed, he instructed them both to stay in the small garret at the top of the house tonight, because of the proceedings outside. He was sure that it would be a matter of time before their house was ransacked, especially if they were stirred with information about his mission to Strafford, the post in the royal guards, or the fact he had turned down that offer of a sea captain's position from Parliament. He thought about all of his neighbours, the man next door being a good friend, and decided to check up on old Jack.

He slipped out after telling the servants of his movements, locking the door behind him, and knocked on his neighbour's. Once he answered, with the usual friendly greeting, Charles stepped into the hall, staying on the perimeter of the building, so as to provide quick access back to his own abode. The narrow passage was like a mysterious portal into Tudor England, every inch of the wood panelling carved with cherubs, fruit or flowers, while a portrait of a matronly lady in widow's weeds glared at the newcomer to the place. Needless to say, Jack had several wall mountings with candles at various points to light up this oak tunnel, like it was the interior of one of those great trees itself, travelling to the roots of England's heritage.

"Sir Charles, thank God we have not gone mad too. If it was not for those living around me, this city would be the bleakest place on earth."

Charles put his hand on Jack's arm. "I brought you this, should you need to defend yourself. Carry it at all times, my friend," he advised, as he handed over a small knife that could be kept discreetly on his person.

"Thank you for the kind thought. The Arrowsmiths were telling me of their trouble with those dogs only yesterday."

Charles shook his head, but it was nice to see the neighbours were still keeping in touch outside of the weekly Sunday gathering at Church.

"Well it is sad we will not be visiting each other for Twelfth Night parties," Jack added.

"Aye, but you are welcome anytime you wish. Just knock if you need me. In fact, I would gladly have you stay with me until this trouble is over," Charles told him.

"Oh, you are all so kind - even Mister Cole over the road has sent some homemade food round the doors. I will not let that mob force me out of my own home though. I will die here if needs must, for I have been here forty years. I see you have sent your good lady away."

Charles nodded. "I cannot have her jeopardised. After the slipshod attempted arrests in Parliament, this lot are ravenous for blood. I will keep an eye open on your safety, Jack," he predicted, as he bid the man good night.

The street was full, like a giant party flooding between the houses. The back alleys acted as narrow fords to this river of people, even children, while all semblance of business, work, time and chores slipped away.

Back home, he was about to try to snatch a few hours sleep when muffled shouts outside alerted his tired senses.

He jumped up, casting the woollen blanket off him, staring at the small brazier that held a delicate, almost shadowy remains of a log. He listened hard. Stampeding drew him to the door and he waited, hearing tales of armies and soldiers apparently coming to overrun the protesters. Then he heard a pounding, followed by the noise of running, as bangs continued to echo out. Impelled to answer the door, he felt the bustle of the crowd flood into his abode as he opened the dam.

"Up to arms, my friend, there are troops to come against us," a fellow insisted, waving his hands around to emphasise the point.

The man ran on, imploring people to be ready to fight off the approaching army. Near enough fifty others sped after him to add to the cajoling, jostling as though it was a race.

"Sign our petition against the use of force upon honest citizens."

He duly added his name with the offered feathered quill, simply because he felt that no matter who a man supported, everyone should wish to keep innocent lives safe. Charles was just going back inside when he glimpsed one scruffy person pointing at him, speaking to a group nearby. The face was hauntingly familiar.

It took barely a few seconds to remember it from the battle he and his men had outside Parliament, when they were converged upon by hundreds of protestors.

Quickly retreating into the house, he bolted the door, first thoughts being for the maids and their safety. Wedging a sturdy chair against the handle, he stood listening again - through the din, he could hear voices.

"That is the home of Sir Charles Berkeley, a notorious King's man."

The reply was drowned out.

"He is no better. I say he pays for his misjudged support."

"Aye, his status does not protect 'im now, after sidin' with tyranny. He be in the King's own guards, went with the King to seize Mister Pym."

He heard the maids talking in the kitchen and ran down the hallway, bursting into the room in front of Louise.

"I told you both to go upstairs, now get to it."

"Sorry, sir?"

"Do it, immediately," he barked as he raced back out. Grabbing his pistols as he went, he pushed one into his breeches, hanging his sword belt around his shoulder. Then he heard a crash as glass shattered, resonating from the dining chamber. He hurried to investigate, shards crushing beneath his shoes, and against the polished wooden floor.

A stone had hit the table next to the smashed window, though the piece had rebuffed the mortar, leaving only scratches and dents.

He drew a pistol and ran to the broken glass. It was the middle panel of the three that had smashed, and a chill chased through the room.

"That's a warnin' you hear me, you royalist bastard. He is in the King's Guard, that man just told me."

He clapped eyes on Cotton nearby.

"You - I might have known," he bellowed, bringing the pistol down onto the stone frame to take aim.

Soon, he heard the door being kicked, and missiles flew into the house, a flaming torch being thrust through the remains of the window. Charles leaped out of the way, before grasping at the base, but fire had took hold of the rug, turning the rich red, yellow and blue patterns to black. No sooner had he flung the danger back out, than several others landed in replacement, and he let a shot off to repel them from sending more. The plume of smoke from the pistol was soon lost in the heat and clouds of the flames. He was desperate, more so than he had ever been. It was his worst nightmare and now it was actually happening.

Taking hold of the heavy oak table, he turned it over with difficulty, letting it fall flat on top of the burning mat to put out the flames. The impact echoed on the wooden floor and the candelabras clanged as they scattered all over. The dull thud struck to his very core, sending a faint tremor around the room. Then the door imploded with a crash and a group of men raced inside with Cotton at their head, his doublet open. Charles was breathless and sweating profusely, but ruthlessly propelled himself on. The last flamed projectile caught a chair and once some of the flames found such rich pickings as the velvet cover, they soared into angry, intense fires. It was rapidly spreading, growing like the anger of this mob. The heat burned onto his body, but in his rigorous defence of his home, he only faintly noticed it, the sensation being overtaken immediately with his determination to fight the intruders off.

"You whoremonger, Berkeley, I have waited for this moment. You are ruined; you chose the King, the wrong side, so you must face the consequences. I have proof this man helped Strafford," Cotton shrieked. His resentment and hatred had increased, even after he had released some anger by taking revenge on Charles with his brief imprisonment.

The burning chair was getting worse and Charles kicked it, upturning it, before he ruthlessly stamped on it, taking several blows to crush it.

Now the mutilated hand of his old enemy held up a piece of paper, the wound no longer hidden, and Charles raised his other pistol and let a shot out again, hoping to take the whole limb this time. Cotton collapsed to the ground, squirming in pain, grasping his arm and holding it close as if it was a baby.

He ran over and took the paper that had dropped with him - the other intruders behind were momentarily stunned.

The scrap was a forged note from Charles to Digby, with a bad imitation signature. The dog had been crafty with his time - if he could not get the real thing, he would make it up, just like Pym.

Cotton managed to get a strained cry out, even though he was still winced up in agony. Charles threw the message into the flames, anxious to exterminate this matter once and for all.

As the surprise faded, the men who had followed Cotton came towards Charles, and he noticed the wounded pile on the floor struggle, pushing himself up in spite of his wound. During this action, the man glared, jaw firm with determination as he withstood the pain.

Then Cotton produced a blade at the last moment. "This is going to come to you first, and then I will share it with your son," he yelled, after he had launched himself at Charles.

Turning away, with no time to defend himself, Charles felt a piercing pain in the side. He grasped at the area and then examined his hand to see blood seeping through his fingers.

Cotton set on him again and Charles held his wrist, pushing the point away from him. The men were locked together, shaking as they battled to repel each other, and Charles managed to force the blade sharply towards Cotton's chest, though only slicing at his shirt before he jumped away. Charles managed to temporarily grab his collar, before losing the grip. Now a golden glow shone onto the portrait of him and Anne, and quickly yanked it from the wall. Leaping onto the desk to escape everyone, he crouched somewhat, facing away from the blaze, which had silently and maliciously caught the curtains.

"Quiet," he bellowed to the crowd.

They ignored him, so he drew his sword and shouted at the top of his voice. The effect was a bloodcurdling cry, which made his vision change momentarily, and caused his temper to soar. Still nobody reacted to him, but Cotton stood motionless for a split second. Charles's hands trembled and a sting shot through him, body tensing together with the sensation that his nerves and arteries had been jerked hard.

Then he saw something from within Cotton's ripped shirt and recognised the rosary beads. He pointed his sword at the man and howled again. The crowd retaliated with some bawling of their own, until Charles bellowed about the Catholic within their midst - this attracted enough attention to draw the focus to his sword end, and then bewilderingly to Cotton. The man realised at the last moment and his hands went to his neck in a defensive reflex, but the sight of such an iconic Papist object ignited the mob, acting in the same way as the flint sparking the gunpowder in Charles's pistol.

"Nay, we have a true enemy to us all, a Catholic," Charles exclaimed, seizing the opportunity.

Those who had not already seen Cotton's reaction, or the religious object, soon caught on.

"This man is a Papist, he comes to murder us all and he has tried to start with me. He must take all Protestants for fools."

Charles pointed at his wound, holding up his bloodied hand.

"I have a Protestant wife and son, and he wants to kill them. Are your family safe from these Papist bastards?"

"Hang him."

More and more people chanted as the crowd erupted.

Cotton tried in vain to stem this rising tide of hatred. "He is bluffing, he is a King's man. He is your enemy, not me. This man helped Strafford and the devil."

Charles felt nothing but revulsion. He wanted to slice his enemy's neck, relishing the bulging eyes and terrified expression.

"I swear to you, I saw him celebrating Mass. He knelt before the Virgin Mary and worships his dangerous faith right here in our city. He is the leader of a plot to massacre us all, just like the forty thousand in Ireland," Charles cried, playing on as much fear as he could in one sentence.

Cotton sprinted to the window, fear getting the better of

him, jumping out of it and slicing himself on the glass that remained, frantic to escape. He chose flight, rather than facing the accusations, and most men turned and left the house to give chase, while a handful of others ran to the window.

Charles glared at Cotton and threw his head back, letting out a torrent of oaths, followed by laughter of relief and satisfaction.

It was scorching in the room now, like the fires of hell where Cotton would soon end up. Charles's shirt was soaked through, clinging to him pitifully. He gingerly struggled down from his elevated position, his injury causing great distress and initiating a chain of hurt throughout his body. Cotton was out of sight in the general mêlée by now, as Charles's adrenaline burst petered out.

"God be thanked, my family are saved from that devil," he vowed bitterly as he spun round to assess the fire. His erratic tackling of it had meant that the curtains, though long gone, were the main incendiaries, leading the fire to the wood panelled walls.

A cry pealed out from the street.

"They arrive; the King's Catholic army are upon us outside the city gates. Let us smash 'em."

The noise from the thousands of people was intense. Arabella's screams barely pierced the din as she ran into the room.

She trembled, crying hysterically and screeching at the fire and devastation, as though it had been the final straw, tipping her whole being over some precipice. Louise rushed in to comfort her, but was out of time, and Arabella fainted. As Charles raced over to them, a shot echoed out and he pulled Louise down to shelter. They lay staring at each other; Louise was determined and he admired her bravery, before quickly helped Arabella to her feet and out into the hall.

She was still shuddering after coming round, but deathly silent and her eyes were wide. Louise stayed with her, holding the girl's head to her chest, stroking the long auburn locks.

During the respite, Charles dragged some remaining furniture away from the wall, hoping to stop the spread of the fire, but soon realised that more was needed. The house was like a huge wooden tinder box, and by taking hold of the wall, the fire had already embedded its claws into the very fabric of the place. Mister Cole put a bucket of water to the destroyed window.

With a shout of appreciation, Charles grabbed it, throwing it at the newer flames, and then tugged the bookshelf time and again until that tipped over, attempting to keep it out of reach.

Books crashed all around him, fluttering around like birds, the cracking and roaring of destruction covering up a more welcome noise. Pitter patter gave way to a stream of rain, rattling down upon the house. Charles smashed the remaining two window panels and that section of the flames began hissing with disapproval. Some neighbours hurried in, and pails came down the line, full of sand or water. Other locals were visible in the rescue party, winding around the house like a lifebelt.

"They have cut open one of the lead water pipes," one man who lived further up the street shouted to him, "If your house goes, the whole of London could."

His wound sent a sharp pain through his whole body and he winced, dropping a bucket of sand. Water was cast time after time, with no apparent effect, until eventually the blaze began to subside in the face of a continuous onslaught. Standing breathless amid the devastation, he leaned forward, no strength to even stand straight, aware of excruciating discomfort.

He ripped his doublet off, shouting with the pain, and pulling his shirt up to examine his wound. It was deep, and only now did he realise the extent.

He cried out and grasped it tight, feeling his legs give way as the red smouldering objects, yellow flames and black charred wood swirled around in his eyes. He whispered Anne's name as he hit the floor.

Chapter 54

When he woke up, Charles was in bed, with Anne standing over him. Though she was an angel to him, he knew he had not died in that split second of consciousness.

"The fire?" he yelled.

As he sprang forward, he grasped his head, which throbbed like an exploding cannon.

"Charles, it's fine," she reassured, taking hold of him.

"Anne, what are you doing here?"

"I arrived a little while ago and it is a good job too. Mistress Arrowsmith helped me tend to your wound."

He stared for a second and she tried to ease his body back, but he was rigid.

"Henry?" he shouted in uncontrolled panic.

"We made it to Lucy's, but I wanted to return immediately. I felt sure you'd be commanding me to stay, so I wouldn't wait around to receive such an order. Now, lie there and I will get some water."

"I cannot. What is the house like? Is it secure?"

She looked at him and struggled to keep her tears back.

"Bloody idle apprentices," he shouted, tears rolling down his cheeks, especially due to seeing her sorrow.

"Charles, you may be master of the house, but in the name of God lie back. Will you rest, you stubborn man?"

Her oath, unusual as it was, caused him to stop and he let out a large sigh as he looked at her, laying his hands on each cheek and kissing her passionately. That tender, loving connection was enough to highlight just what was not lost, and would never be. They embraced, intensely relieved to have each other so close once more. Then after a while, he went to move, but grimacing at the discomfort in his side, he shouted out. He tugged his shirt away to reveal the deep cut; it brought back anger over Cotton, until he remembered how he had been set upon by the mob.

"Cotton is dead, I am sure," he growled, relieved again at the fact, and anxious to tell Anne, adding the positive news.

Without replying, she gently tried to wash his wound, but he resisted and forced himself out of bed, despite the injury, to limp downstairs with her following after him. The black remains of furniture and burned books littered the room, the wall panels a mixture of charred blackness, or wizened. The room was freezing from the broken window, and a smell of smoky firewood remained to haunt the senses. He felt utterly destroyed and let down by those who pretended to aim for freedom, but in fact only wished to cause chaos and revolution in the name of Parliament.

"The picture, did it survive?"

She did not reply. He bellowed for Louise and she ran into the room.

"The painting, where is it? I remember I took it off the wall."

Louise turned to Anne with a look of anguish.

"We have been looted last night; they took some things which Lou could not secure, my love. The constable did not want to tackle the group, so she found Lord Dorset's horsemen, and it was them that finally managed to scatter the thieves."

Taking hold of each side of the doorframe to stabilise his body, he yelled at the top of his voice, "Where is law and order? Is this what they call safeguarding our liberties from the King?"

"Lieutenant Colonel," a call was heard.

Charles looked up to see Colonel Hadleigh and some other officers from the King's Guard.

"I heard about your terrible news. I just want to tell you that the King is leaving London for now, but is extremely saddened by your treatment."

"Leaving, but why, sir?" he gasped, feeling disheartened that the monarch seemed to be fleeing in the face of those outside, who would see it as victory.

"Surely you of all people will understand that, judging by this mess? His family are targets; the attempted arrest has made heroes of Parliament and he has lost a mammoth section of support. Pym and his men could easily take over control of the city now and then he would be a pawn to them. They already issue edicts to be accepted as law, without the King's lawful consent. What else can he do?"

Charles paused and then realising that his thoughts, worries and motives right now were exactly the same as the King's, he made a resolution. For once, he actually felt as though he knew the monarch's situation personally, understood what was motivating him and how he was feeling, and he glanced at Anne.

"When does he travel?"

"Tonight, by water. It is to be quick and discreet and we head for Hampton Court."

"Where can we meet you?" he asked, after Anne's faint nod gave him sanction, before her gaze fell to the floor.

"The King will not stop, but I will tell Major Fanshaw to halt outside the city gates and wait there; the main body of guards are to march to Hampton Court. He shall wait for fifteen minutes. Be there by ten of the clock."

As Hadleigh departed, Charles looked once more to Anne, explaining that it was the only thing left to do. Knowing she understood sealed his determination to go with the monarch.

He felt sure they would be safer and better off there. After all, most of his enemies had declared for Parliament and he was damned if he would stay in the midst of this anarchy.

"What of Henry?" she quickly demanded.

"Is he better off with Lucy, or should we take him on all our journeys? I do not even know where we will end up," he thought aloud.

"And the house?" she asked, raising her hands in despair.

He did not care about the house. "What is left will be here when we get back. We can leave Arabella and Louise."

Anne kept her gaze on him.

"What now?" he asked, sensing something more.

"Arabella left us yesterday. She said her husband did not approve of your political leanings. She stole some of my clothes as she went, according to Lou."

"What? When was I going to be told? I deal with the servants of this house," he reminded her bitterly.

"You were in no fit state since last night, and still would not be if it was not for me caring for you, and trying to persuade you to have more common sense," she told him plainly.

"I will make sure she does not serve again. How dare she steal from me after all I have done. Have I not been a fair master?"

She sighed. "You can only influence a certain group of this city now. Arabella will get employment from a Parliamentarian, where court influence does not matter."

"Have you been to that tailors again? You know more of this battle than me. It is only after gossiping in there for hours that you come back so enlightened."

"Just get us out of this city for a while until tempers calm," she demanded, showing this inner strength that she reserved for the very worst of times.

He rubbed his hand down the stubble on his jaw and neck.

"I am sorry," he said softly.

She stepped slowly towards him and he took her hands in the same way they had done on marriage, hearts beating out the agreement for better or worse.

"My love, I cannot find words to describe how proud I am of the way you have coped and managed this situation while I was out of it."

"Your prophesy about civil war - it is happening, is it not?" she asked, trembling slightly.

Hesitating out of a wish that it was not true, he finally nodded. "Like the King, I fear for my family, so we must go with him. He is the one who has law on his side after all of this."

"Giving so great a blessing as [God] hath now done to the resolute and unwearied endeavours of our soldiers fighting for Him in the maintenance of His truth ... and in the defence of their liberties and the Privileges of Parliament."

Quote from the Parliamentary account of the
Battle of Edgehill
OCTOBER 1642

Chapter 55

The fifty one year old Earl of Essex, Captain-General of Parliament's forces, sat within his canvas tent. His coffin and winding sheet, which would accompany him wherever the march of the army should take him, had recently arrived in the camp. Just then, his Lieutenant General of horse, Sir William Balfour, appeared at the entrance and bowed his head.

"Come in, Sir William," Essex said, with a casual wave of his hand.

He sat back in his chair with a groan, before taking a sip of some fine wine and invited Balfour to partake of a glass.

"What news of the King?" he asked.

"They are coming off the hill and redeploying at the foot of it. Should we attack, my lord?"

Essex made a loud appreciation of the claret he had just sampled. "Nay, we have all the time in the world. I prefer not to attack first; let him do that and be charged with starting this war."

Balfour stood up straight, before letting out a laugh. Essex, for his part, smiled along, lighting up the rather plain and plump face. Having fought in Holland during his twenties, and then as a Vice-Admiral in a naval expedition, he had real experience of warfare, a subject in which a lot of the nobility were virgins. As such, he had been the main choice for this post. Ironically enough, a warlike and stolid reputation made up for his lack of prowess with the opposite sex.

Sir James Ramsey joined them, talking excitedly of the coming battle and his words of encouragement to the men.

"The squadrons of horse are interspersed with musketeers, as per your orders, my lord," Ramsey informed him.

With a nod to the footman, Essex caused another lot of wine to be poured for the newcomer.

"My men were full of courage and trust in God. I told them that the enemy were Catholics, Atheists and Irreligious persons for the most part."

When Ramsey asked whether they were to attack, Essex left Balfour to repeat his earlier thoughts. The three infantry commanders now entered the tent and gathered around Essex's desk. He stood up, taking a taper and igniting it in the candle, lighting his pipe with it. The candle seemed to burn away for that reason alone. He puffed away at the pipe, creating a plume of smoke around him, which was a trademark.

"Gentlemen. We have the biggest advantage on our side - time."

The gathering seemed to focus on the slow rhetoric, not expecting any miracles, or glorious words, but they knew he would have a sound tactical plan. He moved his tobacco off the badly drawn map he had sketched earlier and pointed to a large black square, badly coloured in with ink blotches from his quill.

"This represents our position. We have three regiments of foot, eleven troops of horse and seven field pieces on their way to reinforce us as we speak. The longer the King delays, the better."

The officers expressed agreement.

"He is after Banbury, but our location blocks him from assaulting it. We have Warwick Castle to our backs, a stronghold that will support us further. And finally, as Sir James pointed out, we have the Good Lord on our side."

The men cheered, with the jubilant Scot, Sir James Ramsey, downing his wine in one go.

"Order the men to pray for our success," Essex commanded, "I will be out presently to examine the positions."

The men bowed. Those who wore colourful apparel contrasted well with Essex's, but nevertheless, a sense of comradeship existed between everyone. They were sewn together by a belief that their religion would be forsaken by the King, and they would be turned back to Rome and Catholicism, should they not secure victory today - such a reason for fighting would lie heavily in the bellies of men like Essex; strict, devout Puritans especially.

As they left the tent, the noble called after them, "I will fight at the head of my army, pike in hand like a common soldier.

We battle as one for our belief and our God, not on behalf of an individual being."

Alone, Essex paced up and down the tent, each slow, meticulous step landing as closely in line with the last as possible.

He mulled over his plans. He had roughly fifteen hundred more infantrymen than the King, and nearly double the artillery. This was going to be his trump card, to be exploited, while he made the best of his outnumbered cavalry. He felt sure that the fractured command of the monarch - for he had heard about recent squabbles - would not work together efficiently. Indeed, spies told him that the King had made Price Rupert, Lieutenant General of the horse, independent of the Lord General, causing that commander to resign his post on the spot.

This reminded him of Rupert's imperious demand that he fight a duel to settle the whole matter, and laughed at it, before spluttering as he coughed from some inhaled tobacco smoke. His boy handed him a cloth.

"I used to be close to the King's brother. If he had lived and become monarch, I'll wager we would not be in this situation," he reminisced to the young lad.

Observing the boy, eagerly listening, he instantly dismissed him. He could not dwell upon children anymore, for that was a dream long gone. The King's father had designed a marriage for Essex, though the lady had an affair and later claimed he was impotent. His divorce was excruciating and embarrassing, especially for one who was the son of such a debonair, handsome and witty father as the second Earl of Essex who wooed Elizabeth the First, and eventually lost his head for organising a plot to overthrow her.

He walked outside and stood in the field, filling his lungs with the fresh air. Then, he fell back to his pipe and chatted to his attendants, intending to mount up and inspect the men.

"Westmore, I want more artillery on the left wing facing Rupert, not on our left."

No sooner had he issued that order, than a chorus of cheers and joyful chanting carried down the field with the breeze. He wheeled around and observed the royalist ranks, watching a scarlet flag travelling along the lines.

With his own men silent, about to sing hymns, and being beaten by the King to inspecting the men, Essex felt irritated.

He took his pipe and thrust it down upon a table near him.

"Prepare the artillery to give fire," he bellowed, in gruff, resolute tones.

Chapter 56

C harles sat impatiently on his great steed, one hand protectively stroking the rich, brown mane, uniting himself and his horse as they waited warily.

He searched the ranks of Parliamentarians to the northwest, small figures in the distance with the village of Kineton over a mile behind them. The weather was clear and bright, but a chill hung in the air, as if emanating from the enemy's stubborn opposition. Charles and the royal forces stood in the Vale of the Red Horse, Warwickshire, having descended three hundred foot from the ridge of Edgehill behind, following the enemies' refusal to attack such a strong position. The village of Radway nestled under Edgehill, close behind their lines. Their former post on top of the great slope was apt, considering the precipice of destruction the country continued to stand before; brought to the field of battle, would Englishmen kill their fellow countrymen? The red clay of the area seemed to weld to the hooves of all present, creating a reluctance to move, engage, or fire the first shot to start a pitched battle. Indeed, the twenty eight thousand men of both sides had been facing each other for over four hours, manoeuvring into final positions.

He was full of apprehension, and could not get comfortable in his saddle. Inactivity had ushered in terror, his legs tingling with nervous energy, as he stretched them.

"Three cheers for the King, gentlemen," bellowed one officer, as the order ricocheted from every ear, like a shot.

Charles sat upright, though inside, his heart was still sinking. He was repulsed by Parliament's attempts to claim full power from the King, or to change the religion, yet now he faced these 'Roundheads' he had little wish to fight them; if they were French, or Spanish it would be different.

At the height of the quarrel, he wondered whether they would treat and accept the power sharing, which should have come from the many concessions the King had made over the last two years. Another look at the distant, but great wall of men and beasts opposite made him pray that they would accommodate each other; his life was worth far more than a salary of forty five pounds per month.

"For God and King Charles," was the war cry of the day, finally moving his thoughts to less personal matters.

As he faced around, Charles looked through the ranks of the four hundred and fifty horsemen who made up the troops of Prince Rupert's lifeguard. The standard bearer for his troop dipped the colours forward as a mark of respect to the sovereign. Charles had been acquired by the young Prince, nephew of the King, who recognised the same qualities of honesty and dedication as his own. At that point, a huge, scarlet banner flapped into view, leading a column of the high command. Wealthy nobles as well as Prince Rupert and his brother, Prince Maurice, flanked the King and his two young sons, all riding towards the right wing of the army. Intense cries of joy, respect, and pride manifested itself, floating ghostlike across the seventeen hundred horsemen, making a welcome diversion to the earlier rush of nerves.

The vision of the King was a catalyst for their emotions, whose billowing black cloak twisted and turned to display its ermine lining, and gave the monarch an awesome air. Charles was imbued with a renewed sense of reason for opposing the Roundheads, determined that he was on the side of God and the law, with his monarch clearly ready to spill his own blood with them all in this true and just cause. Only now did the descent of his nerves begin to slow, stiffened by focus on the regal manifestation.

The King drew up in front of their lines and still the hollers and cries flowed, the only noise any man was capable of making anymore, such was the buzz of feeling that gushed through their bodies. But as the cheering eventually tailed away, the monarch began speaking to them and Charles was mesmerised by the words that he could faintly hear, or which were repeated by the officers. His hands shook slightly as they held his horse's reins, and any minute now, he felt that he would be impelled to gallop off, leading the men to the enemy. Anything was better than sitting still.

"Your conscience and your loyalty hath brought you here this day, to fight for your religion, your King, and the laws of the land. You shall meet with no enemies but traitors, who desire to destroy both church and state, and who have already condemned you to ruin for being loyal to us."

These words, which struck to the core of every man's soul, carried through their bloodstream to trigger every sensation, causing ructions of cheering and unadulterated emotion.

Charles's breathing was increasing, his eyes welling up for some time, finally forcing him to release his tension and liberate his own exclamation. Beneath his back and breast plate, cow hide buff coat, doublet and shirt, he was sweating though, jubilant chanting masking the apprehension and worry.

This release of feelings helped his frame of mind, whilst igniting loyalty and confidence, almost subconsciously preparing him for what was to come. He began loudly relaying the message to his men.

"Your King is both your cause, your quarrel and your captain, and come life or death, your King will bear you company, and ever keep this field, this place, and this day's service in his grateful remembrance."

Charles yelled again, now thinking of Anne, who was at the rear of the army, near the baggage train in their own coach. He had purchased it especially to house her as she accompanied the ever winding march of the King, from London to York, before racing back towards the capital, eventually coming across Parliament's forces here yesterday. This love for his brave wife was enough to seal his will to fight, for she had refused to leave his side. He would do her and the family proud with his actions. Despite trying to block it from his mind, thoughts of losing her created a terror that panicked him, bringing his own mortality into question.

The royal message was echoed around again, ensuring that none missed it. The King then continued on towards the ten thousand or so infantrymen in the centre, stretching off in a great line. The sight was magnificent, of dynamic proportions. With his present temperament, this gave Charles strength to see the sheer volume of comrades, and it was easy to miss the near equal length of Roundheads arrayed opposite them. He could only see the enemy's first few ranks, though it was clear they had more cannon and foot soldiers. His own comrades may have been heavier in cavalry and dragoons, but would this be an advantage that could secure victory?

Beyond the Royalist foot soldiers, and at the opposite end of the army, were near one thousand further horsemen, forming up the left flank. The mixture of uniforms and colours in the mass of bodies before him was like a patchwork quilt, interwoven and tied together with their loyalty to the figure who was now riding past to address them. He breathed deeply, anxious to retain some coherence. Despite his appetite deserting him long ago, he regretted not eating earlier when his men were tucking into their bread, cheese and beer, for now he felt the effects of an empty belly.

Then a rapport exploded into the atmosphere, reminding everyone that this was not a unified military parade, but two opposing forces come to fight. As the noise silenced the cheers of approval, Charles immediately looked towards the enemy, seeing a plume of smoke rising. The offending iron round shot then bounced into view, conveying more of a message than any amount of words ever could. It ricocheted off the ground, ploughing into the field near to the infantry, sods and dirt thrown into the air along with a handful of men. It took some minutes to comprehend the attack, proving the end of peace in England, and conjuring up the destructive, grisly spectre of civil war, which had lain at rest for nearly two hundred years.

A quiet stirring and unease was generated from the way the victims had been cast aside like toy soldiers, but also outrage that the Parliamentarians were firing at the King and his party, proving their hostility and downright treason, and adding weight to the King's allegations about them. Charles looked around him at his colleagues' reactions, the mass of cavalrymen and horses practically a blur to his frayed senses, before he sat up straight and glared warily ahead, anticipating the next volley.

He was sure that this would be the start of it all, completely impatient at being idle in the face of such danger. Was he to sit and wait for his head to be blown off, he muttered through gritted teeth. He pulled the visor down on his triple barrelled helmet. Sight of the King again made him think of Holland, who had aligned with the Roundheads, and then of Digby, who was thankfully stationed far away on the Royalist left wing.

He was sure the man was Parliament's secret weapon, for every reckless thing he advised so far had been enough to ruin the King without a single bullet being discharged.

With the propelling vision and drive of a cannonball, Prince Rupert was now dashing through the ranks of horsemen with his officers, exhorting them all to restrain from firing their pistols until they were in amongst the enemy. The giant, slim figure must have been about six foot four, sharp, clean cut features as piercing and demanding as ever. His confidence and knowledge began to be infectious; they had a leader who was committed to them and moreover, one who was capable. Charles focussed on the man and his orders, which restored discipline.

"Do not draw up before the enemy to discharge your weapons, but continue charging into them with swords drawn.

Once amongst them, firearms will be much more effective."

Following the King's ignition of the Royalist reply, judging from the position of the scarlet blanket that fluttered near the artillery, the duel lasted what seemed like hours. Of the six cannons in the artillery battery behind Charles, a pair of demi cannons launched huge twenty seven pound shot towards the enemy. Amidst this thunderous roaring, he steadied his unnerved mount. In an attempt to likewise reduce his own worry, he thought about the multitude of horses that had pulled the huge guns into place; twelve for one demi cannon alone.

At nearly three o'clock, following an age of pounding each other with round shot, and to little avail, the welcome blast of the trumpets sounded, melodiously ordering the right wing to advance. The complete change of tune from the warlike barrage of cannon sent a wave of urgency and readiness through all present. Now that the moment had arrived, Charles hesitated in almost disbelief, waiting for the colonel to move first. Then he squeezed his legs against his mount, walking it forward with the rest of the seventeen hundred cavalrymen of the wing, each step drawing upon every reserve of his willpower and courage, grasping the mantle of honour and discharging his duty.

A quick glance around confirmed that their wing was to launch the first attack, slowly leaving their army behind. He had expected as much, with fiery Rupert in command here. The small standards of the various regiments heralded their movement as they advanced, while he scoured the Roundhead formations, drawn up just over five hundred yards away. He sat rigid, fixated on the array.

Two dirt roads led the way to the Parliamentarians, striking through their ranks, and linking the two armies in the same way they brought together the villages of Radway and Kineton. The horses neighed and snorted as their heads moved forwards and backwards. The line advanced in good order, ready to take on the first few hurdles of ditches and hedges that were scattered over the expanse of countryside. Now, in alignment with the rest of his comrades, he gently kicked his mount with his heels, changing into a trot and trying his best to keep his own motion of rising and sitting with his beast. Still fixated on the lines of horsemen opposing them, little else entered his mind, after a brief prayer for Anne and Henry.

Opposing cannons blew off their indignation at this continuous, steady approach, causing his heart to race each time. A glance to the left gave sight of the Royalist left wing of horse beginning an advance, both flanks now leaving the infantry behind. Then the shout from various officers was a reminder to discharge pistols only when amongst the enemy.

"You must fire only when you are amongst the Roundheads," Charles cried, before drawing his sword with a scraping sound that merged with the mutual actions of so many.

The explosions and dull echoes of the enemy artillery in front had made him inhale sharply each time he heard them, the slow advance giving too much leeway to fear the worst.

He spotted the source of the missiles that flew overheard with an odd whistle. Three falcons were placed with the enemy wing, the field pieces spitting their deathly ammunition out.

With his attention focussed on the guns, he instinctively knew they could reach out as far as three hundred and twenty yards, given the right elevation.

He heard occasional cries of pain from around him; the few early victims of the coming carnage were blown off their horses, limbs either mangled and wrenched off, or bodies pierced by shot that would probably go on to gradually claim their lives as they lay in a pool of blood. Each horrifying shout forced him onwards - to repay comrades' bravery, safeguard his family and prove himself. Cowardice was a fate absolutely worse than death. His father had once told him that those who face danger survived, while those who hesitated were lost. In the midst of this chaos, his mind briefly recalled this unimportant fact.

Beneath his armour he was roasting, legs as heavy as lead.

Now he could make out the full bodies of the horse and men opposite; small divisions of foot were interspersed between their cavalry, a few starting to fire off premature volleys. Charles braced himself and aimed his sword at them, anxious to stop their hostility.

At two hundred yards, a blaring, stirring tune gushed from the trumpeters, signalling the charge, and without so much as a glance to his colleagues, Charles launched himself forward.

Events began to race as two pound artillery shots carved through their ranks with more precision, though the resultant gap was soon filled by other Cavaliers. The quick reaction to the speeding up left any sensations, feeling and cohesion behind as he leaned forward.

A buzz of roaring and yelling grew like a wave as Charles sped towards the rebels, shooting the odd quick glance to his colonel to ensure he followed his lead. A smart noble in front jerked to the side, before his body slumped, converged upon by an attendant, while Charles rode by, his only thought about the matter being to get past this obstacle.

Some firing came from the musketeers that stood within the enemy horsemen. With a hasty guess, he looked at the distance between the two sides and desperately resisted his temptation to return fire. He would still be out of their seventy yard average range and the enemy officers' disapproval of these wasted volleys was clear. Still the Roundheads stood, appearing to be ready to receive the Royalists and expecting them to halt their deafening advance to fire pistols, before engaging hand to hand. As he thought about Rupert's orders to plough into the Parliamentarians, he prayed that they continued their stance.

They grew nearer, clothes, patterns and headgear becoming distinguishable; no longer plain, generic figures, but individual Englishmen. One of his men let a shot off, which encouraged some others to follow, and Charles swung his arm at the man next to him, but much order had been lost several hundred yards ago.

At less than one hundred yards away from clashing with the enemy, their tawny orange scarves gave them a wash of colour. Dirt, soil and smoke rose up, growing as fast as the destruction. Horses whinnied and human wails intermixed with the resolute war cries, while stones, turf and dust from the hooves scattered wildly.

Charles stretched his arms forward, straddling the horse as it carried out a jump over a ditch - his heart hung in the air as the beast pounded back down to earth. While the steed galloped through the field, wind whistled through his helmet, infiltrating his whole body. The blur of the scenery, the motion of the ride and chill of the face began to naturally take the edge off the immense fear he had. It took colossal concentration just to focus on handling his sword, never mind thinking about the savage fighting he would soon face and what he would do when he closed with the enemy. The noise and thumping of the stampede was immense.

He thrust his sword forward, holding it with a grip like a vice. It shook from the vibrations of the gallop and the pressure of the air that was gushing around it. Finally, he let out a blood curdling bellow as he neared his quarries, as if possessed, and anticipating the smashing impact that was coming. The drone of shouting hung in the air around the cavaliers charging impetus, while below him, clouds of dust and earth added to the furious image.

Mostly devoid of their shot from their premature firing, and now observing the looming horsemen, untamed and rampageous, the enemy veritably wavered, horses and riders turning and swivelling from this oncoming torrent. Charles saw the lines breaking up with gaps as some fled, while others wheeled around in panic. Ranks of formerly tight horsemen began to turn and run as the lines crumbled.

"You cowardly traitors, stand and fight," Charles yelled with rage. He had kept resolve and he had no respect for anything less than this.

Then a whole load of horsemen tore off their orange markings and fired their pistols into the ground, moving out of their file and joining the King's men, though some of these who were too slow to declare their new allegiance, were cut down in the unstoppable stampede. This was the final straw to break the back of the enemy wing, and the sight of the deserters caused an implosion as waves of horses swayed around and stamped away. Groups scattered, some riding clear through other formations of soldiers and dispersing them too. Lone musketeers, who had used up their shot too early, panicked and followed their routed colleagues. Only a minority were cajoled into holding their positions.

Many soldiers dropped their weapons and simply fled without putting up any resistance. As one man came close to Charles's path, he slashed his sword right across him, before slicing down the back of another runaway. The man fell to the ground in one go. Charles pulled on the rein, gradually stopping his horse, and turning it to face some more enemy horsemen, part of the few that were making a stand. In front of him was a large gaping hole in the enemy formations, through which an array of Royalists stormed, eagerly pursuing immense amounts of runaways in a blood lust.

Yanking his firelock pistol out of the holster and pointing the eighteen inch barrel forward, Charles blasted one rebel down, covering himself in a resulting smokescreen. The enemy had been blown away by the strength of the royalist advance, and the invisible aura of determination this unstoppable cavalry arm must have exuded. As their troops of horsemen spilled away, racing down the gradient, the vulnerable foot soldiers were left to race around uncontrollably. As easy prey, they littered the area; a reminder of how complete the destruction of their lines had been.

At long last, the nerve shattering blasts of these few field pieces had come to an end for good, as the Royalists drove off the cannoneers and overtook the guns. Charles vengefully approached one of the iron killers, yelling at one of his horsemen to dismount and nail the cannons to disable them. He clashed his sword against the object, scratching the dolphin-shaped lifting handle, to claim them for the Royalists. His mind was in a maelstrom of emotions at this split second, while he thought about turning it around to use it on the Parliamentarians, or getting some troopers to wheel the six foot falcon away to their own army. It took no time to get back to battle thoughts though, leaving such premature and overeager thoughts aside.

He fired his other pistol at a musketeer who he noticed was making ready to shoot. A flash came from the weapon, his arm jerked back a little, and smoke engulfed his hand while the musketeer screamed and rolled to the ground.

In the confusion and disarray, carnage and destruction was the inevitable rule. Musket fire snapped through the cloudy air, screaming, yelling and groaning competing with the bellowing orders from the officers of both sides. It was near impossible to know where the firing was coming from. Standards waved around, attempting to call men back to their colours, without much success. The cavaliers attacked and chased madly, while a minority reformed, their allegiances sketchy at first glance in the murky atmosphere of hell. Noises of frantic, violence, clashes and clangs resulted from the fighting all around, horses panicking in the scene of horror, while Charles rode around the area. His adrenaline was all that was keeping him going.

Blood appeared on the next opponent that Charles assaulted, and seeing him go down was the signal to move on and check his own position, though this part of the field was rapidly emptying. He noticed a horse standing over a dead rider in the distance, while other mounts raced around within the bulk of the action, still caught up in it despite having no trooper. With every pause, he regained his senses and took stock. An enemy musketeer vainly swung his flintlock at a horseman, letting out a yell as he was run through. Other Royalists fired their preserved pistols, Roundheads staggering, hands in the air, their bodies rolling to the ground and leaving destitute families behind. The casualties were not always on the battlefield.

"Stop, damn you, regroup here," Charles bellowed to as many Royalists as he could.

His horse now turned at his command, and with his rapier held high, he clashed with an oncoming enemy trooper, the two swords clanging as they met each other, sending numbness up his arm. He panted, snatching some gasps of murky air.

A royalist cornet rattled past, chasing after his regiment as it pounded its way onward, ornate blue doublet, saddle and white mount a blur, though the long lance and the black colours it held with their golden crowns, was as clear as day. Following this interruption, Charles glared at the foe he was pitted against and moved forward, bringing swords together again. He slammed the other blade out of the way, before thrusting the handle of his sword into the trooper's black helmet, stunning him for a second. This was enough to give an opportunity to force him off his horse in an almighty struggle. The man fell to the ground, armoured body and legs now without mobility. Charles raised his visor, wiping a flood of sweat out of his eyes with the leather glove and lace edge, as the din drew away from the climax it had reached earlier.

"You dog, get up and fight," Charles roared, at the top of his voice, while the man held his hands up in surrender.

The continued capitulation of the foe brought the chance for sober judgement; he did not want to kill the fellow mercilessly. Breathless, Charles searched around the confusion, smoke eerily hanging in the air as he inhaled the pungent smell of gunpowder. Bodies lay scattered around the ploughed fields and grass, their final acts now played out once and for all. Shouting and orders came as officers desperately tried to redirect the assault, and Charles was unable to spot the bulk of his men. In fact, now that he had the chance to focus, out of the sixteen hundred horsemen of the right wing, he could barely see one third of them here. He looked back, expecting the second line of the wing to have remained, ready to attack the exposed Parliamentarian foot soldiers, but that body had vanished too.

"Where in God's name have the bastards gone?" he cursed.

"O Lord! Thou knowest how busy I must be this day. If I forget Thee, do not Thou forget me."

Sir Jacob Astley, Sergeant-Major-General of the Royalist Infantry. Prayer said on his knees before he ordered his men forward into the Battle of Edgehill.

Chapter 57

King Charles the First patted his white steed, watching the ranks of his infantrymen engaging with the rebels. His forces still had the advantage, with ten thousand men to verse six thousand, even though his cavalry had all but completely left the field.

"My perspective glass, Walker," the King commanded of his footman.

After taking hold of the telescope, the monarch held it up and carefully surveyed the battle, taking particular note of where the Earl of Essex's standard was, being commander of the rebel forces. From the ridge he was on, he could see most of the formations in front of him.

Then he stopped, catching sight of horsemen moving out from behind the enemy infantry.

"Horsemen? Richmond, where have they come from?" he demanded.

"I know not, Your Majesty. Essex must have kept some in reserve."

King Charles resumed his examination of the force, as they slowly emerged in their entirety and began to charge towards the left wing of the royalist foot regiments. The entourage surrounding the King began to scrutinise every movement in the battle, the Earl of Dorset bellowing out the names of the Roundhead commanders leading the cavalry reserve.

"Stapleton and Sir William Balfour."

As the horsemen clashed into the royalist foot, the King tensed.

His heart pounded as he scoured around for any trace of his own cavalry, as though in disbelief that this enemy force could upset the balance of the battle so easily. He glanced at Lord Dorset, an experienced cavalry officer. He wanted to ask what they could do, starting to fear for the victory he had so expected before this.

"Aha. God bless those lads," Dorset growled, thrusting his fist into the air.

The King, breath held for a second, watched with eventual relief as the cavalrymen were driven off. Some of the men around him cheered and he smiled. This was his first battle, and he was rapidly learning that the fortune of war was as fickle as any ambitious courtier.

"Your Majesty, their second lot of horsemen are attacking now," Sir William Howard warned.

King Charles turned, seeing the rampant cavalrymen smash into the centre of the Royalist line, breaking into Colonel Richard Fielding's men. The infantrymen of both sides eventually disengaged bit by bit, leaving a gap between the two as for a welcome the lull in hand to hand combat. Musket fire now crackled out from both sides, smoke emanating like ghosts from the weapons as they poured lead balls into each other at close range. Considering the lines were packed with men six or eight deep, this fire began to take its toll.

The Roundhead cavalry pressed on their advantage, scattering a lot of royalists in green tunics. As the men fled back towards the rear of the Royalist army, the horsemen began surrounding another regiment of foot, though some of them simply chased after fleeing Royalist soldiers, pursuing them towards Edgehill and the King's cannons in the rear.

"The devil does look after his own," Lord Dorset said bitterly.

"We could withdraw the men so that our cannon can fire on the enemy, Your Majesty?" suggested the Duke of Richmond.

The monarch watched as Colonel Nicholas Byron's regiment now began to break up, causing a line of retreating soldiers to stretch from the battle, right up to the rear of the army. For a time, his eyes followed the ranks of deserters, until he broke from this glare and looked at his two sons nearby.

"Escort the princes to the top of the hill, my lord," he ordered his cousin Richmond.

"May I beg to remain here, sir, for I do not wish to leave your side at such a crucial point," Richmond pleaded.

"Lord Dorset, can you carry them to safety, for I will not have them exposed to danger," the King demanded.

"Sir, I will not be thought a coward for any King's sons in Christendom," Dorset responded bluntly.

The King was in a rage, feeling his face flush with that rare, but sharp temper. Apart from his sons' safety, these men, his closest advisors, were shunning his direct orders.

"It is my express command that you remove my sons to the safety of the hill. I will not accept any excuse to the contrary," he snapped at Sir William Howard, who hastily acquiesced.

After only a few seconds, the King commanded them all to advance, and he threw his black cloak over his shoulder, pointing his golden marshal's baton at the foray.

"I will steady my men and bolster their confidence," he shouted, with a firm resolve that seemed to manifest itself from his anger.

The odd protest was lodged, but the monarch ignored them, obdurately scorning to answer now that his mind was made up. As the great, white steed advanced, the King pulled his black visor down and then noticed Sir Edmund Verney following him with the huge royal standard. He was sure that the magnificent sight would restore his men, and was anxious to play his part. Dorset's sentiment was right in one respect; cowardice was a sin. The small party with the fifty men of the bodyguard made their way towards the remains of the infantry, of which the far left and right wings were the only ones remaining after the centre had been destroyed.

A blast rang out so close to the King, that he was sure he had been hit. Screaming pierced the air around him. His horse panicked but he soon got it under control, despite his hands shaking as he looked around him. Taking quick breaths, he glanced down to see blood on his horse, the same bright colour as his saddle with its gold embroidery. He jerked his head to find his footman clenching his face, rolling around on the field in agony.

"Take him back with the princes. Commit him to my physician, Doctor Harvey," the monarch commanded, as he continued to advance.

As the royal party approached, two regiments of enemy foot now advanced towards the gaping hole in the centre of the royalist ranks and pushed forward. With the King's men about to be split in two, he rode amongst the men, causing great cheers and ructions to spread from the beleaguered troops.

"Your King is with you. Stand firm and God will see you through," the King yelled. The Banner Royal was enough to advertise the royal presence, though it seemed to also attract unwanted notice, for now the two rebel foot regiments were approaching the King's position. On the ground, he struggled for a moment to move across the debris of bodies, pikes and equipment.

"Your Majesty should withdraw to safety, I urge it."

King Charles did not look to see who said it. Instead, he found himself staring down on the corpse of a loyal soldier.

That man could not withdraw to preserve his life. Withdraw and lose, or stay and fight to victory; only the last option was available in the King's mind.

As the lifeguard rushed forward to barricade the King from the advancing enemy, Sir Edmund Verney who held the royal standard was assaulted. Firing enveloped the whole area and powder smoke plumed around, while yells and cries rang out. Sir Edmund and his servant were fighting off some men now, killing two of them. The King went to draw his sword, though the divide between them was too great to intervene. As he held the handle of his sheathed blade, he could not bring himself to use it; rebels they may be, but they were still his people, and killing them with his own hand was too much for him to contemplate.

Sir Edmund's servant went down, and the standard bearer himself, now converged upon because of his precious load, used the pole of the banner to fight them off. With no armour or leather buff coat, Sir Edmund presented a unique figure amongst the battle that raged around him. His vow from when he joined the King's cause now rang in the royal ears. 'I have eaten his bread and served him near thirty years and will not do so base a thing as to forsake him now.'

Sadness struck the King's heart as the loyal servant defended the banner like a lion, arms extending out, before falling slowly backwards from a musket shot.

"They have the colours," Dorset cried in disbelief.

Deep within the turmoil of the King's mind, he knew the Roundheads had got more than that. The flower of his most loyal servants, officers and men were being lost. He looked back for his two sons, anxious now for their safety - if he should lose his life, the succession needed to be secure in the Prince of Wales. With horror, he saw that some of the enemy horsemen had pushed as far back as Edgehill and were in pursuit of his flesh and blood.

"We need to stop those traitors from undoing us," the King instructed in vain, as he watched helplessly. For the first time in the battle, worry for the outcome had truly overcome his soul.

Chapter 58

A large flash emanated from beyond the Parliamentary lines and a terrific explosion followed, dark, ominous plumes of smoke billowing up from beyond. The sight all but signified the destruction of the enemy wing. A renewed clatter of hooves drew Charles's attention as he turned to see Prince Rupert leading near one hundred horsemen towards him. The young man sped on as furiously as any summer storm, his troops racing along like menacing, dark clouds.

"Gather our men together, for God's sake, sir," the young commander yelled.

Charles scoured the area around him for stray Royalists, checking for progress of the battle at large, and reacting to the stark words. In a flash, Rupert and his men were gone again, the silver, blue and black personal standard soaring like a bird across the field and out of the Parliamentarian positions. If Rupert could only get a handful of men back from their victorious marauding, then nobody else had a chance.

He set off in the direction of the royal, towards the centre of the field, where the opposing large scrums of foot soldiers were charging each other like an army of stags.

Eyeing the ranks of pikemen and musketeers in the middle of the arena brought his attention back to wider tactics. The formations were interspersed and locked together in desperate battle, long lines of men condensed into a pack of bodies, the wooden pikes of both sides now pointed at each other, then forced up over as they came together to charge each other viciously, desperate for the other side to give way.

"You dogs, do you run? Get back to our soldiers, they need you," Charles commanded of some friendly horsemen galloping by.

As he spouted rallying cries to his crazed colleagues that swirled around, he attempted to get back to the army, eager not to be cut off behind the rebel lines. A sharp pain alerted him that his own leg was cut, just above where his unfolded leather boots ended at the upper thigh, though he had no idea when it had occurred. While his horse slowly trotted, the fastest it could go by now, he looked mournfully at the bodies that lay nearby, until one caught his attention. He tugged the reins, stopping his horse as he looked at one man.

"James," he said, the words quickly lost in the rapports and echoes of firepower, along with the commands and incessant bellowing.

The man glanced up in silence, aware that someone was hovering over him.

"It is me, Charles Berkeley. Your leg, what happened?" he observed of the cut and bloodied limb.

"Cut down like a dog. Best to lie still until all your bloody cavaliers have gone."

"You need a surgeon."

"And you need to get on with your battle. Move off for the love of Christ, I will go back to my lines soon and get this damn thing treated," James snapped, making it clear that Charles's allegiance barred him from helping his friend.

An overhead noise proceeded from a thump that shook his

whole being as a cannon fired nearby. A handful of cavalrymen hammered past, distracting the two of them, and reminding them of the fractured activity that was still ongoing in all parts of the field. The speeding comrades drew Charles away, reluctantly admitting he was powerless to help James.

"I will return after the battle," he vowed as he moved off.

His weary horse had savoured those few minutes of respite, and neighed out sad recognition that it was over as Charles tried to take command of those passing troopers. He checked his sword, making sure it was still attached to his wrist by a cord, and gripped it tightly once more.

Next, through the smoke clouds, he saw a few horsemen with red scarves chasing after a band of Roundheads, the King's standard being with the rebels. The sight of the royal banner, which he had been close to when serving in the King's guards in London, made him fear the battle could be lost. He made towards the thieves, clashing in from the opposite side to the other Royalist group, until a friendly commander finally recovered the talisman. The horse was beginning to falter again, no longer able to speed around, or respond to him. His own legs and rear ached too, and he panted as they came to a halt, eager to refill his lungs for his next action.

"Help me escort the banner royal back to its rightful home," the colonel exhorted.

Charles aligned himself with Colonel John Smith without hesitation and the thirty or so horsemen steadily made their way back to the main Royalist army, to do whatever they could there. The nearer they got to the foot soldiers, the worse the melee seemed, as he glared at the interlocked lines of men now close in front.

"What has happened to the second line of cavalry on our left wing?" Charles questioned, as he watched the vulnerable infantry.

"Digby led them off the field to pursue the Roundheads,"

Smith said, causing Charles to curse with a mouthful of oaths.

The two forces jostled and pushed each other, both sides heaving with compressed bodies, while some fresh Parliamentary soldiers marched up to support their forces, adding extra pressure that the teetering Royalist men could do without. From his initial jubilation when Parliament's horsemen capitulated, he now realised that victory was far from certain. The thin, twelve foot forest of poles jutted out in every direction, some shattering as the tension became too much, casting shards of deadly splinters across the fray. It was a melting pot of yellow buff coats and colourful sleeves. The infantry standards showed just how many different regiments were in this desperate conflict, with their red crosses in the corner and colourful decorations peering above the ranks, drowning in the deadly crush. A small body of enemy horsemen had passed the whole pack by, overwhelming the artillery and playing havoc in the undefended rear of the lines. With the King in the mix, riding around and encouraging his infantry, Charles saw this foray as a dangerous threat that needed to be checked.

"We should destroy those, sir," Charles yelled to Colonel Smith, above the din.

"You take them out. I will return this standard and boost their morale, for our men are losing heart."

Without further delay, Charles leaped off his horse, ordering a colleague to swap mounts, and gaining a fresher steed. Smith agreed to split the force in two, clearly focused on returning the flag. As Charles shouted commands to his small band, his new mount faced all ways but where he wanted to go, and the animal would not move. He kicked it sharply, bellowing out a lot of oaths before finally it set off, thundering along erratically.

As he drew closer, he watched some of the enemy now moving towards the position of the twelve year old Prince of Wales, and his younger brother the Duke of York. The cannoneers were being slaughtered, defenceless as they were, and their demise would make the field pieces useless; a mere handful of horsemen could jeopardise the whole Royalist position.

"The sly bastards. If we had not chased the rebels from the field, we could have trampled their whole damned army," Charles cried with frustration.

When he checked, he found that ten men had accompanied him, enough to drive off the intruders from the cannons, but little else. The enemy did not seem to move or respond to his approach though, and he guessed that they took his party to be colleagues, and the small Royalist group powered through them, chopping them down or scattering them. Without any respite, he waved his arm, demanding they reform and continue, testing the stamina of even the best of horsemen with his demanding nature. The main rebel troop were further on.

Edgehill lay ahead, in all of its glory. Charles was desperate to catch the bulk of the enemy, whose intentions soon appeared to be on securing the two princes as bait, or indeed to murder them. He thought of his own son Henry, and worked himself into a passion that the royal children were threatened. A small barn lay further on, and the entourage of the young royals were frantically making for that shelter, though the enemy were hot on their heels. Charles kicked the horse mercilessly, determined to show it who was master, as it continued to snort and shake around at rebellious intervals.

As the royal party drew behind the barn, which was flanked with hedges, the Roundheads slowed, aware of the pursuing group of Royalists behind.

"Will you stomach those traitors in our ranks any longer?" Charles roared, his voice deep and outraged.

He perceived their actions, and from the interruption of their advance, surmised that they thought the barn was fortified. The dark shadows of the riders - for daylight was escaping fast - turned about, their shouts and jeering carrying in the cold, crisp air. Charles's face was numb as he galloped onwards, drawing his rapier again and aiming at them. As if battling with these troops was not enough, exhaustion was chasing him once more.

One of the enemy party was unperturbed and continued on with his intentions to seize the royals. The princes' attendant rode out to meet him, exchanging pistol shots, before the Roundhead was dismounted with a clatter. The full body armour made it difficult to rise up at first, but he was immune to the sword blows, allowing him to relentlessly pace along on foot. At this point, Charles lost sight as he collided with the enemy horsemen who had charged at his men. One colleague to his left was run through, sliding off his horse, and Charles sliced at the victor, lashing out as they passed alongside each other.

Now his horse began to rebel violently, whinnying and jerking. Charles kicked it repeatedly, catching sight of the unassailable, stubborn iron clad man. Then his horse reared, low at first, but it repeated it and he panicked, tugging the reins in his alarm and desperation to get it back down. As if to solve matters, the beast span to the right, tipping over and flinging him off, though clear of the rolling horse. Charles crashed to the ground, right onto a dead body, flat against the freezing armour breastplate of the man. His ribcage stung, and his head rattled around in his helmet like a ball. As he looked up, disorientated for a moment, the corpse's bulging eyes seemed to be glaring at him, and he shouted, pushing himself off the body.

"Damned sword won't do a job with him," the Prince's attendant cried with frustration, as he once more assaulted the frustrating Roundhead trooper.

The attention of the immune cuirassier was attracted and Charles got to his feet as the enemy man approached him, walking slowly and confidently, seeming to easily repel the attendant. It was now that Charles realised his sword had gone astray during the tumble, and he drew back, pain in his chest shooting through him with every movement. A pistol shot rang out, and Charles's leg went from under him as he fell once more, the sudden action making him believe it had been blown clean off. He grasped it, yelling loudly, unable to do a thing about the relentless march of the fearsome opponent, already brandishing his sword triumphantly. He squeezed his eyes, howling with the excruciating pain, sweating, gasping and squirming.

"The Lord hath brought you here to pay, you heathen. Now I will be the victor and you can hand over my medal that you wear," a familiar voice demanded.

"Cotton. How many lives do you have?" he barked.

Charles was freezing, and his heart thundered as much as the galloping troops that sounded like they were withdrawing. A quick glance around showed that the rebels had cleared his puny force away. He tried to push himself backwards, but could not. Cotton began to loom over him, relishing the last minutes as he raised his sword, ready to pin him to the ground.

The shining, black, iron shell of the man's armour was a work of art. From his waist, rung upon rung of impregnable strips, held together by gleaming nails, stretched down each leg to his leather boots.

Then Charles saw a pole axe lying in the grass, a remnant of some earlier struggle, and he reached out, but was just too far away. He clawed desperately, seizing the shaft and jerking it back to him, the reflex action enhanced by the intense discomfort that also recalled his arm. Cotton had no sooner seen it, than Charles let out a roar of anguish and final determination, summoning up every ounce of strength his body could rally and thrusting the point of the head upwards.

The sharp, long spike skewered the plating of Cotton's chest. The metal resisted at first, but once pierced, it slid into Cotton's body with ease.

As he was impaled, his foe dropped the sword, but stayed standing. Charles kept hold of the pole, taking no chances, unable to believe he had succeeded. The figure was silent, which unnerved him, and Charles pulled the weapon with what little energy remained. Cotton fell to his knees as it began to withdraw; still the long shaft connected the two men, until Charles yanked it from the body, shouting at the top of his voice as he did so, before his vocals faltered, and he was overcome with tears. Cotton fell flat on the grass. A deathly groan escaped from the cladding, which now acted as a coffin for the corpse within.

Charles's weary body could do no more and he fell back, clawing the ground, fingers delving into the soil with anguish. In the darkness of his tightly closed eyes, now seeping with quiet tears, he saw Anne and Henry. His battle was over.

Character List

King Charles I

Aged 41 in 1641, born in Dunfermline, Scotland. King since 1625, he is the Grandson of Mary, Queen of Scots. His father is the first monarch to rule over England and Scotland from 1603. As a child, he is not expected to live, but an immense determination helps him overcome these frailties. Devoted in his faith to the Church of England, he has a hatred of Puritanism. King Charles becomes heir to the throne when his elder brother dies in 1612. The King is an intelligent, refined man and very reserved. Impeccable manners and a complete love of his wife and family are what he is known for.

Queen Henrietta Maria

Aged 32 in 1641, born in Paris, France. Youngest daughter of King Henri IV, who converts from Protestant to Catholic when he becomes monarch and is eventually assassinated in 1610 by a Catholic. Queen Henrietta marries King Charles in 1625. After an unhappy start, the marriage is blissfully happy and she is unrivalled as the person most trusted by the King, who relies upon her. The Queen lives and breathes Catholicism and is tactless, wilful and demanding.

Prince Rupert of the Rhine

Aged 22 in 1641. Born in Bohemia, he is a nephew of King Charles I. Rupert's father is the Protestant Elector Palatine, who is invited by the rebellious people of Bohemia to be their King, overthrowing the Catholic monarch. He accepts, but this decision leads to war between Catholic and Protestant powers in Europe. The new King of Bohemia is defeated and all of his lands, both Bohemia and the Palatinate, are seized by the Catholic Holy Roman Empire. King Charles I is desperate to help his sister and family regain the Palatinate, but Parliament begin to challenge royal authority, rather than vote money. Rupert comes to England in 1642 after the English Civil War has broken out and is given a crucial post in the King's army. He is energetic, efficient and proves to be a military marvel, the best general the King employs. Handsome and charming he may be, but his brash and headstrong manner alienates many older and experienced men in the King's service.

Prince Charles Louise of the Rhine

Aged 24 in 1641. Charles Louise is the eldest nephew of King Charles I and brother to Prince Rupert. With his father's death, he becomes Elector Palatine, though in exile, still desperate to get the family lands back in the Palatinate. He is in England during 1641, trying to enlist the support of his uncle, the English Parliament or anyone who could help with this. Possessing little charm, he is dour and stands on the sidelines, waiting to see whether King or Parliament come out as victors in the power struggle.

James Stuart, Duke of Richmond

Aged 29 in 1641, Richmond is a cousin of King Charles I. With an honest, sensible core, his honourable nature is well known.

Thomas Howard, Earl of Arundel

Aged 56 in 1641. Catholic peer, whose family plotted against Queen Elizabeth I. Restored to the family titles in 1604, he holds many posts within government and as Lord Steward, presides over the trial of the Earl of Strafford, who he has no regard for. Famous collector of art, sculptures and marbles.

Robert Devereaux, Earl of Essex

Aged 50 in 1641. Very quiet and sober, he is a Puritan, eventually picked to lead the armies of Parliament. Although endearing, he is not an able commander, nor very inspiring. King Charles I's father match made a marriage for Essex, which failed miserably and publicly. Essex is the son of the famous second Earl of Essex who had been close to Elizabeth I, eventually executed after rebelling against her.

Henry Rich, First Earl of Holland

Aged 51 in 1641. Holland had been sent to conduct the marriage negotiations between King Charles I and Queen Henrietta Maria. He is adept at politics, enjoys the finer points in life and is good friends with the Queen. When Parliament call for more power, he supports their point of view and eventually this leads to his alienation from the royal family. Holland commands the cavalry in the Bishops War and gives patronage to the main character.

Robert Rich, Earl of Warwick

Aged 54 in 1641, he is the older brother of the Earl of Holland. A strong Puritan, he has business links with the New World and holds a senior position within the Royal Navy. He fully supports Parliament and goes on to become leader of the Parliamentarian Navy.

Thomas Wentworth, Earl of Strafford

Aged 48 in 1641, born in London, England. His family have Yorkshire roots and as a young Member of Parliament, he initially opposes the King until concessions were made. After this, he takes up royal service in government and rises to become Lord Lieutenant of Ireland. Strafford is a figurehead of the King's government and is efficient, effective and intelligent, but has a blunt, forceful and strong character. When the King goes to war with Scotland over plans to impose a prayer book on that nation, the monarch recalls Strafford to England in a bid to use his immense talents to restore order. He eventually becomes a target by Parliamentary opposition to the King and is arrested by Parliament and held in the Tower of London, pending trial.

Archibald Campbell, Earl of Argyll

Aged 34 in 1641, Argyll is John Pym's opposite number in Scotland. He becomes the leading member of the Scottish Parliament and closely watches events in England, wresting power from King Charles and practically ruling Scotland in the monarch's absence. A merciless streak lies at his core.

Lucy Hay, Countess of Carlisle

Aged 42 in 1641. Daughter of the Earl of Northumberland, she is a wealthy widow and lady of the bedchamber to Queen Henrietta Maria. Rumour has it that she is the mistress of the Earl of Strafford, but when he is on trial, she begins to turn her attention to John Pym. Celebrated for beauty and wit, she loves court politics and intrigue, using her position with the Queen to betray the royal family and carry secrets to John Pym. Her ability is so good, that this two-faced, double dealing goes unnoticed until far too late.

Lord George Digby

Aged 29 in 1641. Son of the Earl of Bristol, he is manipulative, ever optimistic and self confident, prepared to say and do anything to further himself. With no military or government ability, he begins by supporting the Parliamentary calls for more power, until the Earl of Strafford is put on trial. At this point, he begins to move towards the King and speaks out against the trial. He is a destructive force within the royal party, for his suave manner allows this incompetent man much influence. Digby is often involving the main character in plots.

Sir Thomas Lunsford

Aged 30 in 1641, Lunsford is an experienced soldier and supporter of the King. Rash, bad tempered and brutal, he is described as someone who fears neither God, nor man. Aged 22, he attempts to kill a neighbour over a quarrel and flees the country for a time, returning to fight for the King in the Bishops Wars with Scotland. Rumours, gossip and hatred spread fast within the populace, claiming he eats children and commits other such atrocities. In 1641, the King installs him as Lieutenant of the Tower of London, thus securing the arsenal and fortress for royal use. London erupts in opposition to this choice and the King is forced to replace him with someone equally as loyal, but with a better reputation. After this, Lunsford is given command of the King's guards.

Sir Charles Berkeley (fictional main character)

Aged 27 in 1641. Born in Colchester, Essex, his English father - an innkeeper - was a staunch royalist, whereas his French mother, whose family fled religious persecution in France, was quite the opposite. From early childhood, Charles enjoys the military tales his uncle tells him and longs to follow in his footsteps. Life changes when his sister, Lucy, elopes and marries without their father's consent, creating a rift in the family. Not long after this, Charles's mother passes away. By 1639, when English troops are fighting in the Bishops War against Scotland, Charles is determined to buy a commission as a minor officer and fulfil his ambitions. Scotland is resisting the

King's attempt to bring their religion further in line with the English, and the resulting ignominious 'Bishop's War' is where Sir Charles achieves a minor victory, the rarity of it bringing him to the attention of the high command. He is promoted and knighted, moving to London under the patronage of the Earl of Holland. It is here that he meets his wife, Anne and not long after the marriage, the power struggle intensifies.

Sir Arthur Cotton (fictional)

Aged 31 in 1641. Born in the Scottish highlands, Cotton fights in the Bishops Wars against the English. During the Bishops War he is wounded and captured. Taken to London, he is soon released when peace is declared and the Scottish appoint him to negotiate and liaise with the English Parliament, causing him to stay in the capital. Cotton is a proud man, been married for some time, though without children. He is an excellent swordsman and has a striking appearance, adding to his womanising ways. Ruthless, ambitious and violent, his temper is enhanced with the short period of English captivity and he soon enters the political scene, thriving on intrigue.

Sir Richard Warrington (fictional)

Aged 59 in 1641. He is the colonel of the red regiment of the London Trained Bands, and the main character's commanding officer. Gruff, haughty and arrogant, he has no ability in running the regiment, preferring to hold and enjoy the post, though with as little effort as possible.

Sir George Hadleigh (fictional)

Aged 42 in 1641. He is the colonel of the King's Lifeguards, under Sir Thomas Lunsford.

Sir Arthur Haselrig

Sir Henry Vane

William Strode

John Maynard

John Glynn

All men are supporters of Parliament, assisting John Pym.

William Laud, Archbishop of Canterbury

Aged 68 in 1641. Born to a humble tradesman, he begins to climb the ranks of the church. Laud has high church views such as creating a uniformed Church of England and introduced more ceremony and ritual into religious services. The beauty of holiness was something else he promoted, with paintings, or golden crucifixes added to the fabric of churches to emphasise this. Additionally, he supported the role of Bishops and tried to eradicate Puritanism. This forced many to travel to the New World for both a fresh start and freedom of religion. The Archbishop's views mirror those of the King and Laud uses the royal courts to fine and punish any who oppose the policies. When Parliament are called in 1640, the primate is arrested by them and imprisoned in the Tower of London.

Edmund (Mun) Verney

Aged 25 in 1641, Edmund is the son of Sir Edmund Verney, Knight Marshal to the King. He is a great friend of the main character and serves in the Bishops Wars against Scotland. Honest, loyal and courageous, he is an ardent supporter of the King.

Lucius Cary, Viscount Falkland
Edward Hyde
Sir John Culpepper

All are men who supported Parliament initially, but after the many concessions made by the King, transfer to the royal cause because they feel Parliament is going too far in its actions.

John Pym

Aged 57 in 1641. From Somerset, Pym is as sturdy looking as his unflinching Puritan views. Described by one as 'an Ox' due to his build and appearance, he enters Parliament in 1614 and experiences the eleven years when King Charles I ruled without recourse to a Parliament. In 1640, when Parliament are summoned after this long recess, Pym comes to the fore and is looked upon as a natural leader. After the Bishops War, when the King is financially drained and needs Parliament to grant subsidies of money, Pym uses many ingenious plans to gradually wrest power from royal hands.

John Hampden

Aged 46 in 1641. A member of the gentry, Hampden is first cousin to Oliver Cromwell. From the start, he opposes the King in clear terms when he refuses to pay the Ship Money tax that the monarch orders to be collected, without the sanction of Parliament. Hampden is convicted by the narrowest majority by the royal judges, highlighting the depth of feeling during the time that the King rules without Parliament.

Lucy and Edward Hungerford (fictional)

Sir Charles Berkeley's younger sister and her husband. Lucy elopes to marry Edward, against her father's wishes and this creates a rift in the family which has lasted ever since.

Brief Historical Background

England remained at peace while Europe was ravaged by a war over religion (The Thirty Years War 1618 - 1648) The English and Scottish crowns were united in 1603 when the Tudor Queen Elizabeth I died. King James of Scotland now became King of England, Wales and Ireland too. So in effect, Great Britain was formed with King James as monarch. Following the Gunpowder Plot in 1605, when Catholics (known as Papists) tried to blow up the King and his government, the population became ultra suspicious and intolerant of all Catholics. Religious tension simmered under the surface. King James died in 1625 and his son, Charles, was crowned.

King Charles I had tried to get involved in the Thirty Years War in support of the Protestants, hoping also to restore his Protestant sister and brother in law to their domain in the Rhineland. They had been driven out by the Catholic Holy Roman Empire. Past military campaigns against France and Spain had failed miserably though and depleted the English treasury, so that when he had asked Parliament for money for fresh hostilities, they would not grant a penny before he listened to their grievances about the government of the nation.

The King held all executive power except for that of finance. His power was called the royal prerogative, allowing the monarch amongst other things, to declare war and peace, appoint ministers, bishops and control any armies raised. Parliament had the fundamental right to levy taxes. It was an assembly which had never been regular, and was only called when needed. Their unprecedented demands and complaints about his government incensed the King and he dismissed them.

England was changing though and the long era of peace boosted trade and industry, making the country prosper. As a consequence, the middle classes expanded and now wanted more of a say in government, resulting in Parliament aiming to secure greater rights and take some of the monarch's power. This brought them into a collision course with the King and they decided to limit his income to give them leverage. The royal government was starved of funds and Parliament began to question the suitability of the royal ministers.

King Charles I and the majority of the nation believed he was appointed by God to rule the country and he took his coronation oaths to protect the laws, church and his people with the utmost seriousness. As such, King and Parliament were inevitably going to clash and the King finally dismissed Parliament in 1629. They would not meet again for around eleven years, during which time the monarch resorted to dubious methods of raising money and relied upon the prerogative courts and judges to uphold his government. One of his aims was that the Church of England should be mid way between Puritans and Catholics and began making changes to achieve this. Churches were adorned with paintings, gilded crucifixes and rails were put around the altar.

Matters came to a head when King Charles I attempted to unite England and Scotland further by introducing a new

Prayer Book for the Scots, more in line with the English one. His beautification of churches and services created suspicion, for people saw similarities too close to that of the Catholics. There was a rise in the Puritan faith in England too, and these people were very plain and sober in worship, so were alienated by these actions.

When Scotland rebelled and rejected the prayer book, King Charles raised an army of his own to impose it. The English were completely defeated in the First Bishops War of 1639 and a peace was agreed. Now devoid of funds, the monarch called Parliament in 1640, the first time in over a decade, and summoned his greatest minister, the Earl of Strafford, to help manage the situation. Parliament refused to levy taxes for the King, until he had heard their complaints and requests for more say in government, so the monarch dismissed them and set about planning another invasion of Scotland. The second Bishops War was farcical and the English had no hope, eventually suing for peace, but not before Scottish troops occupied much of Northumberland.

The only way to raise enough money to buy off the Scots was to summon Parliament again and the King's hand was forced.

Parliament, consisting of the House of Commons and House of Lords, recognised their vital role and this secured their existence. Rather than deal with the Scots, they began to focus on the royal government and lay out their grievances. Ministers such as the Earl of Strafford and the Archbishop Laud of Canterbury were imprisoned on their orders and they began to demand more rights and powers. Bit by bit, the King granted concessions, though this only seemed to make Parliament want more. It is during the height of this crisis that the story begins.